DON'T LET HIM IN

ALSO BY LISA JEWELL

Breaking the Dark

None of This Is True

The Family Remains

The Night She Disappeared

Invisible Girl

The Family Upstairs

Watching You

Then She Was Gone

I Found You

The Girls in the Garden

The Third Wife

The House We Grew Up In

Before I Met You

The Making of Us

After the Party

The Truth About Melody Browne

31 Dream Street

A Friend of the Family

Vince & Joy

One-Hit Wonder

Thirtynothing

Ralph's Party

DON'T LET HIM IN

LISA JEWELL

ATRIA BOOKS

NEW YORK AMSTERDAM/ANTWERP LONDON
TORONTO SYDNEY/MELBOURNE NEW DELHI

An Imprint of Simon & Schuster, LLC
1230 Avenue of the Americas
New York, NY 10020

This book is a work of fiction. Any references to historical events, real people, or real places are used fictitiously. Other names, characters, places, and events are products of the author's imagination, and any resemblance to actual events or places or persons, living or dead, is entirely coincidental.

First Atria Books hardcover edition June 2025

ATRIA BOOKS and colophon are trademarks of Simon & Schuster, LLC

Interior design by Erika R. Genova

Manufactured in the United States of America

1 3 5 7 9 10 8 6 4 2

Library of Congress Cataloging-in-Publication Data has been applied for.

ISBN 978-1-6680-3387-6
ISBN 978-1-6680-3389-0 (ebook)

DON'T LET HIM IN

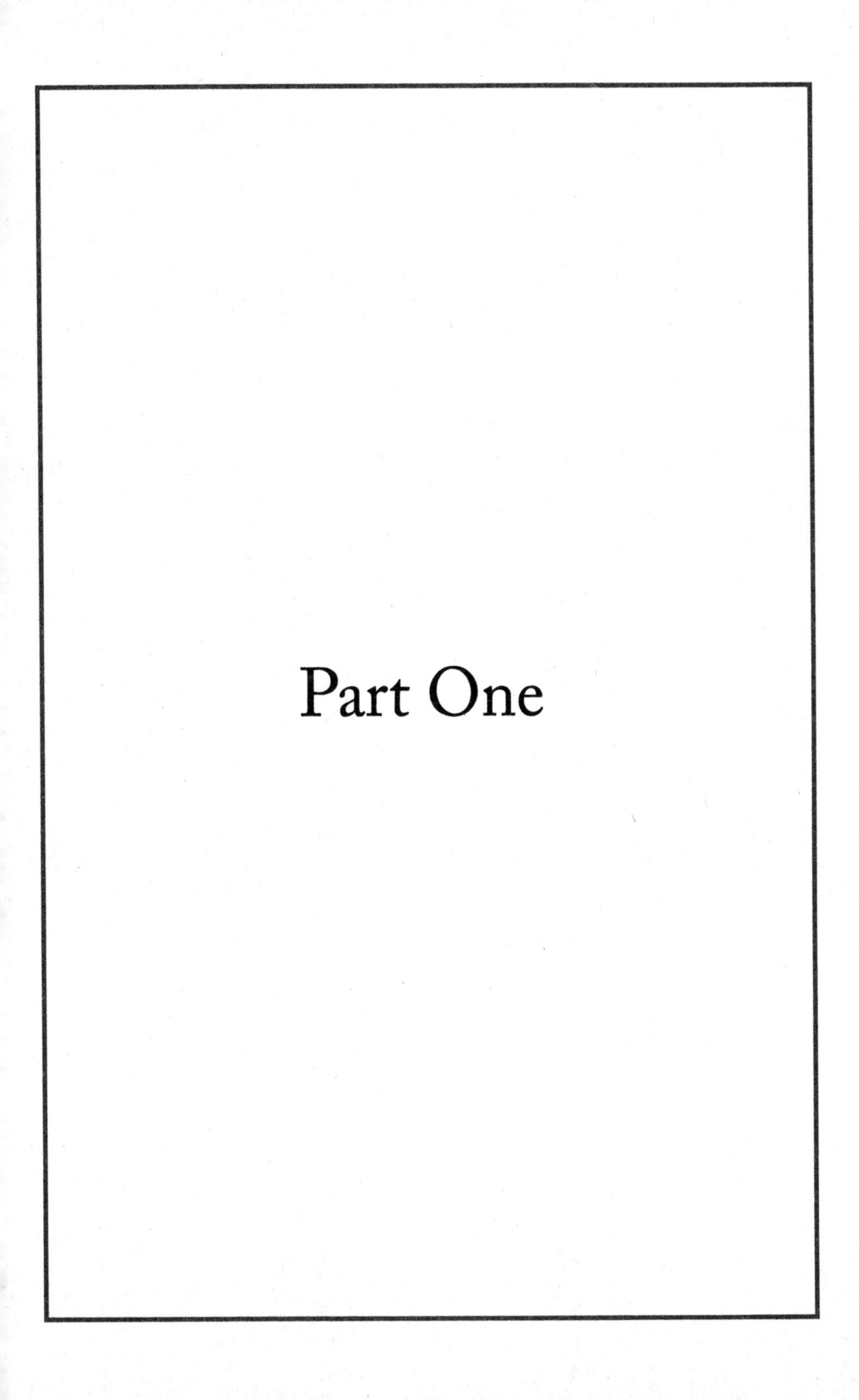

Part One

ONE

NOVEMBER

The house is spectacular. A huge white stucco villa on three floors plus attic rooms, and a direct view of the sea visible through tall windows that frame the vista at the back and the front. I imagine that a wall must have been taken down at some point to offer up that level of open-plan space in a Victorian house. Steel beams put in. Expensive stuff. Just to give the owners more light and space. I feel an uncharacteristic twitch of jealousy. It's not like me to envy others. I rarely, in fact, give a thought to them. But this is a different case altogether. I turn off the van's engine and sit, just for a moment, readying myself. Through the window, on the other side of the house, I see the shadows of movement and as I pull on a baseball cap and open the driver's door, I hear the muted murmur of chatter. There are four cars parked outside and clearly the day is still going strong. I go to the side of the van and pull open the door. There it is, my last delivery of the day: an extra-large bouquet of white hydrangeas and roses, no expense spared, in a pink bag. On the envelope is the inscription "Nina Swann & Family."

I walk toward the front door, peering in subtly as I pass the kitchen window. A small group sits around the table, a mix of younger and older people. They all have wine, are dressed somberly. There is music playing, candles are flickering. I see art and photography and graphics on the walls; I see a designer kitchen in midnight blue and pink, with flashes of brass and copper, big globe light bulbs hanging at irregular intervals from golden chains, plants on shelves. Through a door at the back of the kitchen, I see huge velvet sofas, a mixing desk, a Gorillaz poster.

It's the home of a Gen X man who has made good decisions, made a success of his life, piled his building blocks one on top of the other with precision and care. But also, the home of a man who made one really bad mistake that his wife and his family are going to pay for, over and over again.

I keep moving past the window and then I put my finger to the doorbell.

TWO

Ash thanks the delivery driver, then closes the front door behind her and carries the flowers to the kitchen. Here, her mother, Nina; her brother, Arlo; her grandmother; her uncle; her aunt; her three cousins; and her best friend all sit around the big wooden table, which is littered with wine-stained glasses, dirty plates, the gelatinous-looking remains of the canapés. The atmosphere is both brittle and unburdened. The worst of it is over, the day is done. Now Ash is shoeless in black tights, her heels abandoned earlier, once most of the other guests had left.

"Who are they from?" asks her mother. Her voice is ragged.

"Er . . ." Ash feels around the pale pink bag for a card, peels it off, and hands it to her mother.

"Please," says her mother. "You do it."

Ash pulls a small card from the envelope; it is the same shade of antique pink as the bag and has a linear rose embossed on the front, over which she subconsciously runs her fingertip. Inside is a note scribbled in messy florist's handwriting with a water blotch on the ink.

Thinking of you all
Love and condolences,
The Tanners

"Who are the Tanners?"

Ash's mother sighs. "Literally no idea. Can you put them in some water?"

"We've run out of vases."

Her mother sighs again, and Ash knows that she must not mention anything more to do with flowers today. She sticks them in a vase that already holds a bouquet—the two bouquets look wildly mismatched, aesthetically unpleasing—then joins her family at the table.

Ella slops some white wine into Ash's empty glass. Ash makes a kiss at her.

The sun didn't come out today, not once, which is ironic as Ash's father was obsessed with sunshine, chased it around the garden, chased it around the world, kept a UV lamp in his home office for gray days, studied forecasts religiously, insisted on barbecues at the merest hint of spring. He'd wanted this house because it was south-facing; he had his favorite suntrap spots in the garden, one in particular where he could sunbathe even in February, which he referred to as "Ibiza." "I'm going to Ibiza for a bit," he'd say on a sunny morning, a coffee in one hand, sunglasses on his head. There was always a bottle of sun cream by the back door. All year round.

But today, the day they said goodbye to him, the sun stayed away. Ash liked to think maybe he'd taken it for himself. But on the other hand—no. She very much believes that dead people have no influence.

He was fifty-four.

He was killed by a stranger.

Pushed onto the tracks.

Under a train.

He was on his way home from a restaurant opening, not one of his but a friend's, in Soho. He was very drunk. He'd been drinking tequila slammers, according to his friend. The life and soul. Always the life and soul, Paddy Swann.

The man who pushed him was called Joe Kritner.

There. Done. One moment. Two lives. More, if you include the train driver, the witnesses, the paramedics who had to pull the bits of him off the tracks.

There's a photo album on the table; Ash and her brother, Arlo, had put it together. They'd left space in the final pages for guests to add their own photos of Dad, of Paddy. Ash opens it at a random page and sighs at the sight of her dad wearing a bucket hat and sunglasses, holding a pint of beer in a plastic cup at some kind of festival. Peak nineties, Ash thinks. He was born in 1970, so must have been about twenty-five here. Same age as she is now.

"Where's that?" she asks her mum, turning the album toward her mother.

"Ha, Glastonbury. Of course."

"Of course," says Ash drily. "Were you there too?"

"Yup. Oasis. Pulp. The Cure. Boiling hot. We went with Lena and Johnny. Dad got very, very . . ."

"Drunk?" Arlo suggests.

"And the rest."

They all smile wryly. Everyone knows what Paddy was like. He liked to drink, he liked to take party drugs, he liked to get stoned. He liked to listen to music all the time, always walked around in headphones. He liked vinyl, liked T-shirts, liked live music, liked people, liked food.

Paddy Swann was the most uncomplicated human being in the world, and then, two weeks ago, a very complicated person used Paddy Swann as a character in his own very complicated internal story and pushed him under a train. And now he is dead.

The remains of his clan are loud now, they don't know how to be quiet, even in the fading light of the day that they buried him. But the noise is riven through with something piquant and terrible. The lack of his voice, his laugh, his bulk. The fact that at the other end of today, everyone's lives will continue without him.

Ash slams the album shut and grabs her wineglass, tips it back, ignores the sugary, cloying warmth of it in her mouth, the way it leaches into the stale insides of her cheeks. How will they go to bed tonight? How will they say that this day is over, and the next bit begins?

Part Two

THREE

JANUARY

Ash picks up the card that is propped on the sideboard in the kitchen and reads the greeting inside.

Dear Nina and family

I just heard the news about Paddy. I am so devastated to hear of his death last year. Paddy and I worked together in a restaurant in Mayfair many, many moons ago. He was one of the nicest guys I ever knew, and one of the best chefs I've ever worked alongside. A few years ago, I chanced upon his restaurant in Whitstable and didn't realize it was his place until I saw him passing across the floor. I stopped him and we had a chat, and he looked so well, so full of his usual bonhomie and generosity of spirit. He pulled up a chair and joined me for the rest of my meal, forced good wines upon me. We caught up a little on our lives, his spent growing a family and a restaurant empire on the south coast, mine living the bachelor life and running a wine bar not far from where we first met in Mayfair. I always thought our paths would cross again someday, that I'd go back to Whitstable and enjoy another hour or two in his delightful company, eat another one of his delicious meals, but it never happened, life got in the way, and now it is too late.

Anyway, I just wanted you to know how much I adored Paddy and how sorry I was to hear that he had gone so young and in such tragic circumstances.

Yours, with sympathy and with love,
Nick Radcliffe

Ash waves the card at her mother, who is standing by the kettle, waiting for it to boil.

"Nice card."

Her mother turns. Her eyes are dull and tinged with gray circles.

"Oh," she says. "Yes. Very sweet."

"You ever met him?"

"No. I don't think so. At least, not that I remember."

Ash pulls her phone out of her pocket and googles the name, adds Mayfair to the search terms. His name pops up on LinkedIn and she clicks it.

Nick Radcliffe is listed as the "Co-founder and Owner of Bar Amelie in London W1." In his profile photo he looks about fifty, has pure white hair, a trim white beard, very blue eyes, and a pleasant smile. She turns the phone toward her mum. "Look," she says.

Her mum glances distractedly at the photo and says, "Nope. Never seen him before. He's quite hot, though."

Ash throws her mother a look of horror.

"What?" says her mother. "There's no law against it."

Ash googles "Bar Amelie" and finds a glitzy website for it. It's just off Curzon Street and is sleek and beautiful—brushed brass and pale velvet, three different types of caviar on the bar menu. It's the antithesis of her dad's restaurants: sandy-floored, rough-hewn, chalk-boards, tongue-and-groove cladding, smoky chowders and chargrilled lobsters.

"We should go there," Ash says, showing the wine bar's website to her mum. "Get him to tell us more about what Dad was like back then, before you met him."

"Your dad knew hundreds of people before I met him."

"I know. But he sounds really nice. He might have stories."

"Well then, you can go there," she says. "I'm sure he'd be thrilled to meet Paddy's lovely girl and share his stories with you. And you might get a free dinner. Or a job."

This last sentence is clipped and raw and there follows a small, tense silence.

"I might," says Ash. Then she puts the card back on the sideboard with a slightly haughty snap of her wrist. "I might."

Ash works at the fashion exchange boutique in the village. People bring in their old clothes; she and the shop's owner, Marcelline, steam them up in the back room to get the smell off them; then they hang them on expensive hangers next to displays of silk flowers and snazzy cabinetry. If the item sells, the customer gets 50 percent; the shop gets the rest.

It was meant to be temporary, this job, just a stopgap for the summer after coming back to live at home when London didn't work out for her, while she sorted herself out. But then it had been September, then October, then her dad had died and now it is January, nearly February, and she is still working in the fashion exchange boutique and still sleeping in her childhood bedroom, and she will be twenty-six soon and did not expect to still be here.

But as much as she knows she shouldn't be here, she doesn't want to move out. Not now. She wants to be in this beautiful house where she grew up, which still smells of her father.

She has regressed. She is going backward. She is falling.

FOUR

FOUR YEARS EARLIER

I kiss my wife on the lips. Her breath smells of last night's toothpaste mixed with sleep. But I kiss her every morning. It's what I do. It's part of the thing, the illusion, the rhythms that have formed the percussion of the last four years of our lives. If I did not kiss her on her lips in the morning, then she would wonder . . . and I don't want her to wonder. If she starts to wonder at the little things, then she will eventually start to wonder at the bigger things. So, I manage the little things forensically to make sure that everything is the same. Until it isn't.

"Morning," she says, curling into me, an arm reaching across my chest, her face nestling into the space between my shoulder and chin.

"Morning, my love." I kiss her hair. It smells of her laundry, and also slightly of her scalpy essence, which I don't love, but it's part of the deal. I snuggle into her, and we lie like that for a moment, as we do every morning. And then I peel myself away from her and stretch and yawn and climb off the bed, find my gown where it is slung across the armchair in the window, and slide my arms into it. The sky through the window is a rich blue, more like July than February. It sends a shiver of hopefulness through me. My time here in this stultifying, unsatisfying place is drawing to an end. I can feel it sliding away, like a dropped silk scarf running between my fingers.

I turn and smile at my wife. "I love you," I say.

"I love you too," she replies.

Then I say, "Oh, by the way, I'm speaking to George today."

George is my fictional financial advisor.

"He wants us to put a little more into our pensions. Just a thousand or two. He's found a little wriggle room."

Fictional pensions too. For the fictional future that we will be spending together.

"Oh," says my wife. "That's good. But I don't really have the cash to hand right now. Not after paying for your knee surgery."

I feel my jaw clench.

"I really think we should do it, though. Darling." The word almost hurts to utter. "Think about our future. You don't want to be doing this forever. You work so hard. We both work so hard. We need something soft to fall back onto, and the sooner the better. Every penny we put into that pension now, the closer we get to what we both want."

I hear her sigh, and I know it's a sigh of acquiescence and I feel my jaw unlock. The picture of the future I have painted for us is so exquisite that I almost wish it could be real. We will sell this house, this stupid house she bought when she left her stupid husband (nothing makes me happier than talking about how stupid her ex-husband is), and we will buy a house in the Algarve and she will paint and I will potter, and her children will come to stay and all of this, this dreadful day-after-day toil and drudgery, it will be over and we will be happy, forever.

"I'll see what I can do," she says.

"Thank you, darling," I say, and this time the word doesn't hurt because this time I mean it. She is my darling. My darling wife who would do anything for me. Absolutely anything.

FIVE

MARCH

Two days after Ash's twenty-sixth birthday, a parcel arrives. Ash sees it on the front step as she arrives home from work. It's not an Amazon parcel, it's in a smart box with a handwritten label, and at first she assumes it's for her, a late gift. But she looks closer and sees that it's addressed to her mother, so she scoops it up and brings it into the kitchen.

"Mum," she calls out. "There's a parcel."

"I know," Nina replies from her office at the top of the landing. "I asked the guy to leave it. I was in a Zoom."

"Looks interesting. Can I open it?"

"If you like."

Ash unloops her bag from across her chest and pulls off her teddy bomber jacket and oversized scarf. She gets scissors from a drawer and slices through the tape. As she folds back the arms of the box, she sees another box inside, pale antique pink with a teal satin ribbon.

"Er, Mum. I think you should open this. It looks like a present."

"Give me a minute."

Nina appears a moment later, taking AirPods from her ears and pulling a cardigan on over her work shirt.

"Ooh," she says, glancing at the pretty box. She looks at the writing on the address label and shrugs. "Don't recognize that."

Then she pulls the lid off the box and peels back some tissue paper to reveal a scuffed-up copper Zippo lighter and a note in a small envelope.

She glances at Ash, and Ash shrugs. Then she opens the small envelope and reads out the note:

Dear Nina,

I was going through old boxes the other day, looking for some letters from my late mother, when I came across this. It belonged to Paddy. He left it at the restaurant one night and I took it home to make sure nobody else snaffled it. When I mentioned it to him, he told me to keep it. I think he was intending to give up smoking, but I'm not sure that he ever did.

Anyway, I thought you might want it. A little bit of history.

I do hope you are holding up OK?

All my very best, as before,
Yours
Nick Radcliffe

"Wow." Her mum holds the lighter in the palm of her hand and stares at it.

Ash can see tears glistening across the surface of her eyes and touches her arm gently. "That's wonderful," she says. "Isn't it?" She picks up the letter and sees that Nick Radcliffe's email address is written under his signature. He clearly wants a response. "Can I?" Ash glances at the lighter in her mother's palm.

Her mother passes it to her, and Ash is taken aback by the weight of it in her hand.

"Everyone had these in the eighties and nineties," says her mother. "The smell of them—it takes me back."

Ash lifts it to her nose: a hit of butane, burnt metal, smoke. "Will you write to thank him?"

"I suppose so," Nina replies, her chest going up and dropping down with a heavy sigh. "Yes. I should."

"He wrapped it so nicely too. Do you think he's gay?"

"Ash!"

"Just joking! But it is so beautiful. The tissue paper. All of it." She hands the lighter back to her mother, who curls her fingers around it. "Can I keep the box?"

"Of course," says her mother. Then she sighs again and says, "I've got another stupid Zoom in a minute. But I'll be down after that. Maybe we could light the fire and watch some trash?"

Ash smiles and nods. "Yes. That would be nice."

Ash takes the box up to her room. She puts it on her dressing table. She'll fill it with something. With trinkets. Mementos. She goes to the window of her room, which overlooks the sea. The sun has just set, the sky through the bare trees is a dark, haunting gray, lacy with pale clouds catching the ends of the daylight. She feels the thud and canter of time running by as her early twenties bleed into her late twenties and thirty appears heavy on the horizon. She hears the drone of her mother's tired, end-of-the-week professional voice talking about staffing issues with the people who run her dead father's restaurants, the restaurants that her mother now has to run, even though she has another job, albeit a part-time one that she can do in an hour or two a day, but still, it's a lot. Her mother is tired and sad and alone. And so is she.

Four months and eight days since her dad died.

She thinks of Arlo, her baby brother, far away from here, living a life unaffected by the echoes of devastation that still ring around their home. He has his big, messy house full of friends, his high-paying job, his pub nights and club nights, his girlfriends (a different one every week), his weed, his tattoos, his normal life. He has the same freewheeling, formless starter life that Ash had been living up until eight months ago, but while Arlo takes it in his stride, hers had nearly broken her.

She flops onto her bed and goes onto Hinge, scrolls mindlessly for a while, thinking that a boy might save her, but they all look ugly to her, stupid and ugly. Then she goes onto Airbnb and looks at expensive apartments in stunning European cities that she can't afford to visit. Then, and only then, does she go to her camera roll, scroll backward through February, through their hideous Christmas, past the funeral and into the summer before, when she was lost and broken by a sequence of events that she still can't explain, and back further again until there she is, a year ago today, before any of the bad things had happened, and she stares at herself, that girl with slightly shorter hair, with a mouth wide open in the throes of laughter, her arm around her father, his arm around her, a glass of wine in his other hand, an apron tied around his waist, and a smile, that smile, the one he always had when it was sunny, when there was food, and especially when he was with her and Arlo, because he loved them both so much.

She lets her phone drop onto her chest, and she cries.

SIX

FOUR YEARS EARLIER

I look at my wife across the breakfast table. She looks tired. She's been looking tired a lot recently. It's probably my fault, but there's not a lot I can do about that. She was forty-four when I met her, a youthful forty-four. She's forty-eight now but looks closer to mid-fifties. She's put on a few pounds, keeps going on about "perimenopause" when she's ten years younger than Jennifer Aniston, who doesn't appear to have any problem keeping herself in shape. I want to tell her to put less butter on her toast, but I can't because that would be unpleasant, and I am a very pleasant man and a very good husband.

"You look like you could do with a holiday," I say.

She glances up at me, her tired eyes suddenly bright. But then they dull again. "We can't afford a holiday," she says. "You know that."

"Well, what if I told you that I'd had a bit of a windfall." I put it out there with a flourish.

"You have?"

"Yes, just a few hundred. Money I lent a friend a couple of years ago, they finally paid me back."

"A friend?"

"Yes. Peter Tovey. Remember I told you? He needed it to keep his child at that special school?" There is of course no such person as

Peter Tovey and this never happened. But what difference does it make?

She shakes her head vaguely. "No," she says. "I don't think I remember. But that's good, then. I mean, maybe we should put it toward one of the loans instead, though. A holiday would be nice, but the overdraft could really—"

I cut her off by reaching across the table and grabbing both her hands, smiling up at her with the brightest, warmest smile I can muster. "Darling, come on, look at you. You're exhausted. You need this. I'll book us something. Leave it with me."

I slide the box across the kitchen counter the following day. It's sky blue, her favorite color, and tied up with a silk ribbon. She looks at me, her tired eyes filled with curiosity and anticipation.

"I hope you haven't done anything silly," she says.

"Might have," I reply, and rock back on my heels, eye her with affection. "Go on."

She slips the lid off the box and there it is, the printout from the internet for the weekend in Lille I've bought for us, which includes an eight-course tasting dinner and travel on the Eurostar. "It's a Wowcher thing," I say. "We can use it any time before December thirty-first. So, shall we get our diaries out? Find a date?"

It only cost a couple of hundred per person, and she's paying for it, of course, even though she doesn't know that. I used the money she transferred into my account last month to put into our fictional pensions. But it's the thought that counts and the expensive gift box is all part of the illusion. A basic husband would just have forwarded the email, but a top-notch husband, the sort of husband a woman yearns for, prints it off and puts it in a box in her favorite color, presents it with a soft smile, and suddenly it's more than just a cheap Wowcher deal, it's a display of love and adoration.

She opens up her phone and beams at me, then scrolls through to her calendar app. "How about June?" she says. "Maybe the middle? The seventeenth?"

I pull out my own phone, find my diary, and scroll to 17 June, and of course there's nothing there because my life doesn't work like that, it doesn't have markers and delineations, it doesn't hang on dates and plans, it just hurls itself at me in disjointed chunks that I have to somehow knit together into something that looks like normality, and it's why I work so hard to maintain my charming exterior, because my interior is a chaotic hellscape beyond anyone's possible imaginings.

"Yes," I say, typing it into my phone, nodding, pretending to sound organized. "Yes. Perfect. Leave it with me. I'll book it tomorrow."

I kiss her on her cheek, breathe in and then quickly out again to expel the slightly sour, slightly salty smell of her skin, that end-of-day, officey smell that she sometimes has.

"You go and have a shower," I say. "I'll do dinner."

"Are you sure?"

"Of course I'm sure. Go. It'll be on the table in half an hour."

I kiss her again and smile at her, tenderly, softly, so genuinely that I can almost make myself believe that I adore her.

Then I turn and pull some garlic from the fridge, put it on a board, find a sharp knife, and hum something French under my breath as I cut it into thin, thin slices.

SEVEN

NOVEMBER

They have passed through a whole summer without barbecues, without noisy late-night parties, tents on the lawns, and Dad behind his decks. They have passed through Dad's fifty-fifth birthday, Arlo's twenty-fourth. And now they have passed through the first anniversary of Paddy's death. A full turn of the cosmos. A full complement of birthdays and anniversaries, seasons and holidays. A full year without him.

Ash glances up as Nina dashes into the kitchen, looking a little frantic.

She's wearing her dyed brown hair up in a topknot, big hoop earrings, red lipstick, a black crew neck, and cropped indigo jeans, platform-soled boots. She's fifty-one, but she can still get away with dressing like that. As she passes, Ash gets the backdraft of musky perfume.

"Are you going somewhere?"

"No, not going anywhere. Staying in. With Nick."

Ash exhales and closes her eyes slowly at the mention of his name.

Nick Radcliffe.

He's so lovely.

Such a lovely man.

But he's arrived too soon.

"What time is he getting here?"

"Half an hour ago."

Nina pulls a bottle of Dad's wine off the shelf and shoves it in the freezer, embedding it between packets of frozen peas and spinach and vegan nuggets that have been there since Paddy was still alive.

A year since he died. That's not very long. Not after thirty-three years together, twenty-eight years of marriage, two children, a devastating death. It's not very long at all. Nick seems lovely, but if only he'd arrived in their lives another year from now. Maybe even two. Maybe when there was nothing left in the freezer from when Paddy was still alive.

But Ash can't say anything, she can't make a fuss, because she is twenty-six and a half years old, and she should not be living at home. She should be out in the world, not sitting here watching her mother shove wine in the freezer drawer, not having to smell her mother's special perfume or watch her mother trying really hard to be wonderful for a man who isn't Ash's father.

The doorbell rings.

"Shit," says Nina, trying in vain to get the freezer drawer to shut.

"I'll do that," says Ash, getting to her feet.

Her mother smiles and goes to the door.

"Hello, you," she hears her say. Then, "Oh! Thank you! They're beautiful. Come in!"

Ash has just got the freezer drawer to close when he walks in.

Nick is six foot two. Dad was small. Only five foot eight. But what he lacked in stature he made up for in charisma. Nick has a full head of thick white hair. Dad's was thinning and had just started turning gray, about 20 percent of the way there, mainly around his ears. Nick wears a shirt and a jacket. Dad never wore a shirt or a jacket, he wore T-shirts and hoodies and denim jackets. Nick has white teeth. Dad's were a bit discolored. He'd had them bleached once, for his fortieth, but all the coffee and red wine had taken them back to normal again in under a year. Nick has piercing blue-gray eyes. Dad's were a deep golden brown, like brandy. Nick is handsome. Dad was just nice-looking.

"Ash," he says, striding into the room, all teeth and good hair and expansiveness, kindness, warmth, and glow. "Lovely to see you again. How are you?"

"I'm good," she says, offering herself up to his shoulder hug and cheek kisses. "You?"

"Good, yes! Busy. Mad. But good. And all the better for seeing you both."

Nina is arranging the flowers in a vase. They're very beautiful. Nick waves a bottle of champagne about and says, "It's ice-cold—we could just open it now?"

Nina smiles. "Yes. Good idea! I forgot to chill the wine, so it's only just gone in the freezer."

Nick plucks champagne glasses from the open shelving in the kitchen and turns them deftly the right way up using the stems, the same way Dad used to, a restaurant-trade flourish. He puts a cloth around the bottle, just like Dad always did, like a cloak, and tips the bottle just so toward the rims of the glasses, fills them perfectly, gives the bottle a small twist before putting it in the wine cooler. Because that is one thing that Nick does have in common with Dad. The restaurant trade.

Nick and her mum had started messaging each other after she'd written to thank him for sending Dad's Zippo six months ago. Nick had replied and then she'd replied and so it had gone on and somehow at some point it had blossomed into something, but Ash hadn't known about any of this. Nina hadn't said anything until suddenly, a month ago, she told her she was meeting someone for a drink.

"Someone *who*?"

"Nick Radcliffe," Nina had said, tentatively. "Remember? The man who sent me Dad's Zippo. The man who owns the wine bar in Mayfair?"

"Oh," Ash had said. "How come?"

Nina had smiled a smile so uncertain that Ash had physically ached at the sight of it.

Now Nick passes her a glass of champagne and she smiles at him and says, "Thank you." He pulls out a chair at the kitchen table and folds his long form onto it. Most of his height is in his legs and they stretch out across the tiled floor toward her, ending in a pair of expensive-looking suede trainers. "How's it going?" he asks in that pleasant way he has of asking things.

"Jobwise, you mean?"

"Yes. Did you hear back from the literary agency?"

She shakes her head, even though it's not true. She did hear back from the literary agency. They said that though they were very impressed with her qualifications and found her to be a "very engaging and likeable candidate," sadly there were others whose experience was more suited to the position and therefore they would not be pursuing her application any further.

"Ah," says Nick. "I'm sure there'll be another agency in touch before too long, biting your hand off."

She smiles tightly. "Yeah," she says. "Maybe."

"But meanwhile you've still got the boutique?"

"Yes, still got that."

Nina joins them, and Ash watches the sparkle appear, the sparkle that is only there when Nick is here, the sparkle that always used to be there and then died along with her father. Her mother is beautiful when she's with Nick. Her neck is slender, the curve of her cheek is pronounced, her spine is straight, her shoulders back, everything where it should be. The light catches the lowlights in her hair, the loose strand next to her ear, the gold hoops. Nick has eyes only for her.

Ash tips the end of the champagne down her throat and stands up. She makes her face soft and smiles. "I'll leave you to it."

She glances once behind her as she walks through the door into the hallway. She sees Nick's hand on her mother's hand. She tries to make herself want this for her, but she can't.

EIGHT

Alistair said he'd be home by five p.m. to help Martha empty the flower delivery van. Or at the very least to stay indoors with the kids and the dog while she emptied it. And now it's gone six o'clock and the last thing she wants to do is go out and empty the van.

She types in two question marks under her last message to her husband:

When home?

She looks at the kids. Troy is on the sofa, his legs outstretched, staring at his phone with his AirPods in, the dog on his lap. Jonah is at the dining table, his iPad propped up in front of him, doing some kind of art on the painting app. Weird stuff he puts on there, anime-type stuff. Nala, the baby, is in her walker, staring at the TV screen. Something to do with dogs with superpowers. The sky outside is black now, the last of the winter sun petered out a few minutes ago.

She calls over to Troy, who turns awkwardly and removes an AirPod.

"Will you keep an eye on the baby? I have to go and sort out the van."

He shrugs.

"And that means taking out your earphones, I'm afraid."

He sighs and shrugs again and then takes the other one out. The dog sits up perkily at the suggestion that something is happening and his face appears over the back of the sofa.

"No, Baxter," she says to the dog. "You need to stay here."

She puts on her jacket, grabs her bag, and walks onto the driveway. The van is pink. A classy, faded pink named California Rose on the color sheet. On the side panels, in black cursive, it says: "Martha's Garden. Fresh Flowers & Gift Baskets, Delivered to Your Door." It's an eye-catching van and it makes Martha something of a celebrity in the local area. Usually she'd be working tomorrow, but Alistair's taking her away for the weekend, two nights in a hotel in Normandy, just the two of them, so she's leaving Milly, her assistant, in charge of the shop, and her brother in charge of the kids.

She drives the van the three minutes to the shop on the high street and parks outside. She moves fast: Troy's a good boy, but he's likely to forget that he's meant to be watching Nala. He's a dreamer. Milly is still behind the counter, tidying up for the night. "Give me a hand, will you?"

Milly follows her out to the pavement and together they unload anything that Martha doesn't want to die in the van over the weekend. Martha looks at the time on the vintage clock above the counter. Six twenty-six.

"You get off now," says Martha. "I'll do the rest."

She sees Milly perk up. Milly is twenty and it's Friday night. It's been a long week, and she has a boyfriend she yearns for all the time.

"Are you excited?" asks Milly. "About the weekend?"

"I am," says Martha. "Slightly worried about leaving the baby with my brother. But, yeah, I'm sure it'll all be fine."

She and Al haven't been away together since before Nala was born. They were meant to be going away last month too, but Al had got called away by work. His job is like that. Sometimes he's at home all the time, other times they call him in at the last minute and he's away for days. He's a good man, but his job is a pain in the arse.

She looks at her phone. Still no reply. For God's sake.

She climbs into the van and does a three-point turn before heading home. The high street is lit up now with the first of the Christmas lights: twinkling puffballs hanging from the trees, narrow trunks wrapped in more lights, angel wings strung across the street at three separate points. They'd cost a fortune, those angel wings; all the local shopkeepers had pooled together to buy them a couple of years ago. But worth the money. Enderford High Street is one of the prettiest high streets in Kent, a mix of Victorian bow-fronted shops and pastel-colored Georgian town houses, coffee shops, antique shops, delis, and estate agents. The shops go all out for Christmas. Martha's is festooned with pale pink baubles and looks a treat.

At home everything is quiet. Nala is still transfixed by the super-powered dogs, Jonah is still drawing scary things on his iPad, Troy is still staring at his phone.

"Is Al back?" she asks Troy, even though she already knows he isn't.

Troy shakes his head and slowly replaces his AirPods.

It's nearly seven.

She mouths "fuck" under her breath, then she goes into the kitchen and gets some food on for the kids.

When Martha wakes up the next morning, she is happy for a moment because it's the weekend and it's not dark outside as it normally is when she rises at this time of the year. For a moment she enjoys the warm, luxurious glow of a lie-in, thinks of hot tea and buttered toast, and then it hits her—she's meant to be going to Normandy today, with Al. Her brother is due in two hours. Her favorite dress is hanging from the wardrobe, ready to be folded into her weekend case to wear at the lovely restaurant Al's booked them into for dinner tonight. But Al is not here.

A darkness descends.

`Sorry,` the message he'd finally sent her at eight last night had said. `Big blow-up at work. All hell let loose. Going to need to stay here overnight. Should be home by tomorrow afternoon. We can still make the dinner booking!`

She hasn't replied. She knows exactly what it means; should be home by tomorrow afternoon means I have no idea when I'll be home. Her stomach churns with anxiety.

She pulls back her bedclothes and puts on her silk dressing gown, then heads into the baby's room. Nala's still sleeping—she's a good little sleeper, much better than the boys ever were—so she leaves her and goes to the top of the stairs, smiles at Baxter lying at the bottom, wagging his tail furiously at her, and heads past him into the kitchen.

She met Al four years ago. She was pregnant two years after that. Not what she'd been expecting as a forty-four-year-old divorcée with a ten-year-old and a thirteen-year-old. Not how she'd seen the next chapter of her life. But then she hadn't seen a man like Al in her future. She hadn't known then that she was going to meet the perfect man.

She quells the fury and the disappointment, swallows back the nauseating anxiety of what the next few hours or days are going to feel like, fills the kettle, and switches it on.

NINE

Ash takes her morning toast into the living room and sits with crossed legs on the oversized sofa in the picture window that overlooks the sea. Sometimes you can see France from here, sometimes you can even make out the shapes of individual houses. But today there's a pall hanging over the channel and no sign of anything on the horizon. There's a chill in the air and she covers her bare legs with the fluffy blanket that sits on the back of the sofa, then picks up her phone and begins to scroll. She stops scrolling at the sound of breathing in her periphery, the whine of a floorboard underfoot, and turns to see Nick walking toward her. He's in boxers and a T-shirt. The sight is quite alarming. Boxers are basically underwear. They're pale blue with a cream windowpane check. His legs are slim and hard, deep dips carved into the point where his quads meet the flesh on the back of his thighs. His reading glasses are on his head, nestled into his thick white hair.

"Good morning, Ash," he says. "How are you?"

"Oh," she replies. "Good. You?"

"Yes," he says, rubbing at the back of his neck with his fingertips. "A little rough around the edges but otherwise OK. I was trying and failing to work your coffee machine."

Dad's coffee machine, she wants to say but doesn't.

"Oh," she says, peeling the fluffy blanket off her lap. "Sure. Let me . . ."

"No," he says. "Please. Don't. You look so cozy there. Just give me a quick pointer and I can work out the rest."

She explains the vagaries of the machine to him and when he goes, she toys with the idea of tiptoeing out of the other door and escaping to her bedroom. But she's twenty-six. She's not a moody teen. She straightens herself and waits.

When he returns a moment later, he's holding one of Dad's coffee cups.

He sits himself down next to her and she clears her throat, holding back the stupid fury and the stupid rage.

"This view," he says dreamily. "I mean, I have never seen anything like it. It's almost as if you're in the South of France. Hard to believe it's Kent."

"It's the cedar tree," she says, pointing into the middle distance. "That's what gives it that Mediterranean feel."

"Ah, yes," he says, nodding. "I can see that. It's beautiful. And you've lived here all your life?"

"Yes. Since I was a few weeks old. Apart from the bit when I was at uni in Bristol."

"Well, lucky you. What an incredible place to grow up."

She shrugs. "I guess."

It *has* been a wonderful place to grow up. Close enough to London to feel connected to a metropolis, but still with the old-fashioned charms of a Victorian seaside resort, the higgledy streets, the independent coffee shops and pizzerias, the pebble beach with sweeping views across the channel and around the coast toward the sinister, lumpen outline of Dungeness. It is wonderful. But she should not be here still, and her childhood idyll has lost its luster.

"Your parents," Nick continues, "very astute. Buying here before it was fashionable. I mean—this house." He gestures around himself at the high ceilings, the large, airy room, the rolling grounds. "What a place!"

She shrugs again. "I know," she says. "It's beautiful." She pauses, looks at him briefly. "What about you? Where do you live?"

"Oh, I'm in a temporary situation at the moment, renting a flat in Tooting."

"Tooting?" She is surprised, had imagined owning a wine bar in Mayfair equated with owning property somewhere in a smart Zone 1 postcode.

"Yes." He smiles at her playfully. "Something wrong with Tooting?"

"No. I just thought . . ."

He continues to smile at her. "Just thought what?"

"Nothing," she says, hearing the sound of her mother's steps down the staircase. She turns fully so that she can see her walk in and when she does, she feels a sense of relief. Her mother has her hair tied up in a bun and is wearing a gray oversized cardigan over her pajamas, thick socks on her feet, her big square reading glasses on top of her head.

Nina yawns and smiles and says, "Morning, angel," to Ash, then leans down and kisses the top of her head. Ash grabs her mother's hands and holds them for just a moment, long enough to anchor her, to center her, in the eye of this weirdness.

She hates how right her mum and Nick look together.

It had long been a running joke with her dad's friends that Paddy was punching when it came to Nina. But Nick isn't punching. She and Nick make a perfect match.

"Right," says Ash, pulling back her blanket, getting to her feet, picking up the empty plate she'd eaten her toast from, "I'm going to get ready."

Her mother strokes her hair again and then slides onto the sofa next to Nick, her legs pressed up against his, the fingers that had just been in Ash's hair now brushing gently against the hairs on his arms.

Ash turns and leaves the room.

TEN

FOUR YEARS EARLIER

On my way home to my wife from the train station, my attention is caught by the kind of wide-eyed, almost alien-looking girl I used to lust after when I was a young man. There is a disproportion between the size of her eyes and the structure of her face. She is wearing a beanie hat and a short puffa coat with yoga-type leggings and trainers. These elfin girls are no longer a threat to me or to my male ego now that I'm not a young man. Where once this girl might have thrown me into a tongue-tied state of desperation, now I can see her for what she is: powerless.

The sky is newly dark and she will of course be feeling less confident on this quiet back street than she would have an hour ago when the sun was still up. The thought of her fear plus the large vodka tonic I had at the station bar give me a quick, cheap thrill that I decide to follow through on by walking just a little too close to her, making my breath leave my body just a little more heavily than I normally would, and when she slows to check her phone, I slow too, and when she speeds up to try to put some space between me and her, I speed up, and I can smell it coming off her and it makes me feel so alive that by the time I get home I'm ready to fuck my wife, and I do, slowly, tenderly, like the perfect husband I am, making it all about her, but in fact it's all about the Bambi girl and the way she made me feel with those jerky little movements of her head on her tiny, delicate neck.

Afterward, my wife snuggles herself into my body and says, "Well, that was unexpected. What brought that on?"

And I say something trite about how I'd been thinking about her all day, and she likes that very much. So easily pleased. Most women are. Because most men are just so utterly dreadful. I don't understand why men don't realize how little effort is involved in making women happy and how many benefits there are to making women happy.

I help my wife cook the dinner. I throw a tea towel over my shoulder and we put on music and I dance a little with her and make her laugh and I keep her wineglass topped up and make sure the light is low enough for me to look at her and think she's pretty (she's not particularly, but she has a softness about her that's quite appealing, and a charming smile).

"Oh," I say, bringing my napkin to my lips to blot the buttery sauce. I wince to prepare her for the fact that I'm about to say something she won't like. "I'm really sorry. But it looks like I'm not going to be here for the drinks party."

Her face is pinched, and her fork hangs limply from her hand. "Our drinks party? On Friday?"

It was my idea. I thought it would stop her feeling bad about the fact that we don't really go anywhere or see anyone because I have her sold on this idea that the two of us don't need anyone else. But I also don't want her to feel trapped and lonely and turn those feelings against me. So I'd said, "Let's have a little get-together. Your family. A few friends." Her face had lit up like the dawn sky.

"Yes," I say now. "I've got to go up to Edinburgh, the whole weekend. I'm really, really sorry." I sound so sincere I almost believe it myself.

"But I ordered all those expensive canapés from M and S."

"I'm sure you can cancel the order," I suggest softly, my eyes limpid with sorrow.

"That's not the point," she says with an uncommon hint of crossness. She lets her cutlery drop onto her plate. "Why are you going to Edinburgh?"

"Work. The new place I was telling you about. They're having teething troubles and they're sending me in to work with the new crew."

"But—" She stops, her face changing color a little, and I can see anger building deep inside her and here it is, I think, the line we keep getting to and not crossing, the line where if she crosses it, she will look at me and think, *Who the fuck are you?* and demand answers and truth, and at that point, of course, the relationship is doomed, because I am no longer her perfect man, I am a problem. One small chip is all it takes, after all, to ruin a Royal Doulton teapot. I need to turn this back, quickly, so I manufacture glassy eyes (it's a neat trick an actor friend once taught me. I trigger myself with a memory of a childhood dog) and I take her hands and I say, "Darling, I can't bear letting you down. You know I can't. It kills me. And this—this is why we need to have a plan for our future, so I can stop all these stupid hours, stop having to leave you in the lurch all the time like this. So we can have a proper life together. A quality life."

Her hands yield to my touch as I speak. I feel her melt.

She sighs and says, "I'll see if I can cancel the order."

"Thank you, thank you so much. I don't deserve you, I really don't."

We got married three years ago, six months after our first date. It was low-key. Very low-key. Neither of her adult children attended. Her elderly mother came under duress. Her best friend, Fleur, was her matron of honor. Her mother died a year ago and I don't know what happened to Fleur. My wife's children visit quite regularly, especially her daughter, Emma, who is currently pregnant with her first child and about to make me, I assume, some sort of *grandparent*? I can tell this makes Emma very uncomfortable as she doesn't really see me as a true member of the family. She doesn't like me at all. Neither of Tara's children does. I don't care too much about that. I can't say I particularly like them either. I don't need to like them, and they don't need to like me. The most important thing, the key to everything, is that my wife trusts me. And she does. Implicitly. I have her passwords to everything. She lets me look at her phone. I have access to absolutely every last aspect of her existence. And she to mine. Or at least to the traces of mine that she knows about. I am a compartmentalized man—I have to be. In order to give women what they want, I need to juggle things, and juggling things necessitates secrets and, occasionally, lies. I can't give her access to everything. Obviously.

After dinner, I tell her that I'm going to have a shower and I leave her at her laptop, canceling food orders for our drinks party and messaging our guests. I squeeze her shoulders sympathetically as I walk past her and head upstairs. Then I pull my bag from the bottom of the wardrobe. It's a doctor's bag. It belonged to my father once upon a time—he was a GP—and is a concoction of compartments and pockets and zipped-up slots. Inside the innermost section of the bag is yet another compartment and inside that is my other phone. I pull it out and turn it on, my heart beating steadily as I type:

> *I've sorted it out, am free next weekend, can be with you at 8 pm on Thursday. Are you still up for it?*

I stare at the phone, waiting for the ticks to turn blue, which they do, immediately; the ticks always turn blue immediately. She is quite besotted.

I see that she is typing, and I glance at my reflection in the mirror inside the door of the wardrobe as I wait for her reply to appear. I'm looking a little rumpled, but my eyes are still bright, I am still better looking than most men I know of my age (I'm nearly fifty-one). I push out my chest and check that my pectorals have not begun to soften into man breasts, feel reassured by the strong outline of them through the fine white cotton of my business shirt. I run my fingers over my jawline, my manicured stubble doing a good job of masking some of the encroaching softness. Then I return my gaze to the phone and see that she has finished typing her response.

> *8 pm Thursday is perfect. Can't wait to see you. I'll meet you at the usual place. The kids are with my ex until Sunday lunchtime, so I'm all yours. Mx*

All yours.

I smile. She's younger than my wife. Only by four years, but it feels like a substantial age difference. Her children are younger. She's perter. Her waist still has that tightness to it at its narrowest point. Her skin still has a suggestion of dew. Not yet perimenopausal, I suppose. Though not far off. She lives in a picture-postcard cottage in a chichi market town in Kent, a world away from my wife's slightly sad new-build semi in a soulless development outside Reading. She is a successful businesswoman who can pay her own way in life, and she is lovely, with her cloud of soft blond curls, turquoise eyes, unusually long eyelashes, and soft rose-pink mouth, in a way that my wife, I'm pretty sure, never has been. But also—and this is key—she needs me in a way that she doesn't even realize she needs me. She still thinks of herself as the dashing divorcée, effortlessly juggling kids and a career whilst keeping her house beautiful, herself physically appealing. She has an active social life, great hair; she thinks she has it all and that she doesn't need a man. But she does. The way those blue ticks appear so quickly tells me that she does; the way I can still feel the sticky residue of a hasty wax on her inner thighs when we meet up at the last minute; the way she is sometimes clumsy in my presence, fumbles over simple things; the way she plays down her kids, even though I've never made the merest suggestion that I would prefer her if she came without them; the way she looks at me with a mixture of lust and terror—terror that I will cool off, lose interest, extinguish this thing I've lit here in her life, and leave her to smolder and then die.

She didn't think she needed a man until I turned up in her life with my Reiss overcoat and my suede Chelsea boots and my extravagant gifts, and the way I look at her as if she and only she is real and everything else is cheap wallpaper, and now she is addicted to something she didn't know she wanted. To me.

I smile at my reflection in the mirror and then look down again at her message.

All yours.

I reply with a single red-rose emoji.

See you on Thursday, beautiful Martha, I think. I cannot wait.

ELEVEN

Nina is dropping vegan croissants into the air fryer, wearing her business jacket (she had never owned a business jacket before Dad died, now she has a special one, dark blue with red-trimmed lapels, which she wears when she has to see people who are used to dealing with people who look professional). Her phone buzzes and she picks it up distractedly, looks at the notification on her screen, and Ash sees a hot smile pass over her face.

Nick left only an hour ago. Ash had heard the click of the front door, then glanced out of her window to see Nick heading away in the direction of the train station.

Three nights he'd stayed in the end.

The whole weekend.

And now that air all through the house of sex and newness and hormones.

"Did you have a nice weekend?" Ash asks.

"Yes," her mother replies softly, discreetly. "Yes. It was lovely."

There's a pert silence. It feels as if neither Ash nor her mother is breathing.

"Are you . . . ," Nina begins. She turns to face Ash, looks directly at her, and says, "Are you OK about it? About Nick?"

Ash shrugs and feels a little adrenaline spill into her blood. It's not a confrontational question, but if she answers it truthfully, it could lead to a row. "I guess." There's another silence. Ash ends it by saying, "Are you . . . I mean—are you OK about it?"

Nina nods. "I am," she says. "I mean, it's very unexpected. Obviously. I thought I was still grieving. I *am* still grieving. I really, really am. My heart is still . . ." She exhales audibly as if she's just been kicked in her gut. "It hurts, all the time . . ."

"Even when you're with him?"

"Yes. Even when I'm with him. But it's like . . . it's almost like I have a new heart alongside the old one, and the new one is fresh and unused, and it can be excited to be with someone and enjoy them and want to get close. If that . . ." She pauses, looks up at Ash. "If that makes any sense?"

Ash nods. It does and it doesn't. But she's not going to question it. What does she know? She's never been in love once, let alone twice. The only man she has ever loved is her father and he is dead. "So, is this going to be a regular thing now, do you think?"

"No idea," Nina replies. "He says he wants to book a weekend away, maybe get the Eurostar to Lille? But I don't know. He's a very busy man. Hard to pin down. We'll see."

Ash feels a pulse of anger toward her mother. She broke her year of mourning her husband of twenty-eight years to spend the weekend shagging a man who may or may not be taking her to Lille. Ash doesn't want to judge, but equally she expected more of her mother, a self-proclaimed feminist.

"So, you don't know when you'll be seeing him again?"

"No. But I'm sure it will be soon."

"And do you definitely want to see him again?"

There it is. The really big question.

Her mother nods. "Yes," she says. "I do. He makes me feel good. He makes me feel like . . . like there might be a part two? That my book didn't end?"

"You know he lives in Tooting?"

"Yes. He told me that."

"Wouldn't you think someone like him would live somewhere a bit posher than that?"

"Yes, well, he's having some financial problems with his wine bar, apparently. He did have a flat in Pimlico. But he had to give it up. The place in Tooting is just temporary."

A red flag jumps into Ash's consciousness.

Her father's restaurant business is worth a lot of money, she is sure, as is this house, which her parents bought for nothing when they were young and this village was unfashionable. Now her mother owns all three of her father's restaurants as well as this house, and in many ways could be seen as something of a unicorn in the middle-aged singles market.

"Has he ever been married?"

"No. But he was engaged once. In his twenties. No children."

Ash thinks of the tall, handsome man who spent the weekend in her mother's bed, the man with the easy smile and the nice way about him, the man who smelled good and had neat cuticles and defined muscles and a brand-new haircut, and she thinks, Why has this man never been married? And why does he have no children?

"Hmm," she says.

Nina raises an eyebrow at her. "Hmm what?"

"Nothing," says Ash, taking the hot croissant her mother is passing her and then heading to the fridge to get her vegan spread. "Just looks like the sort of man who'd have had a family. Some kids. Seems strange."

"The woman he was engaged to, the one he was going to marry and start a family with. She died."

"Oh." The sound leaves Ash's mouth, sharp and dry. Suddenly Nick is thrown into relief. Not only does he have a good reason for being single, but he also has a reason other than her mother's financial assets to want to be with her. They have their grief in common. "That's really sad."

"Yes," Nina says. "It really is. Anyway . . ." She picks up her phone and looks at the time. "I need to run. I'll be back this afternoon. I can bring you something for your dinner from the kitchen? Vegan burger, maybe? Or the vegan Halloumi thing you like?"

It's what her dad used to do, bring her back treats from work.

"Just anything that looks good," Ash says. "Thank you."

Ash heads down the hill into the village at ten o'clock. Marcelline is just unlocking the shop as she arrives. "Good morning," says Marcelline, her words leaving her mouth in clouds of icy breath. "How was your weekend?"

Ash shrugs and smiles. "It was OK," she says. "How was yours?"

"Not so bad."

The shop feels cold and unloved. It's housed in a three-hundred-year-old building that sits on a corner and leaches all its heat out through gaps and cracks every weekend and then takes the whole of Monday to warm up again. Marcelline plugs in the blow heater near the shop desk and turns it on, rubbing her hands together. Ash takes off her coat and hangs it in the staff room at the back of the shop, fills the kettle and flicks it on.

"Mum's got a boyfriend," she calls out to Marcelline. "But . . ." Ash pauses, realizes she's just said more than she should, that people want to know how Nina is getting on and that Marcelline might tell someone who'd inadvertently spread it around the whole village. "Don't tell anyone."

"I won't." Marcelline appears at the door of the staff room. "But that's . . . good, isn't it? It's been . . . ?"

"A year. And twenty days."

"Well, that's quite a long time. And your mother is a very vibrant woman, very warm. It doesn't surprise me really that someone would have made a play for her. What's he like?"

"He's nice. I think."

"Think?"

"Yes. I mean, I was the one who told my mum to write to him in the first place, because he sounded so lovely in the card he sent her. He used to work with my dad, thirty years ago. Saw the story about Dad in the papers and got in touch."

"That's sweet."

She tells Marcelline about the Zippo in the pink box, and the wine bar in Mayfair and the dead fiancée, and then she shows her Nick's photograph on LinkedIn.

"He looks lovely," Marcelline says approvingly. "Tall?"

"Six foot two–ish?"

"Wow, the full package." Then Ash sees her flinch when she remembers that Paddy was not a tall man. "Sorry. I didn't mean to . . ."

Ash smiles. "It's fine. Who doesn't like a tall man?"

"So, are you feeling OK about it? I know how close you were to your dad."

"I'm feeling happy that my mum's happy, you know. She's such a good person and I like seeing her happy. But I'm also worried. I mean . . . what if he's not what he seems? What if he's after her money?"

"Er, you said he owns a wine bar in Mayfair."

"Well, he co-owns it. And it's in a bit of financial trouble at the moment, according to Mum."

Marcelline sighs. "I'm sure it's fine."

"Yup," says Ash. "I'm sure it is. It's just . . . weird."

"Of course it is."

And as she speaks, Ash's gaze is caught by something to her left, on the desk where Marcelline does all her paperwork.

It's a pink box, filled with pens and pencils. It's exactly the same as the pink box that Ash has on her own desk in her room, the box that Nick had sent Dad's Zippo lighter in.

"Where did you get that?" she asks, pointing.

Marcelline glances at it and then back at Ash. "That pink box?"

"Yeah."

"God, I don't know. I think it was a gift box—it was . . ." She snaps her fingers. "Soaps? Maybe? A couple of years ago. Such a pretty box, I kept it. Why?"

Ash shrugs. "Nothing," she says. "No reason."

TWELVE

Alistair finally comes home on Monday evening. He appears to have had a haircut and is clean-shaven. Martha narrows her eyes at him as she watches him walk through the front door with his overnight suitcase, his overcoat, his work bag, the smell of outdoors on him, the smell of trains and unknown places.

She sucks down hard on the urge to yell at him. Instead, she stares at him passive-aggressively and says "Hi" with a chip of ice in her tone.

"Martha," says Al, removing his bag from his shoulder, unlooping his cashmere scarf, "darling. I am so, so, so sorry."

She can't find words, so she shrugs petulantly.

The boys are at their father's, Nala is in bed, the house is quiet and still.

"So, what was the emergency this time? I see you had time to get a haircut."

He absent-mindedly puts a hand to his head. "Ah, yes. There was a barber's in the hotel. Seemed a good use of my time."

"You stayed in a hotel with a barber's?"

"Yes, the same one I always stay at."

"I didn't know it had a barber's."

"Well, it's more of a hair salon, really. But they do very good men's haircuts."

"I could have cut it myself." She hates the way she sounds, the sourness of her voice. She imagines it in his ears, ears that have been away from her for three full days, filled with the sounds of other people's voices, fresh, interesting people, probably women too, women who don't work eight-hour days in a flower shop and come home with red-raw hands and burnished cheeks, women who wear tailored office attire, fitted sweaters, heels even, who straighten their hair and contour their faces and look like they just stepped out of a magazine. And then he comes home to a messy cottage and a wife with a voice like acid, and this cold, hard silence.

"I didn't want to ask," he says, his voice soft and kind. "You're always so busy. I thought it would take one more job off your plate."

The softness of his tone takes the top layer off her anger and resentment. "I just wish . . . Al—why can't you be more organized? Why do you just . . . disappear? Not give me at least some warning? It makes me feel so powerless. Like you hold all the cards. Like you have the controls."

He sighs and lets his head flop. Then he looks back up at her again and she sees a sheen of tears across his eyes. "I am so, so, so sorry, Martha. I can't even find the words to tell you how sorry I am. I'm hopeless. It's this stupid job. It's my ADHD."

Oh *God.* Martha bites down on her need to shout again. The ADHD. He was diagnosed a couple of years ago and now he uses it as an explanation for every last fuckup and oversight. And she wants to sympathize and be kind, but sometimes she just wants to tell him that she knows people with ADHD, she knows *children* with ADHD, who are more considerate, organized, and reliable than he is. That he cannot use it as an excuse for absolutely everything. But she can't say that, because that's what an uncaring bitch would say, and she does not want to be an uncaring bitch.

She tucks her hair behind both ears and stands up. She had resisted the temptation to get into her bed clothes when she showered after work. Part of her wanted to do it just to fuck him off, to make a statement about her mood. But another part wanted to look delicious for him, to make him relish getting home, wonder why he ever went away, make him forget about the women in formfitting clothes. So, she's in a cashmere sweater and skinny black jeans and her curly hair is up, how he likes it, and she wears golden hoops and has bare feet, her toenails painted a creamy beige, scent behind her ears, a glass of wine in her fragrant, moisturized hand.

"How was it?" she says. "The work thing?"

Al works for a hospitality company that provides training for hotel and restaurant staff at high-class establishments. He's a director there: he doesn't have to do much fieldwork and mostly works from home since Covid. But sometimes they call him in, like the big guns, and he has to drop everything and travel across the country at short notice. He gets put up in fancy hotels and treated like a demigod. And then he comes back here, to dirty nappies and moody teens and a wife who is finding it increasingly difficult to hold back her resentment.

He sighs, picks up some letters from the console, and leafs through them noncommittally. "Fucking nightmare," he says. "Fine-dining brasserie in Glasgow. Staff are all school-leavers. Sweet as pie, but not a clue." He puts the letters down and sighs, then stops and stares at Martha. "I really missed you," he says. "I missed you so much."

Martha blinks slowly. "I tried calling," she says, "but it just kept going to voicemail."

"Yes. I had it on silent. I'm so sorry. It was intense. And I've messaged the Airbnb in Normandy. She couldn't give me a refund, but she's given me a credit, so we can go another time."

He had time to message the Airbnb, but not enough time to message her?

She can't. Not now. She shakes her head slightly and then sighs loudly. "Great," she says. "Let me look at my diary."

Then he opens up his arms to her and she walks into them, glad he's here, glad it was only three days, not three weeks, glad that he still loves her. And she wonders what happened to the woman she used to be.

THIRTEEN

FOUR YEARS EARLIER

We're outside the station near Martha's house and I don't want to say goodbye to her. This weekend has been perfect. We stayed holed up in her cottage with her dog, Baxter, and a fridge full of the fancy wine I brought with me. We ordered in food from the chichi Italian in the chichi village where she lives and watched movies and walked her dog and had sex and I stared into the bluest eyes I have ever seen and smelled skin that bloomed like rose petals and felt the sweet heat of her breath in my ear saying my name. Her home is so warm. Her bed is so soft. I could fall in love with this woman, I really, really could.

"When will I see you again?" she asks, and it's brusque, to the point. It takes me aback a little. I'm not used to women asking for exactly what they want.

"Soon," I say. "Very, very soon. But you know it's a bit tricky."

She nods and sighs. I've told her that I'm based in a hotel in Edinburgh for the foreseeable, until they open its doors next month. It's almost true. Except that the hotel is in Essex, and I am only there for three days.

"I understand," she says, and I smile.

That is the first hurdle crossed.

Martha, it seems, has an understanding nature.

On the train, I turn on my phone and see five missed calls from my wife and a series of voicemails, all saying the same thing: "Where are you? You need to come home. It's urgent."

I don't call her. I don't want to hear her voice in my ear, the ear that still tingles with the feel of Martha's breath. I'm not ready to face her yet; if my feelings toward her were diminished before this weekend, they are now annihilated. There is nothing left. Anything I ever felt for my wife is dead. So I pull up some music on my phone and I put in my earphones and for the rest of the journey, I listen to songs that make me feel alive.

My wife greets me at the door of our sad house in our sad road. She's wearing a sad jumper with sad trousers and her hair, after my weekend lost in Martha's wild curls, looks so defeatedly and disappointingly straight. I feel sure I once loved her hair, the hints of hazel and gold in it when it catches the light, the way it sometimes flicks inward toward her mouth, like a comma or a speech mark, before she peels it away with a fingertip. But not now.

Her face is contorted and I feel a blunt thrill of excitement, and then a tang of fear. For a moment I think she is going to start crying, or worse, that she is going to make a scene, lambaste me in some way, pull down the crumbling edifice of this awful marriage.

But she does neither of these things. Instead, she opens her mouth just a crack and half whispers the words: "Jonathan, the police are here."

I feel the blood drain away from my face, away from my heart, away from my stomach. I feel weak for a moment, as if I might pass out, and then the adrenaline kicks in, the fight-or-flight response, and I know that I can do neither of those things. If I run, it looks like I have something to run from; if I get angry, it looks like I have something to be angry about. So, instead, I feign wry surprise and say, "Oh dear, what have you been up to now?"

My feeble joke does not, of course, elicit a laugh, it wasn't meant to, but it does neutralize the moment and means that when I step into my home my breathing is steady and I appear the very picture of a decent, upstanding human being.

There are two of them, both women, one very young, the other one fortyish. They stand up and I tell them not to, a wide smile across my face.

They introduce themselves: the older one is called Beth and does all the talking. My wife passes me a cup of tea and I touch her hand, affectionately. "Thank you, darling."

"Mr. Truscott. We would like to talk to you about complaints made by two women who have come forward separately to report a man matching your description following them at night."

The slight I feel is real and raw and my voice is surprisingly emotional as I put my hand against my chest and say, "Me?"

"Yes, sir. One of the women involved asked a neighbor whose house she passed while she felt she was being followed if she could see her doorbell footage the following day. The man following her is seen very clearly at close quarters to the woman in question and does very much match your appearance. The woman in question posted the clip to a neighborhood app and another woman saw it and recognized the man on camera as a man who had behaved the same way a few weeks earlier. And then someone posting under what appears to be a false name claimed that they know you well and offered the women your name and address in private messages."

I blink furiously. "Sorry. This is . . ."

The woman's eyes go to my shoes, my suede desert boots with the contrasting tan elasticated side panels, my long legs, my distinctive, black-framed glasses. She sighs and shows me a still on her phone of a man who does indeed look a lot like me, but who is not definitively me, not by any stretch. It's dark and the footage is fuzzy and really, I could be any leggy man with white hair and black-framed glasses.

I analyze the photo for something that will make it clear that this cannot possibly be me, but then I notice the distinctive shape of the elasticated panels on my desert boots, and I gulp silently. "This is not me," I say. "I don't even know where this is."

"The boots, Mr. Truscott, look at the boots."

Her fingertips sit against the screen of her phone as she pulls the image wider, zooming in on the boots, and I breathe a sigh of relief. "Those are not my boots," I say. "Look. They're black. These are gray. And that man has much smaller feet than me. Mine are a size thirteen. His are . . ." I shrug dismissively. "A ten?"

The policewoman called Beth cocks an eyebrow. "Are you a detective, Mr. Truscott?"

"No," I say, "but I do have an eye for detail. And everything about that image is wrong. The shape of his shoulders. His height. All of it. And like I say, I have no idea at all where that footage has been filmed."

"Where were you, Mr. Truscott, at two minutes past six on the night of the twelfth of February?"

"God, I have no idea." I turn to my wife, hoping that she'll say something helpful. Or at least not say something that will entrap me or trip me up. "Darling? Do you remember?"

She glances at her phone and scrolls back to the date on her calendar. "You were in Gloucester."

I turn back to the police detectives and blink, nodding my agreement with my wife's information. "That's right," I say.

"And what were you doing in Gloucester, Mr. Truscott?"

"Business. I'm a hospitality trainer. I was working with a young team at a boutique hotel."

"And can you prove that's where you were?"

"Well, yes," I say. "Of course. The whole team was there. They'd be—"

"Oh," my wife interjects suddenly, dreadfully. "That was the day you came home. Now I think of it. Because I remember going to collect your shirts from the cleaners that day, so they'd be hanging up for you . . ."

I blanch. Everything about this is terrible. The fact that she has now placed me back here in Reading on the day in question, and the cringey way she talks about my shirts, as if she is my housekeeper, my lackey. I feel the mood shift, the eyes of the two female officers on me in a way that feels a little less neutral.

"How did you travel home, Mr. Truscott?"

"On the train," I say.

"And which train would that have been?"

And here it is. The train puts me in exactly the right time and place to conceivably have been following that stupid girl down the street. So I tell her the train I was on and tell her, yet again, that I have never been on that street before, that that man is not me, that that girl is mistaken, and that they are wasting their time.

The police officers leave a moment later and then it is just me, and my wife, in a quiet house full of awkward, unasked questions.

"That was weird," says my wife, picking at the skin around her fingernails.

"Yes," I agree. "Bizarre. But that was not me. You know that, don't you?"

I see her eyes flick toward me and then away again.

"Oh," I say, "come on . . . seriously? You seriously think that might have been me breathing down the girl's neck like a total freak?"

"No. Of course not. But . . . God, he really, really looked like you, Jonathan. I mean he did, didn't he?"

I want to break her jaw. I want to feel it shatter under my hardened knuckles. Instead, I smile gently, I put my hands on her hands. "Yes, he did. But it's just a crazy coincidence. That is all."

She nods, and I lift her face by her chin and kiss her exquisitely gently on her lips. I expect her to melt into the kiss, but instead I feel her freeze, her lips harden.

This is it. I can smell it, feel it, taste it. We've reached the end. She might not know it yet, but I do. I've been here before. The tipping point. Except usually it is not precipitated by a visit from the police accusing me of being a sex pest. (And to be accurate, I am not a sex pest. I was merely invading that woman's personal space because I was annoyed by her energy. I wanted to ruffle her smug, implacable feathers, not rape her.)

We have dinner and the mood is strained and odd. And then I feel it coming from way down the line, like the chirrup of a distant train. She pushes her food around her plate and then she suddenly stops and looks at me and says, "Jonathan. Who are you? Who are you really?"

I blink at her. "I'm sorry, I don't . . . ?"

"Because there are things, Jonathan, things that don't make sense, and I've been so patient, so very patient, waiting for everything to fall into place, for all of this"—she gesticulates wildly between the two of us—"to make some kind of sense, for all the money to make a difference to everything, for us to move on to the next stage, but it's like we're swimming in circles and it doesn't matter how many loans we take out or how many hours I work or how hard you work, there's never any money. And sometimes, Jonathan, sometimes I just really feel like I have no idea who you actually are."

I let my head roll back slightly and I observe my wife, this new version of her, the one who has stopped living in the moment and has started putting the moments together.

"Who have you been talking to?" I ask softly.

"Nobody. I haven't been talking to anybody, I've just been . . . thinking."

"You know that's mad, don't you? I'm your husband. Of course you know who I am. I've lived here in this house with you for nearly four years. We know everything there is to know about each other."

"No, Jonathan. You know everything there is to know about me. I barely know anything about you. I've never met a colleague, a friend, a relative—I mean, how do I even know you were where you said you were this weekend? I have nothing. No way of contacting you. No one to call if there's an emergency—"

"Emergency?" I deflect. "What sort of emergency?"

"It doesn't matter. I just feel, Jonathan, as if there's a dark void here, in our world, and that you emerged from it and now I'm being sucked down into it too."

Her eyes are wide as she ends this strangely poetic statement, as if she has scared herself by finally speaking her truth.

I sigh and close my eyes slowly, then open them again and look deeply into those dark, scared eyes. "Tara," I say, "I love you. I adore you. Just keep the faith. Stay strong. Please, Tara, don't give up on me. Not now."

FOURTEEN

Ash goes to the cute little café across the street from the boutique and buys her usual lunchtime avocado, tomato, and vegan pesto panini. The couple who run the café are thirtyish and have a small, scruffy dog that sits in the window in a plaid jacket, watching the world go by. They are both smiley and comfortable in each other's company. Ash watches the way they negotiate the narrow space behind the counter like a choreographed dance and she thinks, How did you meet each other? How did you know? How did you find the money to start a café? How did you know that was what you wanted to do? What is it like to be *you*?

She taps her card to the contactless reader and smiles at the woman, who is probably only five years older than her but so clearly a woman and not a girl, and she takes her panini from the café, petting the dog as she passes. She sits on a bench on the promenade overlooking the sea, which is gray and frantic in the wind rolling in from the south.

It's not, she thinks, as she unwraps the paper from around the sandwich, that she wants a husband, or even a boyfriend. She just wants to know that the boyfriend or the husband will arrive at some point. That the job will arrive. That the career and the dog and the flat and the whole deal will arrive. It doesn't have to be now. But some sort of guarantee would quell the fear.

She sees two girls she went to school with walking past, one with a red cockapoo, the other with a golden cockapoo. The friends, who are wrapped up in similar full-length puffa coats and are wearing similar bobble hats, clutch coffee in paper cups and are lost in a deep conversation. As they pass, Ash sees that one of them—she thinks her name is Lauren, she's not quite sure—is pregnant. They don't notice her as they pass and she is glad; she realizes that she has let them all go, all the local friends, because she thought she was gone from this place, thought her time here in this small seaside village was done, that she didn't need them anymore. But then she clearly didn't have any idea who she was back then, what she was capable of, how badly she could possibly mess everything up.

She'd thought she was normal back then.

And now she knows she's not.

The house is empty when Ash gets home that afternoon and she patrols it for a while, looking at all the places that Nick had been that weekend, looking for bits of him. She doesn't know why. It's as if, she suddenly realizes with a shot of dark dread, she's obsessed with him.

She goes to her mother's bedroom and opens the door, looks at the bed, loosely made in that way her mother always makes beds, like she doesn't really believe in making beds but does it anyway. She goes to her mother's en suite and stares at the shelves above the sink, the rows of lotions and serums and cotton buds, HRT patches in a little pink packet. She opens the cabinet and looks for her father's razor, which is still there where he left it the day he went into town to help celebrate his friend's restaurant opening and didn't come back. Her mother said she would never move it, that it would stay there forever.

But now there is Nick Radcliffe, and how will Nick Radcliffe feel about this razor, still with flecks of Paddy Swann's wildly multicolored stubble in it?

The toilet seat is up, she notices, then pulls the sleeve of her jumper over her hand to pull it down. How rude, she thinks, to leave the lid of your new girlfriend's toilet open in the bathroom she once shared with her dead husband. How incredibly rude.

She goes to the head of her mother's bed and looks at the pillows, hastily plumped into a haphazard pile. She sees a single white hair, so white, the color of fresh snow. She shudders, thinking of Nick Radcliffe's head on the pillow, his body in these sheets. Why did he have to come here? Why couldn't he have invited Ash's mother to his place, in Tooting? Why, she wonders, would anyone want to have sex in the bed of a dead man?

And then her eye is caught by something on the floor by her father's side of the bed. It's buried in the thick shag pile of the lambskin rug that covers the wooden floorboards: a simple gold ring. Big. Too big to be one of hers or one of her mother's.

She jumps at the sound of the front door banging open and closed and then her mother's voice up the stairs: "Ash! Are you home?"

"Yes. I'm here. Coming down."

She picks up the ring and stares at it for a moment, then tucks it in her pocket and heads downstairs to greet her mother.

FIFTEEN

Martha doesn't notice it's gone until the following day.

"Al," she says, staring at his hand holding a cereal spoon at the kitchen table. "Where's your ring?"

Nala is on Martha's hip, drinking her morning milk bottle. Troy and Jonah are getting ready for school. Al glances down at his hand and then up at her. "Ah," he says. "Yes. I think I left it in the changing rooms at the gym."

"What gym?"

"At the hotel. It's the only explanation. The only time I ever take it off is at the gym. I called them and they said they haven't seen it, but the manager who was there at the weekend will have a look when he's in tomorrow. I'm really sorry, darling."

Blood rushes through Martha's brain, making her feel light-headed for a moment. He finds time to go to the gym, but not to call her. There's time for haircuts, but not to reply to her messages. The baby wriggles in her arms and Martha slots her into the high chair, puts a finger of dry toast on the tray in front of her.

"What will you do?" she says. "If they can't find it?"

"I don't know. Replace it, I suppose."

"But, Al, that cost nearly a thousand pounds. I . . ."

"Maybe the household insurance will cover it?" He looks up at her sheepishly through his black-framed glasses. "I'm really, really sorry. But I feel like it will turn up, you know, that . . . that the universe will return it to me." He smiles and she smiles back.

"Well, I hope you're right," she says, turning to the dishwasher to put away the boys' breakfast things. Her gaze goes to the view through the kitchen window, out across her tiny garden, stripped now of all the magical foliage and greenery that make it look like a fairy tale during the spring and summer months: the curved bench under the lilac tree, the firepit surrounded by low-slung teak armchairs with floral cushions. Just then, a flake drifts lazily past, then another and another, and soon the sky is filled with them, and she turns to Al and says, "Look! It's snowing!"

The boys gather at the window too, and Al plucks Nala from her high chair and brings her over. The five of them stand together watching the wonder of it, the luminescent, airless flakes cascading across the garden, and for a short while, Martha forgets about her lost weekend in Normandy, about the ring, about the haircut, about all of it, and just feels so glad she found a good man who will stand with his baby in his arms and show her how to love the snow.

SIXTEEN

FOUR YEARS EARLIER

The atmosphere is sour now in our sad little house in Reading. My wife pretends that everything's fine, but of course it isn't. Nothing will ever be the same following that visit from the police, and even though they have not found enough evidence to bring harassment charges against me, the backdraft of it lives on in this house, in the space between my wife and me. Also, there's something strange about the way her daughter, Emma, has been acting since the police visit. She's over more frequently, usually leaving just as I get home from work, or arriving just as I leave, almost as if she's timing her visits specifically to avoid seeing me. Sometimes I see the extra mug in the kitchen sink when I get back from work and I know that she's been, but my wife doesn't mention it to me.

I know what all the secrecy means. It means that my wife is discussing the next stage of her life with her daughter, planning her exit strategy, and that, I'm afraid, I cannot countenance, absolutely not. This marriage ends when I am ready for it to end, and not a moment sooner.

On Wednesday afternoon I had been going to tell my wife that I had to travel to Belfast on Friday, for the weekend. I was going to tell her that there had been a bust-up between the general manager and the housekeeping manager of a boutique hotel there and that I was being called in to broker peace. In reality, I had planned to take Martha to Cambridge for the weekend: punting, the Bridge of Sighs, the splendor and awe of it all. But now I don't feel safe leaving the house for a whole weekend; it will give my wife too much space to plan and plot, to change locks, call in the cavalry. But I can't not see Martha. I ache for her. I can't remember the last time I felt like this about a woman, and I wonder, maybe if I'd met Martha when I was younger, then none of the other bad stuff would have happened. All the bad marriages.

But maybe it's not too late for my happy ending?

I walk to the end of the garden and call her.

"Martha," I say. "It's me. I'm really sorry, but I don't think I'm going to be able to make this weekend after all. Something's come up at work."

"Oh," she says, and I can hear the flutter of disappointment in her tone. "Oh, that's a shame."

"I know. I'm gutted. So gutted. I've been looking forward to it so much. I had so much planned. This amazing seafood restaurant." He sighs. "But listen, what are you doing now?"

"Now?"

"Yes, right now, this very minute. I could be with you in . . ." I pull my phone briefly away from my ear to glance at the time " . . . two hours, three maybe. I could bring wine, food, whatever you want. I just need to see you so badly."

"Um," she says. "I mean. I was just about to start dinner for the boys. I haven't washed my hair. I'm . . . I need to . . ."

"You don't need to do anything. Please. Just let me come. I miss you."

"Are you sure this isn't a booty call?"

She laughs drily, but I don't respond with humor. I respond with ardency.

"Martha. I want you to know . . . I need you to know . . . the way I feel about you, it's so much more than the physical. I mean, the physical is amazing, of course, it's utterly amazing, but it's you, Martha. It's you I crave. I don't know how this has happened, and happened so quickly, but you are already so important to me. I've never felt like this before."

My voice is soft and emotional and it's not fake, it really isn't. This is more than physical. And this woman is remarkable. She really is. I can feel my destiny is to be with her.

"Oh," she replies simply, and I can hear that soft vulnerability in her voice, the softness that tells me she's the right woman, "that's . . . lovely."

"So," I say, "please. Can I come?"

She says yes, of course she says yes. And I go straight upstairs to throw some things into a small backpack, and I leave by the front door without saying goodbye to my wife.

Martha's older son eyes me from the dining table, which sits in a nook at the far end of her living room. I can't remember his name—Travis, I think, or something American-sounding like that. He's a nice-enough-looking boy, clearly takes after his father as he looks nothing like Martha. His parents split up eight years ago, so I assume he's seen other men flit in and out of his mother's life. He doesn't seem too disturbed by my presence here, even manages a small smile, which I appreciate greatly, especially coming from a thirteen-year-old boy. Young men should never underestimate the power of a good smile.

He's doing some kind of homework and if I were in a film about a guy coming to the home of his brand-new love interest and seeing her son hard at work on something, I would saunter over and say something like, "What's that you're doing there?" and offer to help, but no, just no, that makes me shudder. I know kids, and I particularly know kids of single mothers, and no, they do not want some fly-by-night random smarming all over them and offering to help with their homework. So I merely eye him back casually, give him a nod, and return his small smile. That will do, that is plenty.

Martha beckons me through to the kitchen. She designed this kitchen herself. It's all moody blues and patinated brass, things hanging from racks, shabby bistro chairs, floppy-headed flowers in pale glass vases. She seats me at the table, and I watch as she lifts champagne glasses from metal shelves and passes them to me. I squeeze the cork from the bottle and study her face as I do so. She's just exquisite. Her curls are tied up this evening into a puff on top of her head, her huge blue eyes set off by the pale blue blouse she's wearing with baggy jeans. The cuffs of the blouse are elasticated and pushed up her forearms, revealing her narrow wrists, delicate hands, fingernails kept short and unpainted because of her job, but I've always liked plain fingernails on a woman.

"Champagne on a school night," she says. "What a treat."

"You know," I say, pouring the champagne carefully into the two glasses, "I've never understood why people keep it for special occasions. My mother had a bottle"—I've told this story so many times before, I can almost believe it's true—"that she won in a raffle in 1987. It was still in the back of her fridge when she died in 2002. And my mother loved champagne. She just never felt it was the right moment to open it."

"That's very sad," says Martha. "How old was she? When she died."

"Sixty. No age. No age at all."

"Oh, I'm so sorry. What was it?"

"Cancer. Ovarian." I wince as the words leave my mouth, as if the pain of the memory still lives inside me.

"What about your dad?"

"God knows. And I don't care. He's a horrible man."

"Really?"

I nod sadly. "A sociopath. A narcissist. An abuser. I could blame him for everything if I chose, but I do not choose, because that would give him power, and he has no power. Not anymore."

Martha looks alarmed, but also tantalized. I can tell she wants to ask me questions about my horrible father, but also that she's not sure she should, that she doesn't want to appear insensitive or ghoulish. "When did you last see him?" she asks instead.

"A while ago. Ten, maybe twelve years. Around the time that Ruth died. He turned up like a bad smell."

Ruth. It's a solid name. The sort of name you would associate with someone with integrity, heart, intelligence, beauty. It's the sort of name that makes women feel the weight and impact of my loss.

I could describe Ruth in minute detail, from the top of her auburn head to the soles of her size-six feet. I could even show you a photograph of her. I have one just in case anyone asks, but it's not of Ruth, because she is not real; there never was a Ruth. I just need her to reassure women that there's a reason I've never been married before, a reason why I'm single, that there's not something horribly wrong with me.

Martha smiles sadly at the mention of Ruth's name, as she always does.

The evening is soft and gentle. The champagne takes the edge off all the stress and angst I've been feeling about things at home. Martha's youngest walks in. He's wearing pajamas and is slight and fey with a shock of blond curls, just like his mother's. He looks like the type of boy to be targeted by bullies at school. He presses himself against his mother's side and looks at me distrustfully.

"Go on," says Martha, "go and brush your teeth. I'll be up soon."

The boy keeps his gaze on me and then sighs and tuts and leaves.

Martha looks up at me. She doesn't apologize, and I'm glad. She should not apologize for her child. Instead, she smiles and says, "Shall we eat?"

I jump to my feet. "Let me," I say. "You've been busy all day."

As I find my way around Martha's kitchen, assembling the ingredients I brought with me, to the background of a pleasant soundtrack that she's found for us on Spotify, I think of my kitchen at home in Reading: the sharp, hard corners of it, the plainness, those shiny white cupboard doors, the mean window overlooking the immaculate oblong garden, the metal sink, the neat rows of matching brushes and scrubbers, the cold marble tiles underfoot. I think of my wife, sitting on one of those plain wooden chairs at the plain oak table with the fabric runner down its center; all so simple, all so modern, all so soulless and cold. I don't want that kitchen anymore; I don't want that life. I want this kitchen, this woman, this life. My phone buzzes mutely in my trouser pocket and I pull it out.

Where are you?

I turn my phone to flight mode and tuck it back in my pocket.

SEVENTEEN

It's snowing when Ash wakes up on Tuesday morning, a soft, lazy snow, the type that looks like it won't settle. She stands for a few minutes at her bedroom window and watches the flakes floating past. She wants to run and tell someone: "Look! Snow!" But there's no one to tell. She can hear her mother's voice drifting from her study off the landing—on a Zoom already and it's not even nine o'clock.

By the time Ash leaves for work an hour later, the snow has all but stopped and she feels a pinch of disappointment. Snow changes things, even for just a short while, makes the world seem different, a run-of-the-mill Tuesday memorable. And now she has nothing to pin this day down with in her memory, nothing to stop it feeling like yet another pointless twenty-four hours in her already pointless existence.

"I've been obsessively googling him," says Marcelline when Ash walks into the shop. "Your mum's new chap."

"Oh," says Ash, surprised. "What did you find?"

"Nothing much. And I did a reverse image on his profile photo. But nothing there either."

"Do you think he's dodgy then?" Ash asks.

"Dodgy?" says Marcelline. "No. Why would I?"

"Because you googled him."

"Nope. Just being nosy. I google everyone. Don't you?"

Ash shrugs. "I guess."

She'd shown the ring to her mother that morning.

"Oh," Nina had said. "That's weird."

"Yeah, that's what I thought."

"Where did you say you'd found it?"

She couldn't tell her she'd found it deep inside the pile of her mother's bedroom rug whilst snooping around looking for traces of her mother's lover. "It was on the landing outside your room, just sitting there."

"Wow," Nina had said, turning the ring around with her fingertips. "How did I miss that? I guess it must be Nick's."

"But . . ." Ash had paused, blinking hard enough to make black shadows in her vision. "It's a wedding ring, don't you think?"

"Looks like one."

"And he hasn't been married?"

"No. He hasn't. Although it was only two weeks before the wedding that his fiancée died. Maybe they'd already bought their rings and now he carries his around as a memento?"

The theory was sound and Ash had nodded. "Yeah," she'd said. "That could be it. Anyway, you should let him know you have it. He must be worried. Give him a call?"

"No," Nina had said. "He's at work. He won't be able to talk."

"He might."

"No, I'll just message him."

Ash had wanted to put him on the spot, to hear his explanation for the ring and for it to be fresh.

"I'll call him. Give me your phone."

Nina had looked at her with narrowed, questioning eyes. "Er, Ash. It's fine. I said, I'll message him."

Ash had backed down. There was no way to explain to her mother what was going through her mind without sounding like a needy, insecure child who couldn't deal with the fact that her recently widowed mother was seeing a new man.

Now she tucks her phone away in her pocket, gets to her feet, and says to Marcelline, "I'm going to go into the back, do some steaming."

The afternoon is slow and only three customers come in. One buys a Dorothy Perkins summer dress, another buys three pieces of identical knitwear, and the other is a regular who arrives with two glossy carrier bags full of castoffs and stays for tea, which kills an hour of the day until finally it is five thirty and Ash can pull on her jacket, sling on her bag, head back up the hill to the big white house, and chalk up another pointless day waiting for everything to make sense.

EIGHTEEN

Martha walks into the bedroom at six thirty, holding their morning coffees. Al is in his boxer shorts and a T-shirt, just tucking something into the wardrobe. He looks flushed, as though she has just caught him out somehow. Martha sees the shape of the bag he keeps in his side of the wardrobe. It's a strange, battered leather thing with a big metal clasp and a brass padlock and belonged to his father, apparently, the narcissistic sociopath who, ironically, had been a GP in a small rural Yorkshire community, well loved by his patients. It's all he has left of his father, Al told Martha a long time ago. He keeps it to balance out the hatred he feels, to remind him that his father had also been a good person, and that maybe if a hundred people remember you as a good person, then it doesn't matter about the one person whose life you destroyed with cruelty and disinterest.

"What are you up to?" she asks him.

"Oh, nothing. I was just looking for something."

His energy is strange, there's color in his cheeks. She wants to push, but she doesn't want to spoil the nice mood that's been between them since that morning early in the week when it had snowed for a few minutes and they'd felt for a brief moment like a special family, the sort of family you dream about belonging to.

"I'm taking Nala to the childminder's at eight today," she says. "Are you still going to be able to open up the shop for me?"

He looks up at her and smiles and nods. The awkward color has gone from his cheeks. "Absolutely," he says. "I will be there."

Martha smiles back at him gratefully. He's been helping out at the shop more and more recently. He's taken over deliveries too, a few days a week. He says things are quiet at work at the moment. He says he enjoys helping her out and it's the least he can do since he lives in her house rent-free. Martha has never had a proper grown-up colleague before, someone to whom she can hand over everything and trust implicitly. She's always worked alongside young adults; she likes giving them the opportunity to learn a trade. But they don't last long, these Gen Z–ers—the early starts, the hours on their feet, the weekends, the low pay, the cold. They usually stay long enough to get something decent on their CVs and then they're gone. She has sweet Milly at the moment, but Martha can already tell she's running out of enthusiasm. Floristry is vocational, nobody does it unless they love it, and she can see that Milly doesn't love it, that she lives for her days off and holidays. Having Alistair involved is like a breath of fresh air. Having adult company, a driver she can trust to get to the right place at the right time and deliver with charm and professionalism, has been a game changer for Martha. She used to hate leaving Nala at the childminder at seven in the morning, particularly at this time of year when it's still dark outside. It felt cruel and inhuman, but now that Alistair opens the shop for her most mornings, she can take Nala at eight instead, or even nine, like the other mothers do.

Nala and the boys are still asleep, and the world is soft and quiet. Al gets to his feet and stretches, then kisses her as he passes on his way to the shower. He has that sugary, slightly doughy smell of sleepy men and his nighttime breath has become trapped in his stubble, but she likes the way he smells even now. She climbs on the bed and drinks her coffee, looks at the time: 6:36 a.m. Al hums in the shower and her heart is filled with gratitude for her man.

But then something inside her warps slightly, a burn of wrongness, the image of Al pushing that weird bag into the wardrobe. She moves quietly off the bed and kneels in front of the wardrobe, slowly opens the door, and pulls the bag toward her. The padlock is undone; he must have pushed it back hurriedly. She snaps the metal clasp and the bag creaks open on rusty hinges. The main body of the bag is empty, but there are numerous compartments, all of which appear to be locked too. In one of the compartments is a small bulge. She fingers it and makes out the edges of what feels like a phone. The minute she feels it, her stomach hits the base of her spine. A secret phone. There is no lock on this compartment and her hands shake as she starts to open it, peering upward as she does so to gauge the sound levels of Alistair's shower. But just as she is about to pull the zip open, she hears the water stop, the squeak of the Victorian-style knob being turned. She closes the bag and pushes it back in the wardrobe, angling it just so, her heart racing hard under her pajama top, her coffee cup shaking slightly in her hand.

NINETEEN

FOUR YEARS EARLIER

Do I have a job? Yes.

Am I a hospitality training director?

No, I am not.

It matters not what I do for a living, but let's just say that it's sporadic, ad hoc, I can do it whenever I want, cash in hand, under the radar, and it's very useful in terms of filling gaps in my finances. And right now, I have a massive hole in my finances, a hole so big that no amount of ad hoc, cash-in-hand work is going to fill it. I've just bought a car.

I'm in it right now, breathing in the aroma of a fresh valet service, my hands gripping the steering wheel as I drive home to my wife. It was an impulse purchase. I took Martha and her boys to the big used-car dealership near their house and we spent three hours wandering around. I bought them all lunch at the American-style diner there, then we returned to claim the Tesla that the boys had been so keen on. I paid for it on a card, £25,000, making sure that they were nowhere in earshot as the man at the sales desk conducted his conversation with me as "Mr. Truscott."

Buying a car was easy enough to do. Paying for it is a problem I will have to deal with later. You might think it's stressful living as I do, from one credit card to the next, one lie to the next, but it really isn't. I'm not like other people, you see.

The boys asked if they could drive back with me from the dealership. I could tell that at the very least I had cracked the older one, who I now know is called Troy. The younger one, Jonah, is still cagey, less impressed by flashy cars. I can see him now in the rearview mirror, strapped in on the back seat, the seat belt cutting in at his neck because even though he's ten, he's still so small. His hands are spread out on the upholstery at either side, and he stares resolutely ahead.

"What do you think?" I say, playing up the soft northern tones of my accent. "Do you like her?"

"Her?" says Jonah.

"Yes," I say to his reflection in the mirror. "Cars, boats, airplanes, they're all girls. Not sure why. And maybe that's a bit old-fashioned now. Maybe nowadays it's a 'them'?"

The inappropriate joke hits the spot with Troy, who snorts with dry laughter, but I clock a red flush passing across Jonah's cheeks, and I store it away for the future.

Martha smiles as she watches her boys pile out of my fancy new car outside her cottage. "Came on a train, leaving in style," she says with a smile but a note of sadness. "Are you sure you can't stay?"

I've already stayed longer than I meant to. My phone's been on flight mode since Wednesday night and now it's Saturday afternoon and I have no idea what my wife is doing or where she is and it's making me anxious and edgy. I should have gone home yesterday. I could not tear myself away, but now I must. The boys head back into the house and I look at Martha, framed by her picture-postcard cottage, her curls held back with a floral band, in baggy jeans and a bomber jacket. She smiles at me and it's so sweet that my heart burns with affection and with desire. "I wish I didn't have to go. I wish that more than anything, but I'm already five hours late for work. I'll get the sack if I don't leave now."

"I understand," she says. "Of course I do."

She holds her arms out to me and I go into them. I rest my cheek against the crown of her head and give her a bear hug, squeezing her with all I have.

"What are you doing next week?" I say. "I want to take you for dinner. Somewhere amazing."

We arrange to meet again on Wednesday night. I tell her I'll have my company send a car for her, I'll meet her somewhere in town, it will be a surprise, she should dress up. Her face glows. I am bringing things into her life that she didn't know she wanted. But then she, too, is bringing things into my life that I didn't know I wanted. I didn't know I wanted *this*. This rural bohemia, wild curls, mismatched crockery, flowers, all this bloody pink. This woman with her full mouth and big teeth and quirky kids, her cute dog, her knitted throws and old Britpop Spotify playlists, clumpy boots—all of it, *all of it*.

But first I have to work out what to do about my wife. And before that, I need to work out how the hell I'm going to find the money to pay for this stupid fucking car.

My wife stares at the car as I climb out of it two hours later. I see her between the curtains at the front window and my stomach clenches. On one hand, I'm relieved that she's still here; on the other, I am sickened by her, the meanness and spareness of her. But I find a smile from somewhere deep inside me and I climb from the car with an apologetic flourish, pluck the flowers I bought for her on the way here from the passenger seat, then my bag and coat from the back seat, and I stride up the garden path as if there is nowhere on God's earth I would rather be right now, as if it is only the universe conspiring against me that has kept me from here. From her.

"Darling," I say in that voice I use when I'm with her: clipped, elegant, private school, not the soft, swollen, northern lilt I use when I'm with Martha. "I am so, so sorry. I cannot even begin to tell you the whole thing. It's been . . ." I've had two hours to work out what I'm going to say to her and I think I have it straight, but I need a minute just to put myself back together. Her eyes go over my shoulder to the shiny black car, and then back to me.

"Let's go inside," I say. "I'll explain everything."

Inside, I hang up my coat, put my bag into the cupboard in the hallway, and pass the flowers to my wife, who takes them uncertainly and then silently moves into the kitchen, where she dutifully puts them in water, which I take as a good sign. I had half expected her to throw them in my face or beat me with them. I was ready for that, deliberately hadn't chosen roses. I'd also half expected her to have left or changed the locks. I feel my breathing steady. I am Jonathan Truscott again.

She's sitting at the kitchen table, with a gin and tonic by her hand. She doesn't usually drink unless she's socializing.

"We need to talk," she begins.

"Let me just pour one of those first," I say, softly.

The silence between us as I pour my gin and tonic is profound. I rest my drink gently on the table in front of me and then I sigh heavily.

"I am so, so sorry. I am . . ." I bring tears to my eyes; I know they look extra blue with that glassy layer. "I just think . . . I think I'm falling apart, Tara. I think . . . I don't know. I feel as if I might be going a bit mad. It's work, the stress of it. And on Wednesday, I just had this horrible, overwhelming fear . . ." I turn my wet eyes up to her. "That I was losing you."

She wrinkles her small nose. "Losing me?"

"Yes. I've been feeling lately, since that stupid business with the police, that you've been backing away from me. Closing down. And I don't know what to do about it. I just don't know what to do." I let the tears come now, hard. I shove my fist into my nose, and sniff and gurgle. I wait, just a beat. Is this right? I wonder. Is this going to do it?

She blinks, so slowly that I wonder if she'll ever open her eyes again. When she does, the coldness in them chills me.

"And you decided that disappearing for three days, switching your phone off, and coming home in a weird car was the solution?"

I don't have to fake the existential chaos that goes along with finding an answer to her perfectly reasonable question, because I'm in it. "I know," I croak loudly. "I *know*! I can't explain it. I've just been driving around, for three days, driving endlessly. I've barely slept. I've been trying to clear my head, find a way back to myself. I think I'm burning out. I've been feeling it coming for years, to be truthful. This job is just . . . it's killing me, darling. I can't keep doing it . . . I need to escape. With you. Just the two of us. Sell this stupid house—we don't need such a big house—cash in our savings, go somewhere quiet, start again, live off the land if we have to. But I simply cannot do this anymore. I can't."

I am channeling all the angst I'm feeling about my overwhelming need to be with Martha into this story of my desperate downsizing dreams. "Please, darling," I say, "please. Help me."

She picks up her gin and tonic, takes a slow, measured sip, then puts it back again.

"The car?"

"Oh God, yes. The car. It's my friend's."

"Your friend?"

"Yes, a guy at work. He lent it to me. I need to . . . well, I suppose I need to give it back to him. Although he did say I could keep hold of it for a while."

"So, you didn't *buy* it?"

"Buy it?" I ask tearfully. "Of course I didn't buy it. How could I have *bought* it?"

"I don't know, Jonathan. I really don't. I don't understand anything, really, about the way your finances work. Where does all the money go? You work all these hours and yet still . . ." She sighs.

I jump on her words. "Exactly, darling, exactly. I work my guts out, I sacrifice time with you just to be at the beck and call of these people, and even then, there's never enough money. So come on. Let's do it. Let's sell up and cut ourselves loose."

"Jonathan," she says, grimacing at me as if I am a moron. "I'm about to become a grandmother. The baby is going to be here in under a month. How can I possibly think about selling up and moving now? Em needs me. And not only that, but I *want* to be here. This is where I belong, where my friends are, my family, my job, all of it."

She's done it, I can feel it. She's cut the rope that tethers her to me, but I know there are still a few strands intact and I grab for them. "Tara. Please. I can't live like this. You know I can't. It's killing me. Help me."

I make my eyes big, and I see a flicker of pity across her face. But then the coolness returns. "What do you want me to do?" she says. "I don't understand. How can I help you if we both want different things?"

I turn it round. "So, what, darling, what do you want? What would make you happy?"

She pushes her tumbler round in a tense semicircle with her fingertips and then back again.

I gulp, silently, as I stare at her. She suddenly looks beautiful again, the light catching the hazel streaks in her hair as she lifts her head and says, "For you to leave, Jonathan. For you to just *leave*."

TWENTY

"So," Ash asks Nina a few days later. "What did Nick say? About the ring?"

Nina is scrolling through the Deliveroo app on her phone, choosing a pizza. She glances up at Ash quickly and then back down again, her finger still on the screen. "He said exactly what I thought he'd say. It's the ring he bought for the wedding to the dead fiancée."

"And why did he have it with him?"

She sees a muscle in her mother's cheek twitch and knows she's getting on her nerves.

"I don't know. I didn't ask. None of my business."

"Well, it sort of is."

Nina blinks slowly and Ash hears her exhale. "There," she says, passing Ash her phone, "your turn."

Ash sighs and takes the phone, scrolls through to the vegan section, selects the Mozella with wild mushrooms, and hands it back again.

It's Friday night and Ash has declined an invitation from Ella to spend the weekend at her place in Brighton, said she was tired, thought she might be coming down with something, but she wasn't coming down with something, she just couldn't face it. Ella's two flatmates were so full-on and always did that thing of trying to impress upon her how well they knew Ella, as if they were insecure about the fact that Ash had known her since they were both seven. They constantly threw out desperate in-jokes and you-really-had-to-have-been-there stories and Ash found it exhausting. So here she is on a Friday night, ordering pizza with her fifty-one-year-old mother instead.

"Twenty to forty minutes apparently," says Nina, turning off her screen.

"Can I open wine?" asks Ash.

"Sure. There's a fizzy one, I think, in the door?"

Ash opens the door, her eyes find the fizzy wine, and she pulls it out and stares at it for a moment, giving herself a beat to frame her next question. "So," she says, "when are you seeing him again? Nick?"

"Well, actually, I think he might be coming over tomorrow night."

There's an edge to her mother's voice, a dryness. She knows that Ash doesn't want him there, that it is an intrusion, that it is weird and strange for her. But Ash can also hear the resolve in her mother's voice, the note of "It's my house and I'm a grown woman and I can do what I like under my own roof," and she is, of course, entirely right. Ash makes herself smile and says, "Oh, that's good."

"He's taking me to that new place in town, the one where Luc Martin cooks—you know, who your dad used to love?"

Ash shrugs. She's not a crazed foodie like her parents, or at least, she likes food, but she's not fussed about who cooked it. "Is it going to be expensive?"

"Yes. Probably."

"I hope he pays for you."

Nina throws her a surprised look. "I can afford to pay for my own dinner," she says.

"Yes, well, just don't pay for his."

Nina pushes her reading glasses off her nose and into her hair. She appraises Ash quizzically. "Why did you say that?"

Ash shrugs. "I just want you to be careful. That's all. He might be . . . you know, after you for your money."

Nina laughs. "Oh God, Ash. No! No no no! He is most definitely *not* after my money. No, he's very wealthy."

"So why does he live in Tooting?"

"It's just temporary. I think he inherited it from someone or borrowed it or something."

"So he must have a property somewhere? That he owns?"

"He's in between. He had that house in Pimlico he sold."

"Why did he sell it?"

"To release some capital, I suppose. To invest in the business."

"Doesn't sound that wealthy to me."

"He's got other interests. He owns land. He wants to build a country club on it one day, you know, like a Babington House type of thing. And he's a shareholder in lots of companies. I actually quite like the fact that a man like him is happy living in a one-bed flat in Tooting. It shows that he's not up himself, hasn't lost himself in the rarefied ether, you know."

Ash nods as she peels the metal foil from the top of the bottle. "Did he tell you anything," she says, "about Dad? About what he was like when he knew him, back before you met him?"

"No, not really. Nothing that you wouldn't have expected him to remember. The smoking. The swearing. The food obsession."

"Did he ever meet Jane?" Jane was Dad's girlfriend when he met Ash's mum. They'd been together since they were both eighteen and the breakup had been a mess. Dad had totally broken Jane's heart and the whole thing had made the early days of her parents' relationship really hard.

"No," says Nina. "Well, at least if he did, he didn't mention her."

Ash has always been slightly obsessed with the concept of Jane. She'd been half hoping she'd turn up at the funeral in a blaze of drama. The stories she'd heard about her over the years had thrilled her heart: her tragic, loveless childhood, her modeling career, the time she cut all her hair off with blunt scissors, her nervous breakdown, her pet rats. She'd married an earl or a lord or something and sounded like someone from a movie about mad, posh English people. Her mother always talked about her in a soft, slightly pitying voice, an unspoken "poor Jane" behind every mention of her. Her dad had one photo of her; he'd kept it in a box of mementos. Black hair, a pointed chin, saucer eyes, floaty georgette baby-doll dress with a rosebud print.

Young.

Lost.

Troubled.

Just like Ash.

TWENTY-ONE

Nick arrives late in the afternoon on Saturday. He has, as always, brought flowers. The last ones are just beginning to die on the kitchen sideboard and Nina throws them away with a flourish, cleans out the vase, and refills it with fresh water while Nick stands and watches, leaning louchely against the kitchen counter, his arms folded across his chest, his large feet crossed at the ankles in desert boots. He's telling Nina all about his week and Nina is girlish around him, tipping her hair over her shoulder as she laughs at his jokes, a coquettish angle to her head as she tweaks at the flowers to get them just so, before Nick steps across her and takes over.

"Here," he says, "you want the big ones here, the smaller ones there."

"Never met a man who has thoughts about how to arrange flowers."

"I used to work in floristry," he says. "Back in the day."

"Is that how you learned to gift-wrap too?" Ash asks from where she sits at the kitchen table, pretending to do something on her laptop.

"Indeed it is," he says, turning to hit Ash with one of his amazing smiles full of teeth. "I can curl ribbons with the edge of a scissor blade like you wouldn't believe."

She smiles and turns her eyes back to the screen of her laptop. She wishes he'd stop being so fucking nice.

A minute later, Nick and Nina have gone to sit in the living room and Ash is alone. She stares at Nick's jacket where he's left it hanging on the back of one of the kitchen chairs. It's black, a kind of zip-up thing with a high neck, woolen. He was wearing it with a scarf when he arrived, which is now hanging over the top of it. She doesn't like the way he dresses, it's all so proper and grown-up. She's not used to fifty-somethings who dress like grown-ups; all her parents' friends dress like they're thirty years old. She hears laughter coming from the other end of the house and with a brief look over her shoulder, she steps quickly toward the chair and runs her hands deftly in and out of his coat pockets. A tissue. A fifty-pence piece. A ballpoint pen. A . . . She peers at it more closely, trying to work out what exactly it is. It's unrecognizable to her: a plastic circle with a cartoon of a ladybird on it, attached to a piece of blue nylon, with a plastic clasp at the other end. She stares at it, and then quickly grabs her phone to photograph it before shoving it back in Nick's coat pocket. In his other pocket she finds something slinky and slithery. She pulls it out and sees that it is a doggy poo bag. She didn't know that Nick had a dog. She wonders who looks after it when he comes over here to see her mother.

Just as she tucks the plastic bag back into Nick's pocket, he appears and she jumps, grabbing hold of her heart with her hand. "Shit," she says.

"Sorry," says Nick. "Nina sent me for crisps. I didn't mean to make you jump."

"That's OK," she says. "I'm a jumpy person."

She ponders his back as he leans down to the cupboard where he already knows they keep the crisps. She says, "You know when you worked with my dad? Back in the nineties? Did you ever meet his girlfriend?"

She sees him pause before collecting two bags of crisps by their corners and pulling them out. He straightens and turns. His face is a picture of hard remembering. "No," he says. "No. I don't think I did. I mean, he must have had a few back then, a guy like your dad. So gregarious, such a live wire."

"No," Ash responds simply. "No, he only ever had two girlfriends. My mum was the second. He was still going out with the first when he met my mum. There was a messy overlap."

Nick nods. "Right," he says. "Well, he never mentioned her to me in that case."

She nods, doesn't say what she wants to say, which is that Jane was all over every element of her dad's life back then, sat in restaurants where he worked, waiting for him to finish, came to meet him at one in the morning after his shifts, called him constantly on the restaurant phone, five or six times a night.

"How long did you say that you and my dad worked together?"

"Oh, only a few months, you know. Maybe not even that. I couldn't hack it in the end. Your dad had the gumption for it. I just didn't."

He waves the crisps at her and taps the kitchen counter twice with his index finger before smiling, somewhat uncertainly, and leaving again.

TWENTY-TWO

It sits in Martha's gullet, the absence of her husband; it makes a dense puddle of adrenaline that eats away at her gut. He'd left yesterday morning, an emergency call, a mission. She'd let him go, shown kindness and patience about the fact that she'd have to take Nala to the shop with her. It's his job, she'd said to herself. You knew what you were taking on when you got together with him. But then the promised message to tell her what time he'd be back didn't come; none of her messages were opened, let alone replied to; her calls went through to voicemail; and soon it was ten o'clock, eleven o'clock, the day was over, he was not coming home, and she found herself at her laptop, googling "hotels with hair salons Glasgow." The search whittled the dozens of Glasgow hotels down to seven, only two of which were boutique hotels. When she perused their websites, she saw that though they had hair salons, neither of them had a gym. She slammed down the lid of her laptop as if it might burn her.

He gets home on Sunday night looking bedraggled and broken. Martha stares at him as he falls through the front door in his black jacket and scarf, his chin opaque with extra beard growth, his reading glasses perched on top of his head.

"What the fuck, Al."

"Yeah, I know. And I'm sorry."

She closes her eyes and sighs. "Sorry is what you say if you're a few minutes late for something, Al. Sorry is what you say if you forgot to pick up some milk. It's not what you say to someone when you've ghosted them for a full twenty-four hours." Her stomach roils with adrenaline, her heart races under her rib cage. "Are you having an affair, Al?" she says, her voice harsh and sore. "Just tell me. Please."

Al looks at her with shock and horror. "What?" he says. "Are you . . . God, *no*! No, of course not. What on earth made you think that?"

"Your phone being switched off. And, Al, the secret phone you keep in our wardrobe, in your father's medical bag. I saw you shoving it back in there on Friday morning, just as I walked into the room."

"A secret phone?"

"Yes. I saw you putting something into that bag, and then I found it, in the inside compartment. A phone. Why is there a phone in there?"

His brow furrows and he pinches his stubbled chin between his thumb and forefinger. "Are you talking about my father's phone?"

"The phone in that bag."

"That's my father's. I don't know why I kept it, but I did. Look, do you want me to get it for you—show you?"

His bright blue eyes are wide and eager. But she's seen the brightness of his eyes enough times before to know that it's a trap, designed to be fallen into. "No," she says. "No. I don't care about the phone. It's more than that. It's—where've you been? Why didn't you call? Why didn't you reply to my messages?"

He sighs wholeheartedly. "It's been a nightmare, Martha. I mean, I can't even begin to tell you. That hotel is broken. The management is toxic. Five members of staff had walked out before I even got there—I had to wait tables, I had to man the front desk. I was on the phone to recruitment agencies, interviewing temps. I didn't eat, Martha. I literally just had fruit out of bowls, stale croissants, cold coffee . . ."

He's talking and he's talking, and there are words and words and words, and they keep coming out of his mouth, but not one of them explains the lack of a simple *I'm not coming home tonight, I'm so sorry* text. It takes longer to eat a stale croissant than to send a message like that.

"You could have texted," she says. "You could have called. You've sat in a car for three hours, Al, with a phone. You could have called to say you were on your way back."

"I know. You're right. But I just ended up on back-to-back calls with the team the whole journey. And by the time I got off all the calls, I was fifteen minutes away and I just thought there was no point."

Martha doesn't want any of this drama. She wants a quiet Sunday night in with her dreamy husband. She wants to open a bottle of wine and find something to watch together, to tell him about her weekend, hear about his. When things are good between them, she genuinely believes that there is nothing in the world that is better, and now she is sitting here making a conscious decision to rob herself of a pleasant Sunday night with the man she loves. But it's too urgent inside her, the need to ask questions, to get answers. It hurts.

"What was the name of the hotel," she says, "the one where you stayed when you left your wedding ring in the gym?"

She sees him twitch. "What?"

"What was it called?"

He gives her the name of one of the hotels she googled earlier. It's one of the two that doesn't have a gym.

She picks up her phone and googles it again. He stares at her questioningly. "There," she says, pointing at the section at the bottom of the page where it says *Other amenities.* "No gym."

"When did I say the gym was in the hotel?"

"When you told me about it. When I asked how come you'd had time to go to the gym. You said it was on-site."

He shakes his head slightly. "No," he says. "I didn't say that. Why would I say that?"

"I don't know, Al. But you did."

"But I didn't. Of course I didn't. I used the gym in the shopping center over the road."

"You definitely said it was in the hotel. That was the whole point of the conversation. Why would I misremember it when you said something so specific?"

"I have no idea. Genuinely. But . . ." He puts his hand into his jacket pocket and pulls something out. "Ta-da." He uncurls his fingers. And there inside his hand is his wedding ring.

"Where did you find it?"

"In the car."

"In the—?"

"Yes. Weird. I know."

"But you said—"

"Yes. I know. And maybe that was just wishful thinking, because, really, and if I'm being totally honest with you, I wasn't sure I'd left it at the gym in Glasgow. And the manager said it wasn't there. So I did a sweep of the car, and there it was, just wedged inside the gearbox."

Martha shakes her head and sighs. She doesn't know what to say, how to react. Her head spins.

"It's good, isn't it? I thought you'd be happy . . ."

"Yes. I am happy. I mean, I'm happy it's not lost. But I don't know, there's so much that doesn't make sense, and I can't have someone in my life who I can't trust. I just can't."

He flinches and his blue eyes shimmer with hurt. "You don't trust me?"

"I don't know, Al. But the way you've been recently, the last few weeks, it's been weird. That's all."

She feels herself run out of steam. She feels the promise of the sofa, of wine, of softness and fun and love, begin to overwhelm her. She wants to park her suspicions for now. It's the ADHD, she tells herself. It's his stupid job. It's all the emotional baggage, the death of his fiancée, the death of his mother, the estranged, narcissistic father. He carries a lot of burdens. He's unusual. She has to look at him as a whole, not just as fragments of behavior. He's better than any other man she knows.

She needs to give him another chance.

TWENTY-THREE

FOUR YEARS EARLIER

This isn't meant to be happening. Not yet. If Tara makes me leave now, I will have nothing. I will have nowhere. I will be on the streets. I've been careless—it's Martha, she's got under my skin, made me rush things, made me move too fast, and I thought there'd be time to get more out of this marriage before I abandoned it. But as it is, I have nothing: an overdraft, credit card debts, a stupid £25,000 car.

"I can't leave, darling," I say. "Where would I go?"

"That's not my problem, Jonathan. You came into my life from nowhere, I suppose you'll just return to nowhere."

I swallow down the panic. I don't like the way it makes my voice sound. I have to regain the upper hand here.

"Darling," I say, softly, lovingly, "I think I understand what's happening here. I think I know what's going on. And I can fix it. OK?"

"I don't want you to fix it. I want you to go."

She's steely. She means it. She reminds me so much of the woman I met four years ago. The one who looked me up and down when I arrived for our first date and said, "I thought you'd be younger—are you sure you're only forty-seven?"

I'd laughed and said, "It's the silver hair. I promise I'm forty-seven."

And that much had, at least, been true.

"Just give me some time to prove myself to you," I say now. "Give me a week. I'll go and stay with a friend, or at a hotel. I'll get out of your hair, out of your space, give you some room to breathe. Please, darling. Give me that much at least."

I see it leak out of her, the resolve, the certainty, and I know it was planted there by Emma in the first place. It never belonged to her, not truly. My wife adores me. My wife has built her whole life around me. What will she do without me?

She nods. "OK. One week. But, Jonathan, there's nothing you can do, not really. I have made my mind up."

I head upstairs to pack. I grab my father's medical bag from inside the wardrobe and fill it with underpants and socks. I go to my wife's jewelry box and I pluck something small from the bottom of it; it's a ring, her mother's, I believe. It is set with sapphires and diamonds, and she once told me she was going to get it reset one day because it was a bit old-fashioned for her tastes. I have no idea of its value, but I also have no idea how I'm going to pay for anything once I leave this house and even a couple of hundred would be better than nothing.

I zip some jackets and shirts into a hanging suit bag, and I snatch a towel from the airing cupboard. I shove toiletries into the medical bag and then, listening carefully for the sound of my wife, I unzip the internal pocket and pull out the phone that lives in there.

`I have a week's leave,` I type to Martha, `starting now. We could go away somewhere? What do you think?`

I picture her as she looked when I left her a few hours ago, a piquant sadness in her eyes, her cheek brushing against mine slightly awkwardly as she tried not to let me see how much she didn't want me to go. I picture her in her kitchen, hearing the vibration of her phone, picking it up, seeing my message, a whoosh of joy surging through her, and then I picture her pausing. She has children. She runs a business. Of course she can't go away at such short notice. I watch the phone for a moment or two. Nothing. That's fine. She'll need time. And actually, I, too, need time, time to clear up some messes, put things in order. I know now that I was never meant to be here with Tara, that I was under some kind of spell.

We met on a dating app, Tara and I. I rarely use them. I much prefer the electricity, the magic, of meeting someone's eye across a room, a street, an aisle. Or in a flower shop, in the case of Martha. I am tall, I am well built, well dressed, and with my white hair and blue eyes, I am eye-catching. You can't quite appreciate all that in a photo on a screen, and it is the same with women, though often it's the other way round: photos taken in the best possible light, photos taken after a trip to the salon, contouring makeup and filters—good God, the filters. The women, even the good-looking ones, never look as good in real life as they do in their online profiles: they're catfish almost to the last one. But Tara, I could tell, was a natural beauty. Not a knockout. Not a *ten*, as the young people say. But she looked healthy and natural and groomed, and for fun, in one of her photos she'd held up that day's newspaper, like a hostage in a ransom video, just to prove that she was the age she said she was. It made me laugh and I'd messaged her and soon realized that she was dry and clever and financially independent, that she lived in a smart new build on a top-notch estate in a decent suburb of Reading, that she had no baggage, just two grown-up children, both financially independent from her, and an ex-husband with whom she was on good terms.

We met in a wine bar, and I told her I was thinking about buying it, though of course I wasn't, it's just always been a fantasy of mine for some reason. She looked like her photos: fresh, clean, vital, and I saw her eyes glitter with triumph when she saw me; no doubt she'd worried that I too might be a catfish, that the "six foot two" on my description might have had a few extra inches added, that the blue eyes might have been enhanced with a filter. I saw her draw herself up, pull herself in, lick her lips very slightly to put a sheen on them suggestive of youth and virility. And then the dry put-down. I'd loved it. I can take a joke at my expense. I'm not as serious as you might think. It broke the ice, and she flicked at that hazel-hued hair with her fingers and eyed me up and down and soon we were in a frenzy of mutual attraction, and not long after that, I was through the door of her post-divorce new build that still smelled of paint and new carpets, and at first it was incredible. I still had some money in the bank when I met Tara, enough to sweep her off her feet here and there, to bring champagne to her door, take her fine dining, take her on city-break weekends, buy her perfume and flowers. All the flourishes, all the suggestions of a self-made man in need of nothing but the love of a beautiful woman.

But the money ran out and soon, as always, I needed to think on my feet to explain away the change in my circumstances. Investments gone bad. Always, always someone else's fault. We'd sit and talk about how bad these other people were, the nasty money people; poor us, the victims of this greed and malpractice. *Poor you.* I garner sympathy, I foster team spirit, and then I find ways to extract money. Money, quite often, that my wives did not know they were able to access until I told them exactly how, when, and where. Personal loans. Home equity loans. Payday loans. Debt consolidation loans, credit cards. Even pawnshops. But always, always, just as a temporary measure. And I need you to believe me when I tell you that I always, *always* take this money with an intention, a true, deeply felt intention, of finding a way to repay it. I am a proud man and I have drive and ambition, I have a vision of my future and it involves me making money, owning assets. That vision exists over the next hill, around the next corner, it tantalizes and it glitters and it makes me sick with longing, and it often, I'm afraid, leads me to making rather bad choices.

In total, Tara has contributed over £200,000 toward our marriage, and she is, I know, currently £89,000 in debt, including a small remortgage and the car she doesn't yet know she has paid for. I wish I could do something to help. I wish that I could pay her back somehow—but I can't, because that money is gone.

And now I am penniless. Homeless. About to be destitute. My timings are all out of whack. Which means . . .

I groan inwardly when I think about what it means.

My phone buzzes and it's Martha.

`I'm so sorry,` her message says. `I wish I could, but I'm stuck here with work and the kids. Could do something next weekend? If you're still free?`

I sigh. It's no more than I'd expected. It's too soon for me to land in Martha's life right now. I'm still finding my way with her. I need to sidle in, not crash it.

I type a light-hearted reply and tuck the phone back into the medical bag. Then, with a deep timbre of sorrow and regret, I say goodbye to Tara before I head out into the night.

TWENTY-FOUR

Jane has a Facebook page. Her name, despite two marriages, is still Jane Trevally, which is how Ash's parents had always referred to her, with both names, as if to distinguish her from other Janes. Her privacy settings leave very little to view apart from shares of other friends' posts about lost dogs or GoFundMes or videos of scientists and statisticians during the Covid years. Her bio says that she lives in Dorset and her profile photo shows a very striking-looking woman with intensely red hair, very wide eyes, a strong jaw, and a dress with a ruffled neck. The background photo shows a collection of gun dogs lined up against an ivy-covered wall.

Ash knows that if she sends Jane a message here, it will fall into the black hole of Facebook's "other messages" folder, where messages from strangers go to die, so she finds her on Instagram instead, another private account, and contacts her there.

> Hi Jane.
>
> My name is Aisling Swann. I am Paddy's daughter. I don't know if you're aware, but my father died last October. He was pushed onto the tube tracks by a man suffering from paranoid schizophrenia. The man is in a secure psychiatric unit now, and he was given

a life sentence, but we (me, my mother and brother) are not close to feeling any closure. The whole thing felt so pointless and wasteful. My dad used to talk about you a lot, about your relationship, which sounded crazy and colorful and kind of amazing! I'd love to talk to you about him, about your memories of him, things you know about him that maybe I never knew before. It's a big ask, I realize that, and I know you've moved on with your life and maybe never think about him anymore, but it would mean a lot to me. Maybe you have photos I've never seen before? Stories I didn't know?

Anyway, I'm sorry to barge into your DMs like this. Please do reply either way.

Yours, with hope, Ash

She sends the message and within thirty seconds it has been seen, and Jane is typing a reply.

A moment later, her message appears.

I am sitting weeping 😢I did not know about Paddy. I have been abroad since lockdown and only returned home a month ago 🏠I would love to talk to you about him. Either in person (I'm based in Dorset but spend a lot of time in London) or over the phone/Zoom/whatever. Do write back so that we can make a plan 🙏 And I am so sorry for your loss 💔💔💔

Two days later, on her day off, Ash takes the train into London. She has arranged to meet Jane for brunch at a restaurant in the new development at King's Cross, one with a terrace that spills onto a beautiful, landscaped piazza with fountains and avenues of bare-branched cherry trees.

It's the first time that Ash has been to London since she left under a cloud eighteen months ago. She feels panic grip her gut as she steps off the quiet train and heads into the maelstrom of St. Pancras. It's not the number of people that is making her heart race, it's the possibility of one of them being one of her former colleagues from the lifestyle magazine where she used to work. Or worse still, one of them being her ex-boss, Ritchie Lloyd.

It's easy to spot Jane with her shock of bottle-red hair and a contrasting shaggy green cardigan. She gets to her feet as Ash approaches and holds her at arm's length for a moment, scanning her face.

"Yes," she says to Ash, "I can see him there. I can see Paddy."

Then she brings her close for a hug and Ash smells something that reminds her of a holiday in Ibiza when she was a child.

Jane's a few inches taller than Ash, which means she must have been roughly the same height as Paddy, possibly even taller.

"I'm afraid I already ordered," says Jane, pointing at some kind of smoothie and half a buttery croissant. "I was starving. Here"—she passes Ash a menu—"order whatever you like. My treat. I know you poor millennials can't afford nice things."

"No," says Ash, "it's not that we can't afford nice things. It's that we can't afford *important* things. And I'm actually Gen Z, just."

Jane widens her eyes. "Are you really? I thought they were all at primary school!"

Ash can't tell if she's being disingenuous or not. "Do you have children?"

"Step. I have stepchildren. Two sets. Ha! I am rather more of a dog person than a children person, it turns out. Anyway, I am so sorry about Paddy. About your dad. I googled after I heard from you—I saw all the stories online. It sounds quite horrific."

Jane is very posh, but not in a grating way. And she is mesmerizingly beautiful: hollowed cheeks, a wide, expressive mouth, a long neck that she touches a lot with elegant fingers.

"It was," Ash says. "It is. It feels like a nightmare that never ends. Every day. I can't close my eyes without picturing it. Without imagining how he must have felt when those hands connected with his body. When he knew he wouldn't be able to pull himself back. That it was done. That he'd never see any of us again."

Ash blinks hard and rolls her head back as the darkness nudges at her temples, trying to worm its way into her being. She makes herself smile and glances down at the menu. "Anyway," she says, her eyes scanning the words that swirl and fade as she tries to process them, "I should probably have something to eat too." A waitress approaches and she asks her for a cappuccino with oat milk, and a coconut yogurt with berries and chia seeds.

"You know," Jane says, eyeing Ash gently, "Paddy was the love of my life?"

"Yes," says Ash. "I did know that. He told us quite a lot about your . . ." She reaches for words that won't offend. "Your time together."

"Did he say I was mad? Oh God, I bet he did. I bet he made me sound like a total lunatic. And in many ways, I suppose I was. But I was so young, and really, young people shouldn't be let loose on relationships. Those really should just be left for the grown-ups. And I did behave quite terribly on occasion. I know I did. Did he tell you?"

Ash scratches the side of her face where a stray hair has tickled her skin. "Kind of. I mean, yeah. But only because . . ." She inhales deeply " . . . because I was going through something similar. With a guy. A guy at work. Who I was kind of . . ." She feels a flush rise through her from her gut " . . . obsessed with. Yeah. I was obsessed with him, and I did some mad stuff, and my dad told me some stuff that happened when you two were together, I think basically to try to make me feel better. You know? But he only talked about you with affection. With kindness." This wasn't strictly true. There had also been some dark humor in the way her father spoke about Jane Trevally, about the way she was perceived by the Swann family.

"Oh," says Jane, pushing the cuffs of her cardigan up her forearms and tossing her head slightly. "I'm sure he did. Paddy was a very kind man. He was always very nice to me, even when I didn't deserve him to be."

"How long were you together?"

"Four years. From eighteen to twenty-two. Blink of an eye from this perspective. But it felt like a marriage at the time. You know. Four years. Nowadays, four years happens when you're in the shower." She sighs. "I'm not so crazy now. Or at least, the edges have been worn off me. In a good way. Weird to think that if I'd met Paddy now, I'd probably be sane enough to keep hold of him." She darts a glance at Ash. "Sorry," she says. "That sounded weird. Inappropriate. Forgive me."

Ash shakes it off. "It's fine," she says. "I get it. I really do." Her coffee and yogurt arrive, and she smiles and says thank you to the waitress. "What was he like? Back then?"

"Oh, pretty much as he was when he was older, I'd imagine. He was solid, steady, you know. Just regular, decent, grounded. It was me that made things complicated." She shivers lightly.

"Do you remember a man called Nick? Who worked at the restaurant in Mayfair where Dad used to work?"

She cocks her head. "Nick what?"

"Radcliffe. He's kind of tall, slim. His hair is white now but was probably dark then. Slightly northern accent." She swipes her phone screen to find Nick's LinkedIn page, then does a double take and grimaces when she realizes it's gone. "Oh," she says. "His LinkedIn page has disappeared. How weird. But look . . ." She scrolls through her camera roll to the screenshot she has of it. "This is Nick. Do you recognize him?"

Jane peers at the photo and shakes her head. "Not that I recall. Why do you ask?"

"Oh, I don't know, he's just kind of landed in our lives. Said he knew Dad from back then. He sent us Dad's Zippo. Here."

She pulls it out of her bag and slides it across the table toward Jane.

Jane eyes it curiously. "Whose is this, did you say?"

"Dad's. Apparently this Nick guy found it back in the day. My dad left it in the kitchen one night and Nick put it in his pocket for safe-keeping, but then Nick left and forgot to give it back to him. He saw the story about my dad in the papers and then somehow found our address and mailed it to us. Well, to my mum, really. And now he's kind of, well, he's dating Mum. And it's all a bit weird."

Jane reaches out for the Zippo and turns it over in her hand.

"Not Paddy's," she says decisively.

Ash flinches slightly. "What?"

"Paddy never had a lighter. It was a thing, you know? He was always cadging lights off people, always had pockets full of those flimsy match-books from restaurants and bars, or shitty old Bics that never worked. He never had a proper lighter."

Jane pushes the Zippo back across the table toward Ash, slowly, with a kind of apologetic tilt of her head.

"Are you sure?"

"Oh yes," Jane says decisively, comprehensively. "I was the world expert on Paddy Swann, remember. I was obsessed with every last detail of him. I could have written a book." She sighs. "Sorry," she says. "Inappropriate again. I'm not very good at . . ." She gestures at the space between them, suggesting delicate human discourse.

"So, you think this guy is lying? About the Zippo?"

Jane pulls the lighter back toward her and examines it at close quarters. "It doesn't even look old enough, to be frank. It looks quite new." She pushes it back once more, leans into her chair, and blinks slowly.

Ash shrugs. "Maybe he thought this was Dad's, but it was someone else's," she says, her hand covering the Zippo. "Or maybe Dad did own it for a while, and you didn't know. But it just feels . . . I dunno. It all feels *off*. Somehow."

Jane nods, her mouth open slightly, as if she is pondering whether to speak her mind. "I know people," she says, leaning toward Ash. "People who can run checks. You know. Run him through systems. Police records. That kind of thing." She ripples her fingers. "Which makes me sound kind of mysterious and exciting, which I'm not, I just come from a very wealthy, very paranoid family who trust no one, and I have two paranoid wealthy ex-husbands who also trust no one. I could ask someone to check him out? If you'd like?"

Ash inhales sharply. "Yes. Please."

"What do you have?"

"Not much. A name. Nick Radcliffe. A wine bar that he says he co-owns. A deleted LinkedIn profile. He lives in Tooting. He's fifty-five. He has a dead fiancée. No kids. Although I did find something in his coat pocket the other day and didn't know what it was at first, but turns out it's the thing that clips a baby's pacifier to their clothes, so they don't lose it?" She shrugs and takes a sip of her coffee. "And, oh," she says, putting the cup back down on the table. "A poo bag, for a dog. I mean, you wouldn't have one of those in your pocket, would you, unless you had a dog, and he never mentions a dog or brings a dog, and *anyway*. He's just very . . . sus."

"Leave it with me," says Jane, picking up the last section of her croissant and popping it in her mouth. "Now," she says, rubbing her greasy fingertips together to dislodge the crumbs and leaning down to pick up the bag at her side, "I brought some photos. Of your dad. When he was a young thing. Do you want to see?"

Ash feels her stomach turn to liquid and she nods eagerly. "Oh," she says, forgetting for a long moment about Nick Radcliffe and all his disquieting loose ends. "Yes. Yes, please."

TWENTY-FIVE

FOUR YEARS EARLIER

She comes to the door very quickly. Her blond hair is fried with too much bleach—I used to tell her all the time to take it easy, that it was ruining her hair—and piled on top of her head. She's wearing yoga pants and a hoodie and is chewing the remains of something, suggesting I've caught her halfway through a meal. It's half past six, so that makes sense. She always did like to eat her dinner early. It's clear she was expecting someone else, her posture is too easy, she seems as if she'd already decided what she was going to say to the person she'd assumed would be at the door, and when she sees me, it takes a split second for it to register—then she opens her mouth and I have to clamp my hand down firmly over it and push her back hard into her hallway. I'm aware of the sound of the TV in the background, or is it someone on a phone? I'm pretty sure she's alone—I've been watching for a while from across the street—but at the suggestion of there being another person in there, I clamp my hand tighter around her mouth and manhandle her into the darkness of a room just to my left. I click the door closed behind us both, and then I throw her into a chair, my hand still hard against her mouth. I wait until her eyes are less wide, until her breathing is less ragged, and then I release it. Her hands go to her face, moving spit-covered hair from her cheeks, then they rearrange her clothes, but her eyes stay on me all the while.

"Damian?" she whispers hoarsely.

I nod.

"What the fuck? What the . . . I don't understand."

"Just stay quiet," I say. "Is there anyone here?"

"No! Just me. But . . . what is this? Is this some kind of sick joke?"

"It's not a joke, Amanda. It's very far from a joke. I need you to help me, OK? It's very important."

I see her eyes fill with tears; I see her bunch her hands up into small fists and bring them to her mouth. A convulsion passes through her then and suddenly her arms are around me and she is sobbing. "Is it really you, Damian?" she keeps asking. "Is it really you?"

"Yes," I say, rubbing her bony back through the cheap cotton of her hoodie. "Yes, it's me."

"But we . . . Jesus Christ, Damian, we had a fucking *funeral*. Your kids were there, at your graveside, they did speeches, bought suits. Where have you been, Damian! Where the fuck have you been?"

Part Three

TWENTY-SIX

Nina's taking Nick to the Paddy's in Ramsgate, not the one in the village down the hill where the staff feel like family and where the presence of this tall, silver-haired man in suit trousers and a rumpled work shirt with Paddy's widow on his arm might create ripples and start the gossip mills turning. The other restaurant is brand-new; Dad had only just opened it the month before he died. It's the one where Nina spends the most time as it was finding its feet when Paddy went and still doesn't have a proper team on board. The staff there aren't as familiar with the Swann family as the staff at the other two restaurants. But still. It's *Dad's restaurant.*

"Why are you taking him *there*?" Ash asks.

Nina sits on the edge of her bed, her magnifying mirror in her hand, her makeup bag on the bed next to her. She unclicks the lid from a concealer pen and throws Ash a look.

"Because he's going to offer me some professional advice. You know that was Nick's job? Before he bought the wine bar? He was a hospitality trainer. That branch isn't working, you know it's not working, and if I can't get to the bottom of what's broken there, we'll have to shut it, and that will put eighteen people out of a job. Not to mention letting down your father's legacy."

Ash blinks and sniffs, lowers herself next to her mother, and sighs. "Has Nick got a dog?" she asks.

"No," says Nina, dabbing concealer beneath her eyes. "Why?"

She wants to tell her mum about the poo bag, but she can't, because that would mean telling her she'd been ferreting around in Nick's jacket pockets. And she *should* be able to tell her mother things like that, obviously she should; her mother is robust, their family is excellent at communication, talking things through, transparency, always has been. But Ash feels as if she has lost ground with her mother since the events of the summer before her father died. She has shown her mother a side of herself that her mother cannot relate to, and she has behaved in ways and done things that her mother does not and never will fully understand. She did a "Jane Trevally" and put herself in that bracket—the bracket of the weak-minded, the crazy, the not-to-be-trusted. So, she doesn't tell her mother about the poo bag. Instead, she exhales, loudly, and says, "Nothing. No reason. Just wondered."

Ash eyes Nick across the kitchen table. He got here about half an hour ago, all suited and booted, direct from work, so he says. He's staring at his phone, one long leg crossed high upon the other, his shirt unbuttoned to the second button down, showing a small puff of white chest hair. Nina is still upstairs, getting changed. Ash feels she should offer Nick a drink, or a glass of water, just to be polite, but she can't bring herself to.

She clears her throat. "Do you have any pets?"

Nick doesn't seem to pick up on her edginess and answers warmly. "No. Sadly not. I'd love a pet or two. But with my job, my lifestyle, all the traveling, it's simply not fair. I have to make do with my neighbor's dog instead."

"Oh." Her gut plummets, and she is glad now that she didn't say anything to her mother earlier. "What sort of dog do they have?"

"It's a Shiba Inu. You know, those little foxy-looking ones. I take her out sometimes—we get a lot of fuss. Or rather, *she* gets a lot of fuss and I just lap it up vicariously." He laughs. "She's a lovely dog."

Ash nods and plucks at a loose thread on her sleeve. He's talking in too much detail. It's almost, she thinks, as if he *knows* that she looked through his pockets, knows that she saw the poo bag. And if that's the case, then he must know that she saw the baby's pacifier clip too.

"Lovely couple," he says. "Young. They have a toddler too. Little boy. Max."

There. She feels it hit the base of her spine like a hammer. Too much information. She gulps drily and a small wave of nausea passes through her. She thinks of this man walking into her dead father's restaurant tonight, with her dead father's wife on his arm. This man who *lies* and stares deeply, unwaveringly, into her eyes as he does so. Whose body language does not betray him. He lies with passion and self-belief, this man. He lies like a man who has never been caught out in a lie, who thinks he is invulnerable.

"That's nice," she says, her voice a little dry. "Do you like children?"

"I adore them," he replies warmly. "The greatest regret of my whole life is that I never had a child. Truly."

She nods, chewing at the inside of her cheek, and then she looks up at the sound of her mother descending the stairs. Nina walks into the kitchen and they both, she and Nick, gasp softly at the loveliness of her. She wears a huge mohair cardigan over leather leggings and a camisole top. Ash looks at Nick and sees that there is no doubt or uncertainty, no subliminal flinch as he realizes how lucky he is. He merely smiles at Nina conspiratorially, as if she and he were members of their own exclusive club, made for one another, a perfect fit, too good to be true.

Her mother looks at her phone. "Ooh," she says, "taxi's one minute way. Shall we walk to meet it at the corner—save it doing a three-point turn?"

She turns and grabs her bag, smiles at Ash, and says, "Bye, darling. Have a good night. See you later."

For some reason, Ash finds herself wanting to shout, "Stay! Stay with me!"

But she can't, because she is twenty-six, so instead she says, "Have fun. Love you."

And then there is the bang of the door. And then it is silent.

TWENTY-SEVEN

Martha pulls Nala out of her crib. Her face is red-raw, blotchy, slick with tears. Her skin burns to the touch, and then suddenly she is vomiting again, so forcefully that it spatters down the side of her cot, down the legs of Martha's jeans, and into the shaggy pink rug on the floor.

"Oh," says Martha. "Oh God. Oh, baby." She pulls Nala to her and then Nala is screaming, violently, like she has never screamed before. Martha is about to rush Nala to the bathroom when she looks down and sees that Baxter has got into the room and is busy licking up globules of fresh vomit from the pink rug and she roars at him, "Baxter, no!" and pushes him roughly away from the rug with the side of her foot. Her shouting at the dog makes Nala scream again and Martha carries her to the bathroom and lays her down on the bath mat. She takes off all her clothes, then her nappy, which is worryingly dry. Nala writhes and wriggles on the floor and her body feels red-hot. Martha grabs the electronic thermometer from the bathroom cabinet and touches it to Nala's ear. She waits for the high-pitched beep and then looks down at the reading: 104 degrees. She pulls her phone from the back pocket of her jeans and googles "toddler temperature fever."

The internet tells her that she should take Nala to the hospital, but Alistair has disappeared with the car and the car has Nala's child seat in it and she feels sure there is a spare one somewhere in the garage but she can't go hunting around in the garage in the middle of the night with a sick, screaming child in her arms and the boys are at their dad's and Martha is old, she suddenly feels old, too old for this. She is nearly forty-eight and she should be sitting with her feet up, watching TV, enjoying the solitude of a night to herself, not dealing with a feverish child, a child she hadn't even wanted, not really, not at this stage of her life, with the boys finally breaking free, a child that Al had talked her into having, and why? What for? So he could go cold on her? Disappear every week? Turn off his phone, come up with strange excuses for his absences, act weird?

She brings his number up on her phone and calls him. It rings twelve times and then goes to voicemail.

"Where are you? Nala's sick. I have to take her to A and E, and you've got the car seat. I need you to get back here now!"

She picks up her boiling-hot child and holds her to her chest. "Oh, my baby, my poor, poor baby."

Nala goes rigid in her arms and Martha holds her to the side of the bath. The next load of vomit hits the enamel. It's clear now. Is that better or worse, Martha wonders, than opaque vomit? She soothes Nala again, wipes her mouth with a towel, wraps her in it, rocks her, whispers to her, reaches for the Calpol, the syringe. The first attempt to get her to take it ends up with a slick of pink down the white towel, a view of Nala's throat as she screams her disapproval. The second attempt is more successful. She holds Nala's mouth closed and feels limp with relief as the medicine disappears somewhere, does not reappear, at least.

She will give it twenty minutes, she thinks, and then she will take Nala's temperature again. If it is still 104 degrees and she has not managed to find the spare child seat, she will call her friend Grace, who lives one road away, and ask her to drive them. She mops Nala down with a damp flannel and then puts her into a fresh set of pajamas. Please, she thinks to herself, please don't be sick again. She pulls Nala's hair off her face and kisses her hot, red cheek and then she takes her down through the house, the TV still flickering, the sound muted, the dog staring up at her from the kitchen, slightly worried after being shouted at. She slides her feet into slippers and heads down the pathway toward the garage.

Nala cries, the garage is damp and cobwebby, and Martha uses the flashlight on her phone to pick her way through plastic storage containers, metal shelving racks, cardboard boxes. Finally, Nala sobbing in her arms, Martha finds the car seat she's been looking for and then groans when she sees that it is far too small for Nala, it's for a newborn. She turns off her phone torch and slams the garage door shut behind her, crunches hard across the driveway and back to the house, where she takes Nala's temperature again. It's 105.8.

In a silent rage, she calls Al again, even though she already knows he won't pick up. "Fuck's sake," she hisses into his voicemail. "Where the fuck are you, Al? Just . . . fuck's sake." She ends the call with an angry jab of her finger against the screen. She looks at the time. It's been twenty minutes since she told herself she'd wait half an hour. She takes Nala's temperature again; it's still 105.8.

She sighs and finds Grace's number in her phone.

"I'm really sorry," she says. "I really am. But please. I need a huge favor."

Grace's fingers are tight around her steering wheel eight minutes later. Martha sits in the back with Nala on her lap, an overnight bag on the seat next to her, just in case.

"This isn't right," says Grace, "you know that, don't you? This just isn't right."

Martha purses her lips and nods. "Yup," she says. "I know that. Of course I do."

"Do you . . ." Grace pauses, looks into her wing mirror, then flicks her indicator to the right to pull into the next lane. "Do you think he might be having an affair?"

"I've thought about it, of course I have."

"And?"

"And . . . I have no idea. He just says it's the nature of his job."

"So—where did he say he was going tonight?"

"He didn't. He was meant to be home from work at seven. We were going to have our usual Wednesday-night dinner. You know, when the boys are at Matt's. He was going to bring something from the place where he's been working. So I didn't even have any food in."

"That's terrible, Marth."

"I mean, not that I'm bothered about that. I've put on so much weight recently, since I stopped breastfeeding. Quite happy with a girl dinner, y'know. But it's the principle, isn't it?"

"Try him again," Grace says, eyeing Martha in the rearview mirror.

"No point. He won't answer."

Grace sighs. Then there is a poignant silence before she says, "Have you ever thought about using a tracker on him?"

"What!"

"You know, one of those things you can use to track your luggage, or your dog. Just drop it in his pocket, or in the car, so you can see where he actually goes when he's abandoned you at home."

"That's a horrible idea," Martha says, and she means it. She has never been the sort of person to overstep boundaries, to infringe on other people's privacy.

"Well, no more horrible than what he's putting you through."

"Yes, but why should I lower myself to his level?"

"Because he left you without a car or a car seat for your baby, Martha. That's why."

They fall silent as Grace pulls up outside the hospital and turns off the car engine. Martha sighs softly but doesn't reply.

Nala has gone quiet and limp in Martha's arms as she carries her into the emergency room, which worries her more than the rigid screaming.

They don't have to wait long, are triaged quickly into the children's waiting room and from there quickly into a doctor's consulting area, where Nala is prodded and poked and touched and tested, and an hour later Martha has a diagnosis for her baby of norovirus and severe dehydration. She is taken away to be put on a drip and Martha is left sitting on a squeaky chair in a brightly painted room with a harsh strip light overhead that makes her head pulse with tiredness and sickness and fear.

It's nearly lunchtime the following day when Martha and Nala are finally home again. The shop is shut and customers have had their orders canceled, and Martha has spent the entire morning fielding calls from irate people who have been mildly inconvenienced because her child was ill and because her husband was not around to pick up the slack, and she now knows, without a shadow of doubt, that she can't do this anymore; she can't do any of it. She can't do the shop, she can't do the business, she can't do the juggling of it all, and she can't, she really cannot, do Alistair Grey, her stupid fucking husband with his stupid fucking job and his stupid fucking phone that he never switches on when he's not at home. She needs a break from everything, from all of it. She wants to go to bed, and she wants to sleep for a hundred years and wake up and find that everyone has sorted out everything while she was gone. That there is nothing left for her to do. That she can finally, *finally*, sit down.

Martha won't be able to take Nala to the childminder now for at least a few days as she has an infection. She will have to keep her at home or take her to the shop, and it's cold in the shop and Nala is ill and needs to be in a warm house with a television and toys and her mother sitting on a sofa with her. She'd opened Martha's Garden seven years ago and had seen it as her ticket to midlife contentment, her dream come true, the thing she was always destined for. She thinks back to those early days, getting the keys to the shop, choosing paint colors with the boys, her first drive to a customer's house with a van full of table displays for their daughter's wedding. It was hard work, it had always been hard work, but it had been going somewhere, building toward something. She'd thought of another branch, maybe two, maybe a small empire, a soft landing into retirement with money in the bank and a legacy. But then life had taken over, and now this . . . a sick child and a husband who has disappeared in the car with the child seat in it.

And where is all the money going? Why does it not matter that however hard she works, however many hours she slogs, there is never any money?

She puts Nala into her cot and for once Nala is asleep immediately, her face a picture of relief to be home. She turns onto her side and Martha stares at the curve of her cheek, the kick of strawberry blond hair, the curl of her fists, and she aches inside with it all: her choices, her decisions . . . Al.

There'll be no caving when he gets home this time. No submitting to the allure of wine on the sofa and cold toes buried under his lap. Not this time. Not this time.

He returns an hour later. He is rumpled and smells like he slept in his clothes, which, he tells her, he did. He was so tired at the end of his day's work, he says, and there were no empty rooms at the hotel where he was working, so he took a sofa in the staff room, he says, took off just his shoes and socks and slept in his shirt and trousers. His stubble looks unwashed, his breath is stale.

"Please," he says. "Can I just go up and have a shower?"

Then and only then does he look at Martha and say, "How come you're home? Who's looking after the shop?"

She sighs and shakes her head.

"Go and have a shower," she says. "I'll tell you when you come back down."

TWENTY-EIGHT

FOUR YEARS EARLIER

Amanda stands barefoot in her tiny galley kitchen, stirring a tea bag around a mug that has a picture of a cat on it. She was always mad about cats, but I never let her have one because I personally don't like them very much. I hate how it's up to them whether they like you or not. Like you should be grateful for their attention. It annoys me, the same way that young women annoy me. They make me feel cruel.

"There," she says, passing the mug to me across the small table shoved up against the bare brick wall. She stares at me as I pick it up and take a sip, and I cock my head.

"What?" I say.

"I'm watching a dead man drink tea," she says. "What do you think?"

She looks so much older. I might have walked past her on the street and not recognized her. Maybe I have? I have walked through London quite brazenly in the years since I pretended to have died in a water sports accident in the Philippines. I didn't have white hair when I was married to Amanda; it was brown and I kept it long and floppy, kept my chin shaved soft and baby smooth. I was probably a little heavier then as well, young dad around town that I was, going to the pub with friends after work. I was less bothered about my appearance then. And maybe, given my relative youth, I didn't need to be. I didn't need to try as hard as I do these days to stand out from the herd.

"How are you?"

"How am I?" She pulls out the chair on the other side of the table and sits down on it slowly. I see the crepey skin of her décolletage. What is she now? Fifty-six? She's a few years older than me, I think. She was thirty when we met. She was an interior designer, living in a mews house in Chelsea with the living room upstairs and the bedrooms downstairs, and designed rooms for minor royalty and celebrities I'd never heard of. Now she lives in Tooting in what appears to be a one-bedroom flat. She's made it look very nice, of course she has, but it's still a big step down from where she was when I found her. For some reason I thought she had more in her; for some reason I thought she'd thrive without me.

She eyes me with a steely gaze. "How do you think I am, Damian? I mean, really? Tell me?"

"I don't know. That's why I asked."

"I'm . . . Jesus Christ. I'm a fucking *grieving widow*. I've spent nearly twenty years guiding our sons through living without their father. Their father who died leaving me with ninety thousand pounds' worth of debt. I've lost everything, the business, everything."

"This place looks nice enough," I say, my eyes taking in the kitchen that's only big enough for one person to cook in at a time.

She groans. "You know, all these years, I've wondered. Thought maybe you'd faked it. It just seemed so . . . The timing of it. The way we were then. The weird things that happened to my business. I thought, Maybe he faked it. I even did some research into it, found out that there are people in the Philippines who do this, that it's a . . . a *thing*. Y'know? But every time I got to the point of actually doing something about it, I'd just think, No. There is no way, no way on God's green earth that Damian would leave his boys deliberately. He might leave me . . . but he would not, not ever, leave his boys. His beautiful, beautiful boys. But . . ." Her next two words come out as a soft gasp. "You did."

I exhale loudly through my nostrils. Of course she is going to want to understand. Of course she is. I lean toward her and eye her tenderly. "I can assure you," I tell her, "I didn't want to. But, Amanda, I *had* to. I had no choice. They'd have killed all of us. You and the boys were in danger. It was the only way out. I would never have left you all otherwise."

"'They'? Who the fuck are *they*, Damian? What, like the Mafia or something?"

"No," I say, grasping for her hands, which she snatches away from me. "No. Not the Mafia. Of course not. But . . . I borrowed some money."

She opens her mouth to interject, to tell me that she knows about my debts because I saddled her with them, and I talk over her forcefully. "I borrowed some money. Remember. Remember back in 2002, when we lost that big project, the development? The one up in Paddington?"

She looks confused, her mouth hangs slightly ajar, her brow furrows. "The—?"

"I can't remember what it was called. You pitched for it. It was going to be huge. Seven figures. And you got so close, and I suppose I started . . ." I pause and let my head hang for a moment before looking up at her, my eyes glazed over with those magic tears. "I started to get ahead of myself. I started putting money into . . ." I sigh again. "Well, essentially it turned out to be some kind of super-sophisticated Ponzi scheme. But I thought—I really thought it was going to be amazing. I thought it was going to make us rich, pay off all our debts, we'd have enough to send the boys to private school. You know—holidays, a decent car. I did it for us, and I was an idiot, Amanda. A total idiot. I got suckered into it. And of course it was gone. Then I had to pay the money back into the company and I took out a loan from a friend of a friend and, well, it turned out this friend was not quite the genial moneylender my friend had led me to believe, and the interest rate was a joke and before I knew it, I owed them half a million."

I glance up at her, making my eyes as big and regretful as possible.

"They said they were coming for me, coming for you, coming for the boys. I had no choice, Amanda. I had no choice."

"Twenty years, Damian! You had twenty years to let me know you were still alive! To say something to the boys."

"You were all better off without me, don't you see?"

"No! No, we were not better off without you! We were lost without you! Whatever it was, we could have worked through it. We could have moved away. Together."

I simply shake my head and turn my hands palms up, as if to express the dead end of the conversation. There is nowhere else to go. What's done is done. The past is in the past.

"So," she says defeatedly. "What's going on? Why are you here?"

"I need somewhere to stay. Just for a few weeks."

"How did you find me?"

I bat the question away. You have to be actively trying to keep your location secret these days if you don't want anyone to be able to find you. "I've known where you live for years, Amanda. I've been keeping an eye on you."

She shudders, as if a chill has just run through her. "Oh."

"And the boys. I've seen them. Over the years. They look great."

And they do. Grown men now, of twenty-two and twenty-four. The older one, Sam, he looks like me. Tall and rangy with great hair. The younger one, Joel, he's a bit of a shrimp but has that swagger in his walk that some smaller men have. I can tell from looking at him that he has no problem finding girls, have seen him once or twice with some very good-looking ones. The boys are fine. I know they're fine. They didn't need me then, and they don't need me now.

"Oh my God, Damian," she gasps, letting her face drop into her hands. When she raises her head again, she's smiling, but it's a kind of warped smile, like her face doesn't know what else to do. "This is all too much. All way too much. I can't deal with this. Where've you even been?"

Such a good question. Truly. Where have I been? I'm not even sure myself.

"I've been living with a woman," I say. "Outside London. She has grown-up children. Older than the boys."

"And?" She eyes me coolly.

"And . . . she's trying to kill me."

She rolls away from me slightly and blinks. "I'm sorry, what?"

"She's not accepted the end of the relationship. She's been stalking me. Threatening to kill me. She's changed all the passwords to our bank accounts so I can't get my money. She's conned me out of thousands and thousands. She's mad, Amanda. Totally mental. And I have a heart condition—it's, well, the prognosis isn't great, and the stress, it's taking its toll, and today I just knew that it was enough. It was over, I had to get away. I burned everything, Amanda, everything that could identify me, and I came here."

"You came here? With a dangerous woman in pursuit?"

"But that's the thing. She doesn't know me by my real name. I changed my identity. She doesn't know about you. She doesn't know about my past. And I have a new consultant. For my heart. He's based at St. George's. I can get there so easily from here. And I promise you, Amanda, I promise, it will only be for a few weeks. Not even that. Maybe even days. But I beg of you, please, please just say yes. I will pay you back. I will make things right. Just tell me what you want from me, and I will give it to you."

She stares at the tabletop; her fingers are splayed out in front of her, and she ripples them gently as if playing the piano. "I don't want anything from you, Damian. I just don't want to ever feel the way I felt when they told me you were dead. Ever again."

"You won't. I won't. Those days are over. Those people are gone. I'm here now, I'm back. I can be in your life. We could even . . ." I shake my head and smile wryly, as if such a thing would never be countenanced. But it will be countenanced. I know it will. Amanda was always nuts about me. She adored me. And I can see it even now, in the way she tilts her head at me, the way her fingers find her hair, the way even now, during this ridiculous conversation that should have her running for the fucking hills, she's holding in her stomach.

TWENTY-NINE

"Where are you off to?" Ash asks her mum on Saturday morning.

Nina is wearing a huge raincoat and full makeup and sliding her feet into chunky walking boots.

"Nick's taking me to look at something."

Ash's stomach turns. "To look at what?"

"I don't know. He just called. Said to dress for the weather. I'm meeting him in Bangate, near the beach."

"Bangate Cove?"

"Yes."

"But there's nothing in Bangate. It's literally just a pub and some houses."

"Well, apparently not."

Ash glances at her mum from where she stands halfway down the stairs, still in her pajamas. "Can I come?"

"What?" Nina sounds annoyed. "No," she says. "I'm already late as it is."

"I'll be, literally, like a minute and a half. I just need to throw on some clothes. Please. I want to come."

"But why?"

"I just do. I want to see whatever the thing is. I like surprises!"

Ash does like surprises, but that's not why she wants to come. She wants to come because she keeps picturing Nick Radcliffe throwing one of his fancy silk ties around her mother's neck and pulling it harder and harder until she is dead. And what better place to do that than the windswept nothingness of Bangate Cove?

"Well, please, just be quick. I should have left ten minutes ago."

"I will. I promise!"

Ash hurtles back to her room; pulls off her pajamas; throws on joggers and a T-shirt, old high-tops, a fleecy hoodie; tucks her hair into a plastic claw; and runs back down to where her mother waits outside in the car, staring at her phone.

Nina doesn't make eye contact with Ash as she jumps into the passenger seat, just puts the car into drive and pulls away.

It's still raining when they pull into the tiny car park by the cove forty minutes later, and the graveled surface is pitted with deep puddles. Nick is already there and climbs loftily from the low seat of some kind of performance car that Ash didn't know he owned. He wears a waxed jacket that Ash hates on sight and opens a fancy golf-type umbrella as he walks toward them. He leans to kiss Nina tenderly on the cheek and then he looks at Ash, unfazed by her unexpected presence.

"Hello, you," he says. But he doesn't lean in to kiss her, and Ash is relieved. "Lovely day." He eyes the heavy, wet skies facetiously and smiles, and his face does that infuriating thing it does when he smiles of looking kind and handsome and just the sort of man you'd wish for your beautiful, recently widowed mother. He looks nothing like a necktie-strangler as he leads them genially across the scruffy car park and down toward the beach. It's empty, of course, at eleven forty-five on a dour Saturday morning and the sea is a heavy, dank gray as it hits the pebbled beach. There are a few forlorn beach huts on one side of the cove, not like the ones on the beach in the village where Ash and Nina live, which are all well maintained and painted perfect ice cream shades, strung with fairy lights and lanterns; these are peeling and weather-beaten, all of them abandoned.

As they move around the cove, Ash sees an old pavilion, clapboard-clad and falling apart. An old Wall's ice cream board sits outside, sun-bleached and attached to the railings with rusty chains, and Ash's mind, yet again, flits to thoughts of cable ties and gags, and God, why does her mind work like this? But then she remembers the wedding ring, the Zippo in the pink box, the slippery response to her question about dogs. She glances at her mother, sees her doing that thing she does around Nick, the elongation of her neck, the slight pout of her lips, jut of her hips. She does not look anxious at all. Her thoughts are not dark.

"So," says Nick, turning half a circle on one foot to face them both, "this little gem is up for sale. What do you think?"

Ash and Nina exchange looks. Nina laughs lightly. "Think of what?"

"Of Paddy's next venture."

The sound of her father's name on Nick's tongue makes Ash shudder. "What?"

"A fourth restaurant in the chain. I mean, it's ripe, isn't it? Imagine this . . ." He strides up the two steps to the front terrace. "Outdoor seating. A canopy. Maybe just lunchtimes to start with. Pop-up dinner nights in the summer months. Boardwalk to the car park. Fairy lights. An upturned fishing boat just here—lanterns, rope, the works. Come on, tell me you can't see it. Paint it white and Aegean blue—it would be like a little slice of Santorini. Yes? Yes?"

His face is aglow with his vision, but a pendulous silence hangs in the air.

"Er," Nina replies eventually. "I mean, God, yes, obviously it could be adorable, I can see that. But Bangate—I mean, it's just not that sort of location. It doesn't have that kind of, you know, *appeal*."

"You mean it isn't middle-class?"

"Well, yes, basically. It's kind of the forgotten village."

"Exactly!" Nick snaps his fingers. "That's exactly it. You've got this string of pearls on this stretch of the coast—Paddy's already has stakes in three of the best locations. You have a brilliant, brilliant brand. I mean, of course you have, it's Paddy's baby and the man was a genius. I always knew he would do something incredible, and he has. But why stop now? I mean, Padstow wasn't chic when Rick Stein opened his first restaurant there. Rick Stein *made* it chic. Paddy's will bring people here. I promise. And see these." He points at the abandoned beach huts. "All for sale too. You could turn them into boutique accommodation. Get them wired up, plumbed in, little wet rooms in each one. Seriously. And the whole thing under the well-loved Paddy's brand name. How amazing would that be?"

Ash can see her mother softening for a minute, her eyes misting over as she pictures the chichi wet dream of a mini resort that Nick has just painted. But then she shakes it away and says, "You'd never get planning permission."

"Well," says Nick, smiling, "that might not be true. I know someone on the council, or at least my colleague knows someone on the council, and they are planning to regenerate this area. They're investing. Heavily. You could probably push this through in record time. You might even get a subsidy. Worth a shot, huh?"

"What are they asking for it?"

Nick eyes the pavilion and says, "Two hundred for that, another one fifty for the huts."

"So, three fifty in total. Plus renovation, etc."

"Yes. But we could probably get them down from that, I reckon. I mean—look at the place."

They all turn to look at the place. A huge gust of wind blows a sheet of rain at them, the ice cream board rattles on its rusty frame, the whole building creaks a little.

Nina smiles and says, "It's amazing, Nick. But I don't have that kind of money."

He nods, smiles. "Sure," he says. "I didn't expect you would. But you have something else. Assets. You could borrow against things. Just like Paddy was doing. Like Paddy would have continued to do. That's how businesses grow, Nina."

His eyes are so bright they look like they could set fire to something; there's an urgency, a crazed energy about him. It reminds Ash of her dad, the way he would be when he was starting something new. But this man is not her dad; this man is a stranger, and he's using the word "we" in relation to her mother's money.

"Mum," she says. The word comes out as a whisper.

Nina turns to her, looks at her inquiringly.

Ash shakes her head. "Nothing."

She waits until they are on their own in the car a few minutes later, then she looks at her mother and she says, "You're not going to do it, are you?"

"What? Buy that wreck?"

"Yeah."

Nina laughs drily. "No, of course I'm not! Bloody hell. We're this close to having to shut down the new branch and the last thing I need right now is more debt, more risk, more stress. No. But Nick can buy it, if he likes." She pats Ash's knee and smiles widely into the small blade of sun just breaking through a crack in the clouds.

Ash swallows up the moment: the sun, her, her mother, just the two of them; Nick being othered, painted as an outsider.

Good, she thinks. Good.

THIRTY

Martha glances at the clock. Five p.m. Al had left this morning at eleven saying he had a quick errand to run at a brasserie near Folkestone. He'd left without any bags, saying he'd be back before 6 p.m. Usually this sort of last-minute work arrangement would put her into panic mode, but today her breathing is regular, her mind is clear, because yesterday she dropped a dog tracker under the back seat of Al's car and now she can see exactly where he is. And where he is, right now, is outside a restaurant just along from Folkestone Harbor called the Harbor Lights. She has googled the restaurant and seen that it is temporarily closed but about to reopen next month with a new name and under new management. Before that, Al was on a beach between Folkestone and Dover called Bangate Cove. He parked there for around twenty minutes before getting back into his car and driving to the restaurant, outside which he has been parked for the past three and a half hours, leading Martha to assume that he is hard at work in there. She switches her iPad back to the app connected to the dog tracker and is gratified and delighted to see that Al's car is moving, and then, ten minutes later, that it is traveling in the direction of Enderford. Google Maps tells her that the journey will take him just under an hour, which means he will be home at ten minutes past six. Which means that today, at least, Al has been doing exactly what he told her he would be doing.

He looks relaxed when he walks in an hour later. He tells her he has had a good and successful day. Martha smiles and says that she is glad. She hands him the baby and he takes Nala from her arms with a smile of unfiltered joy. Martha checks in with herself briefly, questioning her feelings in this moment. She had given herself an ultimatum after Al's disappearing act last week when Nala had been so sick. She'd made an agreement with herself when she planted the tracker in Al's car that the moment she saw any real-time deviation from the narrative Al gave her to explain his absences, she was going to walk away. Or rather, she was going to make him walk away. She doesn't care if he's been having an affair, she doesn't care if he's been trainspotting, she doesn't care if he's been sitting in a dark room staring at a wall, she doesn't care *what* he's been doing when he's away from home as long as it's what he told her he was doing. And today, at least, he has proved that much to her. Today she can breathe out, relax, open wine, thank her lucky stars for a man like Alistair.

"Oh," Al says, sitting Nala on her playmat inside a horseshoe-shaped cushion. "By the way. I have big news."

"Oh yes?"

"I think I've found a new venture for us. Well, for you, but for both of us."

"A new . . . ?"

"A new Martha's Garden spot. I've been thinking about this for a long time. I know having the baby has held you back a little lately and I know you had all these amazing plans for the business when we first met, and I know our finances have got a bit sticky and things have been . . . well, things have been rough. I've been absent. I've been shit, let's face it. And last week was a wake-up call for me. To have left you here like that, with Nala so ill, it just makes me die inside even thinking about it." He sighs, heavily, and then sits down on the sofa and passes toys to Nala as he speaks. "So, I've decided. That's it. I'm quitting my job. I can't do it anymore. I can't treat you like this anymore. You deserve more. We both deserve more. And frankly, your business deserves more."

Martha had told him about all the canceled orders, all the irate customers, the long-standing account with a wedding planner that had been terminated overnight, the one-star review on Trustpilot. He'd hung his head and said he hated himself.

"We need to focus on Martha's Garden again, and I have found the most fantastic site—coastal, an old beach café near Folkestone. It's been empty for twelve years. But the local council is about to invest a small fortune in the resort to try and bring it up to scratch. They've approved plans for a small estate of New England–style luxe housing, and an upmarket shopping area. And imagine, Martha"—he turns on his phone and shows her his camera roll—"imagine this, painted in California Rose. Imagine a flower shop here, and a café right here. A shopping area selling gifts and branded goods. And these little beach huts—we could convert those into rooms, plumb them in, put in mezzanine beds: 'Martha's Bedrooms.'" He makes the shape of a sign with his hands. "Just imagine that. A boardwalk with integrated lighting joining it all together. Can you see it?" he says, slightly breathlessly. "Wouldn't it be incredible?"

Martha blinks slowly and nods in rhythm. Yes, she thinks to herself, my goodness, yes. It could be stunning. A café! she thinks. She has always fantasized about a café. Pistachio and rosewater muffins on vintage plates. Tea from pink pots. Wildflowers in old jars. They could plant pampas grass and sea thrift along the boardwalk. She would be able to expand her branded stock. And finally, she thinks, get herself some proper staff, not just teenage girls. She could kick back a little, work from an office, not be up at five o'clock every morning.

Her heart races with excitement and she flicks back and forth through the photos on Al's phone, neatly filed away in a folder called "Martha's Garden on the Beach," which she finds sweetly touching.

"Wow," she says eventually, handing Al his phone back. "I mean, yes.

Obviously, yes, I can see it, it could be stunning. Literally amazing. But, Al, we don't have any money."

"Well, that is not entirely true. I might have found a way to come up with finances. Well, half the finances. And the council will subsidize some of the renovation expenses. You just need to find a hundred grand. A hundred and fifty tops. That's all. And you could borrow that easily against the house."

Martha feels a lurch at the pit of her stomach. Al's talked to her before about borrowing against the house, and she's always refused. She already borrowed against it eight years ago to finance Martha's Garden and has been trying to get her mortgage back to zero ever since. The thought of going back to square one and beyond terrifies her.

"God, Al, I don't know. It's all a bit scary."

"Yes!" His eyes are laser bright. "It's terrifying! I know! But, Martha, we need this. I need to get away from my bloody job, and you need more than this"—he gestures around the room, but is suggesting her current life—"to get your teeth into. This is the moment, Martha. You're nearly fifty. I'm going to be fifty-six any minute. We've got another twenty good years. Let's make them count. For God's sake, let's make them count."

Martha smiles; her stomach feels soft.

Suddenly the dream that has recently felt so bruised and tarnished feels bright and new again. She nods. "OK!" she says. "Yes! I'm in."

THIRTY-ONE

FOUR YEARS EARLIER

I see a small bruise on Amanda's cheekbone. I realize that it correlates with the exact location of my fingertips across her mouth two days before and I feel a twinge of guilt, but it soon dies away. It was for her own good, and what choice did I have? I am not a violent man; I have never, ever hit a woman.

"So," she says, eyeing me from the door into the living room, where I have been sleeping on her sofa. She is wearing a voluminous T-shirt, her skinny bare legs pale and scrawny beneath. Her parched blond hair is in a pile on top of her head and there are dark smudges beneath her eyes. She used to be so beautiful, I'm sure she did. Or maybe Martha has ruined my concept of beauty forever. "What are you up to today?" she asks.

"Hospital appointment," I say, feigning some kind of nonexistent pain as I bring myself up to a sitting position. "And then I have some business to attend to."

"What sort of business?" Her eyes narrow as she looks at me.

"I've been back working in the restaurant industry," I say. "For a few years now. And I recently met a guy who wants me to go into business with him, to help him run a new wine bar in Mayfair. I've invested a few thousand. I'm trying to raise a few more. So. We're getting together to crunch some numbers."

Amanda shakes her head, just once, a small gesture of disbelief. "What time's your hospital appointment?"

"Eleven," I say, and then wince again as I move.

"What is it that you've got?" she says, the distrust thawing slightly into concern. "Exactly."

"Hypertrophic cardiomyopathy. Thanks, Dad," I add for good measure.

"Is that what . . . ?"

I flinch, suddenly blindsided by a flash of doubt. I'm usually so good at this stuff, but now I can't remember what I told Amanda about my father. It appears from her response that I told her that he died of a heart attack, and I recover my cool and say, "Yes, that's what killed him." And then I remember our wedding back in 1998, how much Amanda had wanted my father to come, how she had wanted me and my father to be reunited in the glow of our romantic union, and I'd stupidly said I'd invite him, and she wouldn't let it go, would not let it go, so in the end I told her he'd died. A massive heart attack.

She nods sadly, and I breathe a sigh of relief. Yes, I think. That's right. That's right.

Because meeting Amanda was such a long, long time ago, I was a young man and I was not as slick as I am now, I hadn't learned the ways of the world, how to navigate riptides, how to manage sudden changes to the script. I have learned so much about life in the succeeding twenty-nine years. I have learned so much about people. I made huge mistakes with Amanda, but I never allowed her to fall out of love with me. That is the biggest lesson I have learned. Don't let them hate you. Once they hate you, there's no way back, and there always, always needs to be a way back.

"What's the prognosis?" she asks. "Will you have to have surgery?"

"Hopefully not. Meds for now. Keeping an eye on it. And, of course, staying fit and healthy." I pat my firm stomach and smile.

"You look good," she says, and there's a hint of sourness in her voice, as if she is cross that I haven't fallen apart as she has, that if anything I look better now than I did when we were together.

"I work at it," I say, getting to my feet, letting her see the full grandeur of my physical form in boxer shorts and a fitted T-shirt.

"I like your hair white like that. Is that from your dad too?"

I laugh wryly. "Yes, in fact it is. He was quite the silver fox."

"And now so are you."

"I suppose I am." I make my voice soft and sweetly surprised, as if the concept of seeing myself as physically alluring has never occurred to me before. "Except without the filthy narcissism and casual cruelty," I add, reminding Amanda of my dark and traumatizing past.

She sighs, removes her hand from the door frame, and says, "Anyway. Let me get you a coffee."

Tooting High Street is generally unprepossessing but is not as bad as it sounds. Most places in London these days are half-decent; where there are Victorian houses there is the chance of gentrification, and where there is even a touch of gentrification, there is at least one nice place to get breakfast. And that is where I go when I leave Amanda's flat an hour later. It's all sage green and hanging plants in raffia pots and matcha this and matcha that and I order a cappuccino and a slice of something with blueberries in it and sit in the window and enjoy watching the world go by for a few minutes. I was sure to take a spare key with me before I left Amanda's flat and the ease with which she gave it to me shows me that I already have her trust. I'm really hoping that this sojourn with Amanda in her tiny flat, sleeping on her not-very-comfortable sofa, will be brief. I really hope that it won't take long for me to nurture my relationship with Martha to the point that I can move in with her. But before I can focus on the next steps, I do still need to deal with the previous situation.

I told Tara I'd give her a week. I told her it was for her, this time apart, to gather her thoughts, decide about our future, to give her the space to make choices. But it wasn't for her, it was for me. I need a week to secure my future, away from Tara.

I know Tara's schedule intimately, and I know that on Mondays she works from her company's head office in central Reading, and I know that she leaves home at ten to be in at eleven for a coffee at her desk before a department meeting at eleven thirty, and then she works until six and returns home at seven. I know that the house will be empty all day and I will have all the time in the world to do what I need to do.

The blueberry loaf thing is delicious, the nicest thing I've eaten in days, and I chase the crumbs around the plate and tell the pretty girl who clears my table that it was wonderful and I look at her with hopeful eyes, because I am feeling hopeful, I am a man in love, after all, but she does not register it, nor my compliment about the food, she merely nods and says thanks in a flat monotone and I want to say something harsh, but I don't. I just think that she is young and stupid and that it is not her fault. But I take a mental note of the name on her badge. *Kadija.* I have a good memory for names and faces.

It is 9:08. I have some time to kill, so I head up the road to a pawnshop I'd noticed as I was walking to the coffee shop. It was closed then but is open now and I step inside. It's not my first time in a pawnshop. Behind the counter at the back is a tall, broad-chested Asian man with a closely clipped beard, smartly dressed in a waistcoat over a shirt fastened at the cuffs with gold links. I show him Tara's ring and he looks at it closely and offers me £300. I'm tempted. I barely have enough money to pay for my train fare to Reading, but I know I should hold out. I can do better. I smile and thank him, put the ring back in my pocket, and leave.

The house is quiet. Tara's car is not on the drive, though my stupid £25,000 Tesla is still there, gleaming smugly in the morning sun.

Except it's not technically mine anymore; it belongs to Tara now. I transferred the payment to a card I took out in her name a few days ago. She doesn't know yet. I'd been planning to intercept the statements before she could get to them, but obviously that will be tricky if I'm not living here. Hopefully, by the time the first statement arrives, I will be long gone, sucked away into Martha's world with a new name and a clean track record and there will be nothing Tara can do about the car or the credit card or, frankly, any of it. And I feel bad, of course I do, but that's life. She made choices, she allowed it all to happen. I don't want to say that she was stupid, but yes, fuck it. She was stupid. Stupid for love. Stupid for the status quo. Stupid for whatever it is that women get from having a man like me in their lives.

Over my lifetime I have developed the unique ability to see and understand within a second exactly what sort of man a woman is looking for and to offer it to her. After that it is up to the woman to set her boundaries, because if I am giving a woman what she wants, then she has to give me what I need. That doesn't seem unfair, does it?

I turn off the Ring app remotely from my phone and let myself into the house. It's tidy, it smells extra clean, almost as if Tara scrubbed my essence from it the moment I walked out of the door.

I go to the fridge and cut myself a hunk of cheese from a block of Cheddar and eat it as I pace about. It has already stopped feeling like home, this modern house that Tara loves so much. I can't believe that this is where my life has played out for so long. Four years. And nothing to show for it. Not one thing.

It's Emma's fault. If she hadn't got pregnant, I could have persuaded Tara to sell this horrible house and I would have had half a million pounds—maybe more—to play with now. But because Emma got pregnant, Tara refused to countenance it. So, instead, I am reduced to seeing what else I can salvage from the depressing wreck of our marriage.

I go to the corner of the conservatory that Tara uses as her home office, and I open up the lid of her laptop. I'm not sure what I'm looking for. Tara will have something squirrelled away somewhere, and I know for a fact that she has a good life insurance policy because she took her husband's name off it when we got married and added me. Unfortunately, there is only one way for me to access the money in that policy and, well, clearly that is not going to happen. What do you take me for?

I go into Tara's bank account and type in her password. It says it has not been recognized, so I tap it in again, switching on the small eye icon to check I don't mistype it, but it still doesn't recognize the code. I feel a blast of fury pass through me at the realization that Tara has changed her password.

I spin round in her office chair to the filing cabinet behind me. It usually has a key hanging from the lock, but I notice that it's gone. I flinch as I grasp the fact that in the two days since I left, my wife has changed the password to her bank account, cleaned the house to within an inch of its life, and taken away the keys to her filing cabinet.

Black rage starts to build at the base of my spine and I reflexively lock out my finger joints, lacing them together and pulling them apart. The feel of the bones cracking restores me to calm. Now is not the time to get angry. No time is the time to get angry; that is another thing I've learned. Anger is a derailer. It never solves anything, ever.

I sigh and run my hands through my hair and then I stiffen at the sound of a key in the door. I quietly close the lid of Tara's laptop and step toward the hallway.

It's Emma, Tara's daughter. I see her put the key she used to let herself into the house into her pocket, and then slowly take off her coat. I back into the conservatory, my breathing silent. Then I notice my raincoat hanging on one of the hooks by the back door in the kitchen and I walk quickly toward it. By the time Emma comes upon me in the kitchen, I have it in my hand and my face is arranged into a pleasant smile, my other hand clutching my chest in a slightly fey *Ooh, you gave me a start* gesture.

"Emma!" I say. "What are you doing here?"

She eyes me inscrutably. "I thought you were going away for a week."

"Yes. I am. I'm staying with a friend, in London. I just came back to get my raincoat. Weather forecast looks horrible."

"You came all the way to Reading to get a raincoat?" Her hand goes absent-mindedly to her pregnant belly as she speaks, a gesture that inexplicably annoys me. Something about the superiority of it.

"Yes. And a few other things. I packed in a hurry, I wasn't really thinking." I pause for a moment and then I say again, "What are you doing here?"

"Mum said she saw something on the Ring app. Asked me to come and check."

I know this is a lie. I deactivated the app before I arrived. It occurs to me that Emma has been charged with "keeping an eye on the place."

"Oh, right, well, that would be me, then." I shrug and grin, all Hugh Grant, affable and unthreatening, but I don't see even a chink in her demeanor.

"Have you got everything?" she says, glancing at my raincoat.

"Yes," I say. "I have. Are you going to escort me off the premises?" I ask this with humor, but also in the knowledge that that is exactly what she wants to do.

"No," she says, "but it's probably best if you leave."

"You do realize I still live here, Emma. I've only moved out temporarily."

"Yes. I do. And you do realize that this house is in my mother's name and that legally you have no right to be here."

There. There it is. This is the open face of the secret conversations that have been playing out here during the days when I've been at work. It's oozing through the cracks now for me to see.

I keep my face neutral. "Oh yes, Emma, I am well aware of that.

Your mother has been very careful to ensure that I never forget that fact." I sound bitter, and I am bitter. Whilst Tara has always shown me full trust (hence me having access to her bank account), she has always kept something back from me, and it's only now that I feel the full force of that reserve.

"I think you should go."

She has a hard face, Emma, she's not feminine like her mother. She looks like her dad. I want to punch that face, just once, dead center. *Bang.* I've wanted to punch her face since pretty much the first time I met her four years ago. It's her fault that Tara has held back from me; she put doubt into her head from the very beginning. Questioned my motivations. Googled me. Told her mother she thought I was "dodgy."

As far as I was concerned, Emma had been watching too many stupid documentaries. There is nothing dodgy about me. What you see is what you get. I can be a good man, a good husband, a good person. I can give women exactly what they want. But I do have to be creative with my finances, yes. I just don't have that *thing* that some people have, that ability to streamline and think ahead and get my ducks in a row. It's just a bit haphazard, that's all, but the women in my life have benefited from this just as much as they may have suffered as a consequence, because when I do have money, I am generous to a fault. There is always champagne, luxury travel, there is always silk and satin and caviar and the sorts of truffles that are placed in boxes one by one with silver tongs. So, nobody is a loser, not really. And the women in my life know that. Or at least they do until people around them start planting these stupid doubts in their heads.

"You know," I say carefully to Emma, "your mother adores me. I make her happy. So, I don't know why you are so keen for her to cut me out of her life. It makes no sense. I can only assume, Emma, that you are jealous of me somehow. Jealous of the bond I have with your mother."

The minute the words are out, I regret them. I have just given her the key to the door.

I see her face contort. "Are you serious? You think I'm jealous of you? Jonathan—I am nearly thirty years old. I left home ten years ago. I have a husband and a home and a job and a baby on the way. All I want in the *whole world* is for my mother to have a bond with a man. All I want is to go to bed at night knowing that my mother is safe and loved. That I don't need to worry about her. But all I have done, Jonathan, for the last four years is worry about her. I worry about her from the minute I wake up till the minute I go to sleep. I worry about her finances, her mental health, her physical health. I think you're a psychopath, Jonathan, I actually do. I'm sorry, but that's just the truth."

Her cheeks are flushed and I can tell her body is pumping volumes of industrial-strength adrenaline through her system and that, I assume, of her unborn child. I can't imagine that it's very good for either of them.

I arrange my face into the softest shape I can make it into and say, "Emma, you know I have always loved you, from the minute I first met you. As if you were my own. You know that having never had children of my own, I always hoped I'd meet someone who was a mother, and it's always made me sad that neither you nor your brother had any interest in having that kind of bond with me. But I get it. I really do. I don't trust men either. You know about my father. You know the kind of man he was, how abusive he was, and I know that men can be awful, so I see why you want to protect your mother from me—well, not just me but any man. But, Emma, honestly, you have to just trust me when I say I'm one of the good guys, seriously." I turn my hands palms up and make a small, sad sighing sound. But she appears unmoved by my appeal. I see her face contort and her eyes flash.

"It was me," she says triumphantly. "It was me who told the girl on the neighborhood app about you. I saw that footage and I messaged that woman, and I told her your name and your address. And I do not know how you got away with it, truly I don't, because it was so obviously you. And not only that, but it was so obviously the sort of thing that you would do. I have waited all these years for my mum to finally wake up to you and your bullshit, and then she did. Because she knows it was you as well as you do, whatever crap you told the police. There is literally nothing now that is going to make her want to be with you. She's over you, Jonathan. It's done."

The big mental fist in my head smashes into Emma's unpretty face over and over and over as she talks. In my mind's eye, I see her face turn to pulp. But my expression remains impassive. I sigh the small, sad sigh again and say, "I'm sorry it's ended like this. Truly. But you are wrong about the girl on the street, and you are wrong about me. All I ever wanted was to be accepted by you. All I ever wanted was this . . ." I gesture around the soulless new-build house that I have come to hate so much.

Her face is a picture of disdain. "Christ, Jonathan. You are such a bullshitter. Literally every word that comes out of your mouth is a lie."

I simply smile, sadly, and head for the front door.

As I pass Emma at the threshold, she faces me; she is so close to me that her pregnant bump brushes slightly against my body and I shudder with revulsion. Her face is inches from mine as she says, "It's over, Jonathan. OK? You're not coming back. And, Jonathan, if anything bad ever happens to my mum, anything at all, I will be going straight to the police. I won't even wait one minute. Do you understand?"

I hold her gaze as coolly as I can and then I nod, just once, before picking up the key for the Tesla by the front door and slowly leaving the house.

THIRTY-TWO

Jane Trevally messages Ash a couple of days after the impromptu viewing of the beach pavilion in Bangate with Nick. `I have news,` she says. `Can we meet up?`

They arrange to meet again at King's Cross, this time for cocktails. Ash feels the same rush of nervous energy as she disembarks from the train. Her eyes stay low to the floor as she walks, her pulse racing with terror at the thought of catching the eye of someone she knows, someone who remembers her, someone who knows what she did. She sees a pair of soft leather men's shoes coming toward her and a pump of adrenaline goes through her. Ritchie's shoes? But no, they belong to a young man, not much older than her. She pulls in her breath.

Calm down, Ash, she tells herself. *Calm the fuck down.*

She finds Jane in the tiny jewel-box bar above the station where they had arranged to meet, and they face each other on small velvet armchairs across a copper-topped table. Jane looks younger in this soft light than she did outside the brasserie by the fountains in the cold light of day. Ash finds older women's faces fascinating, the way they morph and wax and wane, how they can look five different ages within the space of a minute. Jane looks about thirty right now as she flirts with the waiter who is depositing their cocktails onto paper coasters.

"So," Jane begins, when the waiter has gone, "I did some digging. And frankly, I don't know where to start."

Ash's flesh tingles. "Go on."

"I called the bar in Mayfair. I asked for him. The person who answered the phone said they'd never heard of him."

Ash blinks slowly and gasps. "No way!"

Jane throws her a look that says, *That's just the beginning—buckle up*, then scrolls down the screen of her phone and turns it toward Ash.

It's a photo of Nick Radcliffe. Except the name in the caption under the photograph is not Nick Radcliffe, it's Justin Warshaw, and he's not described as a restaurateur, but as a life coach.

"What!"

"Yes. Exactly. I've googled him extensively and found very, very little. But it appears that this 'Justin Warshaw' guy ran a life-coaching consultancy from a suburb of Cambridge for many years and was then never heard of again."

"But why the weird name?"

"I have no idea. But it fits in with your theory that there might be something off about him."

"Are there any customer reviews? Of his life coaching?"

"Yes. There're six on Google. All five stars. Frankly, I wonder if they're even real." She sighs and takes another sip of her cocktail. "Do you want food, by the way? Snacks? Olives? Anything? You're very thin."

"I am not very thin," Ash replies. "I'm totally normal. I would probably have been thought fat back in your day."

Jane raises an eyebrow and nods. "That's true. Anyway, I'm going to have some rosemary-salt fries and . . ." Her finger, with its chipped nail polish, runs down the small bar-food menu ". . . Padrón peppers. We can share."

She beckons the waiter over and flirts with him again as she places the order, and Ash watches entranced as the waiter, who is a solid thirty years younger, flirts back.

"So, there was a link to a website for Justin Warshaw's life-coaching services, but it hits a dead page now, a 404. Long gone. And I did a reverse image search for this photo and I cannot find it anywhere else. But here, look . . ." She zooms into the photo. "Look at that. A wedding ring."

Ash stares at the ring. It's a plain gold one, like the one she'd found in the pile of her mother's bedside rug. "Is there an email address?"

"Yup. I tried it. It bounced back. Tried the mobile number too—dead tone."

"Have you googled any of the women who left reviews for him?"

"Yes. They all have stupidly common names—I'm going to say *deliberately* common names. But I googled them all, and there is a Sarah May who lives in Cambridge and has an Instagram account that suggests very much the lifestyle of a person who would use the services of a life coach. So I messaged her, but she hasn't replied yet."

"When did you message?"

"Oh, about an hour ago."

"Check again."

Jane nods and switches screens to Instagram. "Ooh." She breaks into a smile and turns the phone to face both of them. "Here she is."

They both look down and read.

> *Hi Jane. Thanks for your message. Yes, I did used to see a life coach called Justin Warshaw, many years ago. He sort of disappeared as far as I recall. What was it you wanted to know about him? He was very good I thought.*

Jane turns the phone back to herself and types:

> *He's going out with a friend using a different name and we're a bit sus about him. Saw you left him a*

review and wondered what you could tell us. Happy to chat on the phone or Zoom or whatever.

Sarah replies a moment later:

Not sure there's much to tell you. But sure. Let's Zoom or something, maybe tomorrow? I wfh so any time works for me. 10 ish?

Ash nods furiously at Jane, who responds with a thumbs-up emoji and her email address.

Jane slides her phone away from her and smiles at Ash. "Well," she says. "That was a good start. But there was something else that my guys uncovered. Not sure what it means. But apparently, Nick Radcliffe does not exist anywhere in the world in any official capacity. I mean, obviously there are *Nick Radcliffes*. Lots of them. But this particular one? The one that claims to co-own Bar Amelie and lives in Tooting and used to work with your dad in a restaurant in the nineties? Nope. Nothing. Same for Justin Warshaw. He exists only in the capacity of a life coach in Cambridge roughly ten years ago. Nothing before, and nothing since. Your Nick Radcliffe . . . he's some kind of a . . . of a . . . *pop-up man*. And listen. We checked the reg plates for his car. It's on a lease. We're trying to get hold of the leaseholder details, but it might take a few days. We do know it was leased from a dealership in Vauxhall, about three weeks ago."

"Right," says Ash. "OK."

"So, that's it. All we have as of now."

"No. That's great. Really."

"Are you going to tell your mum?"

Ash flinches. "Yeah, no. I mean, I want to. But on the other hand—I mean, it's all a bit vague and I don't want her to . . . worry."

Jane looks at her blankly and says, "Why not?"

"Because she'll think I'm, I don't know, trying to spoil it for her, you know? I'm probably slightly overbonded with her these days. Since Dad died. And yeah, even before, to be honest. Overattached to both of my parents. When I left home, after uni that is, I kind of imploded? Had a sort of, erm . . ." She pauses and fiddles with the base of her cocktail glass, then looks at Jane, registers the understanding in her eyes, and continues. "A breakdown? I came home under a bit of a cloud of shame. Had a pretty major mental health diagnosis. And ever since then, I've been treated like a wayward child. And then Dad died, and I just clung on to Mum and kind of policed her a bit? If that makes sense? Policed her grief? Made her take on mine too? It's been an intense year and I think she wants me to go now, but I'm not ready to go and, honestly, the way I feel right now, I don't think I will ever feel ready to go. I look at other people my age and I don't get how they're doing it? It doesn't compute? And this guy, whoever the fuck he is, he makes her happy and when he's around it's like she's young again. Her best self. And if I go home tonight and say, 'Oh, Mum, by the way, your new boyfriend is dodgy as fuck,' she'll just think I'm projecting some kind of stupid, unevolved kidult angst onto her happiness. Do you see?"

All her words have tumbled out of her in a spew. She didn't know they were there until they were there. Jane stares at her and then suddenly places her hands over hers. Her eyes fill with care and concern. "Oh, you sweet thing. You are so, so sweet. And I get it, I really do. I am always the unreliable narrator in my life. People always question my motives, question the accuracy of my opinions or retelling of things. You know? They always think I'm trying to twist the narrative or something. As if I'm even clever enough! Ha!" She turns her smile to the young waiter who delivers the Padrón peppers and the fries, which are served in a silver cone with a twisted knot of roasted rosemary on the top. "You are amazing," she gushes to the waiter, taking a fry and biting into it as she speaks. "Thank you!"

He smiles and flushes and tells her that she's welcome.

"Listen," Jane continues, turning her attention back to Ash. "Leave it with me. I'll do some more digging. And maybe you could do some digging too. And we'll talk to this Sarah May girl tomorrow. And then maybe, once you've got a dossier of stuff, you can confront your mother with it. All the irrefutables. But for now, let's keep this between the two of us. I will help you any way I can. I see you, Ash. OK? I see you."

Ash feels a shiver run down her spine at Jane's words. She smiles and squeezes Jane's hands. "Thank you," she says. "You have no idea how much that means to me."

THIRTY-THREE

Al has quit his job, just as he said he would, and now, on a bright and hopeful December morning, ten days before Christmas, they are working together in the shop. Al is doing the accounts and Martha is attaching jingle bells to holly wreaths. Christmas music is playing through the speakers and she feels a swell of joy in the pit of her stomach. This is it, she thinks, no more stupid job. No more last-minute emergency chases across the country. No more overnights. No more switched-off phone. Just her and her husband, side by side, sharing their space, sharing their beautiful life.

The door opens and a customer walks in. Al straightens up and takes off his reading glasses. "Good morning," he says to the middle-aged man, in his most welcoming tone.

"Good morning," the man replies, his stern face softening. "Can you help me? It's my wife's birthday. The big five-oh. I want to take something home tonight that will knock her socks off."

"In which case," Al says smoothly, "I will hand you over to my beautiful wife, who is the most skilled and knowledgeable florist in the southeast, if not the world."

Martha shrugs off his compliment with a dry laugh, but her stomach rolls gently. She likes how proud Al is of her, how much respect he has for her trade, her craft. And more important, right now she really likes Al. Ever since he quit his job a week ago, he's been amazing. So warm with her, so attentive with the children, especially, strangely enough, with her younger son.

Over the past few days, something remarkable seems to have happened between the two of them. Jonah had come home early from school last Friday, feeling ill. Al, who'd been at home with Nala, sat him at the kitchen table with soup and sympathy and then, apparently, had some kind of seismic conversation with him about his gender identity. Jonah told Al that someone at school had said he looked like a girl and that he'd liked it and now he didn't know if he was a boy or a girl, and that someone in his class had changed their pronouns and now he was wondering about it too, and Al had told him that whatever he wanted to be was absolutely fine and that he should not rush into anything and that he and Martha would support him in whatever he decided to do.

This whole episode had elevated Martha's feelings toward Al to a level higher than they had been even at the beginning of their relationship. That her son, who had always been so delicate, so sensitive, so interior, had chosen Al over her or his father to share this moment with spoke volumes about the caliber of Al's character. Martha had suspected for some time that Jonah was troubled by his gender identity and she had just been waiting for the right time for the conversation to blossom. She should maybe feel a little betrayed by being left out of this moment, but she doesn't. She feels vindicated. Justified in her choices. Justified in her decision to give Al another chance.

She goes to the customer and helps him to put together a £100 bouquet of all his wife's favorite flowers, then she arranges them for him and wraps them in brown paper and pink satin ribbons and puts them into a pink card bag with pink rope handles and the winter sun is picking its way across her shop as he leaves, lighting bits of it up as if to remind her how good she has it, how beautiful her life is.

Al looks up from the paperwork and says, "We're so lucky, aren't we?" as if he'd been reading her thoughts.

"Yes," she says. "We really are."

THIRTY-FOUR

FOUR YEARS EARLIER

I'm feeling strangely undone as I wander through Mayfair later that day. I did not like the way that Tara's daughter spoke to me. It was harsh and it was completely unnecessary. Emma has always made me feel like this, but when I had Tara onside, I could keep her daughter out of my head. She was just white noise to me. Now that Emma has pulled her mother over to her side, she is deafening, grating, has made claw marks on the insides of my psyche. I want to spend time thinking up sharp ripostes to her unpleasantness. I want to write her a long letter full of justifications and clarity. And more than anything, I want her to die.

My day-to-day existence is tenuous, even I can see this. It depends on me troubleshooting each moment as it presents itself. I think on my feet and I'm brilliant at it. I call the shots and I make things happen, bend things to my will, if necessary. I've lived my entire adult life like this, it's who I am, it's what I do. But Emma—she has thrown something in the works that I cannot shift and now I am acting in desperation, and I do not like the way it feels. I should still be at Tara's now, slowly extricating myself from the chains of our dead marriage, preparing myself for the seamless transition into Martha's life and Martha's home, hopefully with some of Tara's cash in my bank account. But now I'm penniless on a sofa in Tooting for God knows how long, and I feel untethered.

But as I turn the corner of Curzon Street and see the empty retail unit that a man called Luke Berner and I are going to make into a beautiful wine bar, I feel myself re-forming.

It's on the ground floor of a 1940s building, two doors down from a Soho House club. It used to be a doctors' clinic, but there is planning permission to turn it into a bar or restaurant. There are two huge square bay windows at street level and a view from the front all the way through to the back. The light is spectacular. I see me and Luke Berner as the new Jeremy King and Chris Corbin; I picture us posing outside for the press on opening day, our arms around each other, possibly both with a glass of champagne in hand. I imagine bringing Martha here—my God, she would look spectacular in this setting—and showing her around, pulling out a stool at the bar, asking the bartender to make her the finest cocktail, seeing the look of awe and wonder on her face as she glances around at the beauty of the place. Ever since I was young, it has been my dream to have a restaurant or bar of my own. It has always struck me as the most glamorous business in the world, and I want this so badly it almost makes me sick.

I met Luke Berner three months ago through a client. Luke told me about this wine bar he was planning to take out a lease on and I told him about my long career in the hospitality industry and the half a million pounds that was coming my way from the "sale of an asset." That asset, of course, was meant to be Tara's house, the house that we were going to sell so that we could move to the Algarve and live off the land. So far, Luke has been very patient waiting for this money to materialize, but I can tell his patience is starting to wear thin.

I make it to my four o'clock meeting with Luke Berner with five minutes to spare. I carry my nausea and nerves with me into the tiny lift and all the way down the carpeted corridor to the door of Luke's office, and then, as the door opens and Luke appears, I shrug it off like a wet robe, and by the time I grip Luke's hand inside mine and tell him I'm good, I'm well, and ask him how he is and comment on how pleasant his new offices are and what a nice day it is and yes, I'd love a coffee, actually, thank you, black, no sugar, and pull out a chair opposite his desk and start to talk about the bar and my role in it, I am feeling fully re-formed.

I stare at the way his hair plumes at the front and recedes at the sides into two shiny cul-de-sacs of skin, at the outline of his nipples through a tightly fitting shirt that looks like it is restricting his breathing. He is ten years younger than me, forty-one, but looks younger, mainly because of the way he dresses, but also because of the way he speaks. Lots of "like"s and "you know"s and "kinda"s.

Luke needs £2 million to secure the lease on the building and so far he has a million. My body language betrays nothing as the three syllables of "million" fragment and ricochet around the walls of his office; as if I always think in millions, as if hundreds and thousands never even occur to me.

"Sooooo," says Luke, pulling out the word into a long syllable. "Your asset? The sale? Any signs of it coming together?"

I look him in the eye, and I say, "I have a very keen buyer, a cash buyer. Give me a week or so, maybe a month, I will absolutely be in for it."

He arches one of his eyebrows, which I now see have been professionally groomed. "The full five hundred?"

"Maybe six," I continue. "I just need time."

"Cool," says Luke. But his tone is edgy, uncomfortable. His eyes run down my résumé where it sits on the desk in front of him. "Yeah," he says, guardedly. "There's something . . ." He sucks in his breath, and I know what's coming. "Something that's slightly bothering me. There are a lot of gaps in this résumé. You're not hiding anything from me, are you, Nick?"

I shift a little in my seat. I'd been expecting this. "Absolutely not,"

I say. "Well, nothing for you to worry about. The thing is, I have a lot of baggage. Family stuff. I can't really go into it. And I've used pseudonyms, over the years, to keep myself safe. Including, er . . . Nick Radcliffe."

"That's not your real name?" Luke looks startled.

"Well, it is currently. Yes. I mean my bank account is in that name. My finances are. But my passport is in another name. As are certain periods of my career. It's pure expediency. Just keeping my head beneath the radar. But nothing whatever for you to worry about." I sigh, a deep and ponderous noise that I hope fully conveys how hard my life has been and how little I wish to expand upon it.

Luke sighs too. "I see," he says, although it's clear that he doesn't. "Well, that sounds tough, Nick. I'm sorry. Just goes to show, you never can tell. But listen." He pulls himself closer to his desk. "Here's the thing. I've been talking to another investor. Jensen de Witt. You might have heard of him. He owns wine bars in Saint-Tropez and Dubai, been around for decades, and he's keen to come in for the other million. But he doesn't like the look of you. I'm sorry." He puts his hands out in an apologetic gesture. "That's his take, not mine. You know I think you're a great bloke and I'd love to make this work. But between the patchy CV, the lack of transparency, and the lack of money, I kinda don't think it's going to. Not at this level. So, yeah, Nick. I'm really sorry, mate, but I'm out. I hope you understand."

The rage descends quietly, and as always, I fend it off. I plaster a good smile on my face and I say nice words in a nice voice; I talk about understanding and no hard feelings. I wish him luck. I even manage to make him laugh, and as I go to leave, in a swell of bonhomie and good feelings, he grabs my hand in his and he says, "Go on, then, Nick, you can tell me—what's your real name? I promise I won't tell anyone." He's wearing a cheeky smile, which I return.

I tap my nose and say, "You know what, Luke, it's been so long since I used it that I'm not sure I can even remember it anymore."

I kick the wall when I leave. I kick it so hard that I fear I've broken a toe. I punch it with my fists, and I growl like a dog. "Fuck's sake." I hit the wall again. "Fuck's sake." A woman passing by looks at me with concern, and I breathe in heavy and hard and straighten myself up, clear my throat, run a hand over my hair, soothe myself.

I want to see Martha. I need to see Martha. She is the only person who could make me feel better right now, who could cool this rage, this darkness, this hatred. I haven't seen her for three days, and I am aching for her. But she is busy with work, with the boys, with some birthday party or other that she's helping to plan for a friend. It's all very tedious, but I told her that I totally understand, of course I do. I have promised her that I will take her somewhere amazing next week, a boutique hotel somewhere, or a fine-dining night in London. I told her it will be a surprise. But first I have to find the money to pay for this amazing surprise and unfortunately right now there is only one way of getting hold of it.

Amanda gets home from her job at about 6 p.m. and smiles wanly at me. I think she was hoping I might have gone; there's a sliver of disappointment in her expression. "Hi," she says. "How did it go?"

For a moment I think she means my meeting with Luke, but then I remember my hospital appointment, the one about my heart. I say, "Actually, not good news. It looks like I'll be needing to go in for treatment. For a week or so."

"What sort of treatment?"

I'm not ready to answer the question, so I skim over it, carry on as if she hadn't said anything.

"It's a special unit that's just been built, somewhere up north. I can't remember the name of the hospital. They're going to email me over all the details. But it does mean a lot of travel. By train. They can't keep me in overnight. And you know, Amanda, I have literally no money right now. I'm waiting for things to sort themselves out with my ex. She owes me thousands. Tens of thousands. But in the short term, and God, I am *so sorry* to ask you this, I really am, but do you think you could tide me over, just for a few days, maybe a week or so, just so I can afford the train travel for my treatment, the occasional hotel overnighter? Eight hundred, maybe? That sort of region?"

I see her eyes flicker over my face; she's trying to read me, trying to make sense of what I'm saying. She says, "But, Damian, I'm penniless. You know that. I live from paycheck to paycheck, week to week. I don't have eight hundred pounds. I—"

I cut in over her. "It doesn't have to be eight hundred pounds. Five hundred would probably be enough. Do you not have some wriggle room on a credit card, an overdraft, something like that? Or what about . . . ?" I pause and lick my lips. "One of the boys. They're both working, aren't they? Could you get hold of something from one of them maybe?"

I see her face contort slightly and I cut in again before she can respond.

"I know. It's a tough ask. I get that. And I wouldn't ask if it wasn't an emergency. But it really is an emergency. Without this treatment, Amanda, I might be limiting my life by twenty years. I would be a walking time bomb."

"And this treatment? What sort of—"

"I'll be a guinea pig. It's still being trialed. Just a handful of us right now. Lasers."

"Lasers?"

I can see that the muscle memory from having lived with me for nearly ten years is still there, that alarms are firing, responses are kicking in, but I know, I just know that she will eventually give me what I want just as long as I can keep on talking. So I keep on talking, and as I talk, I inject breathlessness into my voice. I take deep, swooping mouthfuls of air, I pause halfway through a word, close my eyes, and then, when I can see that she is starting to worry about me, I ask her for a glass of water and tell her that I need to lie down for a while, that I am shattered, that my body hurts, and her expression moves from incredulity to concern. And there it is as she passes me the glass of water: the love, the love I knew would never have died, because Amanda always adored me, possibly more than anyone has ever adored me.

"I'll see what I can do," she says, tenderly. "I'm sure I can find it somehow."

THIRTY-FIVE

The screen shows three faces. At the top is Jane, wearing red lipstick and oversized reading glasses. She's being distracted by a large dog who keeps nuzzling at her neck from behind. "You have very smelly breath, Reggie," she says before pushing him gently away. Next to Jane is Ash, and at the bottom of the screen is the woman called Sarah May. She's in her early thirties, Ash would guess; her hair is dark blond and tied back from her face, with a blunt fringe framing serious, dark eyes. Behind her is a heavily curated bookshelf, spines in color order, plants, framed graphic art. She smiles just once and says, "Hi. Nice to meet you both."

Ash introduces herself and then Jane. "Jane," she tells Sarah, "used to go out with my dad in the nineties. My dad died last year, and I got in touch with Jane because I wanted to hear her memories of him, but also because my mum started seeing this guy a few weeks ago. He's called Nick Radcliffe and he kind of came from nowhere with some dodgy backstory about knowing my dad when they were young and—"

Jane interjects. "I could smell the whiff coming off it from the very first moment. It was so clearly not quite right. The restaurant Nick said he worked at with Ash's dad in the nineties shut down twenty years ago, so we can't corroborate that he was ever there. But we've been doing some digging, and we found a photo of the man who currently calls himself Nick Radcliffe on this page for a life-coaching consultancy. With a different name. Justin Warshaw. And a wedding ring. While our Nick Radcliffe claims never to have been married."

Sarah May's face remains inscrutable. "Gosh," she says after a short lull. "That's insane."

Ash and Jane nod in unison.

"So," says Sarah, "let me tell you what I know about Justin. Or whatever his actual name is. I met him in a pub about twelve years ago. I was twenty-two, I suppose. I'd just graduated, I was working in a bookshop, didn't want to go home, but didn't want to start my real life yet. I was going out with a very avoidant man, and I was drinking too much. I was crying in a pub, something the guy had done, or not done—I don't know, I can barely remember—and this tall older man approached me, and I didn't feel threatened by him. He was very good-looking, very gentle, he got me a glass of water from the bar, and he checked in with me. And then he gave me his card. The whole thing felt like a dream, like he was an angel or something. I emailed him that same night and we had our first appointment two days later."

"Wow," says Jane. "And how did it go?"

"Brilliantly," Sarah replies. "He was brilliant. Well, I mean . . . that's how I felt at the time. He was so energetic, full of ideas. He gave me all these incredible techniques to use to get on top of my life, to deal with the man, the job, my stasis, all of that. And at the time I felt like it was all working, like he was changing my life for the better. He gave me my first session for free and then it was fifty pounds an hour, and then, after a couple of weeks, he put it up to a hundred an hour, and then, I don't know, it all got a bit weird, and I didn't quite realize it was weird at the time, but he started asking me to do two sessions a week and I tried to tell him I couldn't afford it, that I worked in a bookshop, so he got me to . . ." She sighs and her eyes drop down for a moment before she looks up again. "He said I should get a loan from my mum and dad."

Jane and Ash both inhale through their teeth. "And did you?" asks Jane.

Sarah nods, and Jane says, "Ouch."

"How long did this go on for?" Ash asks.

"Oh God, about a year, I guess, two sessions a week. And then he got me to pay out for plans and books and . . . accessories. I just paid for all of it and then after it was all over, after we stopped, I looked it up and saw it was all stuff he'd bought off Amazon for like a few pounds, and I'd given him fifty quid for it. You know? And all the while, I really thought it was working, what we were doing together. I thought I was getting my life on track, but when I look back on it, I just wasn't. I was still working in the bookshop, still avoiding going home to see my family, still letting the avoidant man into my inboxes, into my head. At the end of the year nothing had actually changed, but Justin had somehow managed to make me believe that it had. That it was all just one session away, one new exercise away. And it was only a few months later that I could see the only thing which had changed was that I was five thousand pounds in debt."

"He conned you?"

"Well, yes and no. No, in that he gave me the services I was paying for and a lot of the stuff he did with me was great. But yes, in that I don't think I needed two sessions a week, I didn't need all the overpriced books and accessories. He definitely led me to believe I needed to spend as much money as possible to achieve certain goals. Money, in retrospect, I'm not convinced I needed to spend. But I just put it down to being young and desperate, you know? I never felt for a moment like there was anything bad about him. I liked him. I thought he was amazing. Like really amazing."

"So why did you stop seeing him?" asks Jane.

"He moved away. Very suddenly. Said his parents were ill? Or something like that? I can't really remember. But yes, he left. And that was that."

"And you never heard from him again?"

"No. Never did."

"And where did you used to see him? Did he have a clinic, or something?"

"No, he worked from home. He had a little room at the top of his house."

Ash glances at Jane on the screen. "You went to his house?"

"Yes. Twice a week for a year."

"And did he—did he live with anyone else?"

"Yes. His wife."

Jane glances back at Ash—both of their eyes are wide.

"His wife?"

"Yes. She was really lovely. Her name was Laura. And they had a couple of little girls, as I recall."

"Wait. Are you serious?"

"Yes. Of course I am."

"Were they his children?"

"I don't know. I mean, I assumed they were. But they might not have been, I suppose."

"And this house, where was it?"

"It was in Cherry Hinton. Just outside the city."

"Can you remember the address?"

Sarah blinks and shakes her head. "Er, God. No. It's been ten years, after all. But I can still picture the house. It was on a crescent. It had three floors. One of those houses where you walk straight into the living room, no hallway, and then kind of—what are they called?—open-tread stairs up to the next floor and then his office on the top floor. It was tiny, the whole house. Tiny for a family of four and a professional practice. But very pretty. A cottage, I suppose. And in the spring, it had wisteria outside. And there were bollards on the pavement. And . . . a little park over the way, with a tall wall. You could see into it from Justin's study. But God, the name of the road . . ." She shakes her head again. Then she pauses and looks at Ash and Jane. "Are you saying that he's some kind of scammer? Is he . . . is he bad?"

Ash shakes her head. "He hasn't actually done anything bad, yet. He just seems to be a bit . . . slippery? And my mum is vulnerable. And I really need to know that he's not going to take advantage of her, that he's not going to hurt her. We're just—"

"Doing our due diligence," Jane finishes.

"Yes," says Ash. "Exactly."

"Well, for what it's worth, I think he was a good man. A bit over-enthusiastic, maybe? A bit over-the-top. Maybe in over his head a bit with the life coaching. But he always struck me as a great husband, a great father, just a, you know, a really decent human being. I'm sure he doesn't mean your mother any ill will. And I do know that there was some strange family stuff in his background. He used to allude to a dark past that he was trying to escape, which could explain the name change?"

The moment the Zoom is over, Ash switches her browser to maps and types in "Cherry Hinton." Then she spends the best part of half an hour zooming around the map with her little virtual person, looking at all the streets that abut the park, looking for bollards and wisteria branches, and then there it is, finally, she's sure it is. She takes a screenshot and WhatsApps it to Sarah May, who replies immediately and says yes, that's the one, definitely.

The number on the door is twelve and the name of the street is Kingston Gardens. She googles this and finds that the last time the house had been sold was in 2016, but there are no names connected to the house. Nothing on Companies House. She types the address with the name "Justin Warshaw" included and the internet returns nothing at all.

She sighs and closes her laptop.

THIRTY-SIX

On Sunday, Al takes Martha to Bangate Cove. They strap Nala into the back of the car, clip Baxter in next to her, and head toward the coast.

It's a blowy, icy day, but the sky is blue and the sun is a glimmering white orb. They listen to music as they drive, they chat and they make each other laugh, and Nala enjoys the ride, and it is nice, so nice, to be out of Enderford, to have a change of scenery, even if it is only an hour down the road.

Martha's life has become so small and every time there has been the possibility of a night away, Al's stupid job has got in the way of it, but now, finally, there are miles of tarmac and space between her and her home and her shop and the life that has been rubbing her raw for months now. They leave the motorway and drive through a string of lively, characterful seaside resorts before they turn a corner and find themselves in a more windswept landscape: a few chalet parks and caravan sites, a boarded-up pub facing onto the road, a tatty parade of local shops opposite, a hair salon called Curls by Shirl, a pet-supplies shop, a food shop, and a Chinese takeaway called the Golden Rickshaw. The faded sign as they enter the village says "Welcome to Bangate Cove, a Seaside Paradise," illustrated with a picture of a red-and-white-striped sun parasol.

Martha flicks a quick look at Al and says, "Er . . ."

"Just wait," he says, hitting her with a beautiful smile. "You'll see!"

A moment later, he indicates left and they turn into a small graveled car park. There are three other cars here. A middle-aged couple are just getting out of one with two lively brown Labradors in tow. Martha gets out and immediately her hair is whipped around her face by the frenetic wind. She pulls it behind her neck and tucks it into her hood. Al unclips Nala from her car seat while Martha unclips the dog and then they walk across the car park toward the beach beyond. It is framed by a couple of small dunes and opens up into a perfect shell-shaped cove, with firs and cedar trees dotting the low escarpments at each end. And there, to her left, is the old pavilion that Al had told her about. And immediately she knows he's right. Bangate village is quite unprepossessing, but it is sandwiched between two very desirable locales and this cove is exquisite, the light here is unusually soft, the air even feels a degree or two warmer, the sun catches on the tide as it rolls in and out, the sound of it against the small stones of the beach like the hiss of champagne hitting a glass.

The couple with the two Labs throw balls for them and Baxter tugs at his lead to join in. Martha tugs him back and follows Al to the front of the pavilion.

"I love it," says Martha.

"I knew you would. I just knew. The moment I saw it." And there's another one of those electric smiles—my God, he looks so beautiful when he smiles, her husband. It sends a thrill throughout her whole body, not sexual, just joyful, a sense that she cannot believe she got lucky enough to find a man as fine as this, this man holding their perfect child in his arms, standing in front of a dilapidated beach shack that anybody else would have walked past without giving it a glance but which he knew would light up her heart, make her neurons ping with ideas and dreams and inspiration, make her feel alive again. He is everything, this man. He is everything. And she finds herself throwing her arms around him and squeezing him hard to her, Nala between them, the dog tangled around their legs, and she says, "I love you so much, Alistair Grey. I don't know what I did to deserve you. I really don't."

They let Baxter run around while they take Nala down to the tide and let her dip her fingers into the icy water as it busies back and forth. Nala holds a pretty stone in her cold fist as they head back to the car. "Doan," she says, looking at it. "Piddy doan."

"Yes," says Al. "It's a very pretty stone."

It's nearly midday, and Al has promised them a lunch out. They strap themselves back into the car and Al turns left out of the car park and carries on down the coast toward Folkestone. After a few minutes, he pulls off the coastal road, up a windy lane, and parks them outside a gastropub.

"This looks nice," says Martha.

"You go in," says Al. "I'm just going to drop something in with an old client, just in the next village along."

Martha's head rocks back slightly. "What?"

He touches a card folder in the side pocket of the car. "Some paperwork I had with me—they need it back. I said I'd drop it over, since I was down this way."

"Can't we just drop it in on the way home?"

"No. He's going out for lunch too. I said I'd get it to him before he goes out. I'll only be ten, fifteen minutes. He's literally just down the road."

"Well, we don't mind waiting outside in the car for you."

"No, go and grab the table. We don't want them giving it away. I'll be back before you know it!"

A moment later, Martha is outside the pub with the baby and the dog, watching her husband pull away in the car. She has a bad feeling about this. The suddenness of it, the lack of forewarning, his shooing away of misgivings. All the actions of the preceding three minutes take her back to similar moments, moments that tended to end with her not seeing her husband for days on end. She frowns as she sees the back of the car disappear around the corner, then sighs and heads into the pub.

Their table is by a wood burner. Martha straps Nala into a high chair, then sits and peruses the menu for a while. She orders herself a large glass of wine and hands Nala rice cakes to eat. The wine arrives a few minutes later and Martha checks the time. It's been twelve minutes since Al said he'd be ten to fifteen minutes. She takes a sip of the wine and tries to relax, but two minutes later her sense of discomfort gets the better of her and she scrolls the screen of her phone to find the app that shows the information from the dog tracker in Al's car. Her heart rate picks up slightly as she waits for it to load and then she sees the little flashing blob in the center of the screen. His car is not moving. It's parked on a street in a village about a mile or so away called the Riviera. The street is windy, and he is parked at the top, outside what looks like, from the map, a large house. She clicks on Street View and sees that it is a huge stucco villa, detached, the sea view on the opposite side of the house visible through tall windows at the front and back. It's incredible, she thinks, using her fingertips to zoom around it. It looks, she thinks to herself, like the home of a person who might own a restaurant or a hotel and it reassures her, somehow, that he is doing exactly what he said he was doing and has, somehow, been delayed, presumably by the person he's gone to see.

She turns off her phone and takes another sip of wine while she peruses the menu again. She decides on seafood linguine. And waits.

THIRTY-SEVEN

Nina is chatting with Nick Radcliffe through the window of his car outside the house. She laughs uproariously at something he's just said, and Ash moves closer to the window and tries to listen. She hears her mother saying, "Are you sure you can't come in?" and Nick replying, "No, I've got to get back and do some work."

"On a Sunday?"

"Yes. Poor old me. But, listen, I miss you, Nina. I'd love to see you soon. Properly. Take you out on the town. Or maybe even get away for a night or two? What do you think?"

Her mother laughs gently and says, "Well, I don't know. Radio silence for a week. I was starting to think you'd forgotten about me, and now you're here with 'out on the town' and nights away."

Her tone is light, but Ash knows that her mother has found the last seven days tough. She's pretended to be cool about the fact that Nick hasn't messaged or called, and she has certainly been too cool to message or call him first, but his absence has been a soft but ominous tick-tick in the background of everything. Ash had started to feel hopeful that maybe "Nick Radcliffe" was about to disappear as quickly and mysteriously as he'd appeared. But then, twenty minutes ago, he'd pulled up outside and her mother had virtually galloped out of the house to see him.

"I'm so sorry," Nick says now. "I can't begin to explain to you how crazy work has been."

Work? thinks Ash. What work?

"It's fine," Nina says. "Don't worry about it. I've been pretty crazy too. It's just really good to see you."

"Likewise," says Nick. "Anyway, I'd better get going. But leave it with me. We'll go somewhere spectacular. I promise. Let me know which nights work best for you. I'm pretty much around all the time now that the busy stretch is over."

Busy stretch. There it is again. Busy doing what?

"I'll message you."

"I'll be looking out for it," he says, and then Ash looks away with a slick of disgust as Nick and her mother kiss softly and tenderly for a moment before pulling apart, a look of utter bliss on her mother's face as she waves him on his way.

Ash doesn't want to look at her mother when she walks back inside a moment later. "What did he want?" she asks nonchalantly.

"He was just in the area, popped by to say hi."

"That's nice. Did he say why he hasn't been in touch for so long?"

"Just been busy, I guess."

Nina's tone is light, but Ash knows that she is burning with relief and restoration. Ash knows what it feels like when the object of your affections removes themselves from your sphere. She knows that sick ache in the pit of your stomach, that sense of encroaching darkness, the feeling of someone having cut off a source of light, banished you to an endless winter. She knows how it feels.

"Busy doing what?"

The question is loaded to the point of warfare, but Nina doesn't seem to notice. "Work. The bar. The manager is away, so it's very hands-on at the moment."

"When are you going to go to the bar? Is he going to take you there?"

"At some point, I suppose. There's no rush." She's filling the kettle from the kitchen tap as she speaks.

"My friend went there," Ash begins gently.

Her mother turns to look at her. "What?"

"My friend Lana. She lives in London. I told her about you going out with the guy who owns it and she said she wanted to go and have a drink there, just to check it out. She said that . . ." She pauses, plucks at the cuffs of her sweatshirt, uncomfortable with lying to her mother but feeling that she has no option. "She said that she asked about Nick and that he doesn't actually work there."

Even from behind, Ash can see the rise and fall of her mother's lungs through the cotton of her shirt. "Oh, Ash."

"What! I'm just saying! That's what Lana said. Nobody had heard of him. That's all. It just seemed really strange. And there are other things." She feels her pulse quicken.

"What other things?" Nina says the words "other things" as if the possibility of there being any other things can only be pure nonsense.

Ash picks up her phone from the kitchen table and finds the screenshot of the "Justin Warshaw" life-coaching web page from the obsolete site.

Nina pulls on her reading glasses and takes the phone from Ash. "What is this?"

"It's Nick. Twelve years ago. Going by Justin Warshaw. Did he ever mention that he used to be a life coach? Or that he used to be married?"

"What do you mean, married?"

"Look." Ash points at the ring on Nick's finger.

Nina frowns. "That doesn't mean anything. He always has his ring from Ruth with him. And, no, he didn't tell me about being a life coach, not specifically. But I do know he's had quite a colorful career, done a bit of everything, so it doesn't surprise me in the least." She hands the phone back to Ash and sighs. "Baby girl," she says, "what's going on here?"

Ash feels tears building behind her eyes and swallows them back. "Nothing," she says. "Nothing. I just—who is this guy? That's all. He's fifty-five or whatever. He says he's got no children, but someone who used to be a client of his when he was a life coach said he lived in a house with a woman who he said was his wife, and they had two little girls."

"Oh, come on now, Ash."

"Mum! I'm serious! I wasn't going to say anything, I was going to wait until I had more evidence—"

"Evidence? Ash, what on earth are you talking about? You're acting like you think Nick is some kind of criminal."

"Well, how do you know he isn't?"

"And this . . . I mean, this woman who said he was living with a wife and children. Where did you find her? Who is she?"

"She's literally just a woman. And I found her online."

"Oh, Ash." She sees concern flicker across her mum's face. "Is this . . . ? I mean, you're not . . . ?"

"What? Going mad again? No, Mum, I am not going mad again."

"I did not say that, Ash. I never said you were mad."

"Yes, but I was. Clearly I was. And I am many things right now, I am sad and I am grieving and I am lonely and I am lost—but I am not mad. This"—she stabs her finger at the screen of her phone—"this is real. This guy . . . there's something off about him, Mum. And I'm doing this because I love you so much, and I love Dad so much, and I love everything that you built together, and I cannot deal with the thought of anyone coming into this"—she gestures around them—"into Dad's beautiful world, and making a mess in it. Mum, please tell me that, at the very least, you'll talk to him. Here." She picks up her phone and messages the screenshot of Justin Warshaw to her mother's phone. "Just show Nick that. See how he responds. And ask to go to his wine bar. See how he responds to that too. Please, Mum. Promise me you will. Not for me. But for us."

"OK," says Nina slowly. "Of course I will. I'm sure that there's a perfectly rational explanation for everything. He's had a very colorful life. He's had a lot of trauma. A lot of drama. I'm sure this will just be another bizarre episode with a completely benign explanation."

"Yes," says Ash, with a sigh. "Maybe it will be."

THIRTY-EIGHT

FOUR YEARS EARLIER

Amanda and I are sharing a bed again. Thank God. My back could not have taken much longer on that sofa.

I've also been frequenting the café on the high street, the one with the macramé plant holders and the sour-faced girl called Kadija. I go in there primarily for the cake but also to antagonize her. She wears skintight jeans and has one of those backsides that all the young girls yearn for, but which I'm not a fan of. Her hair is always tied back, pulled tight enough to ensure that everyone can see how good her skin is, how exquisite her bone structure. She hates me, and I play on it because it gives me a huge rush of energy, makes me feel like my sex, my age, my height, are my superpowers. All I have to do is sit there and watch her and she is filled with a rage so putrid and raw that I can feel it in the very air. But it's stoking my need for sex. It's been over a week, and I wanted to save myself for Martha, but Amanda is here, literally sharing the same space as me, and she has that look in her eyes when I walk through her tiny flat in my boxer shorts and a T-shirt. I know she has not had sex for years and I know that that's because of me. Because I "died" and left her with the imprint of the perfect husband, the perfect lover, and how the hell was anyone else ever going to step into those boots?

It didn't take much, in the end. All I had to do was tell Amanda she looked good. Tell her she looked better than most women her age. Tell her how hard it's been living with my lunatic ex all these years, how I could not bring myself to have sex with her and how hard it was not to just come back here to her. And Amanda came to me, and shortly after that we were in bed and when I fucked her, I closed my eyes and pretended she was the girl from the coffee shop, and yes, it was a little, let's say, energetic, and frankly, I have not enjoyed sex quite so much in a very long time.

"Darling."

I've started calling Amanda darling again. It's that muscle memory, like the twenty years in between never really happened.

"Yes?" She looks up from the kitchen sink, which she's scouring with a battered-looking sponge.

"I'm afraid I'm going to need to ask for another tiny loan. They need me in for more treatment next week, and I'll have to stay in a hotel. Three nights. Maybe more. And the train prices are extortionate. I'm so, so sorry to ask you, I really am."

I didn't ask her where the last loan came from. She had just given me the bundle of notes with a tight smile, and I could tell she felt conflicted about it but had made her decision and was going with it.

"Oh God, Damian, I can't, I really can't. I borrowed that last lot from Joel. I said it was to cover some unexpected bills. I can't tell him that again. Not so soon. I mean—four hundred pounds, Damian. I can't believe you've spent it already."

"Amanda—my God, do you think I've just been off on jollies with it? I wish I had! And I haven't spent it all, I just don't have enough left to cover the next lot of treatment expenses. Especially three nights in a hotel. I mean, a couple of hundred would do. Three, tops. And then I'll pay you back, all of it. I promise."

"But I don't think you understand. I literally can't. Joel had to really scrape together that four hundred pounds for me and I can't ask Sam, he's already in debt himself. I've pushed it as far as I can. I mean, surely there must be someone else you could ask? What about your mum?"

"My mum? Amanda—she's eighty-one now. She's senile. She's in no position to be lending me money."

"But you think your children are?"

I sigh. I've taken the wrong approach. "Sorry," I say. "You're right. Of course you are. But the woman I've been living with, the stalker, the money she has kept back from me, it's a lot. I mean . . . over five hundred K. When I get that back from her, not only can I pay Joel back, but you and I, we could start afresh. Sell this place, get something decent. I mean—well, bigger," I elaborate, seeing the look on her face. "We could slowly get our lives back together. Bring the boys into the picture. But we can't do any of that if I'm sick. And the only way I'm going to get better is to continue this treatment. And if I miss one appointment, they'll take me off the trial. They have a waiting list a mile long for people wanting to be on it. I have to be there. So is there anything, literally anything, you can think of, any way whatever of getting hold of this money?"

I know what she needs to do, and she knows what she needs to do, but I know that it's the last thing in the whole world she wants to do, that her stomach is probably churning with nausea just thinking about it. I beam the correct answer into her skull with my eyes, which are filled with tears to convey my fear of her not asking this person for this money. She closes her eyes for a beat or two, then opens them and sighs. "I could ask Bella."

Bella is her sister. Bella is incredibly wealthy, and Amanda and Bella fell out horribly in their thirties and no doubt Amanda has taken not a penny off her sister over the past twenty years since I "died." There was a horrible episode toward the end of our marriage when I persuaded Amanda to ask Bella for a loan for the business (I thought she should be expanding into homewares), which she did under much duress from me, and Bella loaned her £50,000, and sadly, I can't quite remember now how the money disappeared. But that was the nail in the coffin of their relationship, which had been fraught for a long time before I met either one of them, I hasten to add.

"You could," I say now, softly. "I know it would be hard. I appreciate that. But Bella—I mean, it's all a drop in the ocean to her. She wouldn't even notice it."

"But what would I tell her it was for?"

"God, I don't know. Could you say you're the one who is ill? Maybe? That you need a private doctor's appointment?"

"But those sorts of lies, Damian, they blow up out of all proportion. She'd tell Dad, and Dad would get involved, and then there'd be endless questions and I would have to keep on lying and keep on lying and the whole thing would just . . ." She explodes the fingers of both hands. "And what about the boys? They'd find out too."

"Just swear her to secrecy. Tell her you don't want anyone to know about it. It's the best solution. It really is. And you could ask for a bigger amount. Enough to tide us both over while we're waiting for my money to clear. We could even . . ." I let a small smile form. "We could go away for a few days. Just you and me. Celebrate the end of my treatment. What do you think? Will you do it, Amanda? Will you ask her?"

I see a hundred emotions play out over Amanda's face as I wait for her to reply. "Oh God, Damian. *God.* I just . . . why was life so much simpler without you in it? Sadder. Emptier. Lonelier. But, fuck, so much easier. What is it about you? Why is there always, always something?"

Her voice is raw and desperate, but I can also see the shape of a reluctant smile on her lips, a smile of deep-seated affection that she is trying so hard to control, but she can't because it's there, etched on her heart, the way she feels about me, the way she's always felt about me. Nobody has ever loved me more than Amanda. Especially not that bitch Tara, who, frankly, I cannot believe I wasted four years of my life on. What was I thinking?

Amanda sighs and pulls her blond hair away from her face, bunched inside her hands. She makes a small animal noise and then says, "Urgh. Fine. I'll ask her. Just"—she turns away from me while she's still talking and heads toward the sink, where she picks up the scouring sponge and holds it under the tap—"just leave it with me," she says. "Leave it with me."

The following day, I am back in the trendy coffee shop on the high street. The girl is there, and as I walk in, I see a strange exchange of looks between her and a man behind the counter whom I assume to be the manager. I head toward him and the girl disappears, leaving the man looking at me awkwardly.

"Good morning," I say. I am about to order my usual, a white tea and a slice of that remarkable blueberry loaf, when the man clears his throat and says, "Sir, I need to have a word with you."

I smile amiably and cock my head to one side as if to say, *Er, OK*.

"Maybe we could . . ." He gestures to the far end of the counter, away from the customers sitting at tables. I make another face to express my puzzlement but also my amenability, and I follow him.

"It's about my colleague. The young woman who works here. She's a very valued employee. She's worked here for a very long time, and I would be lost without her."

"Right," I say. "Yes?"

The young man rearranges his face as he searches for the right words. "The thing is," he continues, "she tells me that you make her feel . . . uncomfortable."

I swallow back the rush of dark anger that floods my nervous system. "I'm sorry," I say, sounding wryly amused. "What?"

"She says that you are always staring at her, that you walk too close to her. She said that you . . ." The man looks away and then back at me, trying and failing to fix me with a fearsome look. ". . . smelled her hair." He loses his bravado almost immediately. "Or . . . the back of her neck. Or something, I don't know. But basically, I need to ask you not to come in here anymore. I'm really sorry."

I look around to see if anyone has heard this preposterous commentary, but no one has noticed and the girl in question is studiously cleaning tables on the other side of the shop.

"Are you actually being serious?" I ask quietly.

He nods tensely. "Yup. I am. I'm sorry."

I am not going to make a scene. I am not going to do anything, apart from get a slice of cake and get out of here. My heart is full of rage, but I do not show it, not one iota. "Well," I say, "that is quite the strangest and weirdest thing I have ever heard. All I have ever been to that young lady is polite, and I have found her to be really quite sullen and—well, unpleasant. But if she has taken my attempts to get her to be friendly the wrong way, then of course I will take the hint and go."

I see a muscle twitch in the man's cheek, and he nods. "Thank you," he says. "I appreciate that. I do. And could I maybe get you something? On the house? By way of . . ." He shrugs. But I know what he means. He means as an apology for being forced to take her side against mine, when I can tell he's now on mine.

"Oh," I say, smiling broadly. "Well, yes. A slice of that cake would be perfect, thank you."

While he turns to find a bag to put the slice of cake in, I pick up the jar of tips on the counter and pour the coins into my hand. When he turns back, I smile widely and put a pound coin in the empty jar. "Thank you so much," I say. "I wish you luck."

I glance toward the problematic waitress, so he is in no doubt about my subtext, and then I leave.

THIRTY-NINE

Martha dumps her bag on the empty chair at the table in the café where she's just arrived to meet Grace for lunch. "Sorry I'm late," she says.

"You're not," says Grace. "I'm early."

Al is looking after the shop with Milly, Nala is at the childminder's, and Martha hasn't seen Grace since the night they had to take Nala to the hospital nearly three weeks ago.

It's the eve of Christmas Eve and the café is playing "Santa Claus Is Coming to Town." There is a vat of mulled wine on the counter exuding the most intoxicating smell and Martha immediately feels herself soften and relax after an insanely busy morning in the shop.

"You look great," says Grace.

"No, thank you, I don't."

"You need to learn how to take a compliment."

Martha laughs and says, "Thank you. You're very kind. Have you decided what you're having?"

They both order and then, as an afterthought, both decide to have a glass of wine too. Martha gives Grace her Christmas gift and Grace says, "Fuck. I didn't get you anything."

"Oh, don't worry, it's just something from the shop. I didn't make any effort, I promise."

Grace laughs in response and says, "Well, let me get lunch at least." Then she tucks the gift in the tote bag hanging from her chair and looks at Martha and says, "So, how are things going?"

"Good," says Martha brightly. "Like, really, really good. I think that night with Nala was a wake-up call for him, I really do. And since he gave up work, it's basically like I've got him back, you know, my perfect guy. He's so attentive, so present. Just brilliant with the kids. You know, he got Jonah to open up about his gender dysphoria. Jonah chose Al to have that conversation with. It's truly amazing."

"Wow," says Grace. "That's pretty special."

Her friend sounds impressed but also slightly skeptical. Martha doesn't push it.

They talk about their Christmas plans. Grace is going to Yorkshire to spend two nights with her in-laws, who live in a huge barn conversion and spend too much on presents and feed them champagne from the moment they get there until the moment they leave, and Martha has always been rather jealous of their Christmases, even though Grace just moans about the car journey and the uncomfortable mattress and the enforced walks after meals. Martha doesn't have any in-laws—well, she has ex–in-laws, but it's a relationship that doesn't stand up very well to divorce and a new partner. She tells Grace that she and Al will be having a quiet one with the baby. It's the boys' year with their dad this Christmas; they'll be back for Boxing Day and then the five of them will have turkey lasagna and do presents. It's going to be mellow, but after the crazy year they've all had, it will be exactly what she wants and needs.

"Sounds lovely," says Grace. "I'm happy for you. I have to say, for a while there I really was quite convinced there was something, you know, really bad going on."

Martha feels herself bristle. "Really bad?"

"Yeah. I thought it was going to end up that he was one of those blokes you read about. The ones who marry loads of women and lie to everyone and steal all their money."

"What!"

"Yes, I mean, obviously he's not. But it was just a bit weird, you know, the way he kept disappearing, the way you've never met any of his colleagues, or friends, or family. He's kind of mysterious. And I read this book recently, about a woman who married a guy like that, and it turned out he was a . . . well, he was a psychopath." She ends this statement with a small shard of nervous laughter.

"Well," says Martha, "I can assure you that Al might be many things, but a psychopath is not one of them. The empathy he has shown to Jonah this last week, it's just breathtaking, honestly. There's no way Matt would have been able to manage the situation as well. I'm not sure even I could have. So, yeah, you know, he has a murky past, I know all that, and he's used to being able to run away when things get tough, I know that too, but now, I think, I really do think, he's starting to feel safe. He's starting to feel settled. He just needed a place to lay his hat, you know. He just needed . . . us."

Martha hugs Grace on the pavement outside the café and Grace hugs her back.

"That was amazing," says Grace. "We must try and do more things like this, now that you've got Al home full-time. Maybe even cocktails in the New Year? How about that?"

Martha puts her hands into her pockets and smiles. "Yes please!" she says. "I'm looking forward to it already!"

She watches Grace meander down the busy pavement toward her street and then Martha turns back toward the flower shop, her thoughts softened by the glass of wine, the twinkling lights of the angel wings strung overhead, the almost tangible feeling of Christmas in the air, and there, just ahead of her, is the soft pink glow of her shop, her world, her creation, her safe place. She feels a sudden rush of butterflies at the thought of seeing Al. She realizes, ridiculously, that she's missed him in the hour and a half that she's been away from him, and her pace picks up a little as she approaches the shop. She pushes open the door and sees Milly beaming at her from across the counter.

"Hiya!" she says. "Did you have a good lunch?"

"It was wonderful, thank you," she replies, "just what I needed." She looks behind Milly and then around the shop. "Shouldn't you be on your lunch break now?"

"Yes. But it's OK. I didn't mind waiting for you."

"You didn't have to wait for me, though . . ."

"Oh, yes. Sorry. I thought you knew. Al had to go somewhere. He left about half an hour ago? I said I'd cover till you got back. But it's no biggie."

"Go where?"

"I don't know. I didn't ask. Work, I assume?"

"But he doesn't—" Martha stops and sighs. There's no point explaining the small print of their lives to Milly, she won't care. "Right. OK, then. Did he say what time he'd be back?"

"No." Milly looks at her with wide, slightly sad eyes. "I'm sorry," she says. "I thought you knew."

"No," says Martha. "No. But never mind. You get on to your lunch. I'll give him a call."

Milly busies herself in the back room for a moment before appearing in her tiny fake fur coat and freshly applied lip gloss, with a small handbag in the crook of her arm. "Need anything while I'm out?"

"No, thanks. No. I'm good."

The moment Milly leaves the shop, Martha taps Al's number into her phone. The call goes straight through to voicemail. She switches to the tracker app to see if she can work out where he's gone, but the flashing blue dot is nowhere to be seen.

FORTY

It's the second Christmas since Paddy died. Ash can barely remember the first Christmas. The house had been full, people rolling in and rolling out, there had been three Christmas lunches, she recalls, all cooked by different people. Visitors whispered behind doors and then looked at her with soulful compassion whenever she walked into a room. Her mother had been gray, glassy-eyed, lost-looking, Arlo had been overcompensating, going to the very edge of gallows humor and tipping over it here and there, filling the house with his rent-a-crowd mates, who all looked the same to Ash with their floppy hair and monochromatic sportswear. There'd been a swim, she recalls. Dry robes. Crocs. Chubby, mottled thighs of middle-aged people. Was that Christmas morning? Boxing Day, maybe? It might even have been the New Year. The whole week is a blur. The whole week was, Ash recalls, nothing but a Paddy-free void of darkness and confusion and too much wine and too many people and not enough space to breathe.

This Christmas will be different. Arlo came home this morning, and tomorrow, Christmas Eve, they will go into the village and have a pizza, just the three of them. Then on Christmas Day, Ash's grandmother Rosalie will drive down from London with Paddy's kid brother, Sean, who still lives at home for various reasons, and their borzoi called Boris, and they will cook beef (Paddy was the only person in the family who could make a turkey taste like it died for a reason) and drink champagne and watch telly and it will be pleasant enough. Nothing special. But it will be intimate and easy, and it will be, Ash is sure, ten times better than last Christmas.

It's just gone four o'clock and the edges of the night are drawing close when Ash hears the sound of tires on gravel, coming to a slow stop outside their house. She thinks it might be one of Arlo's mates, come by to say hi. Then she thinks maybe Arlo has ordered himself a Deliveroo or a Just Eat. And then, a second later, she hears the front door bang shut and, to her horror, the sound of Nick Radcliffe's voice in the hallway. She closes the lid of her laptop and slides off her bed. From the top of the landing, she sees Nick and her mother embracing. Then Nick says, "Oh my God, it is so good to see you, Nina. It's been too long."

"Yes," Nina agrees. "It really has. But what are you doing here! I wasn't expecting to see you until the New Year."

"I know, but I couldn't wait that long, so I bunked off work early, and I know it's short notice, but I wondered if I could take you out for a coffee, or even a drink or two, so I can give you your present and just see you properly. Just for a little while. Is that . . ." Ash sees Nick's face lose its certainty, elements of self-doubt softening the angles of his bone structure. He pulls himself back from Nina and smiles wryly. "Sorry," he says. "Sorry. I don't know what I was thinking, just turning up here like this without notice. Rude of me. Forgive me. I should have called. I should have—"

"No," Nina interjects, her hand resting softly against Nick's chest. "No, it's fine. It's wonderful. I'm genuinely so happy to see you. And, listen, Arlo is here—I'd love you to meet him. Why don't you come in? I'll open a bottle. What do you think?"

Nick's face lights up and there it is, that fucking smile. Ash hates that fucking smile. It's fake as fuck, but how is any woman of a certain age meant to resist it?

"Are you sure? I don't want to intrude on your—"

"I'm sure, Nick. Of course I am. Come in. Come through."

Ash quickly dashes back to her bedroom and checks her reflection in the mirror. She's not sure why. Her hair is dirty—it needed a wash this morning, but because she didn't go into work today, she decided to push it to tomorrow and have clean hair for Christmas Eve. She spritzes it with dry shampoo and ruffles it with her fingers. She peers at her eyes, sees yesterday's mascara still clinging to her lashes in a couple of places, pulls it off with a cotton pad and reapplies it. Then she sniffs her armpits, decides she smells fine, changes her socks with a hole in one toe for a pair of clean ones, and then appears in the kitchen a moment later, looking nonchalant and casually surprised to see Nick.

"Oh," she says. "Hi. Are you—?" She throws her mother a look, and then returns her gaze to Nick. "Are you here for dinner? Or . . . ?"

"Well," says Nick, "no. Or at least, not officially. But your mother very kindly invited me in for a drink."

"You're not at work today, then?"

"No, not tonight. Not for the whole of Christmas, actually."

"I'm amazed," says Ash, pulling out a kitchen chair and seating herself, "that they can spare you at this time of the year."

"If anything," Nick says, "they're overstaffed. Everyone wants to work Christmas. Great tips, great atmos. People fighting for shifts."

Ash doesn't respond, just raises an eyebrow and looks at her mother, who is opening a bag of tortilla chips.

Arlo drifts into the room then, eyes glued to his phone, feet in thick, holey socks, loose sweatpants hanging low on his waist, his free hand tucked into the waistband of his underpants.

"Oh," he says, stopping as he notices Nick sitting at the kitchen counter. "Er, hi." He takes his hand out of his underpants and glances at his mother. "Are you . . . ?"

"Nick," says Nick, getting to his feet and clasping Arlo's hand inside his, a kind of weirdly masculine bro move that doesn't fit with Nick's usual country gent demeanor. "You must be Arlo. I've heard so much about you. It's great to meet you."

"Yeah," says Arlo, "likewise," and Ash knows Arlo well enough to pick up on the uneven note of surprise in his voice. "Sorry, I didn't realize . . ."

"No. My fault. I only came over to drop off your mother's Christmas present, and she very sweetly invited me to stay. And, oh, I have gifts for you two as well. Here." He goes to his large carryall and unzips the top. He pulls out three similarly sized oblong parcels, all beautifully gift-wrapped in expensive-looking paper and finished with pink satin ribbons. "For under the tree," he says, resting them on the kitchen table. "Which is . . . ?"

Nina smiles weakly. "Have to be honest. No tree. None of us could be bothered. It was always . . ."

"Paddy's job?" Nick offers.

"Yes. And it's all just such a faff, for such a short time, and I just thought . . . we thought—"

"Next year," Ash cuts in. "We'll do a tree next year."

"Yes," says Nina, with a note of gratitude. "Yes. Next year. But for this year," she announces, "we are putting presents under the Christmas yucca. We put fairy lights on it. And a bit of tinsel."

She grins and Nick laughs. "Well, that sounds like an excellent compromise."

Nina passes the bowl of tortilla chips and tub of hummus to Arlo, and carries the opened bottle of wine and four glasses to the table.

Ash catches a sideways glance from Arlo and nods back, just a fraction, enough to acknowledge her brother's gesture. She knows what it means. It means, *What the fuck*. Ash has tried to tell Arlo, but when Arlo is not at home, Arlo is 100 percent committed to not being at home, almost as if he enters a portal into another reality every time he goes back to Bournemouth.

Ash tries not to bring her awkwardness to the proceedings, which are already awkward enough as it is, but as she watches Nick chatting with her brother, she sees it. She sees Arlo sit straighter, bring his body closer to the table, share jokes with Nick, look stupidly happy every time Nick laughs at something he's said. She watches her brother's face—he has such a sweet face, a perfect blend of both of his parents: Paddy's boyishness, Nina's bone structure—and she loves her brother and she misses him and she has been wanting him to come home so badly, it has been so long, and now he is finally here, but Nick Radcliffe is stealing away their quiet night of catching up, of being just them, talking about Dad, remembering each other. He's sucking it all away from her and pulling Arlo toward him, and Nina's face is also aglow, and those three oblong parcels sit there at the other end of the table looking like grisly reminders of what is happening here—the further upending of things that have already been upended and haven't yet been put away. And now there is this man with two names, a wife, no wife, children, no children, doggy bags but no dog, pacifier clips but no baby, a restaurant but no restaurant, and a black hole where his backstory should be—and nobody seems to care but her.

"So," she says to her mother, hearing in her own ears how bitter she sounds, even in that one syllable. "Mum, did you want to ask Nick about those things we were talking about the other day? The, you know, the life-coach stuff."

"Oh!" Nick turns his head, whip fast, a genial smile on his face. "Are you interested in some life coaching? You know, I used to do a bit of that."

Nina throws Ash a pinch-eyed look, as if to say, *See, I told you he'd have a benign explanation*, before turning to Nick. "You did?" she asks.

"Yup," he replies. "For a few years. I thought I was done with restaurants. I'd burned myself out. Needed a change of direction and so I retrained in the early noughties. It turned out it wasn't a good fit for me, turned out I'm much better off in hospitality, even if it does feel like it's going to kill me some days. But it's where my heart is. My soul. I'm good for nothing else. Truly."

He laughs self-deprecatingly and then turns back to Ash. "I'd be happy to offer you a couple of sessions, though. Just to go through the, you know, the basics. If you're interested?"

Ash recoils for a second, barely able to believe what she's hearing, but within another split second she realizes that this could be a brilliant opportunity for her to dig some more, ask him questions, work on him. And actually, Jesus Christ, if anyone she knows is in need of a life coach, it's her.

FORTY-ONE

Al gets home at about eight o'clock that night. He smells of wine and looks shell-shocked and vacant.

"What the fuck, Al?" Martha asks.

"I'm sorry. I really am. I just—"

Al's eyes fill with tears and Martha feels her stomach lurch.

"What?" she says. "What is it?"

"I got a call, when you were having lunch with Grace," he says. "From the people who live next door to my mother."

"Your mother? What do you mean, your mother?"

She sees Al flinch. "Yes," he says. "I'm sorry. I was . . . when I met you, I wasn't entirely honest. I told you she was dead and that my father was alive, and actually they were both . . . expedient lies." He sighs. "It just seemed easier than telling you the truth somehow."

Al tells her that he is estranged from his mother, that his mother had somehow blamed Al for the passing of her husband, the horrible GP who used to abuse Al when he was a child. She'd cut Al out of his inheritance, leaving everything to her cousins' children, and had changed the locks to his childhood home when Al was twenty-one. Al hasn't seen her for over thirty years, but she is now eighty-five and living alone in a small house in the Midlands somewhere.

"Her neighbors found her wandering around in their back garden in her nightdress. Her front door had shut behind her and they didn't know what to do, so they called me. I mean, I'm not sure what they expected me to do about it. A hundred and twenty bloody miles away. But anyway . . . there it is. My mother appears to have dementia and nobody else wants to have anything to do with her because she's so generally unpleasant and now it looks like my life is going to be me just endlessly going up and down the M4, whilst also having to find a way to pay for her care."

"But you said she was wealthy. Can't she pay for her own?" Martha tries not to let her selfish fears for the status quo taint the tone of her voice, tries to sound as though she is genuinely concerned about Al's mother and not even slightly concerned about the fact that her husband, who has only just rid himself of one situation that took him away from home all the time, has now almost immediately found himself in another. And what about the beach property? And the shop? And Nala? What about Christmas? What about their lovely, lovely life?

"Well, yes and no. She has assets, but now I'm going to have to somehow get power of attorney, which will be hard since she's about to be given a diagnosis of dementia. But without that I won't have the authority to free up any cash, and so in the short term"—he sighs long and hard—"I'm going to have to find the money to cover immediate expenses."

"Oh God," says Martha, her hand held loosely over her mouth, "what a nightmare." But even as she's feigning concern over Al's situation, she's wondering about other things. She's wondering about the smell of wine on Al's breath. She's wondering why he didn't message her or call her, and why he didn't say anything to Milly before he left the shop. She's wondering about his decision to lie to her about his mother being dead all these years. And more than anything, she's wondering about the fact that the tracker on his car has been inactive all day. She's googled it and the only way that the tracker could stop working would be if it was physically destroyed. She searches Al's face for some evidence of his knowledge of her act of disloyalty, some darkness, some sense that he is biding his time and waiting to tell her that he knows that she's been spying on him, that she has broken his trust in the most heinous way. But it's not there. All that's there is tiredness and world-weariness, worry and fear—and love. She sees it in every angle of his body, every line in his face, the way he looks at her so softly. He loves her so much. So what, she wonders, is actually going on here? This man is somehow lying to her, but in no easily discernible way. And certainly, given what he's just told her about his elderly mother, she is in no position to dig or delve. Not now. "So, what are you going to do? I mean, what's happening about Christmas?"

"The woman next door says she'll have her for Christmas Day, but I said I'd go up on Boxing Day, if things look like they're going downhill. I mean, she's still compos mentis. Knows who I am. Can cook for herself. Take care of herself. It's just the wandering that's the problem right now. And the woman next door says she'll make sure the door is always locked when my mum's at home and will keep an eye on her. And ha!" he says. "I was even thinking of maybe putting a little tracker on her, you know. Like they put on dog collars. So I can always know where she is."

Ice runs through Martha and she studies his face again, but still, there's nothing there. Just a soft, tired smile. No edge.

She returns his smile and touches his wrist and says, "Well, if this is going to be an ongoing thing now, which it sounds like it might be, honestly, Al, please just let me help. I can do this with you. Don't cut me out, will you?"

He breathes out gently and takes a step toward her. He wraps his arms around her and he says, "You are the most wonderful woman in the world and I don't know what I did to deserve you. But right now, all I want from you is a cuddle on the sofa. And possibly a glass of wine."

She wants to ask him about the glass of wine he's already had this evening, but she doesn't.

FORTY-TWO

FOUR YEARS EARLIER

Amanda's sister, Bella, comes through. Five thousand pounds. "No need to pay me back," she'd apparently said to Amanda, which I can tell upset Amanda more than Bella asking her to return it would have.

Amanda didn't have to tell me that it was £5,000. She could have said it was a thousand and kept the rest for herself. But, as I say, this woman, this ridiculous, broken, sad-eyed woman who put her life on hold after I disappeared, was in many ways my blueprint for managing women, for learning how to navigate and bypass their natural defenses (so much easier than they want you to think it is). I learned a lot about how to balance it all out so that it always swings back in my favor. I pushed this woman and I pushed her, and still she wanted to be with me rather than without me.

Tara was a different undertaking, I know that now. I never really worked out how to breach her defenses, or at least, every time I got close that daughter of hers would tug her back the other way, and Tara didn't love me enough to resist it.

What I have with Martha has already transcended anything I've ever experienced before. I've used the money that Amanda so generously poured into my bank account to book Martha and me three nights in a boutique hotel in the Cotswolds. Her ex is very kindly looking after their children and her dog. I'm going to drive in the Tesla, of course, and I have booked us in for a six-course tasting menu at the hotel restaurant (£129 a head, not including wine). This trip coincides with my "hospital treatment" and the brilliant thing about the hospital treatment narrative is that it means I cannot possibly have my phone on. Of course not.

Amanda sees me off on Friday morning. She touches my chest with her hand and says, "I hope it goes OK. Just call if you need anything. And here." She hands me a Tupperware box. Inside the box is what looks like a homemade sandwich, a banana, and a bag of crisps. "For the train."

I smile and draw her to me for an embrace. "You are so thoughtful," I say. "You are literally just the best." I kiss her on the forehead and then I head down the road toward the spot a ten-minute walk from here where my Tesla has been parked at a charging port all this time.

I collect Martha from St. Pancras station. She's standing outside the terminal in a soft blue overcoat, jeans, and boots, a pair of oversized sunglasses tucked into her curls and a smart weekend bag looped over the crook of her arm. She breaks into a dazzling smile when she sees me and almost runs toward the curb. She looks beyond adorable, and I cannot believe my luck.

"Oh my goodness," she says, leaning in to kiss me hard and urgently on the lips, "I have missed you so much. I can't tell you how much I've been looking forward to this. It's literally all that's kept me going the past week."

She's aglow. I love it. I love the energy that spills from her. It's golden and it's contagious and it immediately lifts me up and out of the gloomy place in which I've been dwelling since Tara kicked me out.

We listen to music as we drive. The sun shines and Martha's hand sits on my leg. She says, "So, how've you been?"

"Busy," I say, throwing her a warm smile. "I've been busy. I've got a new job. Director of client liaison for a hospitality training company."

This is a real job. I did really apply for it. I didn't get an interview, but the description was tantalizing:

> We are looking for a dynamic and charismatic people person with a plethora of experience working in the hospitality sector, to lead a team of twenty-five hardworking professionals traveling all four corners of the UK to recruit, oversee, train, and advise some of the most exciting new hotels, restaurants, and bars in the business. Hours are flexible, with a lot of working from home and last-minute traveling. This position would suit someone without too many domestic commitments, who has a can-do attitude and can be both a leader and a friend. Car required. Salary £88,000 p/a plus benefits and annual bonus.

It was perfect. Absolutely the dream job, in every respect. But the holes in my CV are always going to be a problem when it comes to conventional work.

"Wow!" says Martha now. "That sounds incredible. When do you start?"

"Next week," I reply. "Monday. So I am going to make the most of every minute of the next few days."

"I'm really happy for you, Al, truly. That's brilliant. But God, how the hell are we ever going to see each other now, between your fancy new job and my shop? It's going to be crazy!"

The question is asked lightly, but it absolutely gives me my perfect opening. I sigh heavily. "I have been worrying about that too. It almost made me turn down the offer."

She cocks her head at me. "Seriously?"

"Yes," I answer softly. "Seriously."

She squeezes my leg and smiles. "Sounds like you're getting serious, Mr. Grey."

"Well," I say frankly, "I am. Aren't you?"

She doesn't reply, but I can tell by the way she smiles as she turns to look out of the window that I've just made her heart sing.

Later that evening, we sit side by side in the cocktail lounge at our beautiful hotel. Martha is wearing a black sweater with short puffed sleeves and a pair of fitted black trousers. Her hair is in a topknot, and she has on big golden drop earrings and red lipstick, and she looks, in the soft light of the boudoir-style table lamps, like a Hollywood starlet. I glance around and see immediately that we are by far the chicest, most beautiful couple in the place. Martha has ordered a Dark and Stormy and I have ordered a Negroni and I'm not looking at the prices. Not tonight. Not at all. This is all paying for itself, ultimately. It's all for the greater good, to get me out of Amanda's sad, poky South London flat and into Martha's glossy-magazine Kentish cottage.

"So," I say, after we've made a toast to each other, "how are we going to navigate around our working hours now that I've got a proper job? It is mainly working from home, but a lot of it will be on the road, nights away, quite often short notice. And listen, we could make it work, I know we could, but it would be a compromised existence. And I was thinking . . ." I glance at Martha, just to make sure I'm not jumping the gun, but I can tell by the way she's staring at me so hopefully with her huge blue eyes that she's willing me to say it. "We could try a bit of . . . living together? Hmm?"

"You mean at mine?"

"Well, I guess it would have to be? Because of the boys. Because of the shop."

She nods and looks thoughtful. "Yes," she says, tempering her response. "Yes. It would have to be. And I guess . . . I mean, the boys know you now. They seem OK around you. And there are two basins in my en suite." She tips her head toward me and smiles. "And actually, I do kind of hate it when I'm not with you, if that doesn't sound pathetically codependent and needy." I see a soft pink flush flood her cheeks and I take her hand and smile.

"Er, yes, actually that sounds horrific, and I am about to run for the hills because the last thing in the whole world I want is for a beautiful, loving, brilliant woman to tell me that she misses me when I'm not around."

Gratifyingly she laughs and I get a lurch in the pit of my belly as I sense the deal about to close, the door to the next room of my life starting to swing open.

"I have to be honest," she continues. "I had already thought about it. I'd been thinking of suggesting it. I'm glad you asked first, though, so I can feel at least a little bit cool about how much I like you."

She laughs again and I lean in toward her so that my forehead is touching hers, and then I gather her hands into mine and I say, "There is no way on earth, Martha, that you like me more than I like you, because I like you so, so much. More than I have ever liked anyone in my life."

She tips her head up so that her lips touch mine and I swear, I am not a sexual being, I really am not, but the charge that passes between us at that moment nearly explodes me in half from the inside out and it's all I can do not to drag her up to our room, but I don't because I have put down a £100 deposit on our six-course dinner.

She pulls away after a moment and I look at her through narrowed eyes. "This is going to be amazing," I say. "You and me. The future. We are going to light up the world."

"You think?"

"I don't think. I know."

FORTY-THREE

We get back to London on Monday morning. I drop Martha back at St. Pancras to catch her train down to Enderford. I'm delighted to see that she looks a little tearful as I wave to her through the passenger window, and I can't help but watch her the entire way until she disappears from view. Maybe I was hoping she'd look back one last time, or maybe I just like the way she moves. Either way, I don't move the car until a taxi behind me blares its horn at me, and then I drive slowly back to Tooting, park my car in the same quiet dead-end street, and walk back to Amanda's apartment.

As I walk, I work on my posture, my demeanor. I try to bring myself down from the high I've been on for the past three days and nights, try to look like a sick man who has spent those three days and nights attached to some kind of vague laser-y thing in some kind of vague northern city-center hospital. By the time I put my key in the lock of Amanda's door, I am probably an inch shorter, five years older. She looks up at me from where she sits on the sofa and rests her phone on the coffee table in front of her. She's wearing a weird gray fleecy shawl over her clothes; it looks cheap, and I hate it.

"How are you?" she asks, getting to her feet. "I tried to call a couple of times, but it went straight to voicemail. Was it OK?"

I nod and sigh and sit heavily next to her. "It was OK," I say in a feeble but stoic voice. "Kind of intense. Five hours at a time. No windows. No sunlight. No food or drink until after treatment. I'm kind of shattered, to be honest. I think, if it's OK with you, I might just go straight to bed."

"Oh my God, of course. Yes. I put fresh sheets on for you. It should all be lovely. I can bring you in a cup of tea, if you want?"

"No," I say softly. "Thank you. And thank you, too, for being there for me, for getting the money, for doing all this. I am so incredibly grateful to you. I really am."

She smiles tightly, clutches the ends of her horrible shawl inside her hands, and says, "You are welcome, Damian. Now go and get some rest."

I smile wanly and head to her bedroom, where I lie down upon her crisp clean sheets, and I pull my phone out of my pocket. I want to look at the photos of my time with Martha in the Cotswolds. I should delete them, but I don't want to. They're so beautiful, so full of love, and joy, and hope. I zoom in onto Martha's face, and then zoom in onto mine, and here I linger for a while and think how some men fade with age, some men rot like fruit, some men become florid, their features stop suiting them, their hair thins, their bodies shrink or bloat, but none of those things have happened to me. I have become better in every way.

I am about to delete the photos when I hear the doorbell ring and the slap-slap of Amanda shuffling to the hallway in her stockinged feet. And then I hear the sound of a voice at the door and it's a voice that I have not heard for two weeks: it is the voice of my wife—Tara.

FORTY-FOUR

I jump to my feet and put my ear to the door. I can't quite make out what's being said at first, but then I catch Tara saying the name "Jonathan Truscott" and I start to panic. I can hear Amanda warbling; she sounds scared. I open the door a crack, just in time to see Tara push past Amanda and peer into the living room.

"I know he's here," she spits. "Jonathan!"

"I told you," Amanda says. "I don't know anyone called Jonathan. There's nobody here of that name."

"Look."

I see Tara show her phone to Amanda.

"This is Jonathan. And this is the man I just watched walk into your home about fifteen minutes ago."

I see Amanda's shoulders crumple slightly. "I don't understand," she says. "That's Damian. My husband."

"Your husband? No. This man is Jonathan Truscott. He's my husband."

I know that this is the moment to make my appearance, and I know exactly what to do. I throw open the door and I say, "Amanda, get in the other room. I'll deal with this."

Tara looks at me in disgust. "Jesus Christ."

I bark at Amanda again. "Get in the other room. Now."

"No," says Tara. "Stay. You need to see this. You need to see what this man who you think is your husband, but who is actually *my* husband, was doing this weekend. Look!" She shows her phone to Amanda and I bundle Amanda physically into the living room, but not before I see a photo on Tara's phone of me and Martha getting out of my car outside our boutique hotel on Friday.

Amanda stands in the living room with wide eyes, her chest heaving up and down, saying, "What the hell is going on? Is this that woman? Shall I call the police? Damian?"

I see Tara roll her eyes. She looks like a meme of a woman of a certain age who has run out of fucks to give. I can tell that she is completely calm, not producing any adrenaline, or at least if she is, her system is handling it like a trouper.

"Yes, *Damian*," she says. "Let's call the police. That's a brilliant idea. And I can tell them about the fact that you appear to be a bigamist."

"A—what?" Amanda's eyes are wide with shock. She comes to the door of the living room and I push her gently back again. "Who is she?" she asks.

"My name is Tara Truscott," says Tara, waving her phone toward Amanda. "At least, I thought my name was Tara Truscott. But it turns out that it probably isn't. That actually I'm probably not even married at all. And neither, probably, are you."

And then it happens. Something that has never happened to me before. All my life, I've been able to control my responses to stress and threats. I have a very slick internal switch, or handle, that glides smoothly into gear whenever I feel the fight-or-flight instinct arrive. I recognize the feeling, and I respond to it with elegance and cool. But in this moment, where the unthinkable has happened and two heavily compartmentalized parts of my life have collided in this tiny, claustrophobic space, with evidence of a third compartment on Tara's phone, one person has to be removed from this situation in order for me to think rationally and talk calmly to the other person, and for a moment I want more than anything for that person to be me. I want to pick up my coat and storm past these two awful women, walk out of the flat, get into my car, and drive and drive and drive until I hit the sea, the edge of the world, whatever. But I can't leave, because I need to manage these two women right now before my whole life unravels and I lose Martha.

As all these conflicting and uncomfortable concepts rush through my consciousness, I feel it happen, I suppose what other people might call a red mist, but what I would call a total loss of control, and I hurl myself at Tara and her stupid fucking phone with its stupid fucking photographs. (How, I think, how on *earth* did I not know we were being stalked and watched and photographed? I have such good instincts, finely tuned antennae, for things being wrong, out of place, *off*.) I grab it from her with one hand and with the other arm slam her against the wall, and I say, "Get out of here, before I do something we'll both regret."

She looks at me with pure hatred and says, "It's too late, Jonathan—or Damian—or *whoever you are*. It's over. You're done."

And then I know there's only one way to stop her talking and that is to stop her breathing, and I press my forearm hard against her esophagus, pushing her throat into the wall. I feel her hands, her fingers, tugging at the fabric of my shirt, I see the color in her face change from a hot red to a bruised blue, even her eyes change color, and I find myself mesmerized by her face as it fills with blood, her eyes bulge out of their sockets, and I feel a sense of calm swell through me, a dreadful certainty about what I'm doing, which is that I am killing her, and I want to kill her and she deserves it, she really does, but just as the certainty begins to build into a wave of pleasure, I feel her fight back harder, her fingernails have made contact with my flesh, she is kicking me in the shins, she is wriggling and writhing, and I can feel her begin to break out of my hold and I call out to Amanda, "Help me, stop her, now." And I can feel Amanda falter behind me, sense her breath holding, and then I shout, "Fucking do something, Amanda! Help me, for fuck's sake!"

And then Amanda is there in her fleecy shawl, holding Tara's arms down by her sides, and she's screaming, "Who is she, Damian? Who is she?"

But I can't answer because I don't know what to say, my thoughts are preoccupied with the act of starving Tara's brain of oxygen and I don't have the headspace to explain to Amanda what is happening here, and it feels as though it takes another hour, but really it is only a moment or two before Tara finally gives up her fight, a small rattle issues from her defeated lungs, the tendons in her neck soften, her knees buckle, and she falls toward me in a deathly slump.

"Fuck," I say, cortisol suddenly replacing the adrenaline in my bloodstream, the shock and awe of it pulsing through me, the truth of my actions registering inside my head like a hand grenade going off.

I drop to my knees alongside Tara's spineless form and Amanda collapses alongside me onto her haunches and we are both breathless and pulsating and wide-eyed and I look at her and she looks at me and she says, "Is she dead?"

I feel around Tara's dainty wrist, the wrist she used to dab perfume onto before I took her out to dinner, clasp delicate bracelets around, that I would hold tenderly above her head when we were having sex sometimes, and I push my thumb against her pulse and there is none. I have killed her, I have killed my wife, she is dead and her body sits slumped against the wall next to my other wife, my first wife, who is panting like an overheated dog and staring at me imploringly, waiting for me to answer.

I drop Tara's wrist and I nod and say, "Yes. Yes, she is."

"Jesus Christ, Damian. Who is she? Who the fuck is she? What are we going to do?" She sounds like she might cry.

"Don't," I say. "Do not cry. It's fine. It's OK." I pull myself back from my feelings of slight revulsion and make myself be nice to her. I take her hands and I stroke them soothingly. "This is the woman I was telling you about. The stalker. The one who stole all my money, who's been terrorizing me. For fifteen years, Amanda. Fifteen years. And I've had restraining orders taken out on her and I've changed my identity twice and I've moved, and I've moved, and I've moved, and I really thought, Amanda, I really, really thought she wouldn't find me here, but she did, and I am so, so sorry for putting you in danger like that. So, so sorry. I can't believe she found me. I can't believe she came here. If only the police had done a proper job. *Damn.*" I yell and thump the floor with my fist. "But nobody takes you seriously when you're a man, especially not a man like me."

Amanda nods, her eyes still wide. "But what are we going to do? What the hell are we going to do with her? Can we call the police? We can say it was self-defense. They'll have it all on record, will know she was a danger to you?"

"No! God, no, Amanda. Absolutely not. Jesus. I don't want to go to prison, and I really, really don't want you to go to prison. No. No, we have to deal with this. Just us. Nobody else. OK?" I look deeply into her eyes and squeeze her hands gently and I see her nod, just a fraction, enough to know that she is onside.

"Right," I tell her. "This is what we're going to do."

Part Four

FORTY-FIVE

What do you think of him?" Ash asks Arlo that evening after Nick has left.

"Seems good," he replies with a shrug.

"But don't you think—I mean all the stuff with him being a life coach, changing his name, all of that, it's all just a bit . . . ?"

Arlo shrugs again. "He explained all of that, though."

And it was true. Nick had explained everything, calmly and elegantly, with no hint of anger or defensiveness, his blue eyes glossy with tears. Ash had become almost mesmerized by his words as he talked, as if he was reading to her from a thrilling novel about a man called Nick Radcliffe.

He'd changed his name, he told them, because he'd been stalked by a crazy ex. The woman called Laura that Sarah May said he'd been living with in Cambridge was his girlfriend, not his wife, the two children were hers, not his. He hadn't mentioned this part of his life to Nina, he explained, because he was always having to cover his tracks to protect himself and his identity from the threat of the stalker ex. He was sorry, he said, for his lack of transparency, but he'd had no choice. Nina had clasped his hand in hers and told him that she understood.

"And what about the lighter?" Ash asks now.

"What about the lighter?" Arlo replies.

"Jane Trevally said he never had a Zippo."

"Right, and Jane Trevally is totally the first person you'd trust to remember anything."

"Actually, yes, when it comes to Dad. And you haven't met her, OK. She's cool. She's not like we thought she was. I trust her."

"Yeah, well, I don't think a lighter that Dad might or might not have had when he was, what, like twenty-three, twenty-four, is enough to base a whole opinion of the guy on."

Ash sighs. She hasn't even mentioned the pacifier clip and the poo bag to Arlo because Nick already has stories for those. She rolls her head. She's tired.

"I'm going to bed," she says, sighing. "Night, little brother."

She pats his head, and he pretends to duck and dive, and then laughs and pats her head back and says, "Night, big sis. Love ya."

"Love you too."

On her way up to bed, she stops at the picture window in the living room that overlooks the channel, and she stares out into the night sky, at the moon reflecting bluey-white off the murky surface of the sea and the straggle of stars and the glow of the Christmas lights on the high street down below. She feels an ache in her gut, thinking of the twenty-five eves of Christmas that have come before this one and the slightly different person she was on each and every one of them, but particularly the version of herself who stood here two Christmases ago in the throes of madness, still hiding it from her family. She remembers her father coming to her right here that Christmas, his hands on her shoulders, the smell of wine on his breath, and saying to her, "None of us is perfect, you know, angel, not even me." He'd laughed drily and squeezed her shoulders. "Don't be scared to talk to us. We all make mistakes. Believe me. We really do."

Six months later, the police had arrived at the flat she was sharing with two other girls near Greenwich. She couldn't remember much after that, other than the way her flatmates had looked at her, the brittle air of shock and slight disgust. Her father, of course, when she spoke to him on the phone afterward, had said simply, "Come home, angel. Just come home."

And now here she is again, obsessing over another middle-aged man, maybe about to blow up her life again. But she can't help it. She has to protect her mother, at any cost. She sighs and turns and is about to head up to bed when her eye is caught by the gifts from Nick Radcliffe under the "Christmas yucca." She should wait, she knows, but she doesn't want to wait. What, she wonders, has Nick Radcliffe bought her for Christmas?

She picks up the gift and takes it to her room, where she sits cross-legged on her bed and unwraps it. And there it is. Another pink box. But unlike the box that the lighter came in, this one has a small rose embossed on it. She runs her finger across it and it takes her back suddenly and surprisingly to another moment, and inside her head she is running her finger across the same embossed rose and she cannot remember where or when, but she knows she has seen this rose before, and she has seen this precise shade of pink before, not just on the box in which the Zippo arrived and not just in Marcelline's office at work, but somewhere else entirely. She squeezes her eyes shut and tries to bring it to mind, but she just can't. Then she opens her eyes and pulls the lid off the box. Inside there is a row of three small soaps, each embedded with flower petals, all tucked into pale pink tissue paper. She lifts them to her nose and sniffs. They smell incredible. Ash loves soap. She read somewhere that soap is better for your skin than all the man-made unguents and potions that are designed to clean skin, and ever since then she's made a beeline for interesting soaps wherever she goes. And these, she knows, are top quality, handmade and probably very expensive. She slips the lid back on the box and stares again at the rose. But still, she cannot remember where she saw it.

FORTY-SIX

"Are you serious?"

Ash looks at her mother in horror.

"Ash," says Nina in a tone of voice that suggests she has reached the end of her tether over this exchange within thirty seconds of it beginning. "He is all alone. He's already spent Christmas Day alone. We've all had the most wonderful time together, and now I want to share Boxing Day with someone who is important to me, and someone who has nobody else to share it with."

"But—" Ash stops herself speaking as she catches the look on her mother's face. "Fine. Whatever."

And then, there he is, an hour later, all primped and groomed, wearing a red sweater, clutching his leather holdall, an expensive-looking scarf wrapped around his neck. He smiles almost sheepishly as he makes his way into the kitchen, where Ash sits with Arlo. "Hello again," he says, leaning in to embrace Ash gently, wafting his expensive aftershave all over her, then shaking hands with Arlo and giving him a fist bump. Nina is behind him, smiling the way she smiles when he's around, glowing the way she glows.

"How was Christmas?" he asks them both.

They tell him it was great and then Ash says, "Oh, thank you for the beautiful soaps, by the way. They're stunning. Where did you get them from?"

"Oh!" He smiles happily. "I'm glad you liked them. Wasn't sure if soap was a bit of an old-lady gift for a young woman like you. But I got them from a tiny shop in Mayfair, near the bar."

"Oh," she says. "Right. That makes sense. Do you buy a lot of stuff from there?"

"Well, I wouldn't say a lot, no. But I have bought gifts from there before."

"Right. Because it's the same as the box that you sent the Zippo in."

He looks confused for a moment, but then simply nods and says, "Possibly. Yes."

And there it is, yet again, another conversation that for Ash is loaded with sinister meaning, but which is closed down with a tiny hydraulic puff of a response from Nick.

"I was thinking of coming to your bar in the New Year," she says breezily. "I can't believe you haven't invited us yet!"

"Hmm," he says. "Yes. There's a reason why I haven't invited you. It's a bit . . ." He turns his eyes to Nina, and Ash sees a wave of uncertainty pass across her face—this is clearly news to her too. "Listen," he says, "there's been a bit of a situation at the wine bar. I haven't been able to talk about it because it's kind of a legal thing. But as of a week ago, I'm not actually a co-owner there anymore. So, yes, that's why I've not invited you all there. And that's why I'm scouting about, looking for new ventures, new things. Like Bangate Cove."

There's a tiny beat of uncomfortable silence when Nick finishes speaking. It's the first time one of Nick's explanations has left a bubble of space in which doubt might grow.

Dead fiancées, abortive careers, name changes, wedding rings, pacifier clips, these were all things that could be thrown into the ether and batted away with not even a ripple. But this—this is bigger. He has fallen out with the people he worked with. He lied about why he had Christmas off. He kept something from Nina that he should have told her. And now that it sits stacked on top of all the other, smaller, more easily explained-away omissions, it looks extra big and ungainly.

Ash exchanges glances with her mother and then with Arlo before Nina bounces into the breach with, "Oh, so you're still thinking about Bangate?"

"More than thinking about it," Nick says smilingly. "I've made an offer!"

"What, seriously?" asks Nina, her hand clasped to her collarbone.

"Yes! A couple of days ago. Still waiting to hear back, but yes, the wheels are in motion."

"But I thought you thought I should buy it."

"Yes. But I could tell you were nervous, and I totally understand that, and now that I'm freeing up the capital by selling my shares in the wine bar, well, it makes sense really, doesn't it? And I wasn't going to say anything, but since the conversation came up . . ." He smiles at Ash, and she looks for a hint of malice in that smile, but of course there is none. "Well, I would still want it to be a *Paddy's*. If you'd allow it. I'd still want it to be your restaurant, your place. But I would like to bankroll it."

There's another brief silence. Then finally Nina says, "Oh. Oh my goodness. I mean, that's . . ."

"You don't have to say anything. You don't even have to *think* anything. I've put in an offer. Let's leave the rest of it to fate."

He smiles, and God, it's a good smile, Ash thinks. It's the sort of smile that should settle your soul, warm your heart, make you want to reach for his hand across the table and squeeze it sweetly. It's a beautiful smile. He's a beautiful man. But God, no, she wants to scream at the top of her lungs, God just please make him disappear.

FORTY-SEVEN

It's Boxing Day and Martha stares across the table at her two boys, who both sit anxiously, neither of them knowing why they are anxious, picking up, no doubt, on her anxiety. Alistair left this morning at seven. His mother had gone missing again. The remains of the turkey lasagna sit on the table between them; the gifts from beneath the tree have all been opened, all the wrapping disposed of; and the champagne is still in the fridge because Martha didn't want to drink champagne on her own. It's nearly five in the afternoon and her husband is not here. And no, he is not answering his phone or picking up his messages and she has no idea if he is on his way home, or if he is still there, and why, she thinks, why the hell does he do this? Every single time? Other couples aren't like this. Other couples stay in touch, drop each other messages, even if it's just a thumbs-up emoji next to an `Are you on your way home?` text.

Suddenly Martha feels reckless.

She has spent Christmas Day without the boys and now Boxing Day without her husband, and the shop reopens tomorrow at nine o'clock, she has to be there at 8 a.m. for a delivery and the childminder doesn't start work again until the New Year, so she will have to take Nala with her, and if Alistair doesn't come back tonight, she feels like she will explode.

She tells the boys she is going to the toilet and then heads upstairs to the bedroom. She doesn't give herself time to think about it. She reaches into the wardrobe and pulls out Alistair's medical bag. She feels around for the shape of the secret phone, but it's not there. She'd known it wouldn't be. She'd known he would have it with him. Because suddenly she knows without any doubt at all that Alistair is having an affair. She realizes that for months she's been nudging this knowledge around her consciousness like a football, without ever seeing the goalposts, but she sees them now and she's ready to kick it straight through them. She goes to his jackets and trousers and puts her hands inside all of his pockets, but they come out empty. Nothing. Not a receipt, not a coin, not a peppermint, nothing. Even that, she tells herself, is a sign that something isn't right. Who the hell has empty pockets? She goes down to the hallway and feels inside the pockets of his coats and jacket. She finds a poo bag, one of Nala's pacifier clips, and, crumpled into a ball that she unfurls and smooths out, a receipt from a restaurant called Paddy's.

Paddy's, Martha thinks. Why does that ring a bell? And then she remembers. Alistair took her there for dinner two or three years ago, before they had Nala, possibly just after they got married. It was a cute little seafood restaurant in Whitstable, she recalled, with the most vibrant atmosphere, candles on the tables, graffiti art on the walls, and the owner himself had been there and had spent some time at their table chatting with them. A very charismatic man, Martha remembered. Very charming.

She glances down at the receipt again and sees that this is not from the Whitstable restaurant where she and Al had been for dinner that day, but from another branch of Paddy's just along the coast in Ramsgate. She looks at the date and time—two weeks ago, 9:56 p.m., £55. A single bottle of champagne.

She looks at the diary in her phone to see what was happening on that day two weeks ago and sees with a white-hot flash of pure rage that it was the night Nala was sick, when she had to ask Grace to drive them to the hospital, when Alistair had come home the following afternoon telling her that he'd slept on a sofa in the staff room of the hotel where he'd been working.

Her head pulses hard with anger and she roars so loudly that Jonah appears in the hallway, still wearing the paper crown from the crackers they'd pulled half-heartedly over lunch, his eyes wide with concern.

"What's the matter?"

Martha draws in her rage and her desperation and forces a smile. "Nothing, sweetheart, just stubbed my toe. That's all."

"Where's Al?"

Jonah has become slightly clingy around Al since their heart-to-heart the week before, seeks him out, asks after him when he's not there.

"I told you," she says. "He's gone to look after his mum."

"But when will he be back?"

"Soon," she says. "Maybe tonight. Maybe tomorrow. But soon."

"I want to message him."

She's about to say no, her inbuilt response to protect Alistair's stressful working life from the added stress of family, but then she remembers that Alistair doesn't have a stressful job anymore and that he is currently with either a) his secret lover or b) his elderly mother, and in either case, there is no reason why his stepson shouldn't be allowed to message him on Boxing Day.

"Yes," she says. "That's a good idea. Do you have his number?"

Jonah shakes his head.

"Here," says Martha, "let me send it to you. Then you can message him directly from your phone. OK?"

Jonah nods happily and stares at his phone until Martha's message with Al's contact details appears and then he heads back into the dining room.

"Let me know if he replies!" she calls out to him.

"I will," he calls back to her.

She turns her attention to the crumpled receipt again. Then she goes to the browser on her phone and googles "Paddy's Ramsgate." According to the Google results, it reopens tomorrow at midday. She will be on the phone to them then. But in the meantime, she feels an unsettling wave of relief pass through her, as though she'd been waiting for this moment for a very long time, and now that it's here, she can finally start to breathe again.

FORTY-EIGHT

THREE YEARS EARLIER

I went to Martha's a few days after the incident at Amanda's flat, having laid low in a cheap hotel near Harwich for the duration. I arrived with the bare essentials in my father's holdall and a bundle of cash from Amanda, the rest of the £5,000 that Bella had given her.

I called Martha while I waited for my train to Enderford. "Martha, I am so, so sorry to do this to you, but I am going to need a place to sleep, just for a few days. I know we've been talking about perhaps moving in together, and I know, obviously, that we were talking abstractly and that it wasn't meant to be a plan of action, and I know that you have the boys and the shop to think about, and I would not in a million years ask if it wasn't urgent. But it kind of is?"

She didn't even ask me any questions. She just said, "Yes. Of course. Come now. Stay as long as you like."

And nearly a year later, I am still here.

Life with Martha is everything I'd dreamed it would be. Village life suits me. Martha suits me. She is so uncomplicated and kind. The boys are sweet enough. The seasons come and go through the windows of her cottage like greeting cards: cherry blossom, sunset-hued roses, rhododendron, holly and ivy, a curtain of Virginia creeper on the wall opposite the kitchen window that turns bonfire red in early autumn. I help her out in the shop when I can. The rest of the time I go to work. She still thinks I work for the hospitality training company I told her about last year. She thinks I travel the country staying in snazzy hotels, training up shiny-faced teams of graduates and school-leavers to face the public and provide five-star service. She thinks I'm important. She's proud of me. I can't pretend it doesn't hurt a bit that she's proud of a fictional version of me and not the real me—the me who has spent vast swathes of the last thirty years visiting women around the country, being paid to make them feel good about themselves.

It's a line of work I've fallen back on often over the years. And I never ever get used to it. It's degrading and it's hard and it's ridiculous. It doesn't always involve sex; it frequently involves other things like massages or city breaks or yoga classes or shopping. I charge £200 an hour, £500 for an overnight, and I earn every bloody penny of it. You'd imagine, wouldn't you, that a man would enjoy pleasuring women for money. But that depends entirely on the woman, and frankly, most of these women are not in my league in any way. Some of them are downright revolting. This was bad enough when I was with my previous wives but is even harder to stomach now that I am with Martha.

But one good thing about my line of work is that I get to stay in a lot of hotels in a lot of different places. I get taken out for dinner to some amazing restaurants, and I come home fully versed in the details of the types of places I tell Martha I have been working in as a trainer. I can bring home souvenirs: matchbooks, bathroom miniatures, after-dinner macarons in tiny boxes tied with ribbon. I can describe hotels, high streets, tourist attractions.

But I can't keep doing it. I simply can't. I'm almost fifty-two now and I want more, for me, and for Martha. Unlike Tara, who was ambitious and hardworking, Martha is ambitious, hardworking, and also incredibly creative. Her mind never stops working. She has such plans for her flower shop, such visions, and I want to be a part of them. I want to marry her. I want to make a life with her, but I need to take things slowly, stay under the radar, keep my head well and truly down. Because my recent history is still too complicated to take the next steps.

Emma, Tara's daughter, reported her mother as a missing person about a month after I moved in with Martha. I'd sent Emma a few messages from her mother's phone in the days after she died, told her a long and convoluted story about being in the Algarve, making a fresh start with Jonathan, wanting a clean break, and obviously Emma didn't believe a word of it, her replies to these messages were full of skepticism and unsuccessful attempts to trip me up, but it took her a while to feel uncomfortable enough about it to report it to the police, by which time there was nobody to answer the door when the police came calling at Amanda's flat and I was long gone.

It's almost a year on and Emma is still looking for her mother. She's forever popping up on the news, campaigning for further police investigations into her mother's disappearance, but nothing has ever broken the case.

Amanda, of course, is still a problem, but nobody seems to be looking for her, and for now at least everything feels safe, everything feels perfect.

That is until one crisp morning in late February when the apple trees outside Martha's cottage are bare and gnarled against a sky so blue it looks like gouache and a news report appears on the screen of my phone.

A body has been found in woodland in Essex. A woman's body. No head. No hands. No legs. Just a torso. Roughly fifty years old. No physical identifiers. Could be anyone. But I know who it is. Of course I do.

FORTY-NINE

The day after Boxing Day, Ash heads to Cambridge. She has to do something. The past twenty-four hours have been intense and too much: the claustrophobia of having Nick here on Boxing Day when it was meant to be just the three of them, and seeing Arlo behave as if Nick was his new best friend, saying things like "He's good for Mum, that's the most important thing," even as he put his Christmas gifts into carrier bags ready to take "home" to Bournemouth the following day, after which he won't have to think about any of his family again for months.

She tells her mum she's going sales shopping and gets the ten o'clock train into St. Pancras, goes over the road to King's Cross, and gets the 11:21 to Cambridge, from where she gets a bus from outside the station to Cherry Hinton.

Ash can see the twinkle of Christmas tree lights through the window of the house on Kingston Gardens, and she breathes a sigh of relief. A Christmas tree means that someone is actively living here. She inhales to calm her nerves, and then rings the doorbell.

A youngish man answers. He has close-cropped hair and round-framed glasses, wears a trendy sweatshirt and jeans, and his feet are bare. "Hello?" He has an American accent.

"Oh," says Ash, "hi! I'm looking for someone called Laura? I'm not sure of her surname. Possibly Warshaw? But she used to live here about ten years ago?"

The man turns his head and calls out behind him. "Honey. Can you come here a sec?"

A woman appears a minute later. She wears a similar pair of round-framed glasses, and a similar sweatshirt and jeans.

"Was there a woman called Laura here before we moved in?"

"Laura?" says the woman. "Yes. That rings a bell. She had two little girls. Kind of fortyish?"

Ash nods feverishly. "Yes!" she says. "Yes, that's the one. How long ago did she move out?"

"Well, we've been here for ten years," says the woman, and the man nods along in agreement.

"And do you—do you have any idea where she went? What happened to her?"

The couple look at each other. "Not sure, really," says the woman. "I think she moved for schools? For her children? Something like that. Is there something wrong?"

Ash shakes her head. "No. Just . . . she was a friend of my father's. And my father just passed away. And I just wanted to let her know. That's all."

The couple exchange another look and then the woman says, "You could try asking our landlady?"

"Oh. Yes! Wow, that would be great, if that's OK?"

"Yes. Sure. She's called Petula. She runs the salon on the high road."

"Oh! Great! What's it called?"

"Petula's."

Ash gives them both a double thumbs-up and a stupid grin. "Great. Thank you. Do you think it'll be open now?"

"No idea. But I can't see why not."

Ash thanks the couple and puts the salon into her Maps app. It's a four-minute walk away.

Petula is an older woman with bright blond hair and a nice way about her. She hands her client over to a junior to have the dye washed from her hair and then takes Ash to the sofa in the window, where a small white dog slumbers on a fleecy rug.

"Laura," she says sighing heavily. "Ah, yes, poor Laura. She got well and truly done over. In my opinion."

"What do you mean—done over?"

"I mean that guy, her husband, Justin. He scammed her."

Ash feels a jolt of energy pass through her. "Really?" she says.

"Well," says Petula, "like I say. *In my opinion.* She maintained that he was a good guy, but she put up with all sorts of nonsense."

"Were you friends?"

"Well, sort of. We were neighbors for a while. I own the house next door as well and I was living there when she moved in. I lived there for about a year and we kind of rubbed along a bit during that time. I could hear things through the wall, get an idea of the dynamic, and oof." She blows out her cheeks. "I did not like that man. Not at all. He had this way about him, so charming, perfect husband, perfect father . . ."

"So those were his children? The two girls?"

"Well, yes. Or I assumed so. He used to refer to them as his daughters."

"And they were married?"

"Again, I assumed so. They both wore rings. He referred to Laura as his wife."

Ash gets a slightly panicky feeling in the pit of her stomach and into her bowels. Here it is. It's coming. It's like a tornado or a tsunami, it's over there somewhere, she can't see it yet, but it's getting closer and once it arrives, all hell will break loose. And she wants it to happen, but at the same time she really doesn't, because this, on top of Dad's death, not to mention Ash's own mental health crisis not that long before—all of it might be too much for her mum, might tip her over, because she has been so strong, so brilliant during all of this, but can she take this too? Is Ash going to blow her mother's life into smithereens? In the process of trying to save her from doing it to herself?

"So, what did you hear? What happened?"

"Psychopath."

Ash cocks her head questioningly.

"Classic case," Petula continues. "Gaslighting. Word salad–ing. Love-bombing. All of it."

Ash nods but doesn't really know what Petula is talking about.

"And then, one day, he just disappeared completely. Left her alone with two little girls and thousands of pounds of debt. I mean . . ." Petula blows out her breath and widens her eyes. "You'd think she was a stupid woman, from me saying that. But that was the thing. She really wasn't a stupid woman. She was a clever woman. Funny. Confident. Great company. She had a proofreading business, used to do work for some really famous writers. She was well-known in Cambridge, had a great reputation. She was very well-liked. And this man, Justin, he somehow managed to persuade her that he had her best interests at heart when he really, absolutely did not. Or at least, not in my opinion."

"Where did she go—Laura?"

"Well, she moved out about ten years ago. Couldn't afford the rent as she was having to pay off all of Justin's debts. I don't know where she went, but it certainly wasn't around here. I'd know if she was still in the area. And we weren't quite close enough to stay in touch. So that was that. She handed me back the keys, we had a bit of a hug, she left. Never saw her again."

Petula sighs, then glances down at the photo on Ash's phone screen of Nick Radcliffe's LinkedIn profile. She sniffs. "Slippery fuck," she says. Then, "What is it with some women? I really don't get it. Why can't they see through men like him? What is it that he does? It's like . . . black magic. Like that character from that sketch show, you know, *Look into the eyes, not around the eyes, look into the eyes.* You know the one? And everyone else can see what's happening. But the woman in the middle of it, the woman being love-bombed and bamboozled and lied to and manipulated . . ." She shakes her head sadly. "Make sure your mum doesn't let him at her money. Make sure she stays in control. But better still, make sure she gets rid of him."

Laura Drummond is her name. Not Laura Warshaw. She didn't take his name when they married. Her date of birth, according to the lease she signed for Petula's house, is 28 June 1973. Her daughters are called Lola and Evie. They would be teenagers by now. It's not much, but it's enough. Ash heads back into the city center and finds a nice coffee shop where she eats a slice of cake and has a coffee and plugs in her phone to charge while she googles the hell out of the small amount of information she has to work with, and there it is—Laura Drummond, Proofreading Services, Peterborough PE2.

She finds the address on Maps and goes onto Street View. It's a small office block on a suburban-looking high road. No doubt it will be closed today, nobody needs proofreading services over Christmas and the New Year, but she calls the number anyway and it goes to a voice message, a woman with a very soft voice telling the caller that she is away for the Christmas period and will be back on 2 January and please do leave a message. "If it's urgent," she says, "please send me an email."

Dear Laura

My name is Aisling Swann.

My mother is dating a man called Nick Radcliffe who once went under the name of Justin Warshaw, to whom I believe you were once married?

I'd love to talk to you about him if you feel comfortable doing so, as I have some concerns about him.

Please reply to me here, or call me on the number below.

Many thanks
Yours
Ash

She presses send and hurls the message toward an unknown next chapter.

FIFTY

Al comes home the day after Boxing Day and immediately tells Martha that he will have to go back to the Midlands and stay with his mother until they can get some kind of care plan in place.

"But what about Nala?" she asks. "The childminder doesn't start back until the second. And I can't keep bringing her to the shop. It's a nightmare."

"Surely Troy can look after her. He's going to be eighteen next month. He's virtually an adult. Or Matt? He's not going back to work until the New Year, is he?"

"I can't ask Matt to look after my child!"

"Or your brother? I mean, surely there has to be somebody."

"No, Al. There really isn't."

"Well, then maybe you'll just have to leave the shop shut. Until the New Year."

"Are you serious?"

"Martha." Al sighs and looks down at her. His eyes are sad, a sheen of tears on their surface. "I am so tired. This is so stressful. I genuinely can't bear it, I can't bear that I have to go away from here, go away from you, that I have to sacrifice all of this to be with *her*. You know how I feel about her. You know I hate her. But she has nobody else. I can't just abandon her. I have to do this. It kills me, but I have to." A tear escapes from his eye and trickles down his cheek and Martha resists the temptation to wipe it away with the side of her hand, keeping a tight rein on her emotions in order to maintain her resolve.

"Fine," she says. "I'll shut the shop. Milly will probably be happy. I know Jonah will be happy to have me home too."

Al sighs at the mention of Jonah. "You know he sent me a message yesterday?"

"I know," says Martha. "He asked for your number. What did it say?"

Al smiles sadly. "Here." He passes her his phone.

Dear Al. How are you? I hope things are OK with your mum? We missed you today. I hope you will be home soon? Please send Mum a message so she knows because she gets really worried? See ya! J

Martha's stomach rolls, first with sadness that her son sent such a sweet message, and then with pure rage and fury that Al hadn't replied to it.

She hands him back his phone and sighs. "You couldn't even reply to that."

"I told you, Martha. I just wasn't in the right headspace to look at my phone. It wasn't that kind of day. And you're right. I know you're right. And I know this drives you mad, and to be honest, Martha, it drives me mad too. It really does. I hate being the way I am. I hate being so unreliable and so chaotic. I've been trying so hard to be a better person, you know I have. But every time I start getting myself together, something else comes along and upsets the equilibrium. And I know it doesn't make any sense—it doesn't make any sense to me either. I wish it did, but my brain, it just goes off on tangents, it spirals, it loses the thread, I lose track of time, I forget what I'm meant to be doing, and I know it's not good enough, it's really not good enough, but please, Martha, stay with me on this. I'll have this sorted before you know it. I'll get my mother a carer, I'll get it all tied up, I'll be back, and we can get on with our lovely life, OK? Can you give me that time? Please? And in return, I will try my hardest to remember to reply to messages, to stay in touch, to be what you need me to be, because, Martha, I love all of this so much, I love this life, I love those boys, I love our beautiful daughter, and I love you, Martha. I love you so much it kills me."

The tears come again and for a moment Martha finds herself watching him clinically, objectively, like he's an exhibition or a piece of performance art, not a real man expressing real feelings. And into her head, a word lands, like a brick.

Bullshit.

As it hits her, Martha wants to laugh. But she keeps her face straight, her expression neutral. She nods and she says, "It's OK. I understand. Thank you for explaining it all to me. It all feels much clearer now. I'll shut the shop. It's fine. You go and do what you have to do."

She touches him lightly on the arm and walks away, her chest tight with resolve. She knows what to do next; her mind is clear.

FIFTY-ONE

TWO YEARS EARLIER

For a long while after the news breaks, it remains in the headlines: "The Body in the Woods." Poor, poor woman. No signs of sexual assault, no signs of violence, merely a pile of flesh and bones, left to decompose into mulch and acid, leached away by the forest floor to feed microorganisms, worms, creatures so small that nobody even talks about them. They call her Woman X. Highly unoriginal, but there you go.

I feel edgy, vaguely sick, for quite a few days after the news breaks. Weirdly, I want to talk to Amanda. She occupies my mind almost constantly. The sense of connection to her I feel in those days and weeks is almost tangible and I hate to say it, but there is a moment where I keep her face at the forefront of my mind while I'm making love to Martha, which is revolting, I know, but what can I say? The whole scenario is new to me. I have only dismembered a body once in my life, and there was only one person there to share the experience with me and that's not the kind of thing you can just shake off in a dash. And actually, during those awful hours when Amanda and I did what we did with the remains of Tara's body, I have rarely, if ever, felt closer to another human being. She really was quite extraordinary. Mainly, of course, because I had somehow managed to persuade her that she was the one who'd killed Tara. Or at least, she would be blamed for it if Tara's death ever came to light. We were in that flat for twelve long hours, doing things that were basically unthinkable, but we got into a rhythm, a dance. We even, I seem to recall, put on some music. It still doesn't feel quite real. But when I look back at it, I feel a kind of triumph. Because God it was brilliant, quite, quite brilliant. My mind, which so often operates in cyclones and whirlpools, became entirely still in those hours, I knew exactly what to do and how to do it, and all I had to ensure was that Amanda would go along with it. And she did.

I also have to say that something changed inside me after that day. I evolved. Which is a strange thing to say about something that was essentially an act of unevolved animal savagery. But I did feel like I had tapped into something inside me that I didn't know was there, something vital and energizing, and I would be lying if I said I haven't relived that last moment of Tara's sad, pointless life over and over again, and although I do keep coming back to this sense I have of myself as not being a sexual person, I do feel it is related somehow to my latent sexuality. It's the same, in a way, as how I feel when I follow women in the street. It brings me to life in a way that normal sexual interactions simply don't. During normal sexual interactions, I am usually very mindful of my performance as a loving and nurturing husband or a highly paid escort. I know what's expected and I make sure I deliver it. I have been married to women who weren't interested in sex at all, particularly after having a child, and I was unbothered and patient. But it's different now. I feel different. And right now, two years into my relationship with Martha, I would say, sexually speaking, things are very much alive and well. I've been holding off asking her to marry me until I know that the Tara episode is well and truly over, that they have not identified Woman X, that Emma is not coming after me, that nobody anywhere is putting the two parts of the full piece together. So, for now, for a while longer, we're just freewheeling, Martha and I, while I use my own hard-earned money to treat her as a woman of her caliber deserves to be treated.

This morning, I awake in the bed of a woman called Marie. She is sixty, very well kempt, if slightly too thin and crepey in places. But overall, in the subtle lamplight of her top-floor apartment in a leafy suburb of West London, she is nice enough to look at. She lives alone, with two dogs who share our bed. One of them greets me by sniffing my face and I pat its head and tell it it's a good boy (I think it's a boy). Then I roll over and climb out of the bed. I am wearing underwear. We didn't have sex last night, or at least not the sort of sex that required me to remove my underwear. Marie mumbles something from the depths of a nest of fat pillows and I take her hand and give it a tender squeeze. "Thank you, darling," I say. "That was just wonderful."

In her kitchen, I search her fridge and then make myself a hastily assembled sandwich with some fancy-looking ham and a slick of garlic mayonnaise. I give the dogs some ham too, and then, from its place resting against the toaster, I take the envelope with my name scrawled on it ("André"), check the contents (£500), grab my bag and my coat, and head to my car in the guest parking space outside. Four hours later, I am back in Enderford, where I scrub my face raw in the bathroom with a flannel, soap, and some very hot water.

I use some of the £500 to take Martha out for dinner that night. It's a place I keep reading about in the local press, and then last weekend it was in *The Times*, listed as one of the "top twenty seafood restaurants in the UK."

It's called Paddy's in Whitstable. I tell Martha that it's a surprise and that she doesn't need to dress up, but that she should expect it to be nice. She looks excited as she gets ready. Her boys are staying with their father that night, so we don't need to rush back for a babysitter and will have the house all to ourselves when we return. I like Martha's boys, especially the youngest, who reminds me so much of myself in so many ways, or at least the pitiful version of myself that existed during my childhood, but it's nice to have a night or two every week without them.

When she comes downstairs, Martha has her hair up, just as I like it, and small gold spheres hanging from her ears. She wears jeans, a simple black T-shirt, and a beautiful velvet jacket in a smoky green. She looks exquisite and I tell her so and she smiles, revealing perfectly white teeth, that dimple, a tiny hint of gum. I'm wearing jeans, too, with a smart jacket and expensive new trainers, and for the next hour or so I forget about where the money came from to pay for these nice things and focus more on the fruits of my rather sordid labor.

Our taxi arrives at six o'clock and Martha and I sit holding hands across the back seat, talking easily and lightly, as we always do, and soon we are dropped outside Paddy's, directly onto the cobbles of a picturesque side street just as the sun is going down on the town.

The ambience of the restaurant is evident even from the street: the sounds of laughter, conversation, the smells of garlic and the sea. I'm hungry after all my travels and the late night before with Marie. A young girl shows us to our table. She's not terribly pretty and I am jolly and avuncular as she seats us and passes us menus and explains things to us as though we are children who have never before been out to eat.

"The small plates at the top, we recommend two or three, then here, in the middle, large plates, for two to share, plus some sides, but we also have 'Something While You're Waiting'"—she points out some italicized text at the very top of the menu—"in case you've come hungry." She smiles and I smile back encouragingly, then she talks us through the specials, which are all things fresh from the sea, including a type of fish I've never heard of before that I immediately know I will order.

We have razor clams and oysters and blinis with salmon roe and truffle cream. We have smoked trout and crisp apple slices and a beautiful local sparkling wine from a Kentish vineyard. Our waitress is great, and I already know I'll give her a good tip. I look around at the people who surround us, and I feel a dizzying clash of emotions: pride at the realization that we are the best-looking couple in here by a mile, but a blow of shame at the thought that in order to afford my place here, last night I had to perform cunnilingus on a lonely sixty-year-old woman while her cavapoos looked on. I banish the thought and focus instead on Martha's smile and the spectacular remoulade that comes alongside my exciting new fish with a name that I've already forgotten.

And then I feel the air in the restaurant change. The atmosphere ramps up, diners turn slightly. I see a few people break into smiles as a man appears in a chef's apron and matching hat. He's a small man, barely five foot nine, he has a paunch, he wears scuffed trainers with baggy combat trousers, his hair is stuck to his forehead with sweat, and he glows with the heat of the kitchen. I see him perform a complicated teenage handshake with a customer and then pull out a chair.

"I assume," says Martha, a little breathlessly, "that that is Paddy himself?"

The way she says the word "himself"—it makes me experience a strange burst of rage. It reminds me, I realize, of the way people used to respond to seeing my father outside his practice. The way they'd bring themselves up taller, or, if it was a family, the way they'd form a kind of queue, almost doff their fucking caps at him as if he was important somehow. Purely because he'd learned some stuff that they didn't know. Purely because he could do things that they couldn't do.

And it is the same here with this man in his steaming chef's whites and his name over the door of a popular seafood restaurant in one of the most upmarket seaside towns in the country, who has somehow learned to cook better than most other people are able to cook, but beyond that has nothing to mark him out as deserving of turned heads and hushed awe. I feel ruffled and unbalanced. I see the way Martha looks at him, that flush on her cheeks as though she is in the presence of someone godlike and unworldly.

I look at the man, Paddy, and I see a nobody. And then I look again closer and I realize that I know this man. I've seen him before. An image flashes into my mind's eye: a louche young man smoking a cigarette in the alleyway behind a restaurant in Mayfair where I worked briefly in my early twenties. I was employed by an agency at the time, mainly washing up. He'd looked at me, this man, narrowed his eyes, and then flicked his stub across the alleyway into the gutter.

"What are you doing out here?"

"Just getting some air," I'd said.

"Get the fuck back in there," he'd said. "You're not being paid to breathe."

Then he'd turned and walked back into the kitchen, letting the door slam in my face. I remembered him now, that cocky little man with his tobacco-stained teeth and his mockney accent. I remember the black shame of that moment, the gnawing rage in my gut. And more than anything, I remember the bit of me that died in that moment.

And now I smile grimly at Martha and say, "Yes. I imagine it is."

I see her eyes trailing over Paddy's restaurant, drinking in all the tiny aesthetic details that make it so alluring, and I know that each element represents some small iota of Paddy himself, of his psyche, his soul, and it feels as though she is drinking him in. All of me fills with putrid envy. Why does this man, this small man with his nondescript face, his slack belly, his teenage demeanor . . . why does he have an empire? Respect? What does he have that I do not, apart from the ability to dress a crab?

"You know," Martha is saying, "this is what I've always imagined my fantasy café to look like. The vibe. The colors. The feel of it. Don't you think?" She turns to me and smiles, and I feel as though she has stabbed me in the heart. But I smile back and say, "Absolutely. Yes. I can absolutely see you having a place like this. And one day"—I make sure my attention on her is so focused she will forget that there is anything or anyone else in the world—"you will. It's going to happen."

And then, suddenly, Paddy is by our table. "Hi, guys," he says in his mockney drawl, "how's your night been? Everything good?"

Martha turns and beams at him. "Oh my God," she says, breathlessly. "It's all been incredible. Truly. And this place, it's just beautiful, the look of it, the feel of it. All of it. You're a genius. Seriously." She smiles at him again, showing him all her teeth, her gums, her dimple.

And suddenly something happens. Paddy's body language changes. It becomes sexualized. His groin brushes slightly against the back of Martha's chair, not once but twice. Then he puts his hand on her shoulder and squeezes it. He pulls her shoulder back slightly toward him and he says, with a laugh, "Well, I'm not sure about that. But thank you. I'm so happy you've had such a good time." And I can feel it, I can smell it, the want that is passing through this man's body, the want of her, Martha, my girlfriend. I know that he is inflamed, engorged, that his ego is burnished, and his chest is puffed. I know what he is feeling because he is a man, and I am also a man. And I know that he has forgotten that I exist, that I have pixelated in his peripheral vision into nothing more than a blob.

"I hope you'll come back again?" he asks, and his question is directed at Martha, almost entirely.

"Oh yes," she says. "We'll definitely be back."

I see his fingers squeeze her shoulder again and I hear him saying, "Well, I hope so," and there is a lustful edge to his voice and I'm not imagining it, I promise you. It's subtle, but it's there. And then there is a weird beat of silence and I see him press his groin once more against the back of Martha's chair before taking his hand off her shoulder, performing a small bow, and then finally moving along to the next table.

I have never felt how I feel about Martha about any other woman. I do not want her to smile for another man, feel in awe of another man, be impressed by another man, have any interest of any description in being in the presence of any other men for the reason of their status, achievements, or talents. Especially not this man. This man who once spoke to me as if I was trash and who has somehow, despite being the same age as me, leapfrogged way ahead of me into the life I've always wanted for myself.

Martha looks at me curiously. "Are you OK?"

I nod, then say tersely, "I'm fine."

Martha cocks her head slightly. "Are you sure?"

I nod again. And then I say, "I just think that guy was a bit inappropriate. The way he was touching you."

"Touching me?"

"Yes. His hand on your shoulder."

She laughs and I feel a pulse of anger go through me, but I push it down. "It was more than that," I say. "He was pushing his groin against your chair. Acting like I didn't exist."

"Al," she says sweetly, softly, "I think you're overthinking it a little."

"Well. I didn't like it. I thought it was very unprofessional."

Martha pulls my hands toward her across the table and says, "I love you, you know that?"

I smile and nod, allow a tiny smear of tears to spring to my eyes. "I do," I say.

But the edges of my words are muffled and muted by the deafening thunder of Paddy Swann at the table across the aisle laughing overloudly at something his companion has just said. I turn to look at him, just as he turns to look at me.

Something dark passes between us in that moment, and I know that I am changed.

FIFTY-TWO

Ash goes back to work on 2 January. It is a pleasant day, if a little windy, and she is glad to be away from the house for a few hours, away from the man called Nick Radcliffe, who appears to be living with them now.

She unspools her scarf, unzips her bomber jacket, and takes the cup of coffee that Marcelline hands her.

"Happy New Year," says Marcelline.

"Hmm," says Ash. "Let's hope so. I wish I could say that it couldn't be any worse than last year, or the one before, but I'm not altogether convinced that will be the case."

Ash tells Marcelline about the impromptu visit from Nick Radcliffe, the Boxing Day reappearance, her trip to Cambridge, her conversation with the hairdresser who told her that Nick Radcliffe was more than likely a psychopath, and the email she'd sent Laura, for which she was still awaiting a response.

"I'm hoping she's going to write today," she tells Marcelline, "when she gets back to the office."

"Well," says Marcelline, "I give you permission to check your email compulsively. In between"—she slides Ash a box across the desk—"sale tags."

Ash knows the score. She needs to place sale tags on all the items they're sick of the sight of, which are then removed at the end of January. Ash had once given someone a 90 percent discount on a pair of pink faux snakeskin trousers during the summer sale because she didn't want to look at them for another second.

She grabs the handful of tags and then pulls a box of pens toward her. The pink box catches her eye, and she remembers. What did Marcelline say had come in it originally? She peers at the box and sees that it has the same embossed rose on its lid as the one from Nick.

She waves the box at Marcelline. "Did you say that this had soaps in it originally?"

Marcelline pulls her reading glasses off her face, then looks at the box and back to Ash. "I think so," she says. "Why?"

"Because it's exactly the same as the box my Christmas present from Nick came in. Can you remember who gave it to you?"

"Oh," says Marcelline, cocking her head slightly and returning her glasses to her nose. "I actually think it was a gift from my ex."

"Who's your ex?" Ash has never known Marcelline to have a boyfriend, so this must have been a long while ago.

"Jason. We split up about three years ago. Kind of casual. Too young for me."

"Any idea where he got the soap from?"

"No. No idea. I do remember feeling a little offended that he thought posh soap was a nice gift for a lover. It made me feel very old, and actually, now I come to think of it, maybe that was the beginning of the end."

"Nick said he got it from a shop in Mayfair, but I've done a gazillion hours of googling and cannot find a shop in Mayfair that has branding like this and sells soap like that. This Jason guy . . . where did he live?"

"Oh, somewhere in the countryside. He was a farrier."

"Where in the country?"

"Erm, one of those chocolate-box villages . . . can't remember what it was called. I never went there. But somewhere in Kent."

"What was his surname?"

"Trevor."

Immediately Ash grabs her phone and googles "Jason Trevor farrier kent." A photo comes up on a local website. She turns the screen to Marcelline. "Is that him?"

"Oh," says Marcelline, peering at the photo. "Yes! Gosh, he's aged."

"In three years?"

"Country living, I guess. What does it say about him?"

"It says he's an award-winning farrier who's been working in the north Kent countryside for over twenty years. And it says he lives in Reading Street. And here's a number." Ash pauses. "Can I call him? Do you mind?"

"Erm, oh . . ." Marcelline blanches slightly. "I guess. I mean, don't talk about me. Or you can mention me. A bit. But only if he asks."

Ash gives a tiny, dismissive shake of her head. "No, it's fine. I won't say anything."

Jason picks up on the third ring.

"Oh, hi! My name's Ash. I wonder if I could ask you a strange question?"

There's a taut silence before Jason says, "Right. OK."

"A long time ago, you bought a box of handmade soaps to give to your girlfriend, Marcelline."

"Marcelline?" He sounds uncertain about the name, seems to be struggling to recollect. Then he says, "Oh, yeah. Marcy!"

"Yes, Marcy." She throws Marcelline a quizzical look and she nods in return.

"Sorry, you said *soap*?"

"Yes. You gave her a gift set of soaps, in a pink box, quite fancy. And I desperately need to find out where the fancy soaps came from."

"Oh my days," says Jason. "I mean, no. I really don't . . . And you know, I think, if I'm being honest, they might have been a bit of a regifting thing? To be totally frank? I think my mum might have given them to me? Because I'm going to be honest, I'm not really the type to buy soap. Not for anyone. I can't picture myself doing it. Not ever. So, yeah. I reckon my mum gave them to me."

"And would you maybe have any thoughts about where she might have got them from?"

"God, no. And she's dead now."

Ash blanches. "Oh," she says. "I'm very sorry to hear that."

"It's OK. These things happen. But listen, if you see Marcy, say hi. Tell her I'm still single. Ha!" He issues a nervous laugh. "And don't tell her about the soap, will you?"

The mystery of the pink gift boxes hangs over Ash all day. She spends both her breaks perusing villages in the vicinity of Jason Trevor's address in Reading Street, virtually wandering up and down streets, looking for gift shops that might sell posh soaps in pink boxes. She googles "gift shops," she googles "soap," she googles "pink," she googles everything, but there's nothing. But just as she's heading back to the shop from her lunch hour, she feels a vibration in her pocket and pulls out her phone. It's a notification from her email account. A reply from Laura. Her breath catches and she stops just in front of the shop, her fingers clumsy against the screen of her phone as she opens it up.

Dear Ash

Thank you for writing. I'm sorry for the late reply.

I was in Australia for Christmas seeing my sister and only returned yesterday and am just catching up with my work account.

Your email was a surprise but not a shock. You're not the

first person to contact me about Justin/Nick/whatever his name is today.

Would you like to meet up? I am in London meeting a client on Wednesday. Maybe we could get together somewhere central? Let me know what works.

All the best
Laura

FIFTY-THREE

It is three days into the New Year and Al has completely disappeared.

He went back to his mother's after Boxing Day and at first called Martha every day with increasingly awful updates about the state of her health and the situation in general. But since 30 December, there has been nothing. Not one call. Not one message. Not even on New Year's Eve, which Martha spent alone, drinking the champagne she hadn't had the appetite to drink on Boxing Day. This time, she drinks the whole bottle and wishes she had another one when it is gone.

The childminder has Nala, and the boys went back to school this morning. The shop is open, everything is back to normal. Apart from the fact that Martha's husband is nowhere to be found. For some reason this absence feels different from his previous absences. For some reason, this one feels permanent. Martha doesn't know why she feels this way, but it sits in her gut uncomfortably, like a pebble. She feels agitated and proactive, not anxious and passive as she usually does when he's not here.

The passage from attentive, present husband in the early months and years of their relationship to the constantly absent, unreliable, and non-communicative husband of the past two years had been slow, like water torture: she hadn't noticed it until it was destroying her life.

And then there's the issue of her business accounts. Alistair has been helping her with the finances for Martha's Garden since he gave up his job and started working at the shop full-time. At the time, she'd swallowed down the strange sense of unease she'd felt when handing over the mechanics of her business to him. It was counterintuitive to imagine that your husband, the father of your child, the love of your life, would have anything other than the best and most wholesome of intentions toward the money that paid for the life they enjoyed living.

But there, right in the middle of what had always been a fairly simple balance sheet, is a hole. At first she thinks it is about a thousand pounds. Her stomach roils unpleasantly at the thought that she has cocked up, that someone has ripped her off, that Milly has been milking the till, that something bad has happened, but she immediately calms herself and tells herself that none of these things can be true. And that is when the truth hits her. That it is Alistair. And as she looks deeper into her company finances, she finds more holes: £800 here, £30 there, stock discrepancies that could be put down to shoplifters, but there are genuinely no shoplifters in Enderford, it simply doesn't happen. By the end of that first day back at work, Martha discovers that her business is down nearly £3,000. *Three thousand pounds.* It is all she can do not to run to the toilet and throw up.

Instead, she takes several deep breaths, takes screenshots of absolutely everything, then calls Grace.

Grace comes over that evening with wine. She's a business manager at the local primary school, so has a basic understanding of numbers and knows her way around a spreadsheet. Martha can tell that Grace is yearning to uncover bad things about Alistair, to get some sort of momentum going toward Martha ending her marriage, moving on, cutting free, breaking out.

"You know," says Grace, unscrewing the metal cap from the white wine, "I'm here for you. If you need somewhere to stay, need me to take Nala, the boys, if you need money, whatever it is—you know you only need to ask."

Martha is slightly thrown by this pronouncement. She's not sure she would be able to say the same to anyone in her life. She's known Grace for ten years, since their children joined the local primary school on the same day. She smiles at Grace and says, "Thank you. That's amazing. You're amazing. But hopefully"—she musters a brave laugh—"it won't come to that."

Grace gives her a look that says she doubts very much that Alistair is going to come out of the next hour or so in a good light.

"You need to go to an accountant. First thing," says Grace, an hour and a half later. "And then you need to go to a lawyer. He's been systematically embezzling for weeks, Martha. And he will continue to do so unless you tie a knot in things right now."

Martha nods. She knows Grace is right. But she needs to talk to Alistair first. She needs to hear what he has to say for himself. She sends him a message after Grace has left.

> *I need to talk to you about the company. I'll be seeing a lawyer tomorrow.*

Ten minutes later, Al is on the phone.

"What! Martha! What on earth is going on?"

"What do you mean, *what*? Al, you have been away for seven days. I have not heard from you for four days. You left me alone on New Year's Eve. And today I discovered three thousand pounds missing from my company accounts. And I know it was you, Al. I cannot believe you'd do something like that. To me. To the kids. To *us*."

And then he is crying down the phone. "Oh God, Martha. I'm so sorry. I just . . . it's this thing with my mother. And I couldn't keep asking you for money. It's all so expensive. I thought I could cover it myself, but I've already bled myself dry and—"

She cuts in over him. "Al. Your mother got ill just before Christmas. This has been going on for weeks. And it's not just money—we've got missing stock, high-value things. We've not paid bills, Al. You've signed off invoices to suppliers into cash payments that you've taken out of the business. Three thousand pounds, Al. Who is it for?"

She inhales and waits to hear what he has to say. She can hear his breath down the line, the softness of it. Her beautiful husband.

"Martha," he says. "Listen, there are things, things about me, that you don't know. There are people in my life that I've never told you about. Dangerous people. I made a lot of mistakes when I was younger, I trusted the wrong people. I was on the run so many times. From crooks, from crazy exes, from my psycho fucking father. My whole life I've been scared. I've been alone. I've had to protect myself. Just me. Nobody else. And then I met you and I felt safe for the first time in my life. I felt like I wasn't alone, I felt like I could breathe, Martha. But when I left my job last month, I also felt . . . *adrift*. Unsafe. Like I needed ballast. And the money—I wasn't going to spend it, Martha, I was just going to hold on to it. Just in case. In case you left me. In case something happened. And then something did happen. My mother . . . and now it's all gone, and I am so, so sorry and I will find a way, I promise, to get it back. Every last penny of it. I promise. But for now, I just really need to fix things up here. I need to get my mother into a home. Sort out her finances. And once that's done, Martha, I can sell her house—it's worth about four hundred K, maybe more. I'm working on getting power of attorney before she has her official diagnosis. I'm doing everything I can. And, Martha, please, please forgive me. It was cowardly and terrible of me. It's not who I am. It really isn't. Please, Martha, I want you to trust me. I will never, ever let you down, never again."

And then, in the brief silence that follows Al's last words, Martha hears something in the background of the call. At first she thinks she's imagined it, but then she knows exactly what it is. Somewhere in the close vicinity of her husband who claims to be taking care of his mother in the West Midlands, there is a seagull cawing, and the fizz of waves hitting pebbles.

FIFTY-FOUR

TWO YEARS EARLIER

Paddy Swann is a self-made man. He left school at sixteen, with three O levels. He started working in a local workingmen's caff in Wanstead, near where he was born, and from there he worked his way upward through the dense strata of the London restaurant scene during the late eighties, the whole of the nineties, and into the first year of the new millennium, when he and his wife and their baby daughter took up residence in a big house on the Kent coast. From there he grew a chain of restaurants, starting with a flagship in Whitstable and extending along the coast to two more locations, the newest of which is due to open next year in Ramsgate. He is married with two children, Arlo, who is twenty-one, and Aisling, who is twenty-four. His wife is called Nina and they have been married since 1996. According to the filings on the Companies House website, he made £513K in net profit last year, some of which came from royalties for a pair of recipe books he's written, one in the early noughties and one five years ago.

He has no co-directors apart from his wife. Which means that he has financed his whole micro-operation single-handedly. I'd hoped there might be a rich daddy in the background feeding him fifty-pound notes, fishing him out of choppy waters, making it easy for him. But no, he's a working-class boy from a London Irish family, and his wife appears to have had a similarly unprivileged upbringing.

I think of my own upbringing: the airy, high-ceilinged rooms of the Victorian manor house on the outskirts of the northern market town where I was brought up, the tessellated tiles in the hallway, the ornate cornicing, apple trees in the back garden, an XJ-S in the front driveway, glossy magazines fanned out on tables, fresh flowers in vases everywhere. I think about my mother's wardrobe of designer clothes that were fashionable at the time: Cacharel, Liberty, jeans by Sasson. My father only wore suits, except for holidays, when he wore a selection of extraordinary, now I come to think of it, colorful terry-cloth tops with zips with circular metal pulls. We had money for European holidays, for musical instruments and pony-riding lessons and good cuts of meat, and for mod cons like vacuum cleaners and microwaves and SodaStream machines. I was brought up with everything a boy could need. And I cannot bear that now I have nothing. I cannot bear that I have to sleep with women to whom I am not attracted simply to keep my bank balance healthy enough to make myself attractive to the woman I love. I cannot bear that Paddy Swann gets to live with his wife and children in a big house in a desirable location and earn half a million pounds a year and be lauded and loved and have people turn at the sight of him and say, *Oh, that must be Paddy himself.*

I want to be *himself.* The one who turns the heads. Who sleeps at night knowing that he has created something, built something. Why does everything I try to build crumble on impact with reality? And is it too late for me to start building something now?

The daughter works for a lifestyle publishing house in Bloomsbury. She shares a flat with two other young women in a part of London with which I am unfamiliar, somewhere in the Docklands. She is very slight, has her fine hair tied up, a slick of black liner on the lids of her eyes in a vaguely Parisian style. She wears cropped jackets with pockets set high so that her elbows stick out like bird wings, and huge headphones and leather boots. She is very pretty and very weird.

How do I know all of this? Well, it's very easy to find young people on the internet, especially when they have an unusual name like Aisling Swann. I've been all over her social media and I know what coffee she likes, and I know what she looked like when she had sunburn in Zante in 2019, and I know that she is a daddy's girl and that she bites her fingernails. I know she likes obscure music from the eighties and nineties, that she's vegan, and that she loves Timothée Chalamet. The captions on her posts make no sense half the time and I can't work out if she is pretentious or has some kind of learning disability. But her friends respond to her posts as though she has said something normal, so maybe this is just how they talk to each other these days.

I also know what she smells like. Musky and sweet, a scent that reminds me of a perfume from the Body Shop that all the girls wore in the eighties. I shared a tube carriage with her the other night. I stood very close, but in a way that was unavoidable due to the rush hour crush. I tried not to press myself against her as I didn't want her to notice me, but I did inhale the smell of her, the freshness of her scalp. I did notice the tiny golden hoop pierced into the top part of her ear, the roots of her hair showing her natural mousy tones.

I sat in the same pub as her the week after. I had a newspaper and a pint of cold lager and I wore a baseball cap. I didn't look in her direction. But I listened in to her conversation with the two girls she lives with, and it transpires that she has a crush on her boss. His name is Ritchie Lloyd. He's the publishing director. In his photo on the company website, he has a sharp face, dark hair that flops heavily to one side, good teeth, a casual white linen shirt, a suntan. He is in his forties and looks, it occurs to me, like he could be Timothée Chalamet's father. He is also, according to his bio, married with two children.

I throw a glance across the pub at Aisling Swann and reappraise her.

"You wouldn't do anything, would you?" asks one of her friends, the edge of her lip pinned down by her teeth.

"No," Aisling replies breathlessly. "No. Of course I wouldn't. Genuinely. There's like not one iota of my person that would want anything to happen."

"You know he has a place in Ibiza? With a pool?"

"Uh," says the other girl. "Of course he has."

"Christ," says Aisling. "Stop it. I need to stop thinking things. You're not helping. Tell me he goes kayaking every weekend. Tell me he likes watching trains." She groans, almost orgasmically, and then a large group arrives and I can no longer hear the conversation. I fold up my paper, finish my beer, take the empty glass to the bar, and head home to Martha.

FIFTY-FIVE

TWO YEARS EARLIER

We have a baby now, Martha and I. Nala. She is two months old. It was my idea to have a baby. I do love children. Animals and children are what keep me from the darkness. You would think, possibly, from the sorts of things I've done, that I inhabit a dark place. You would assume that people who do dark things must think dark thoughts and have dark dreams and feel blackness all around them. But no, not at all. Most of the time I would ascribe a kind of muted greeny-blue to the color of my existence. Nothing too bright, nothing too delicate, just a bland midrange color. Obviously, different moods and hormonal changes affect the color, but it is never black. And I put that down to love, to children, to food, to dogs, to finding the perfect pair of shoes, the way the light catches a woman's hair, the top of her cheekbone. I'm not all bad, in other words.

And this baby, this child, my God, she is exquisite. I'd imagined a struggle to get pregnant at our ages. Martha was forty-five when she found out, forty-six when the baby came. All natural. No IVF, no fertility treatment, a smooth pregnancy, a good birth, a healthy baby. She has golden hair and blue eyes and thick eyelashes and soft feet that I can't stop kissing. She makes shapes out of her mouth that delight me and amuse me. I feel sure that she is the best and most beautiful baby in the world. And yes, I know I have had other babies, and of course I felt the same for them as I feel for Nala. But the difference is the way I feel about Martha. The boys I had with Amanda were tainted in many ways by the way I felt about Amanda. The girls I had with Laura were tainted by the way I felt about her, especially toward the end, when I couldn't even bear to look at her. Thankfully, Tara and I did not procreate. But Nala came from me and Martha, a perfect union.

Martha says she is tired. She says that carrying a baby, delivering a baby, taking care of a baby, when you are in your forties is ten times harder than doing it in your twenties and thirties. I can tell she is ashamed of the way her body looks. She told me it took her five years to get it back to normal after Jonah was born, and now she is back at square one, except older. But she looks beautiful to me.

My father was uxorious toward my mother—I always found it quite revolting—and in many, if not all, of my previous relationships I have played the role of the uxorious husband to a T. Subtly, of course, because modern women do not want to feel smothered or controlled. I make my feelings very clear and plain because that is what women want. Transparency. But this is the first time, the very first time, I have not had to play the role. And it scares me sometimes. It scares me that I worry about her leaving me. That I worry about her tiring of me. I've never worried about a woman getting bored by me before. Or at least not before I was bored by them.

I want more for Martha, and more for Nala. I want more for me, for fuck's sake.

I have a client in Hastings. She lives in a penthouse flat in a twenties block overlooking the sea. It's carpeted from edge to edge in a thick cream deep-pile, all the furniture is white and gold, and her bed has a net canopy with lace trim. The whole apartment smells of dead marriages and lonely nights and adult children who never visit. Her name is Jessie, and she is almost seventy. Like all my clients, she keeps herself in good condition, but she is very much at the upper end of what I can stomach, age-wise.

She was in her fifties the first time I met her, not far off the age I am now, and in a way, we have become friends. She doesn't ask too many questions, just enough to make me feel like a human being, and she is very gentle and very clever. Her husband died quite suddenly of a brain aneurysm in his early fifties and she couldn't stomach the dating scene, so she found me. I like her very much. I almost toyed with the idea of entering into a romantic relationship with her in the early days, especially when I realized that she was sitting on all her dead husband's investments. ("I don't need the money," she'd said. "What's the point? I'll let it sit there and gather interest and then the kids can have it when I'm gone.") But I realized that was never going to be what she wanted from me, far from it.

I arrange to visit her a few days after Nala turns two months old. I haven't seen her for over a year—I think she was starting to get used to the idea of life without sex—but I need a reason to be by the coast and Jessie gives me one.

The lift opens directly into her apartment and she greets me sweetly with a hug. I tell her she looks gorgeous, and she tells me I look as wonderful as ever, and she makes us each a G & T, which we drink on her balcony even though it's late January and the temperature is barely hitting double figures. She tells me that she'll pay me for my visit either way, but she's not entirely sure she wants to have sex.

"Nothing personal." She rests her hand over mine and smiles. "Just a feeling I have that I am moving on. Somewhere. No idea where!" She laughs. "But I'm glad you got in touch as I felt bad about not saying a proper goodbye to you, after all these years."

I feel a muscle in my cheek twitch as I sense in the air between us that something is coming. My breath catches and I try to keep my face neutral.

"I want to give you something." She touches my knee and then gets up and heads indoors and I bite my lip to stop myself smiling because I can't help thinking that she is going to give me money, or at the very least something of monetary value.

She returns with something wrapped in a handkerchief. Before she unwraps it, she turns to me and says, "I worry about you, André. I know you say you're happy, but I don't believe you. A man like you should have a family, a life, a future."

My flesh ripples with goose bumps.

"Here." She unwraps the contents of the handkerchief. Inside is a pebble.

A pebble.

She passes it to me, and I throw her a questioning look.

"I picked this up on the beach when I was twenty-one. Just down there." She gestures below. "The day we moved into this apartment. I put it in my pocket, and I said to myself, Jessie Bland, you have your whole life ahead of you, but this pebble will be here long after you've gone. Someone else might pick it up one day and carry it with them for a while. So, I want you to have it now. And I want you to think of me when you look at it. And I want you to think of your future. And once you've found your way, I want you to pass this pebble on to someone else who's lost. Will you do that for me? Do you promise?"

I blink, very slowly, and stare at the pebble. The pebble is nondescript, verging on ugly, and Jessie's accompanying monologue is trite and meaningless. I have no idea what she was thinking, and I have no idea what to say. Rage pulses gently at my temples, my fist closes hard over the pebble, I make my face into a pleasant smile, and I say, "Yes. I promise." But then, from nowhere, more words appear. "Ha!" I say quite forcefully. "For a minute there I thought you were going to give me something valuable! To set me up in a new life!" I laugh, overloudly, so that she thinks I am making a joke. But I can tell she knows I mean it and she gives me a sympathetic look that makes me feel quite murderous.

"Oh, André," she says, folding the handkerchief neatly into a square. "I wish I could. I would love to give you everything. But those wretched children of mine—I can't do that to them. That would be an act of such cruel vindictiveness, I couldn't live with myself."

Her words hit me like a slingshot to the gullet. I picture my mother, although I was not there to witness the moment, sitting at a big leather-topped desk in her solicitor's office thirty years ago, signing the piece of paper that robbed me of my inheritance, that changed the course of my life, that brought me from there to here. And then, in my mind's eye, my mother's face morphs into Jessie's face, and I picture myself forcing the pebble deep down Jessie's throat. I picture it so clearly that for a moment I almost imagine I might do it. But that moment passes, the swishing and swooping in my head subsides, the ringing in my eardrums quietens. I tuck the pebble into my pocket, and I pat Jessie's hand. "I understand," I say. "I was only kidding you. Of course I don't want your money."

"Just my body, yes," she replies with a wink that almost turns my stomach.

"Exactly," I reply. "Exactly."

When I leave Jessie's apartment half an hour later, I remove the pebble from my pocket and toss it forcefully across the beach, where it lands with a smack against the others. It feels symbolic in some way, but I'm not sure how.

In my other pocket is the envelope of cash that Jessie insisted I take with me, even though we didn't have sex—£500. And in the inside pocket of my jacket is a man's watch. In my haste to take it, I could not tell if it was of any value, but I couldn't bear to leave her house with nothing. The watch was in a drawer, inside a box, beneath some paperwork and a tangle of chains and necklaces. She might wonder if it was me, when she notices. She might even report it to the police. And if she does? So what? André doesn't even have a surname, let alone any other form of identification. And how would she explain my presence in her home? A fifty-three-year-old man of no fixed abode. A man who, if traced by the police, would simply tell them what he was—a male sex worker for whose services she had been paying for over fifteen years. And what would her precious children think of that?

I pull the watch out of my pocket once I am in my car and examine it. It's a Cartier. Then I put the car into drive and head for a village along the coast from here called the Riviera.

Nina Swann wears utility-style jeans, quirky knitwear, and oversized reading glasses. Her hair is dyed an improbable shade of dark mahogany with a blunt fringe and she drives an electric car. She is, I should mention, very beautiful, but really not my type. Too tall. Too angular. Too tomboyish, almost. And I have aways preferred blondes.

Every Tuesday and Thursday from twelve until five, she goes to work at an upmarket fruit-and-vegetable importer in Dover where she sits at the reception desk in their rough-hewn, bare-brick warehouse. At three o'clock on these days, she goes to the café next door for an afternoon snack.

I am sitting across from her in that café right now, wearing Jessie's dead husband's Cartier watch and scrolling through my phone. Nina orders a green tea and a muffin to take away. She is chatty with the young man behind the counter and has a slightly flat northern tone to her voice, one I recognize as being from the east of the North, not the west, from where I come. Maybe Harrogate? Beverley? I wonder how she ended up down here with a short man from Wanstead. I wonder how they met. I wonder what it was about him that appealed to her.

A bit of rough, maybe? Or maybe Paddy Swann is somehow, in a way that is impossible for me to register, sexy? He wasn't rich when they met, that came later, so he must have been doing something, consciously or not, to make himself appear desirable. I wonder what Nina Swann would make of me. I feel physically at least we would make a better fit. Though possibly not stylistically. I am more traditional than she is. She wouldn't like my sports jacket. She probably wouldn't like my immaculate pale green polo shirt either. But would she like me? My height? My presence? My beauty? For a moment, I want her to look at me so that I can see how she reacts, but then I remember that I don't want her to notice me, not yet. So I move my gaze away from her and back to the screen of my phone, where I google the value of a Cartier watch the same style and model as the one on my wrist and discover that it is worth only £800. When I look up again, Nina Swann has taken her green tea and her muffin and headed into work.

FIFTY-SIX

Jane Trevally is waiting for Ash under the kissing couple statue on the top concourse at St. Pancras station. She is wearing a huge green parka with a fur-trimmed hood and dark sunglasses, even though the sun has yet to come out this year.

She greets Ash with a hug and says, "Happy New Year," and Ash feels a strange surge of affection toward her, this woman she has known for only a few weeks.

They walk toward the street and cross over to the Standard hotel, where they find three low-slung armchairs in the lounge in front of a large sixties-style open fire. As they watch the door opposite for the woman called Laura to arrive, Ash feels her stomach swirl with anticipation and anxiety—and also a touch of excitement. What will this woman tell them? What will they know about Nick Radcliffe in one hour's time that they do not know now? And how will this new information reshape the landscape of Ash's life, which has already been rendered almost untraversable by the senseless death of her father?

Jane is being chatty, but Ash can tell that she is distracted too. She's telling Ash about her Christmas with her first husband and his new wife and their baby, plus her oldest stepson and stepdaughter, who both hate the new wife and, by extension, the baby, and there are anecdotes about dogs doing unspeakable things and stepchildren doing unspeakable things and it all sounds like she's making it up, just to be entertaining, but Ash is pretty sure she isn't.

And then a woman appears in the entranceway, looking around uncertainly. Jane stands and glances at Ash to check that it's OK for her to take the lead, then gestures the woman over.

"Hi," she says, her hand outstretched. "I'm Jane Trevally. And this is Ash. Thank you so, so much for agreeing to meet us. We're very grateful."

Jane fusses around the woman for a moment, taking her coat, ordering her a coffee and a sparkling water, making the whole thing a little less weird, but then it is quiet and Laura, who is a pale woman with large eyes, a small nose, and fine blond hair that she constantly tucks behind her ears, looks from Jane to Ash and says, "So. What do you want to know?"

"Well," says Jane. "We should probably start at the beginning. How did you meet him?"

At this question, a peachy blush hits Laura's cheeks and her eyes mist over, and she looks like she is revisiting a precious moment. "We met . . . well, he was my life coach."

"Oh," says Ash with a small gasp. "Right. And where did you find him? I mean, was he advertising? Or did someone recommend him?"

"Weirdly enough, he approached me on the street. I thought he was one of those charity collectors at first, but then he said he was offering special rates for his life-coaching consultancy because he'd just moved to the area and needed a new client base. He said my first session would be free and then if I wanted to continue, it would be fifty pounds an hour as opposed to a hundred pounds an hour, and I took his details and did a google on him, saw that he had a few five-star reviews, and thought, Well, I have nothing to lose."

"What did you think of him? When you first saw him?"

The peachy glow reappears, and it occurs to Ash that Laura is still in love with him. "I thought he was preposterously good-looking. Way too good-looking to be selling life-coaching classes on the streets of Cambridge. I thought maybe it was a scam, that he was a front for something because of his looks and I'd end up in a dungeon with a dozen other women, become a sex slave or something." She laughs drily. "But I looked up where he said he worked, and they were lovely serviced offices near the Market Square, and I thought, Hmm, maybe he is legit, and I did actually want a life coach, that was the weird thing. How did he know? When he approached me? It was like he had a sixth sense about me. Knew exactly what I wanted. And that was kind of how it was for all the years we were together—he always knew exactly what I wanted. And he gave it to me. And then, when he couldn't give me what I wanted, he'd find a way to make me believe that I didn't want it. He had this way . . . he used to cry. Well, not cry as such, but his eyes. They were so blue, and they'd fill up with tears and . . ."

She stops, pulls in a breath, aware it seems like she has been getting carried away. "Anyway," she continues, "I went to the first session, and I thought he was good. But more than that, I thought he was the most beautiful man in the world. Beautiful, charming, gentle, interested in me. I went back for a few more sessions and he told me about his fiancée who'd died, just a few weeks before their wedding. Ruth. And I told him about my first husband, who left me for my sister."

"Your sister!"

"Yes. Don't." She pushes the concept away with a wave of her hands. "Anyway, after our fifth session he asked me out for dinner, and of course I said yes because I'm pretty sure I was already in love with him by then. I was nearly thirty. Aching to be with someone. And this man, this beautiful man . . ." She smiles grimly. "What a fucking grade-A idiot I was. Falling for it all."

Ash and Jane exchange looks. "So, when did you know?"

"That he was a bad man?"

Ash feels a sharp chill pass through her. "So, is he?" she says. "A bad man?"

Laura sighs and places her coffee carefully back onto the saucer. "It's not that simple. For such a long time, he made me so happy. Our life—it was perfect. He was attentive and loving. He was a wonderful father. He worked hard. He made us the center of his world. And then one day he just started disappearing. Said his mother was ill, somewhere in the Midlands. Never very specific about where, never let me go with him. Said his relationship with his mother was toxic and difficult, and he didn't want me to be involved. But whenever he went, he'd turn off his phone. He said he had some kind of disorder that meant he compartmentalized too much. Said he'd always been that way. Said he had severe ADHD. He said, *oh*—" She closes her eyes and rolls back her head. "He said so much. He always had answers, always had so many words. But he never got angry, he never shouted. He always knew how to calm me down. He'd get those tear-filled eyes of his. And all I wanted was for everything to be like it was when things were good, and that's what people don't understand about abusive marriages. About toxic relationships. That it's not bad *all the time*. Or at least, it wasn't for us. When he was home, when he was there, life was perfect. He was perfect."

"So, what happened. Why did it end?"

"He just disappeared. *Boom.*" Laura makes a tiny nuclear mushroom cloud with her hands. "Gone. The girls were so young. It was so hard to explain. He sent me a message. Here. Look. I kept it." She fiddles inside her handbag for a minute and brings out her phone. She scrolls to the screenshot on her roll and shows it to them:

> Darling Laura,
>
> My mother is killing me. I can't come back. I am broken. I love you. I love the girls. Please forgive me.
>
> Jxxx

Ash gasps quietly. "Oh my God."

"I assumed he'd killed himself," Laura says, putting the phone back into her bag. "I thought it was a suicide note. I told the police, but there was nothing they could do without knowing where he was. After a few weeks, I reported him as a missing person, but I could tell they didn't think he was in danger. That if he'd killed himself, he'd be found at some point, and if he hadn't killed himself, then he was probably off living his best life without me, and that was that. I was just left adrift. Floating. And then I started getting bills. Credit card statements. Loans I hadn't agreed to take out. Fifteen thousand pounds' worth of debt. All him.

"And then at last I knew. He wasn't dead. He'd scammed me. Can you believe it? An eight-year-long scam! Two children! Memories. Love. Marriage. So much joy. A true, true thing—it was a true, true thing. But all a façade, for fifteen thousand pounds. Jesus Christ, I'd have given him fifteen thousand pounds if he'd asked. And I probably did, all in, over the years. The things—the money for equipment for his business, I gave him thousands for that. And . . . oh God!" she groans. "The student of his who'd been scammed by a con man out of all her life savings! He told me her story and he had the wet eyes, and I said, let's give her something. A thousand pounds! I gave that woman who probably didn't even exist a thousand pounds! When I think back on it, I gave away thousands and thousands, but all of it felt legitimate. All of it felt like it was making things better. Making our life better. And then he fucks off and runs up fifteen grand's worth of more debt in my name, and argh!" She emits a small, animal roar. "So embarrassing. So humiliating. I couldn't tell anyone. I didn't tell anyone. I moved away from Cambridge, so I wouldn't have to answer any questions. And then four years ago . . ."

Ash pulls in her breath and waits for Laura to continue.

"Four years ago, I was contacted by a woman called Emma Greenlaw. She'd done exactly what you two have done. She'd found Jonathan's defunct web page for his life-coaching company on some kind of archiving website and somehow traced it back to me. She'd just reported her mother missing to the police. Her mother, Tara she was called, she'd been married to a man called Jonathan Truscott. Emma told me that Tara had ended the marriage and then followed him to the Cotswolds, where she saw him with another woman. He and this woman were having some kind of romantic getaway together, apparently. Then she followed him back to London, went to a flat in Tooting to confront him—"

Ash and Jane exchange looks. "Tooting," Ash hisses under her breath.

Jane says, "Nick Radcliffe claims to live in Tooting."

"Oh," says Laura. "Well, there's a connection then. Anyway, Emma's mum, Tara, went to confront him there, to tell him she knew about his affair, about him lying. She called Emma to tell her what she was doing. Emma told her not to, told her it wasn't safe. But she didn't listen to her, she went there, and she never came home."

The air chills. A dark shiver runs through Ash, and she exchanges another look with Jane. "Seriously?" she asks breathlessly.

Laura nods. "Emma said her mum sent her a weird message the next day saying that she'd spent the night talking to Jonathan and that they were going to give it another go. Emma didn't believe it at first, but the messages kept coming for the next few days. Then, after a few weeks, her mother said she was in the Algarve, starting a new life with Jonathan, and that was the last straw. Emma went to the police and reported her as missing. There was a police investigation, they found CCTV footage of Emma's mum leaving the flat in Tooting twenty hours after she got there, then more footage of her getting on a train to Reading, but that was it. She never got off the train. She was never seen again. And they saw footage of Jonathan in the area in the hours and days after Emma's mother left, visiting shops, coming and going from the apartment, which meant he had an alibi, but when they went to the flat in Tooting there was nobody there, it was empty. They called off the investigation, or at least in terms of Jonathan Truscott's involvement, and that was that. But Emma didn't want to let it go and she's been building up this, like, dossier kind of thing. A record of all the women she can find who have had any sort of interaction with Justin/Jonathan/Nick/whoever. And there are women in this dossier who have had all sorts of bizarre and unsettling interactions with him. You know he's a street stalker?"

"A . . . ?"

"He follows women at close quarters, strangers, to make them feel uncomfortable."

Ash throws Jane a terrible look.

"Are you serious?"

"Mm-hmm. There's CCTV footage. He was even reported to the police for it once about four years ago. That was why he and Tara split up for a while. The police came and spoke to him, according to Emma, but nothing ever happened. Not enough evidence." Laura shrugs and turns her coffee cup around on its saucer.

"But we have him!" says Ash. "He's in my house. Right now. Living with my mum. I mean . . . this could be it. We could trap him. Stop him getting away again. Stop him doing this to anyone else."

"Don't underestimate him," says Laura, a shadow passing across her face. "Seriously. He's always one step ahead. He can make people do anything he wants them to do."

After Laura leaves, Ash and Jane sit for a moment in a sharp silence.

"What shall we do now?" asks Ash.

"Well, for a start, we need to talk to this Emma Greenlaw. And then"—Jane pauses and touches the arm of her chair with her fingertips—"we need to talk to your mum."

"We?"

"I mean, I could come? If you want? I know that you said you and your mother, your relationship is a bit strained? That she doesn't always trust you? Maybe if I came too?"

Ash blinks hard. What would be worse, she wonders, to come home and tell her mother that she's been investigating her new boyfriend and that he's a serial scammer and a sex offender, or come home and tell her mum that she's been investigating her new boyfriend with the help of Mad Jane Trevally?

She shakes her head, then nods, then says, "I'll think about it."

FIFTY-SEVEN

Nick has been cooking. There is a smell of garlic in the air, something on the hob exuding spice and heat, a damp tea towel on the counter. The recycling bin, when Ash lifts the lid, is full of unfamiliar packaging, and a pan of uncooked rice is soaking in cloudy water next to the hob. She exhales slowly. This man who steals women's money and abandons children and follows women on the street for kicks, this man who lies and finagles and uses people, this man has been in her kitchen cooking food with her dead father's kitchen utensils, and for a moment Ash is subsumed by so much violent rage that her vision turns purple. She resists the urge to lift up the casserole dish with both hands and hurl it across the room and breathes in hard to make herself think straight. She cannot scare this man away. Not yet. She needs to let him breathe, settle, think he's found a place to rest his hat, a family to manipulate. So, when Nick walks into the kitchen a minute later, she turns and hits him with a radiant smile.

"Christ, Nick," she says, "it smells amazing in here. What are you making?"

His face lights up. "Oh," he says, looking pathetically happy. "It's a railway curry."

"A what?"

"Don't you know?" he asks playfully. "It's all the rage. Based on what they used to serve up on the Indian railways. Lamb and potatoes. Pretty easy, just needs some time to sit."

"Well," she says lightly, "it smells amazing. But I'll have to pass, being vegan and all."

"I thought of that," he says, and then goes to the fridge and pulls out a bowl of vegetable curry. "Same spices, no ghee, no meat, one hundred percent pure vegan. You can heat it up whenever you want. Should last a few days."

She smiles at him and says, "God, that's so sweet. Thank you!"

"You're very welcome. Least I can do. I do get it," he says, turning so that his back is against the counter, folding his arms across his stomach, one ankle angled across the other. "I do get that it's a big deal having me here. That it's probably not what you wanted. I get that you're used to having your mum to yourself, having all this"—he rolls his eyes in an arc around the huge open kitchen—"space to yourself. And that me being here is probably really, really annoying. Not to mention that I'm stepping into places that used to belong exclusively to your father. That must be really hard for you. I see all of this. And I see you. And I swear that I will never overstep boundaries. And I will never, ever hurt your mother. I hope you believe me. Your mother. She's . . ." He stops for a beat and sighs. When he looks back at her there is a thin sheen of tears across his eyes. He smiles a watery smile and says, "She's safe with me. Really."

He smiles the watery smile again and touches the corner of his eye delicately with a fingertip, then turns back to the casserole and lifts the lid, sniffs and stirs, closes the lid. Ash contemplates his back.

"Oh," she says lightly. "By the way, that soap you bought me for Christmas? It's amazing! And I want to buy some for my friend for her birthday next week and I've looked all over the internet for the shop, but I just can't find it."

She watches his back and sees a bolt of alarm pass through him, straight up his spine. Then she sees it soften again, but the delay was there, and she already knows that anything that comes out of his mouth at this moment will be a lie.

"You know," he says, turning to face her, his expression soft and thoughtful. "I might have told a little fib about those soaps. Or at the very least been a little economical with the truth. I did buy them from a shop in Mayfair. But it was about four years ago and they were for a woman I was seeing, but she broke it off and I put them away and then dug them out for you, and the shop has probably closed down now, probably another Covid casualty. And yes, classic man. I know. And I'm sorry. But you liked them? Yes?"

"I did," she says with a big smile. "I loved them. That's why I wanted to buy them for my friend too. Never mind."

"Yes," he says. "Never mind."

He turns back to the casserole dish and Ash stares at his back for one more moment before leaving him. Soap does not keep its scent for four years. Old soap smells of nothing but fat. And the soap Nick bought her for Christmas smells so intensely of its ingredients that she can smell it even before she walks into her bathroom.

She grabs her phone and sends a message to Jason, Marcelline's farrier ex.

> *Hi Jason it's Ash again. Sorry to bother you, but can you tell me where your mum lived? Or where she used to do her shopping? Still trying to track down these stupid soaps! And thanks in advance.*

A message appears a minute later.

> *No worries Ash. She lived in a village called Newington. Nearest town was Enderford. But she did most of her shopping online bless her. Parcel deliveries every five minutes. So they could have come from anywhere.*

Good luck. Say hi to Marcy, don't forget to tell her I'm still single lol

Ash goes straight to her browser and types in "shops enderford kent."

She scrolls down looking for a gift shop, a pharmacy, a boutique, any kind of shop that would sell fancy soaps, but there's nothing. Just a butcher, a farm shop, a florist, an art shop, a pet shop, a bookshop, and a delicatessen. She looks at the time: 6:05. All the shops have closed by now. She'll try calling them in the morning.

FIFTY-EIGHT

Martha pulls up outside the empty restaurant in Folkestone. Its plate-glass windows are plastered from the inside with graphics advertising its coming incarnation as a Turkish barbecue restaurant and she can hear sounds of drilling and banging coming from within. She finds a place to park just around the corner and heads back.

It's ten on a damp Friday morning. She's left Milly in charge of the shop and feels a heightened sense of panic about how she should be getting on with the day's orders and deliveries, but she also knows she cannot focus, cannot concentrate, until she has confirmed her suspicions about Al's current whereabouts one way or the other. As if to fuel her resolve, the sound of a seagull cawing overhead breaks into her thoughts, reminding her why she's here.

She stands at the closed door of the restaurant for a moment, knocking tentatively and then a little louder before pushing the door and entering. Three men turn and stare at her. A fourth man, wearing a high-vis vest over a smart jumper and trousers, approaches her and says, "Sorry, madam, you can't be in here, it's a building site. Health and safety."

"Could I just ask you something? Quickly."

The man sighs, puts a clipboard down on a shelf, and gestures to her to leave the building with him. On the pavement, he closes the door behind him and looks at her with polite impatience.

"This place," she says. "Are you in charge of the development?"

"Yes. I'm the site manager. If you have any complaints, or—"

"No," she cuts in. "No. Nothing like that. I just wondered if you knew this man." She pulls out her phone and shows him a photograph of Al. "His name is Alistair Grey. I think he's doing some work with the owners of this place? He's been on-site a couple of times?"

The man peers at the photo and enlarges it with his fingertips. "No," he says decisively. "No. I don't know this man. I've never seen him. He's not involved with this project or with the owners of the project. I'm sorry."

"Good," she says. "Thank you. That's helpful."

He nods and then turns and heads back into the restaurant.

Martha sighs. She'd known already that this place was just a cover for something else Al was doing the day the tracker had followed him here.

She gets back into her car and looks up the big white seaside house on her Maps app. It's a seven-minute drive from here. She presses start on the app and heads out of Folkestone.

The house sits on top of a cliff, up a winding road with three full hairpin bends along its course. It lies between two equally handsome white houses and has a wide portico in its middle and tall windows on both sides allowing dual-aspect views to the sea and, Martha assumes, the coast of northern France. Even on a day like this, with the sky a thick, patchy gray, the sun a milky smudge where the clouds come apart, the sea a pebble-dashed expanse of dirty beige, it is truly exquisite. There is no car parked outside this house, no signs of life inside. Martha gets out of her car and goes to the front door. She rings the bell and clears her throat. Nobody comes. She waits a moment more and then walks from the portico to the side window. Here, she can see into a huge open-plan kitchen, all very trendy and unfitted, with open shelves, jars, rough-hewn pottery, a wine rack built into the wall. There's a large farmhouse-style table covered in family detritus—paperwork, books, a scarf, charging cables, makeup—so a woman lives here, clearly. Her stomach clenches and unclenches. She looks for signs of Al, but can't see any.

She goes to the window on the other side of the house. Through this one she sees a huge double reception room, a large circular dining table closest to the window, a big jute bowl at its center filled with pomegranates and some other unidentifiable fruits. This leads through to a living area—low-slung chairs, a gigantic modular sofa, views through a picture window out to the sea through a frame of cedar trees and palms. The walls are filled with colorful art and there are plants everywhere and it is, Martha realizes, exactly as she would decorate such a house, all so very much to her taste, and as she thinks this, her eye is caught by a cluster of photographs on a cabinet to the side of the dining table and she sees a lovely woman with very dark hair and a blunt fringe, trendy sunglasses, dark lips. She stands behind a teenage girl with pale hair, wide eyes, a pierced nose, and a similar-looking boy, the tallest in the photograph by half a foot. And there, with his arm around all three of them, is a nice-looking man in a band T-shirt and jeans, floppy fair hair falling over his brow, sunglasses on his head, a tattoo of some kind on his forearm, and he is immediately familiar to Martha.

She knows who he is, and whose house this is. It's Paddy Swann. The man who owned the beautiful restaurant Al had taken her to in Whitstable a couple of years ago, that lovely, kind man with the sweet smile who had come to their table and asked how they had enjoyed their meal. He also owned the restaurant where Al had bought a bottle of champagne the night that Nala had been ill, when he said he'd been sleeping in the staff room of a hotel. And Martha knows that this man is dead now, because after she found that receipt in Alistair's coat pocket, she had googled the restaurant and seen the news articles about Paddy Swann being pushed under the wheels of a tube train at Leicester Square on a Wednesday night about fifteen months ago.

Which means this amazing house must now belong to Paddy's widow, a woman called Nina, according to the news articles.

And there it is; it falls into place. Her husband is having an affair with Nina Swann. He is living here in this beautiful house, with its large, airy rooms and its tasteful furnishings and its quirky teenagers and its views and all the money that is clearly a part of the life of Nina Swann. He lives here, pretending, no doubt, that Martha does not exist. That Nala does not exist. That Jonah and Troy do not exist. That her perfect cottage that she is so proud of and has worked so hard on, her business and her life and her choices and her priorities and her body and her hair and her love and her joy, and all the things that make Martha *Martha*, do not exist, that they all pale and fade and shrink and die in the light of all of this. And this is what he wanted, after all. A rich woman. A view of the sea. Another life. This is where he's been. This place. Here.

FIFTY-NINE

TWENTY-ONE MONTHS AGO

How do I explain my obsession with Paddy Swann? I can't. But for a while it takes over my life. I pore over his website, over the details of his life. I buy his cookbooks, which are full of staged "lifestyle" photos of him and his restaurants and his home and his family, and I read them from cover to cover. I want to understand him, this average man with his above-average life. I want to emulate it somehow. But more than that, I want to ruin it.

There. I said it. Call me petty. Call me tragic. But I cannot forget the way he talked to me that night back in the early 1990s when I was just starting out in my life, and I cannot forget the way he touched my wife that night, the way he pushed his body against the back of her chair, the way he acted as though I did not exist. I cannot forget the disgust and the embarrassment of that moment in his restaurant a year ago. I have never felt like this before. Vindictive, I think, is the best word to describe it.

Yes.

I am vindictive.

A few months into my surveillance of the Swann family, I learn that Nina Swann is having an affair.

He is younger than her. Possibly, it occurs to me, the same age as Ash's crush, Ritchie Lloyd. They meet for lunch at a café in Folkestone. They hold hands under the table. I take a surreptitious photograph. He is tall and his hair, although he is young, is on the verge of turning white, just as mine did in my early forties. I'd been appalled at the time, contemplated dying it, I recall, even took to wearing a baseball cap to cover it up. But then, as my early forties drifted toward my late forties and I felt respectably old rather than the wrong side of young, the salt and pepper turned silver and soon I realized that it was a blessing. *Mad Men* was all the rage at the time and the expression "silver fox" was being bandied about and I embraced my silver hair and made it my pride and joy. My USP, in fact. There is a certain type of woman who cannot resist a well-dressed man with a full head of prematurely silver hair. And now, from this side of the busy café, it looks as if Nina Swann might be one of them.

I follow him afterward. He works at a record shop in the trendy, creative corner of the town. I wonder how they met. I wonder how long it's been going on. He seems to be shy and slightly awkward. I can't imagine him having a wife and family at home. It feels more likely that he's a "failure to launch" specimen, maybe even still at home with his parents. They meet again a couple of days later. I told Martha I was working with a fledgling pub with rooms in Folkestone. What I'm actually doing is staying at a pub with rooms in Folkestone. It's cheap and perfectly pleasant, nice touches, stylish bathrooms, a view, if I stretch onto my tiptoes, of the sea. This is how all-consuming my obsession has become—I am spending my own money in order to carry out my surveillance of this man and his family. The awful thing is that I'm quite enjoying it. Maybe I should have been a detective. A spy. I once thought about pretending I was a spy to explain my erratic behavior to an ex, but I realized I had no idea what spies actually do.

This time, Nina and her lover meet at night in a kind of back-street dive bar with vinyl-covered banquettes and movie posters on the walls and a putrid watery-red light over everything. They sit in a dark corner, which I feel is quite brazen—her undertaking a visible affair in this town so close to where she lives, close to the parents of the children her children went to school with, her colleagues, her husband's colleagues. For a moment, I wonder if I imagined the physical contact between them in the café two days earlier. They chat easily now, but I don't see any contact, any touching. Maybe they are just friends? Maybe, when your husband works every single night of his life and your children both live away from home and you are clinging on to the last vestiges of your hotness by your black-painted fingernails, just being in the company of a younger man who thinks you're amazing is enough to fill the vacuum? Maybe it's a little ego boost, nothing more?

I stare at my phone and nurse my gin and tonic and keep my head down. A few minutes later, they finish the dregs of their drinks and silently leave the bar, heading, as I follow surreptitiously behind them, for a door to the side of the bar that leads to a block of three apartments upstairs. I see a window light up on the second floor, then the swish of a drawn curtain.

His name is Ethan. He is forty-one. He does in fact have a child, a ten-year-old daughter who lives in Romania with her mother and comes to visit him once a year. The apartment above the bar is owned by the same man who owns both the bar and the record store where Ethan works. According to the details I found online from a defunct property listing, it is a large studio with a kitchenette, a small bathroom, and steps off the main room to a small terrace and a fire escape at the back. I wonder what Ethan's studio apartment smells like. I try to picture his bedding. I see stains in my mind's eye. I imagine a tidemark on the pillowcase. A fridge full of organic beer and past-its-sell-by-date ham. Toothpaste scum in the bathroom sink. I have formed, very quickly and very easily, a rather poor opinion of Ethan, an opinion that inevitably filters through to my opinion of Nina Swann herself.

I spend a few days at home after that, just to recalibrate everything, to remind Martha what a wonderful life we have together, to reinforce for her that she chose the right man. We work on the garden together, I help her in her shop, I do some van deliveries for her, I pick the boys up from school, I take Nala for a walk. I am perfect. And then I offer to take a look at Martha's accounts for her. I haven't had to ask Martha for money since we got together. My paid activities have been lucrative enough. My age seems to work in my favor; if anything, women seem to want to pay more for my services, which possibly they imagine will be better due to lived experience. I have no idea if this is the case or not, but I'm not complaining.

However, since I started watching the Swanns, I've made less time for work and now my cash situation is in crisis. I have a week away lined up next month: a lady called Annabel, who, thankfully, is the same age as me (in fact, six months younger), is taking me to Porto as her holiday companion. All expenses paid, plus £3,000 cash on top. But until then I'm existing on loose change—literally on the coins I've picked up from around the cottage and the shop, tips from the tip jar, from the delivery van. (It does gall me to have a warm two-pound coin pressed into my palm by someone who is less than me in every way while I smile and look surprised and say, "Well, thank you so much, have a great day," but equally, two pounds is two pounds and I will not turn up my nose.)

Martha looks at me curiously. "What are you?" she says. "An accountant?"

I fold my arms across my chest and say, "Martha, my love, I deal with budgets all day, every day. It's my job."

"Is it?"

"Well, it's a part of my job. And I got a grade A in my maths O level."

She cocks an eyebrow and then sighs and says, "Well, brainbox, it's very kind of you, but I have a perfectly good accountant who I pay perfectly good money to."

"How much does he charge?"

"A grand a year. Roughly."

Now I cock an eyebrow at her. "How about saving that grand a year and putting it back into the shop? And letting me do your accounts."

She looks at me skeptically. "Hmm," she says. "I don't know. Arshad's been doing them for years. It's all so easy. Dump a carrier bag full of paperwork on his desk, walk away, and eight weeks later it's all done and dusted, everything given back to me in nice, neat folders. It's a good system. It works."

"But a grand, Martha."

She shrugs. "It's tax-deductible."

I nod and smile. "Fair enough," I say. "But it'd be great just to have a look. Run an eye over them, just to see if he's missing anything, or if there's anything you could be doing better, working harder, using more, using less. Would you let me have a look?"

I can see that she's still skeptical and it worries me. We've been together for over three years now, we're married, we have a child together, yet for some reason the thought of letting me into her business accounts gives her pause for thought. Is it just a general reaction, I wonder, to anyone asking to look at her numbers, or is it me? Something she can sense about my intentions? A lack of trust? Tara wasn't like this. She was stupidly delighted when I suggested going through her numbers for her. "Would you really?" she said to me at the time. "That would just be amazing."

"Well," I say now, "think about it. I'm not very busy at the moment.

I've got a few free days before I have to go away again. I'd be happy to do it. But only if you're comfortable."

I see her guard lower at my couched suggestion that there is discomfort between us. "Of course I'm comfortable," she says. "Of course. And yes, why not? We can go through them at the weekend maybe?"

"Yes," I say, kissing her lightly on the lips. "That sounds great."

The week in Porto is long and boring and I have to keep my phone switched off nearly all the time because Annabel does not pay three thousand a week for me to be bombarded with messages from my beautiful wife. I tell Martha that it's a conference and I will try to remember to switch my phone on after events and meetings, but that I might not always manage it and to please be understanding.

I see her nod uncertainly. I know she has a million questions she wants to ask me, but I also know that she is controlling the urge, not because she's scared of me, but because she's scared of everything not being perfect.

Annabel takes me for dinner every night and makes a performance of having me ask the waiters for the bill and pay for the meal with a card with her name on it, then thanking me loudly and theatrically. The card is slipped back into her handbag the moment we leave. She is pleasant company and, behind closed doors, is quite happy to sit quietly and read a book. I do manage to send Martha a couple of messages at these times, but the nights are long and Annabel is demanding both physically and emotionally, insisting that I act as if I "love her too much." She asks me to display "toxic love" and though I have a rough inkling what this must look like, I know that what I manage to muster up is not what she was hoping for and by the time we go our separate ways at Gatwick a week later, I have a strong suspicion that she will view the holiday as a mistake and that I will probably never see her again. My finances are about to take another blow.

I have not had a penny of Martha's money since we met, apart from treats that she has chosen to pay for herself. I don't want to start now. But I fear I must.

Two days after my fifty-fourth birthday, on a sunny April afternoon, I stumble upon evidence that Paddy Swann is also having an affair.

The woman is barely thirty, possibly a lot younger. She works in his Whitstable restaurant as front of house, where she is fussy and slightly officious in that way that young people who have been given a job above their station for nepotistic or other reasons can often be. She knows that she only gets to sit up front and tell people more experienced than herself what to do because she is allowing her boss to have sexual intercourse with her, but she absolutely cannot let anyone else know this. Her name is Boo. I have no idea what it's short for, but she looks like a Boo, acts like a Boo, is a Boo.

So now I have both of them dangling on strings. Nina and Paddy Swann are stupidly unaware of the fact that both of them are playing Russian roulette with their marriage for what looks to me like the flimsiest of reasons. Ethan and his tiny paunch. Boo and her thin top lip and nylon blouses. Really? Is that really the best they can do? At the risk of imploding what looks, on the surface, to be a perfect life?

People never fail to amaze me.

But it works in my favor. Clearly it does. They are my puppets now in so many ways, and I am their master.

SIXTY

Enderford is a beautiful village. Ash has heard of it but never visited before, although it's only forty minutes away from the Riviera.

The shop in front of her right now is called Martha's Garden. It's quite charming, with bowed and dimpled windows and woodwork painted an exquisite shade of pink, pale without being washed-out, intense without being gaudy. There are potted trees on the pavement, old wrought-iron guard railings, and fairy lights threaded through everything. An old-fashioned copper bell jingles above the door as Ash pushes it open and then she is ensconced in the warm embrace of a fragrant store full of perfectly displayed plants and flowers, pots and vases. Behind the counter is a pretty young girl in a sleeveless fur jacket and fingerless gloves, her hair piled into a huge bun on top of her head, arranging white flowers into a posy. She smiles at Ash.

"Hi."

"Hi," Ash replies.

"Let me know if you need any help."

Ash nods and walks toward her. "Yes, actually. I was wondering—do you recognize these?" She pulls the box of soaps out of her shoulder bag and even as she does so she sees a display out of the corner of her eye: soaps and handwashes and candles all in the same packaging, the same shade of pink, and yes, she sees it now, the same embossed linear rose.

The girl looks at the box and says, "Yes! These are ours! A woman in the village makes them for us. They're lovely, aren't they? Did you want another set?"

"Er, no. Thank you. It's just they were a gift from someone, and he can't remember where he got them from and—" She stops abruptly, not sure how to continue, or whether to. "Is this your shop? Are you Martha?"

"No!" she laughs lightly. "God, no! I'm only twenty! Martha is my boss. But she's not here today. She's gone off on some mystery mission. Left me in charge."

"Ah. Right. When will she be back?"

"She didn't say. But after lunch, probably."

"Can I . . ." Ash pauses again, not sure if her next question is appropriate, or incendiary. But then she pulls her phone out of her pocket. "Do you recognize this man? He's the man who bought me the soaps. Has he ever been in here that you remember?"

She shows the photograph of Nick Radcliffe to the girl, who says, "Yeah. That's Al."

A blast of shock runs through Ash's system. "Al?"

"Yes. Alistair. Martha's husband."

Martha's husband. Of course, she thinks. Of course.

"Oh." She doesn't let the shock register on her face. "Right. And is he here today?"

"Er, no. He's had to go up to the Midlands," she says in a low voice, as though someone might be listening. "His mother has Alzheimer's and he's taking care of her."

"Oh," Ash says again, struggling now to control the note of surprise in her voice. "Right. So you haven't seen him for a while?"

"No, not since before Christmas. Poor Martha, it's such a stretch with the little one and her boys and this . . ." She gestures at the shop. "And doing it all by herself. She's amazing, actually. One of the most amazing women I know. But . . ." Ash sees the obvious question percolate through the girl and form itself into a quizzical frown. "Why have you got a photo of him on your phone?"

"Oh," Ash replies nonchalantly. "He's a friend of my dad's. An old friend. Yeah. And he got me these for Christmas. And they're so nice. And he told me he got them from some posh place in Mayfair, but I couldn't find them and I think maybe he was just fibbing, because obviously he must have got them from here for free. But don't worry. It's fine. Mystery solved." She flashes the girl a huge grin and tucks the soaps back into her bag.

"Oh," says the girl. "Right. I mean, are you sure you don't want to buy some more? While you're here? They're on sale? Twenty percent off?"

"Oh, no, honestly. It's fine. I know where to come now if I need some more, though, thank you." Ash flashes the girl another smile, and then she turns and leaves.

Married to Martha.

Children together.

A flower shop.

There it is. All of it. She's got him. He's lying to his wife and he's lying to Nina. He's lying to everyone about everything, and Ash finally has him pinned down, limb to limb, inescapably. But now what? She needs a plan. She needs a strategy. She messages Jane from the train back home and tells her everything.

A moment later, Jane replies.

Fuck a duck. 🦆

Then, another moment later:

I have a number for Emma Greenlaw. Do you want to message her, or shall I?

SIXTY-ONE

THREE MONTHS AGO

I take Nina Swann out for our first date roughly a year after Paddy's death. We had been messaging back and forth for weeks beforehand. There were times when I thought she would never take the bait, that she would keep me at arm's length forevermore. But then I said something profound about the nature of loss, or at least I didn't think it was profound, but Nina said it was and I could tell that I had somehow gone up in her estimation, and when I mentioned that I had business on the coast and was spending a night in Folkestone, she finally caved.

"We should meet up," she said. "I can take you out for dinner. If you'd like?"

It is strange being face-to-face with Nina Swann after all those months watching her from a distance or on the screen of my laptop. I find a new appreciation of her face when I'm close up to it and not distracted by her slightly outlandish, masculine style of dressing. Her face has symmetry, and her skin is very smooth for a woman of her age. Her eyes are a very rich shade of coffee-bean brown, and she has a slender neck. She is also, it turns out, utterly charming. I hadn't, for some reason, imagined her to be charming. Seeing her on that seedy night out with her younger lover when she had looked distracted and unhappy, washed-out in the shadows of the tacky dive bar, I had assumed that she would be a faded light.

But the woman who meets me at a lively beachfront pizza restaurant on an unseasonably warm late October evening is glowing, effervescent almost, and the first thought that hits me is . . . *Is she glad her husband's dead?*

I watch her face for her reaction to mine. I'd sent her a selfie at her request and told her that I'm tall, so she would know what to expect. But still, I want to see her take me in. I am not disappointed.

"Wow," she says, as I walk toward her. "You're gorgeous!" She bursts into a billow of infectious laughter and then leans in and kisses me on my cheek. "Sorry," she says, "that was a bit forward of me. I have no filter. Tend to speak as I think. But seriously, you are very good-looking. Objectively."

I smile at her, beguiled and flattered, and say, "Gosh, well, thank you. You're—objectively—very good-looking too. If I might say."

"You might!" she echoes, and then she leads me into the restaurant, which is modern and open-plan, glass on all sides, decking leading from the frontage out onto the pebbled beach. The couple seated next to us have a small dog with them; they tell us it is a shih tzu mixed with something else and I spend some time fussing over it before turning back to Nina, who is smiling at me warmly.

"Dog lover?" she asks.

"Yeah. Better than people. All of them. How about you?"

She shrugs. "I do like dogs, yes. Had them as a kid. But Paddy didn't like them. Thought they were dirty. Didn't let them in his restaurants either. I've already changed that policy." She emits a tiny and very telling tut. "So, we never had one. Kids begged for one for over a decade and then eventually gave up."

"You could get one now?"

"Well, the irony, of course, is that now I'm too busy to have a dog."

"The restaurants?" I ask.

"Yes." She sighs. "The restaurants."

"A lot of work?"

"Unreal. And of course Paddy thrived on it. He loved the stress, the long hours, the high-octane atmosphere, the young people. He *loved* all the young people. He loved being in his restaurants for as many hours a day as he possibly could."

I wince empathetically. "That must have been tough for you?"

She nods, and I sense her effervescence fading a little. "Yup. It was basically as if I didn't have a husband. TBH. And now it's all on me and I'm trying my best, I really am, but it's so hard. I don't know why anyone would choose to go into the restaurant industry, I really don't." She glances up at me and says, "I suppose it's a vocation, isn't it?"

I nod. Of course, Nina thinks that I am a seasoned restaurateur, that the same blood that ran though Paddy's veins runs through mine, and I blow out my cheeks and say, "It is. And frankly, no, I didn't have it. That's why I'm more of a sidelines guy these days—throw my money at them and run. Let them do all the hard work. Because, Jesus, it really is hard work."

And here I do sound authentic because I have actually worked in the restaurant industry. I mean, Christ, I've done most things. You tend to have when you get to my age without having had a solid career. I worked at a tearoom near where I grew up in West Yorkshire. Coach parties of senior citizens came in off an A road and I served them nasty sandwiches and tea in pots. I worked there for just over a year and after that I got a job in town at a posh brasserie-style place (well, as posh and brasserie-like as anywhere in the west of Yorkshire in the eighties could have been), where I served tables in a ridiculous waistcoat and bow tie. I lasted six months before breaking free. And then there were a couple of years of temping in London, washing up and sous-cheffing and such. It was shortly after my interaction with the young Paddy in Mayfair that I met my first client and realized there were more ways of getting through life than chasing stupid careers from the bottom end of the ladder and being spoken to like dirt by small, chippy men with big egos.

"So, tell me about this wine bar of yours."

"Well, I'd not call it *mine*." I'm ramping up the Yorkshire, to create a bond over our shared northern-ness. "It's partly mine. I went in with a young entrepreneur a few years ago. I give him advice. He runs the place. I own shares. It's what I've ended up doing at this stage. I'm basically retired now. Well, semi-retired. But I do like being on the shop floor from time to time, when it gets busy."

"Well, lucky, lucky you. I can't even begin to imagine what that must feel like."

"It feels wonderful. It feels incredible. I just need to sort out the, er, accommodation side of things. I've got this place in South London, belongs to a friend. He's letting me stay there until I can free up some cash to buy a new place. It's a bit of a shithole, to be honest. But it's only temporary, and I've lived in worse places, I can tell you."

We order our pizzas and a bottle of local sparkling wine (have you tried Kentish sparkling wine, by the way? It really is excellent), then chat for a while about our backgrounds, getting into the more granular stuff—we'd already covered the big stuff in our endless WhatsApp messaging of the past few months. And then, when the conversation slows and the first glass of wine has loosened us both up a little, I look at Nina and I say, "How are you doing? The kids? How is it all? Are you any closer to healing?"

She blinks slowly and sighs. Then she looks up at me with those madly brown eyes of hers and says, "We're coping. Well, at least, I'm coping. And Arlo. I mean, Arlo is basically bulletproof, you know. But Ash, I don't know. I'm really worried about her. She has this overly romanticized, idealized vision of her father. She genuinely thinks he was perfect."

"And he wasn't?"

"No," she says bluntly. "Of course he wasn't. Nobody is. But Paddy. My God, he was a difficult man to live with. A difficult man to be married to. And Ash—she was always such a daddy's girl. Actually, more than that, just such a little girl. Ever since Arlo was born, it's like she has clung on to the role of being the little one, the one and only, the center of our worlds, not that she was mean to Arlo, they've always got on very well, but it's like she felt it was her role to give us someone to parent.

"And then, last year, just a few months before Paddy died. Oh, Jesus . . . I probably shouldn't be telling you, but—hold on." She smiles and picks up the wine bottle. "Wait." She tops up our glasses, then knocks back a large gulp and readies herself. "She had a lovely flat-share near Greenwich, two nice flatmates, a great job working for a lifestyle publisher, a fairly OK salary, although it was never really about that because we were happy to keep supporting her here and there. She had an allowance. And it was all going so well. I thought, Finally my girl has grown wings. And then one night, one of her flat-mates called me. She said the police were at their flat, questioning Ash about something, and that Ash was totally losing the plot and the police were saying if she didn't calm down, they'd have to take her in, and could I talk to her. So, they put me on the phone with her and I couldn't understand a word she was saying, had to count her down, you know, eight, seven, six, five, etc., until she was calm enough to tell me that her boss had made a complaint about her. Apparently," she says with a sigh, "she'd been stalking him. She was convinced that he was in love with her, that he'd sent her love letters, that he was going to leave his wife for her. She had the letters, but it turned out that they weren't from him—that they were most likely from her."

I throw her a quizzical look.

"Lots of things didn't add up," she replies. "She'd been sending him letters too, and the police established that they were printed on exactly the same paper as the letters she claimed he'd been sending her. So she must have been typing them herself and sending them to herself. And they were full of instructions from this man of what to do and where to be and she started turning up places where he was and taking photos, and then, oh God, she followed him to his family holiday in Ibiza, just turned up on the beach one day, said he'd invited her, looked shocked to see his family there, and I can't tell you. It was such a bombshell. Our beautiful baby girl, behaving like a lunatic, making this poor man fear for his life. She had a kind of mini nervous breakdown and was hospitalized for a few days, then she was in therapy for a while, and finally she was diagnosed—with borderline personality disorder."

"Wow," I say, thoughtfully. "That's . . ."

"I know," she says. "What can you say? It's one of those things. There's always been something fragile about Ash, an ongoing fantasy, like she was living inside the pages of a novel."

"I'm really sorry," I say. "That sounds very tough. And where is she now? What happened?"

"Oh, she moved home when she left the clinic, got a job locally in a clothes shop. She's let all her friendships wither, has this low-level phobia of going into London, and she's just . . . she's always there, and it sounds harsh, but I'm starting to resent her a little bit? She's quite clingy and immature and she has a tendency to make everything about herself, and I can tell she doesn't think I'm sad enough about Paddy. She judges me for getting on with my life. Which makes me feel guilty. Makes me feel bad."

"And are you?" I push gently. "Sad about Paddy?"

"Oh God, of course I'm sad about Paddy. Of course I am. But also I feel . . . liberated? I know, that sounds terrible. But Paddy was the main character, you know, everything was about Paddy. His music, his food, his moods, his job, his friends, his world. And I loved it, but I also hated it. And he could be . . . quite patronizing? Quite belittling? If you didn't fully subscribe to his view of things, if you didn't like a piece of music, or if you didn't like some weird bit of fish, or a really spicy dish, if you wanted to sit in the shade, or not have a drink, or skip a dinner party or go somewhere different on holiday—no give. No flexibility. He would make you feel like you were an idiot. And

Ash, of course, just fully subscribed to the whole shebang, was just a mini-Paddy, idolized him. Which was, of course, exactly what he wanted. Big ego, our Paddy, as I'm sure you remember." She smiles ruefully and takes another sip of her wine. "Sorry," she says. "I didn't mean to say any of that. I've never said any of that. I'm not sure why I did . . ."

I give her a humble and encouraging smile. "It's fine," I say. "I get it. I really do. He was larger-than-life. And sometimes you just want someone who's the same size as you."

"Yes," says Nina, emphatically. "Yes. Exactly. And you know . . ." She pauses and turns her wineglass around by its stem. "I nearly left him."

I raise a brow and blow out my cheeks. "Wow. When was this?"

"Oh, a while ago. There was a guy. He was younger than me, but he was just . . . well, he was nothing special, but when I was with him, I was just with him? If that makes sense? We talked. We watched TV. We were quiet together. He noticed things about me. Like, for example, at home Paddy was always opening windows because he said it was too hot. Even though it made me cold. But this guy, if I shivered even once, he'd say, 'Oh, let me close the window, you're cold.' Tiny things. But what I needed. That contrast. And he had a nine-to-five job, so he was always around in the evenings, unlike Paddy, who was just never, ever, ever there. And anyway, it went on for a couple of years and then the thing with Ash happened and then Paddy died, and it fizzled out. But there was a moment during that affair when I was mentally preparing to leave Paddy. I really was. And I know I should probably feel guilty now. But I don't. I just don't."

I stare at this woman, and I ache to tell her that her husband had been having an affair too, but I suspect that she already knows that, whether factually or instinctively. She knows. I find myself wanting to reach for her hand. She's so much more than I thought she'd be. And Paddy is so much less. She really does deserve a man like me.

Someone who will close windows when she's cold, spend evenings with her, notice her.

"You shouldn't," I say to her. "You've done nothing wrong. You're a good, good woman."

"Thank you," she says. "Thank you. I really needed to hear that. And you?" she asks, eyeing me. "Are you a good man?"

"I think am," I say. "I really do think I am."

SIXTY-TWO

Emma Greenlaw is a tall, angular woman with the gaunt, shrunken look of a mother who has lost too much weight too quickly after having her children. On the lock screen of her phone there is a little girl with hair in bunches holding a baby inexpertly in her arms. "Sadie," she says to Ash, pointing at the older girl, "and Robyn. Four and one." She sighs. "And my mum has never met either of them."

Ash and Emma are sitting in a branch of Costa Coffee outside Emma's nearest train station. She said she couldn't get into town, too many commitments between the children and her job. She is brusque and dry.

Emma stirs sugar into her coffee and looks up at Ash. "So, he's in your house, is he?" she asks. "As we speak?"

"Yes," says Ash. "According to the girl in the flower shop, he's told his wife that he's in the Midlands looking after his elderly mother. But he's been at our place since the day after Boxing Day. No elderly mother mentioned."

"Wow," says Emma bitterly. "That fucking bastard." Then she lifts her head and looks at Ash. "So tell me the story. Of how he ended up with your mother?"

Ash tells her about the Zippo in the pink box, the impromptu visits, the wining and dining, the wine bar in Mayfair where nobody has heard of him, the flat in Tooting, the soaps from the pretty flower shop in Enderford. The wife called Martha.

Emma nods sagely throughout, her fingertips running around the edges of the tabletop. "And how do you think your mother feels about him? Right now."

Ash shrugs. It's a good question. "I think she really likes him. I think she's into him. You know?"

"Is she in love with him?"

Ash thinks about it. "I'm going to say no? But it's only a matter of time. Whenever she's with him she has this glow, she looks prettier. She looks happier."

Emma groans quietly. "Yup," she says. "Sounds about right. And how has he been with you?"

"Sweet, I guess. Not too try-hard. Just pleasant."

"But still, you feel uncomfortable?"

"I do. I felt uncomfortable immediately. It was like he was . . . too good to be true? Like no man could actually be like that?"

Emma nods. "And in particular a man who has no permanent home, no source of income, and is dating a recently widowed woman whose estate is worth over two million pounds."

"Yes!" says Ash. "Exactly! It was like, who are you? Where did you come from? What do you want? And then lots of things didn't add up and now, well, he's in. Feet under the table and he has an answer, an explanation, for absolutely everything. I've tried talking to my mum about it, but she doesn't really trust me?" Ash pauses before taking a sharp breath in. "I was diagnosed with borderline personality disorder eighteen months ago and I was accused of stalking someone, which I didn't. Not really. But I did do some pretty crazy things and the police got involved and now, well, whatever I say to her, she's going to see it through that lens. Of me being unstable. Unreliable. So I'm waiting until I've got him, fully, a hundred percent. And then I'm going to hit her with it."

Emma nods again, then she opens a folder and pulls out a couple of sheets of paper. "This is my list," she says. "This is what I have so far."

It's a timeline. It starts in the mid-2010s with the words: *Mum and Jonathan meet.*

"How did they meet?" Ash asks.

"Dating app. She resisted his charms for a while—she was slightly unconvinced at first—but he worked really hard on her. He just seemed to know exactly what it was she wanted and then he'd give it to her. And then the next we knew, they were getting married! Some dodgy civil thing at the town hall with three guests. I never liked him, not for one small minute. But he made my mum happy. Until he didn't."

"What sorts of things did he do?"

"Disappearing acts, mainly. And always scrounging for money. He told her he needed a knee-replacement operation, but the NHS waiting list was too long, so she paid for him to go private. He had the op, and then it turns out that he had it done on the NHS and just pocketed the cash my mum gave him. Always emergencies. Everything was always last-minute, and then every time my mum got close to throwing in the towel, he'd suddenly start being Mr. Perfect again. He always knew exactly how far he could push her. But eventually he pushed it too far. He was barely home, never answered his phone, my mum found some weird burner phone in his bag, he came home with a fucking *Tesla* that he said someone had lent him—and then he started talking about selling the house so they could move to the Algarve, and that's when I intervened. I just knew that he had no intention of moving to the Algarve, that he wanted her to sell the house to free up more cash. For whatever reasons. Probably to pay for the stupid fucking Tesla. To pay off debts. To pay for whatever other secret life he was living. And then a young woman reported him for street stalking. Here." She taps the list.

Emma continues. "I saw Jade's post on our local neighborhood app, and I immediately knew it was Jonathan, so I wrote to her and the other young woman, Tilly, who also responded, saying the same thing happened to her, and we agreed to call the police. They paid him a visit, but pah! Nothing. Of course. He wriggled out of it. Just like he always does. But that was the final straw for Mum. She kicked him out a few days later and he came back, so we changed the locks. And then, well, you know what happened next."

They both fall silent for a moment and then Ash says, "What do you think happened to your mum?"

A shadow passes across Emma's face and her jaw clenches with rage. "I think he killed her," she replies tightly.

"Seriously?"

"Yes. Seriously. Remember that woman's remains they found in the woodlands in Essex? About four years ago? I think that was her. But they couldn't formally identify her and so there you go, another dead end."

"Why would he have killed her?"

"Because she was onto him, I guess. She'd caught him in the act. I wish I could track down this woman, the one he was staying with in Tooting. I think she's the missing link. I think she knows exactly what happened that day. But she seems to have disappeared too."

Ash feels a wave of anxiety pass through her gut. The woman sitting in front of her thinks that Nick Radcliffe killed her own mother because she'd worked out his scam. What the hell does she think he might be capable of doing to her when he realizes that she knows his game? "What next?" Ash says, nervously. "What should I do?"

"Keep him home. Keep him relaxed. Don't let anything spook him. And keep me updated."

SIXTY-THREE

"Ash."

Nina is calling to her through the house.

"Yes," Ash calls back from her bedroom.

"Did you see Nick today?"

Ash slips off her bed and goes to the landing. "Nope. Not since this morning. Why?"

Her mother is standing in the hallway, still in her big winter coat, her bag on the floor at her feet, a takeaway for their dinner in another bag.

"Just weird that he's not here. He said he'd be in all day. And now he's not answering his phone."

A chill runs down Ash's spine. *Ah*, she thinks, *it's started.* "Oh," she says nonchalantly. "That's strange. Why don't you have a look at the Ring app? You might be able to see when he left? See if he had a bag? Or whatever?"

"That's a good idea."

Ash descends the stairs and follows Nina into the kitchen. At the table they sit elbow to elbow and look through the clips on Nina's phone. They see the postman come and go, they see a delivery driver pull up in a big gray van and shove something through their letter box, then, in the next clip, they see something strange. At about half ten a car pulls up and a petite woman gets out. She looks about forty-five, with lots of thick, curly blond hair. As she moves closer to the front door and her face comes into full focus in the camera, they see that she has wide blue eyes framed by mascaraed eyelashes, and that she looks wildly anxious.

"What the hell?" Nina mutters. "What is she up to?"

The woman rings the bell and stares into the hallway, her face still contorted with anxiety. She waits for just under a minute and then slowly walks away from the door and goes out of the shot. Two minutes later, she is back in the shot, climbing into her car, and then a moment after that she is gone.

Ash stares at her mother's phone. She's pretty sure she knows who that woman is, but she cannot say. Not yet. They flick through a couple more clips, and then there it is: Nick leaving at roughly midday, a rucksack over his shoulder, his weird doctor's bag (apparently it belonged to his late father who was a GP) in his left hand, his coat on, a woolen hat over his white hair. He leaves quickly and smoothly, without looking back. And then he, too, disappears out of the shot, just the sound of his feet crunching on the graveled road and a note of winter birdcall from a nearby tree before the recording falls silent again.

Nina doesn't say anything for a while after watching the clip. She sighs heavily and pulls her hair off her face with both hands. "I'm a little confused. What did I just see?"

Ash draws in her breath. "OK," she says, "I have an explanation. But you have to promise me that you will hear me out. This is nothing like what happened in London. Nothing. I am completely sane now. I have never felt more sane. Everything I am about to tell you is the truth and I have people who can corroborate it. You have to trust me and you have to believe me. OK?"

"OK," says Nina. "I'm listening."

Ash recounts it all, every last bit of it, from the pacifier clip in Nick's coat pocket to her visit to Martha's shop this morning and her meeting with Emma Greenlaw.

"Jesus Christ," says Nina, her expression stricken. "Jesus fucking Christ! I can't believe I let him . . . I can't believe I . . . Oh my God. I'm such a fucking idiot." Nina slams her fists down against the kitchen table and growls.

Ash touches her shoulder gently and says, "I'm really sorry, Mum. You do believe me, though, don't you?"

Nina's face softens and tears fill her eyes. "Oh, baby," she says, taking Ash's hands in hers. "I believe you. Of course I believe you. But I want you to know that I would never have been one of those women. I honestly never would have. I would not have let him use me and manipulate me. I would not have let him take my money. *Our* money. I just wasn't that into him. Not in that way. Not in the way that I was into your dad." She laughs softly, and Ash smiles. "But I do see how those women fell for him. I do get it. He is a consummate professional. He somehow knows just what buttons to press, just how to play things. He just knows. But it was different with me, the way he was with me, it never quite rang true. It wouldn't have lasted. I would have ended it. Very, very soon. You are my priority, Ash. You and your brother. Always have been. Always will be. And I'm sorry if I've made you feel unwelcome in your own home. Unsafe. I'm sorry I didn't listen to you and I'm sorry I let that stupid man in here. All I want in the whole world, Ash, is for you to be happy. I cannot be happy unless you are."

As her mother says these words, Ash knows she has to share one more thing with her. "There's something I didn't tell you, Mum. About what's been going on. I haven't been investigating Nick by myself, I've had someone helping me."

Nina raises her brow quizzically.

"Jane Trevally."

Her mother frowns. "Mad Jane?"

"Yes. Mad Jane. But she's not mad. She's great. And I didn't want to tell you because I thought you'd believe me even less—I know how you felt about her, how you and Dad both felt about her. And I only got in touch with her because I thought she might have known Nick from when he said he was working in that restaurant with Dad, and of course that was a big lie. But she wanted to help. And I needed help. I'm sorry I did that behind your back, but I didn't know what else to do."

Nina pushes her chair toward Ash and takes her in her arms. She holds her against her heart and Ash hears her sigh heavily. "I don't blame you, angel," she says. "I don't blame you at all. I have not been there for you . . ." She pauses and breathes in hard ". . . for a very long time. I really haven't. I've been very self-absorbed, and I think a lot of that was to stop me from feeling the things I should be feeling. To distract myself from everything that has happened. Because if I think too hard about what happened, I start feeling like I might lose my mind. And I cannot afford to lose my mind, not now."

Ash nestles closer into her mother's body. "Will you come with me tomorrow?" she asks. "To Enderford? To see Martha? Have you got time?"

Her mother squeezes her hard. "First thing," she says. "I'll cancel all my meetings, and we'll go first thing."

She looks down at Ash with a small smile playing on her mouth and she says, "So. Mad Jane. What does she look like these days. Is she still hot?"

SIXTY-FOUR

I drive aimlessly for a while after leaving Nina's, but eventually I end up at Jessie's place in Hastings. I thought I'd never see her again, but I don't know where else to go. She buzzes me in and greets me at the elevator door, then ushers me into her apartment, which is ablaze with winter sun pouring through the plate-glass windows overlooking the sea.

"Jessie," I say, allowing my eyes to mist over with tears. "Something terrible has happened. My mother . . ." I allow a note of strangulation into my voice. "I've been taking care of her. Living with her. But she's deteriorated to the point that she's had to go into a care home and I've had to rent out her house to pay for her care, and basically, Jessie, I'm homeless. I've got nowhere to live. And it would only be a few nights. A week, tops. I have a friend in London who's said I can use their flat when they go back to the States next month. I'd be in your spare bedroom, and I would be quiet and respectful, and I won't use your kitchen, I'll eat out. But I really, really just need a soft bed. And a friend . . . ?" I make a question out of this last statement because of course Jessie and I are not friends. I am a male escort, and she is my client. We have talked a lot over the years. We've been friendly, but we have not been friends. By framing it as a question, however, her natural instinct will be to want to reassure me that of course we are friends, and once she has done that, then how can she possibly deny me somewhere to stay?

I see many emotions pass over her face. She looks stricken, almost, as though I have asked her to donate an organ. But then I see her nod, and with a taut smile, she says, "Yes. Of course. But please, you'll need to be discreet. Very discreet. I've told my neighbors you're a masseuse. They'll be wondering why you're staying here. So just keep a low profile. Stay indoors as much as possible. Are you OK with that?"

I nod and take her hands and kiss their backs. "Thank you, Jessie. Thank you so much. I promise you, I will be gone before you know it."

I rest my rucksack and my bag on the ornate quilted cover on the bed in Jessie's spare room. There is a small pile of plush animals on the bed that I remove and place in the corner. I take off my shoes and I lie back on the bed and stare at the whipped-cream peaks in the ceiling plaster, the tacky art on the walls, the view through the window of the side of the apartment block next door, and I let out a sigh of repressed rage.

How? How had Martha found me? How did she know where I was? I think back to the dog tracker I'd found in the car a few weeks ago. Something to do with Baxter, I'd thought at first, but then I'd had a second thought—was it possible, I'd pondered, that Martha had put it in the car deliberately, to see where I was? I'd decided to be on the safe side and parked myself outside the restaurant I told her I was working at for three hours. The next time I left the house, I smashed it to a pulp with a hammer and dropped it in a bin in a car park off an A road. But how long had it been in my car? And had Martha in fact been using it to follow me? Had she seen it? Nina's house? Had she suspected an affair?

I hit myself hard around my temples with the heels of my hands;

I am livid with myself. But also livid with Martha. What more does she want from me? I'm doing all of this for *her*. To give her what she wants. The dream she craves. Her Martha's Garden empire. And in she blunders like an idiot, ringing on doorbells, ruining everything, and now what? I have nothing. Not one thing. I have a twenty-pound note in my wallet. I have two changes of clothing and some toiletries. I don't know what to do, and I'm furious. I'm absolutely fucking furious.

I get off the bed to throw the curtains closed against the dazzling winter sun, and then flop onto the bed again.

I'm nearly fifty-six, a married man, and I'm here on a single bed in a pensioner's spare room in Hastings with no money and no idea what the fuck to do next. How could I have been so stupid? It's like Tara and Amanda all over again, this grotesque collision of two parts of my perfectly choreographed existence. I can't handle it. Everything needs to be separate. All of it. I'm like one of those fussy kids who doesn't like their food to touch on the plate. I feel itchy, I feel anxious, stressed, enraged. I want to scream and kick things, hurt people, cry. I really, really want to cry. And then I do. I cry hard and ugly. I cry so hard that a moment later there is a gentle rap at the door, and I hear Jessie's voice.

"Are you OK, André?"

"Yes," I snuffle. "I'm fine. Just a bit . . . you know . . ."

"Do you want a hug?"

I nod, but then realize I need to say it out loud. "Yes. Please."

The door opens slowly and Jessie walks in. She perches on the edge of the bed and opens up her arms and I fit myself into them and let her stroke my heaving shoulders and pat my back and I listen to the soft patter-patter of her kind heart through her cardigan and for a short while I feel calm again.

"Everything will be OK, André," she says. "You'll fight back. You'll get back on your feet. This is just a small blip. You're a brilliant man. You'll find your way. I know you will."

I bury my head deeper into her and I hold on tighter to her body, like I'm never going to let go.

Jessie makes us a lasagna. It's not a very good lasagna, but I eat it with gusto. Crying makes me hungry. She talks about her adult children. They've broken her heart. She had them young and sacrificed a lot for them and now they've abandoned her. One lives in Australia. The other lives in Manchester. They are both workaholics and appear to find her annoying. I am empathetic and soothing and tell her that I'm sure they'll come back to her, but inside I'm thinking, Fuck them, just fuck them. They don't deserve you and they don't deserve your money, so give it to me, for God's sake, just give it all to me. With Jessie's money, I could walk away from both of them, from fucking Martha and fucking Nina, and just start again. All I want is to start again. And all I need is money. And why are there so many stupid fucking bitches in this world?

I swallow down the last stodgy mouthful of lasagna with a slurp of white wine and I smile at Jessie. "You're such a good person," I say. "One of the finest I've ever known. You deserve the world. Shall I clear?"

I clear the table for her and I wipe down surfaces and load the dishwasher and top up Jessie's wineglass, and then I tell her I'm going for a walk. It's been dark for hours and the bright morning has faded into a frozen black night. My breath turns to clouds so heavy and dense they linger in the air as I walk the streets around the back of Jessie's apartment block, past all-you-can-eat sushi buffets, microbreweries and pubs, boarded-up shops and clubs. What was Martha doing at Nina's? I ask myself again. What was she planning to do or say if someone had answered the door? And where is she now? What is she doing? What is she thinking? Why hasn't she called me? Or messaged me? All the unknowns make me want to pull my brains out of my head with my hands. I growl gently under my breath, and then I see a young girl across the street, looking at me strangely, her reaction to me triggered no doubt by my inwardly roiling demeanor.

I stop and glance at her, and then I start to follow in her wake. I see her turn a fraction to look at who's behind her and pick up her pace a little, see her breath trapped in the small of her back. She's wearing a camel coat, tied tightly at the waist to show the world how tiny it is, with fitted black trousers and shiny pumps. She's come from an office, and I see her adjust her little handbag in that way women do when they're feeling unsafe, like it's somehow going to protect them. I'm about six feet away from her and I maintain this space. It's optimum. The length of a man. The Covid safe space. Just enough to make her feel nervous, but not enough for anyone else to notice. She turns left and I follow her. I take my phone out of my pocket, and I pretend to look at it as I walk. I put my spare hand into my trouser pocket and let my fingertips graze the head of my penis, just slightly, and only once. I look at the back of her neck where the turned-up collar of her camel coat brushes the baby hairs escaping from her ponytail, then I close the gap between us by a foot and I make a small noise, halfway between a sigh and a groan. She stops and I continue until I am a foot away from her, when I swoop into her personal space, let my nose drop close to the collar of her coat, breathe in hard, instantly dizzy with the scent of her, of fear mixed with flowers. I straighten up and walk right past her, turning briefly to catch her staring at me with her mouth hanging open, not sure what to say, not sure what just happened, caught halfway between fear and uncertainty. Did she imagine it, the tall man walking too close to her? And surely, she's thinking, surely not him? He looks too smart, too respectable, far too fucking handsome.

Meanwhile, I saunter onward, my engines oiled again, my head clearer, my resolve restored. I find a pub and I buy myself a cold pint of lager and I drink it slowly and methodically until I feel ready to return to Jessie's spare bedroom, to the pile of stuffed toys and the cloying expanse of thick, thick carpets.

SIXTY-FIVE

There are two women in Martha's shop the next morning. The first is an older woman with shiny dark hair cut into a blunt fringe, and the second a younger, fair-haired girl wearing a teddy bomber jacket and oversized jeans, a pair of headphones hanging around her neck.

Martha recognizes them immediately.

It's the women from the photo she'd seen through the window of Paddy Swann's house yesterday morning. Nina Swann and her teenage daughter—except the daughter is now an adult. Martha has no idea how they have found her here, but she is ready, so very ready for this to finally begin, to confront the other woman.

She keeps her features even and says, "Hi. Can I help you?"

The woman, Nina, is striking. She's wearing black jeans and platform-soled boots, an oversized fluffy black jumper, and a leather jacket. Martha can't imagine her side by side with dapper Alistair Grey; they seem mismatched, and for a moment she wonders if maybe she's got it all wrong. Maybe Nina Swann is not having an affair with her husband? Maybe it's something else? Maybe it really is just business? Paddy's restaurants? Maybe Alistair is helping her to run them?

But if that's the case, why lie? Why could Al not just say that he's in Folkestone helping a newly widowed client run her dead husband's restaurant empire? Why pretend to be in the Midlands helping his sick mother get back on her feet?

Nina Swann smiles and moves closer to Martha. Her face looks soft and almost charitable. She looks, Martha realizes, as if she is about to tell her something terrible, and surely, Martha thinks, surely she wouldn't come all the way out here with her own daughter to tell her that she is fucking her husband. Who would do that? Nobody, that's who. Is she—the thought stabs at her like a knife—is she going to tell her that Alistair is dead? Her body pumps out adrenaline and for a moment she feels dizzy, like she might pass out.

"Are you Martha?" asks Nina.

"Yes. I'm Martha. What's going on?" Her voice comes out jagged and raw.

"Is there somewhere we could talk?"

Martha grips her elbows and nods, then leads them into the little office at the back of the shop, where there are three chairs arranged in front of her desk. She offers them tea and they say no.

Nina says, "Is this your husband?" and shows her a photo on her phone of a windswept Alistair on a beach somewhere.

Martha's stomach churns and she nods. Al's head is just turning in the photo, not looking at the camera, as though he didn't know it was being taken. Typical Al. He hates having his photo taken.

Martha lifts her eyes to Nina. "What's going on?" she says.

Nina and her daughter exchange looks and then Nina says, "Is he here? Is he with you? Do you know where he is?"

"He's . . . I thought . . . I thought he was with you?"

Nina gives her a small, apologetic smile. "He was with me. Yes. And then you came to my house yesterday?"

Martha flinches with embarrassment and nods.

"Well, we think your husband saw you ringing our doorbell yesterday morning. Two hours later, he left in a hurry. Do you have any idea where he might have gone?"

Martha takes a moment to turn her swirling thoughts into words. "He saw me?" she repeats. "He was there?"

"Yes. And listen, Martha, I don't know what you think is going on, but it's all much more complicated. Your husband—what do you call him?"

"Call him?"

"Yes. His name."

"Al. Alistair. His name's Alistair. That's his name."

"Right," says Nina, "well, Alistair came into my life a year ago, claiming to be called Nick Radcliffe. He wrote to me to offer condolences after my husband died. He said he lived alone in Tooting and had shares in a wine bar in Mayfair, that he'd never been married and never had children. We've been dating since October, and he's been living with me since December the twenty-seventh. My daughter tracked you down via a box of soaps he bought her for Christmas that he told her were from a shop in Mayfair, but which, it turns out, came from here."

Martha's mouth is suddenly dry. She shakes her head just once, trying to settle these new facts into some semblance of order. "I . . . ," she begins, but can't go any further.

"I'm really sorry," says Nina. "Really, really sorry. And listen. I'm afraid there's more."

Martha's mind swoops through the last four years of her life—the holes, the gaps, the weirdness—and she looks up at Nina again and says, "Right. OK."

Then Nina tells her about other wives, other children—abandoned children!—police reports of women being stalked on the streets, a missing wife, suspected murder.

Martha breathes in when Nina stops talking. She blinks slowly and then says, "You know, my husband, Al, he had a thing about your late husband."

"Sorry?" Now it is Nina's turn to look confused.

"Yes. He took me for dinner there, to your husband's place in

Whitstable. About two or three years ago. Your husband was there. He was very friendly, going round chatting to everyone. And then he came over to talk to us and I was a bit starstruck, I don't know why. I mean, he was just a guy, just a chef, not famous or anything. But you know, being in his restaurant, everyone was so excited to talk to him. Your husband was super friendly, possibly a tiny bit flirtatious, he put his hand on my shoulder, though really it was nothing? But Al was so weird after that. I never really worked out why, but then, yesterday, when I came to your house and realized who you were, it came back to me. He bought your husband's cookbook for me for Christmas that year, said something like, 'Thought you'd like it. It's full of pictures of him.' I thought that was weird at the time. But still, none of it fell into place until yesterday. Did he ever tell you that he'd been there? To your husband's restaurant?"

"Well, yes, he did, but he described it like it was a reunion, because he and Paddy had worked together in London in the nineties when Nick—sorry, Al—was a chef."

"Al told me he'd worked in restaurants when he was young—but he was never a chef. Or at least, not that he told me." And as she says these words, Martha remembers that lovely, slightly dreamy, wine-softened lunch with Grace two days before Christmas, when Martha had thought her life was perfect again, and she remembers what Grace had said: *"I thought it was going to end up that he was one of those blokes you read about. The ones who marry loads of women and lie to everyone and steal all their money."*

And now it turns out that Grace had been right. Her friend's instincts, her spider senses, they'd been spot-on, because unless this very pleasant woman sitting in front of Martha right now, looking at her with compassion and concern, is spinning her a crazy web of lies, then the man she's loved for four years, been married to for two, the father of her daughter and stepfather to her sons, is a con artist and a fantasist and a liar and a freak.

But he is also the best man she has ever known.

The cognitive dissonance floors her. She'd been ready to deal with an extramarital affair. Her heart had been hardened, ready for the fallout. But she had not been ready for this.

A lie made of everything.

Every last thing.

"You know," says Nina, "Nick—Alistair—I think he might have been trying to scam me. He asked me if I wanted to invest in a restaurant venture down by Folkestone."

Another wave of nausea passes through Martha. Another tainted memory. That perfect, beautiful day when she and Al took Nala and the dog to the seaside and Al showed her the old ice cream pavilion, the beach huts, he'd held her in his arms and talked about fairy lights and fishing nets and Greek villages and dreams. And then he'd disappeared just before lunch, hadn't he? Dropped them at the pub and driven off to see a client. But it was not, she now knows, a client. It was Nina Swann. This woman, right here.

"What did you say?" she asks quietly.

"I said no way. I'm just about coping with the three restaurants that Paddy left me to deal with. The last thing I want is another one."

"He took me there too," Martha says softly. "Told me we should buy it, turn it into another Martha's Garden, with a tea shop, pop-up restaurant nights, Airbnb rooms. All of that. He said I should remortgage my house to pay for it. I've already spoken to my accountant about it, he was getting me the forms to fill out. I was halfway to doing it." And then, finally, at the thought of the dreams she'd had about the café on the beach, the hours she'd spent obsessing over what color she'd paint the walls, whether she'd have tablecloths or not, how she'd display her crockery—on open shelves or in antique haberdashery cabinets—the tears come.

Nina puts her hand across the desk and cups Martha's inside hers. Her face is pale but set with grit and determination. "We're going to fix this," she says. "We're going to fix all of it. And we're going to get this man put where he belongs, OK? For a very long time. Are you up for it?"

Martha wants to say no. She wants to say, *Leave him alone, he'll come back, he always does. We'll carry on. My lovely life. My lovely man. Our beautiful daughter. Our dreams.* She wants to say this, but she is far too broken to say it and so, instead, against all her basest and most guttural instincts, she says, "Yes. I'm up for it. Let's bring him down."

SIXTY-SIX

A few days later, I receive a message from Martha.

> *Dear Al*
>
> *I don't know what's going on. We miss you. I've been going mad, losing the plot, doing crazy things. I heard a seagull in the background of one of our phone calls and I became convinced you were at the seaside, that you were having an affair. I even went to this house out by Folkestone and rang on the doorbell because I was so sure you'd be there. Of course you weren't there and I felt like an idiot, and of course seagulls don't only live by the sea, I know that, and I'm losing my mind, Al. I understand that your mum needs you too, but please, please come home. We need you, Jonah needs you. I can send you money. Just come back. I love you so much. Please darling. Please.*

Beneath her message is a row of praying-hands emojis and three red hearts.

My stomach lurches and for a moment it all comes flooding back, the joy of life with Martha, her cottage, the boys, my beautiful daughter. But then I think—how did she know about Nina's house in the first place? So I reply circumspectly.

Baby. I'm so sorry. Please forgive me, I love you too. But what is this business about a house in Folkestone? What on earth, you crazy girl! How bizarre!

She replies a moment later:

Please forgive me, I used a dog tracker in the car a few weeks ago, when I thought you were having an affair. The app showed you going to that house when you left us in the pub that day. I was an idiot. Obviously you weren't there. I hope you can forgive me??? Please come home. Please.

More praying-hands emojis. More love hearts.

My heart, which had begun to harden against Martha, softens at the edges. Yes, I think, it is reasonable that she might have suspected an affair. It is reasonable that she might have tried to keep tabs on me. It is reasonable that having heard seagulls in the background of a call I told her I was making from the Midlands, she might have jumped to a conclusion of that nature and then of course it makes sense that she would come to the house, to see for herself. And what would she have seen? As she said, a family home, family photos, no sign of me, of an affair, of anything untoward. My tendency is to forgive her. But I don't reply immediately. I sit on the bed in Jessie's spare room, and I consider my options.

Jessie makes a soup that night: chicken, leeks, potatoes, cumin; it's very warming and much better than her lasagna. I watch her across the table, taking in the bloom of sadness across her face, and I wonder about her future, her life, her money. And then I go to bed to think.

By 2 a.m., I have made my decision.

SIXTY-SEVEN

Ash sees Jane waiting for her outside Bar Amelie. The bar has two large square bay windows overlooking the street, which have been painted a cool charcoal black, and large double doors in the center, with an arched window above and cascades of plants hanging from the ornate balcony that juts out overhead. Ash is wearing something she swiped from the shop today: a wrap minidress in black with a puffy bow at the shoulder. She wears it with boots and tights and her mother's leather jacket and thinks she has made a good attempt at looking like the sort of young girl who frequents Mayfair wine bars.

Jane is elegant in a trouser suit with heels and an overcoat. She pulls AirPods out of her ears as Ash approaches, tucking them into a little canister that she pops into her bag before leaning down to hug her.

"Bloody hell," she says. "This is all mad. And you know, I feel like after all these years I've finally found my role in life. I haven't enjoyed anything this much in ages, to be quite frank, and I'm sorry if that sounds bad, but honestly, I feel reborn. You look gorgeous, by the way," she says. "So like your dad. But prettier, obviously. And I love this dress. With the boots. You're making me sad I didn't have any children now, and I never feel sad I didn't have children. Shall we go in?"

Ash follows Jane through a velvet curtain and into a womb of palest sea green and copper and burnt red and crowds of softly lit people and some kind of background music that sounds vaguely enchanting. Jane finds them two stools at the bar and orders them each a glass of champagne. While the bartender is pouring their drinks, Jane directs a question at her. "So, who owns this place? Is it the guys who did the Ivy?"

"Oh, no," says the young woman, "not them. But two other guys. One of them was called Luke Berner. But he died about three years ago, just after it opened. So now it's just Jensen."

"The owner died?" Jane repeats.

Ash feels a small shock pass through her.

"Yes, really sad. Suicide. He was only forty-one."

"Oh my God," says Jane, clasping her hand to her collarbone. "That's tragic."

"Yeah," says the girl. "I don't really know much about it. But I think it was something to do with money? Debt? I dunno. Anyway"—she smiles sadly and places the second glass of champagne in front of them—"can I get you anything else?"

Jane orders some mini chorizos, bread, and a bowl of olives, and then hands the girl her card, pooh-poohing Ash's half-hearted attempt at paying her share. The moment the girl looks away, Jane starts googling Luke Berner, and there it is, a news report, very low-key: a man found dead in unsuspicious circumstances, no police investigation, an accompanying picture of a vibrant-looking man with slicked-back dark hair, sunglasses, good teeth, a pint of lager on a table in front of him, someone's disembodied hand on his shoulder. A happy-looking man. But everyone looks happy at least once before they kill themselves, Ash thinks. It doesn't mean anything.

Then Jane googles the other owner, Jensen de Witt. He's a much older man, with a swoop of gray hair that curls up at his collar, crinkled hazel eyes, a Mediterranean tan, a gold chain, drinker's teeth. According to LinkedIn, he's sixty-four, has six children, and lives in Geneva with his second wife. He owns a bar in Saint-Tropez and another in Dubai. He reeks of cash, even on the tiny screen of Jane's phone. And then suddenly

Ash feels a sharp dig in her ribs and she looks at Jane, who is pointing with a weird attempt at subtlety to the other side of the bar. Ash looks up and sees steel-gray hair, a turned-up collar, a royal blue sweater tied around the neck, the gleam of a fat golden watch, and she sees it's him, Jensen de Witt, the bar's owner, chatting with two young members of staff and enjoying a joke of some kind.

"Fucking hell," says Jane, grabbing her bag and her champagne glass. "Quick, bring your drink, we're going over. Follow me."

Ash picks up her glass and follows Jane to the other side of the bar, watching as she reaches for Jensen de Witt's hand and says, "Oh my goodness. Jensen, it's you."

Ash watches Jensen's face as he mentally goes through every woman he's ever met who looks and sounds like Jane, a genial smile on his face as he says, "Yes. Of course," in a soft French, possibly Belgian, accent. "And . . ."

"No, sorry, you don't know me. My name's Jane Trevally. I'm here with my friend's daughter, Ash. My friend recommended we should come here. Her boyfriend told her he was a co-owner, but someone else said they'd never heard of him and now he's sort of done a disappearing act and I wondered if you knew of any way of getting hold of him?"

Jensen's brow puckers and his lips purse. "You're not talking about Luke?"

"No. God. Sorry. No. We heard about Luke and that is—that's just terrible. No, this is a guy called Nick Radcliffe."

A dark cloud passes over Jensen's face at the mention of Nick's name. "Oh my God," he says. "That man. Jesus Christ. That man was a crook. He was a madman."

Jane and Ash glance at each other. "Could we possibly ask you a few questions about him? If that's OK?"

Jensen looks at his fat golden watch and then up at Jane and nods. "Sure," he says. "Let's go and sit down."

He takes them to a small booth in the corner and offers them another drink before settling back into the banquette and saying, "So, what's the deal with you and this terrible man? How is he in your life?"

Jane lets Ash tell the story, show Jensen the screenshot of the now-deleted LinkedIn profile page and other pictures of Nick on her phone, and Jensen looks at each artifact with interest and listens intently to the story, only stopping Ash after she says, "He told us he was a co-owner of this place."

"No, no, no, no. Ridiculous. No. Jesus Christ, that man. I don't know where Luke found him. He said he was an experienced restaurateur, but he had a CV that just didn't make any sense. Then he said he'd been on the run from a stalker all his life, had had to change his identity, blah blah blah, and Luke got cold feet and cut him loose. Luke said he'd been OK about it, that he had taken it in his stride and they'd left on good terms, handshakes, etc.

"But then when the wine bar opened a few months later, this guy, Nick, he started trying to sabotage the business, using fake usernames to leave horrible reviews on social media. He even sent inspectors in after claiming to have seen a rat. And fuck me," Jensen laughs wryly, "there was a rat, the cleanest, sweetest rat, and they took it away to a rescue center because as far as they could tell, it was a domestic pet. Three guesses how it got into the kitchen. Then this woman starts complaining about being sexually assaulted by a member of our waiting staff, which was just the most patently ridiculous scam as the guy she was accusing was gay, zero interest in any woman's breasts, let alone hers. But more bad reviews on social media from this woman. Clearly it was him. Nick. And the whole thing, it was . . . it was distasteful. Petty. So petty, so vindictive. All because we didn't want to go into business with a chancer with no money. But this guy, he had this air about him, as if he thought he was more than he was? You know? He thought he was special. Important. And then, in the end, I think it got too much for Luke. He felt responsible for this man and his behavior and the impact it was having on our business. And he took his own life, and as soon as that happened, it all stopped. All of it." Jensen shakes his head.

Ash feels a slick of darkness pass through her at these words.

Jensen sighs. "Such a stupid, childish vendetta. So cruel. So tragic. And now you say your mother, she is dating this man?"

"Well," says Ash, "she was. But he's disappeared."

"Good riddance," says Jensen. "Let us pray, for your sake, that he stays lost."

But Ash is not listening. She is deafened by the echo of Jensen's words, ricocheting around inside her head.

"So vindictive . . . Such a stupid, childish vendetta."

She thinks of Nick Radcliffe's weird grudge against her father and a chill runs down her spine.

SIXTY-EIGHT

The man who killed Ash's father is much smaller in real life than the giant who's lived inside Ash's head for over a year.

He's a slightly built man, and no more than five foot ten. The meaty hands that Ash had pictured over and over again are the size of a normal man's hands, his face is softer, the skin looser, his eyes sadder. He has lost weight. He smiles at Ash as she approaches, raises himself from his seat about two inches and then lowers himself again. There is a strange moment where it looks like he will shake her hand, but he doesn't and she is relieved.

She hasn't told her mother, or indeed Jane, about arranging this visit. The theory behind this visit is so wacky and fantastical that Ash can barely believe she is pursuing it. Having only just convinced her mother that she is behaving rationally and sanely, she does not want Nina to start doubting her again.

He's called Joe Kritner, the man who killed Ash's father. He is thirty-two years old. He has parents who love him but who couldn't keep him safe from himself. His face has been imprinted on Ash's psyche for so long: his pale, wide, fleshy cheeks, a thin line of a mouth, brown hair flopping onto a prematurely lined forehead, eyes filled with nightmares. They'd been shown the CCTV footage: her father in shorts and a hoodie, his headphones on, a little dance in his body as he stands at the end of the platform, glancing back and up at the display every now and again to check the timing of the next train. And then Joe Kritner appears, slow at first, stopping every so often to turn to look at the display, inching ever closer. Then, as the lights of an approaching tube light up the CCTV footage, her father takes a step closer to the edge of the platform and Joe Kritner brings up his pace, and then there he is. *Right there.* For a big man, Joe Kritner moves so smoothly, so effortlessly, the two meaty hands against her father's shoulder blades, the two milky lights of the train . . . and suddenly there is only one man on the platform.

Joe Kritner turns away the moment it is done; he doesn't pause to look at the aftermath, he just turns and stares down the full length of the platform and puts his hands against his own chest, leaving them there for just a second, almost as if he is wiping away the traces of her father's hoodie from his palms. He starts to walk slowly and, in the footage, people appear who had not been in the shot before, they appear and they look horrified and they push Joe Kritner onto a bench and restrain him there as tube workers arrive in high-vis with walkie-talkies, and then the police, and then, finally, finally Joe Kritner is removed and the footage shows an empty, postapocalyptic-looking platform. The drama is over. All that is left is for the clean-up team to arrive.

During police questioning, Joe Kritner had talked about the big "Silver Man" who had made him do it. He'd shown them the money he'd been given—fifty pounds in shiny ten-pound notes. The Silver Man had talked about a bomb. A terrorist attack. The Silver Man had told him what to do. Joe had mentioned him over and over again—but then he'd talked about all sorts of incredible and nonsensical things during questioning. The big Silver Man had sounded just as bizarre as everything else.

"Hi," says Ash. "Thank you for seeing me."

Joe shakes his head. "No, no, it's fine. Honestly. Fine." He speaks with a slight stammer. "How are you?"

The question throws Ash slightly. "Oh," she says. "I'm fine. Thank you."

They are in a small room on upholstered chairs. Joe Kritner has no restraints. According to the officials, he represents no physical danger now that he is medicated, but still, Ash thinks, you see it in films, the prisoner pretends to take their meds, spits them out when no one's looking. There is an officer in the room with them, but Ash feels horribly anxious, on the verge of panic. This is the man, after all, who killed her father.

She clears her throat and makes herself sound brave. "I wanted to ask you," she says, "about the Silver Man?"

She sees something pass across Joe's eyes. "Yes," he says. "I remember that. I remember talking about him. I think, though, that I might have made it up? Because of my problems? You know?" He grimaces apologetically and reaches to scratch the back of his neck.

"Do you really think that? Or is that what people have told you?"

"I just don't know. To be honest. No, that's not right. It's complicated. I feel like there was a Silver Man. But when I think about the Silver Man, my head tells me to stop being so stupid, that there's no such thing as silver men, and what I did to your dad, that terrible, bad thing, it was my responsibility. Fully my responsibility. And I just made up the Silver Man to have someone to blame for my own actions."

"But what if he was real? Is that possible? I mean, does he have a face? Or was he just a voice?"

"He had a face. But I made it up. Like I made up lots of things then—all the time. But, yes, he had a face. A real face."

"And this face you made up. Did it . . ." Ash opens her hand to reveal the folded piece of paper she's brought in with her, and she carefully unfolds it before turning it to face Joe. "Did it look like this?"

It's Nick Radcliffe's LinkedIn photo, slightly blurred in the enlarged printout but still recognizably him. She sees Joe's eyes widen, his jaw fall open. His fingers reach for the sheet of paper and pull it slowly toward him. Then he stares up at Ash, his eyes full of fear and horror, and says, "Where did you get this?"

"It's a photo of a man called Nick Radcliffe. But he has lots of other names too. Do you recognize him?"

He looks back at the photo and then up at Ash and nods, just once. "That's him," he whispers. "That's him. I don't . . ." He pushes himself back from the table with his hands. "I don't understand. He's not real. The Silver Man isn't real."

"But is this him? Is this the man who told you to push Paddy?"

Joe nods. His chair is now a foot from the table, and she can see his breathing has sped up, his chest rising and falling. She sees he is scared.

"He gave me money. He told me the man—your father—was evil. He told me your father was going to explode a bomb. Kill lots of people. He told me lots of things. He just talked and talked and talked. He said so many words. And then he went."

"Where? Where was this?"

"Outside. Leicester Square. I was . . . asking people for money. Because I was homeless back then. Couldn't live with my mum and dad because I was too much trouble. My mum was scared of me. I had to live on the streets. Life was very difficult. I had a lot of things going on. So much noise. I was never quiet. And this man, he gave me money. This one." He points at the photo on the table. "But he wasn't real. He was never real. I know he wasn't real."

"He was real, Joe. He really was. And can you remember, in this conversation you had, which exit you were at? At the station?"

"Where I always was. On Charing Cross Road. Just on the steps where they go down into the station. It was my place. People knew me. Lots of people spoke to me. Brought me things. But this man, this Silver Man . . . he was new. He was friendly. And he was kind."

"How did you get down there? Onto the platform? Did he go with you?"

"No. I can't remember. At least, I couldn't remember before. But now maybe I do. Because maybe he was real?"

"He was. He is. And do you—would you feel OK? To tell people? To say it was him?"

Joe shakes his head vehemently. "No. Nobody would believe me. They didn't believe me then. They won't believe me now."

"What if I could find some sort of film footage, CCTV, to show this man talking to you. To prove it happened. Would you be prepared to talk about him then? To the police?"

Joe glances up at the guard in the corner as though he might have an opinion on the matter. The guard doesn't react, and Joe turns back to Ash. "Yes," he whispers softly. "Yes. I think so. If it was helpful. To you? And your family?"

"It would be helpful," says Ash. "It would be really helpful to me, and to my mother, and to lots and lots of other women and people that this man has hurt."

Joe nods, gently at first, then more and more animatedly. "Yes," he says. "If you can find proof that this man talked to me, then yes. Yes, I will."

Ash collects her possessions from the small locker she'd been assigned at security, her fingers fumbling over her phone as she takes it out of her bag and switches it on, her heart still racing, nausea rushing through her system, making her dizzy, desperate for air. She stumbles through the last of the many doors she went through to reach Joe Kritner and then, as the chilled January air hits the insides of her lungs, the hot skin of her face, she folds herself in half, clutches hold of her kneecaps, and sobs with a mixture of grief and fury.

Then, and only then, does she call her mother.

"I'm calling the police," says Nina. "I'm calling them right now."

SIXTY-NINE

The next morning, I finally reply to Martha:

> *I'm coming home. Very soon. My mother is in a home, and I have some money. I'm sorry I have put you through so much. Let's start again. I will see the GP, get referred for meds for my ADHD. I will be a better person for you. I will be everything you need me to be. I love you so much.*

And I do, I realize as I press send. I do love her so much. But the thing about my love in the past is that it's always been conditional. It's flickered on and off, its trajectory always headed like a dying star toward the dead end of the feeling. But Martha . . . if there is such a thing as the perfect person for a man like me, then it is her. Neither too submissive nor too aggressive, not too clever or too stupid, too kind or too cold. She has no baggage—even her ex-husband is a decent man with whom I have no issues. And her son—he has a place in my heart, because I know how it feels to not belong to yourself.

A moment later, Martha's response comes and my heart fills with joy:

> *We're all waiting, my love. Let me know when to expect you.*

Part Five

SEVENTY

Jane Trevally had messaged Ash the previous day:

> *I know a great geek, a hacker, friend of my stepson. He can unpick the internet like a surgeon He's going to find out where those fake reviews for Bar Amelie came from. Says to give him twenty-four hours*

The online complaints about Bar Amelie from the woman who claimed to have been sexually assaulted there by a gay waiter were easy enough to find. They are everywhere, in every corner of the internet, from Tripadvisor to Google to chat rooms and forums.

Luke Berner himself had replied to her accusations on some platforms.

> Dear Jennifer Smith,
>
> We are sorry that you are still pursuing and perpetuating these unfounded allegations. The member of staff in question has been interviewed by the police and released without caution. We have CCTV footage which proves categorically that you were not assaulted on our premises. We have eyewitness reports. This is part of

a wicked vendetta against myself and our establishment and we will have no compunction about taking you to court over this matter if you do not desist immediately.

Luke Berner
Owner/General Manager

As Ash heads out of the clothes agency now, toward the sandwich shop, her phone bleeps and it's Jane.

He's got her. Jennifer Smith.

LIVES IN TOOTING

Call me when you can 💥😨

Ash gets her usual panini from the nice couple in the shop. She pets their scruffy dog and finds herself regarding the couple a little less romantically as she waits for the panini to come out of the toaster. The world, she now knows, is not what it seems. Nobody is what they seem. Everything is an illusion. Maybe, she thinks, this perfect-looking couple are teetering on the edge of financial ruin, maybe she's having an affair—maybe her partner isn't even who he says he is, maybe he has another wife, has left abandoned children, death, and destruction in his wake. She shakes these dark thoughts from her head as she crosses the road toward the beach, where she sits on her bench by the sea and lets the weak sunshine warm her skin while she unwraps the panini and clicks on Jane's number. Jane answers immediately.

"Don't ask me how he did it. Something to do with IP addresses. I dunno. But her name is Amanda Law, she's fifty-nine, she used to be an interior designer, quite famous in the nineties and noughties, did stuff for It Girls, Britpop stars, that kind of thing. I googled her—quite pretty, very posh. She went bankrupt in 2006 and was last known to be working at an interiors store on Wandsworth Bridge Road. Two grown sons, born in 1997 and 1999. And yes, I have her address. When can we go?"

Ash stares out at the channel, the surface soft and gray on this gentle January afternoon. Her heart is racing with excitement, and also nerves. She says, "I finish work at five. I can meet you at six thirty? Usual place?"

Amanda Law's apartment is in a converted house in a small road off Tooting High Street. The frontage is grimy and sad, and it does not look like the home of a famous interior designer. Jane presses the bell for flat B and Ash feels a flutter of anticipation about what they might be about to encounter. What sort of woman will she be, what sort of story will she have to tell, and how will she react to what she and Jane are about to tell her? A voice comes onto the intercom and Ash jumps with a start. It's a man's voice, and for a brief, terrifying moment she thinks it's Nick—it has a similar tone and quality.

"Oh, hello," says Jane. "We're looking for Amanda Law? Is she in?"

"Who is this?"

"We're old friends."

"What sort of old friends?"

"Back-in-the-day friends. You know. From her Chelsea days."

There's a long silence and then the man comes back onto the intercom and says, "Hold on."

Thirty seconds later, the door opens and there is a young man in front of them, and at the sight of him, Ash gives an audible gasp. He is the image of Nick Radcliffe: tall and broad, with a thick head of hair, a neat beard, those piercing blue eyes.

"I'm Sam," he says, "Amanda's son. Did you want to come in?"

They follow him up a scruffy staircase and through a door on the first floor into a small but very attractively decorated flat. Sam seats them on a sofa in a bay window and gets them glasses of water. Ash watches him in rapt fascination.

"So," he says, eyeing them inquisitively, "you knew Mum back in the day?"

"Well, yes and no," says Jane. "Or mainly—no. But I knew of her. We had friends in common. Lots and lots of friends in common. The nineties. The noughties. London. Chelsea. All of that. You know. And I loved her work. She was brilliant."

"Yes," says Sam. "She really was. Look." He reaches behind him to a pile of books on a shelf and pulls out two coffee-table books, flicks through the pages, points out images of exquisitely designed rooms. "These are hers. Her work made it into a lot of books, a lot of magazines. She won awards, you know." He closes it and then leans back into his chair and sighs.

"I assume," says Jane, "that she's not here?"

A pained look passes across the young man's face. "Ha. No. No, she's not here. She has not been here for a very long time. I live here now."

"Where . . . ," Ash begins gently. "Where is she?"

"No idea," says Sam. "She did a disappearing act. About four years ago? She started acting very strangely. I mean, she was already kind of delicate, you know? She always had been, since my dad died."

Ash shakes her head slightly and says, "Sorry, you say your father died? When was this?"

"Oh, a very long time ago, when I was about seven? He died in a diving accident in the Philippines. Left my mum in loads of debt. Apparently, he took out lots of loans in her name, in her company's name. She couldn't pay them off and that's why her business went under. She had to sell the place in Chelsea, move us here, and she never really got over it. Never got over any of it. But she was doing OK, you know? She was active in our lives, she had her job at the shop, she was OK. And then, yeah, about four years ago she started acting very strangely. She didn't reply to messages, didn't call, she forgot my birthday, she lost weight—and my mum couldn't afford to lose weight, you know? Behaved quite erratically. Then she became quite reclusive, stopped going to work. We tried everything to help her, tried to get her to the GP for a referral for mental health issues, for therapy, you know, for anything. And then one day after this had been going on for a few weeks, she messaged us both, me and my brother, and said she was leaving. She couldn't cope with London life, she couldn't cope with responsibilities, she needed to get away. She said she'd met a man, he lived in the Algarve, she was going to live with him, some sort of hippie retreat up in the hills. I dunno, the whole thing sounded so bizarre. But also—quite Mum? You know? Hippie retreats? So we didn't really question it at the time, but then her birthday came and went, Christmas came and went, my birthday, my brother's birthday, no cards, no messages, nothing. And then my brother wrote to tell her he'd got engaged and there was no reply. And I dunno, we started getting a bad feeling, thought maybe this guy in the Algarve, whoever he was, maybe he'd trafficked her? Killed her, even." Sam flinches as he utters these words. "So we got in touch with the police and filed her as a missing person and they told us"—he pauses and licks his lips, takes a sip of water and then puts the glass down again—"they told us the craziest thing. Apparently, a year earlier, a woman had come to my mum's flat and then left twenty-four hours later and disappeared. It was nothing to do with my mum, or at least I don't think it was. But it did coincide with the time that she started acting weird."

"Did the police tell you anything else about this woman? The one who came here?"

"Oh, only that she was looking for her husband. That she thought he was with my mum. Apparently she'd had a guy staying, according to the neighbors. God knows what happened there or who she'd got mixed up with, but, yeah, this woman was reported missing by her daughter about a month or two later, and when they started to investigate, they got CCTV footage of this woman arriving at my mum's flat and then leaving the next day. Never to be seen again. No idea what happened to the guy either. Case closed. And yeah . . . that was a bit of a shocker. We didn't push it. Didn't ask too many questions, just in case my mum had, you know, got mixed up in something. Anyway, the police dropped the case eventually, although the woman is still on file as a missing person. And I wondered just now, when you said you were here to see my mum, maybe you knew something? Had something?"

Ash's heart constricts with the knowledge that she is about to upend this guy's life even more than it already has been. "Your dad," she says. "Did he look like you?"

"Yeah. Yeah, my mum always said I was the image of him. My brother looks like my mum, but yeah. Look." He jumps to his feet and pulls a photo album from the shelves behind him. He peels through the pages and then turns the album toward them. "Look," he says, pointing at a handsome young man, clean-shaven, with thick dark hair, holding a toddler on his knee. "That's my dad."

Ash hears Jane draw in her breath. "What was his name, your dad?"

"Damian. Damian Law."

"And you say he died, what, twenty years ago?"

"Yeah, round about that?"

Ash and Jane exchange looks and then Ash reaches into her bag and pulls out the printout of Nick Radcliffe's LinkedIn photo, the photo from his obsolete life-coaching page, and a photo from her camera roll of him at their house on Boxing Day, looking hale and hearty in the back of the shot with a large glass of red wine in his hand. She passes them to Sam and watches him anxiously, her stomach churning with the enormity of what she is doing to this human being whom she has only known for ten minutes. She watches a symphony of emotions pass across his face, confusion, amusement, confusion again, then hurt, then anger, and finally he looks up from the photo and says to Ash, "What is this? Who is this?"

"This is a man called Nick Radcliffe who has lied his way into my mother's life by pretending he knew my dead father. He also pretended to be single and child-free, but is in fact married to another woman, called Martha, with whom he has a young child. He has been with Martha for four years and before that he was married to a woman called Tara, who is the woman who was reported missing after leaving this flat four years ago. He was also married to a woman called Laura, and they had two daughters he abandoned when they were very young and who are now teenagers. He also . . ." Ash takes a huge gulp of air before speaking, to stop her voice from cracking. "He also paid someone to kill my dad. And I'm really sorry, Sam, but I believe this man is . . . your father."

Ash sees Sam gulp heavily as his eyes drop back to the pictures. "His hair, though. It's white. I don't . . ." Finally, he nods. "I mean, he got older. Yeah. He looks older—but how? I don't understand."

"You know," Jane says thoughtfully, "I read somewhere that you can pay people in the Philippines to fake your death for you. Apparently, it's a . . . thing? I mean, is it possible that that's what your father did? That he faked his death. And then, for whatever reason, he came back into your mother's life four years ago? That he was the man your mum's neighbors say they saw here, staying with your mother at that time. What did they say he looked like?"

Sam looks up at Jane with cloudy eyes. "They said . . ." He pauses, then starts again. "They said he was tall, with white hair and a short beard, about midfifties." He gulps drily. Then he says, "Fuck."

"I'm so sorry," says Ash. "I just can't . . . I mean, my father was murdered just over a year ago. It was the worst thing that ever happened to me. And I can't imagine what it's been like for you, growing up without your dad. And to know that—"

Sam shakes his head and puts up a hand to ward off the rest of Ash's sentence. Then suddenly he is on his feet, sprinting, hurtling out of the room, feet heavy against the wooden floorboards, followed by the sound of a door opening, knees falling to the floor, and Sam vomiting thunderously into a toilet bowl.

Ash and Jane sit silently as he vomits three times in succession. Ash has her eyes closed, Jane leans into the sofa and lets her head roll back. This is awful, thinks Ash, just the most awful, awful thing. To be here, to be present for it, to witness it, to be, however tangentially, a part of it. It is overwhelming and terrible and too, too much.

"Oh God," Ash whispers into the silence. She rocks forward and then back again. "Oh God."

Jane reaches for her hand and holds it softly but firmly in hers.

"Are you thinking what I'm thinking?" Ash whispers.

"You mean Amanda? Dead?" Jane replies in a matching whisper.

Ash nods. "And killed by . . . ?"

"Nick?" Jane mouths silently.

Ash nods again.

Then Sam appears, sallow, tear streaked, clammy. Jane passes him his water, helps him to his seat.

"Are you OK?" Ash asks.

He nods and then he clears his throat and says, "Where is he now? My father? Where is he?"

Jane looks at Ash and then back at Sam. "He disappeared," she says. "About a week ago. He realized that Martha, his current wife, had worked out that he was with Ash's mum and he did a runner. But we have a plan. OK? We're working on it. Would you want to see him? You and your brother?"

Sam nods. "Yeah. I want to see him. Of course I want to see him."

"Well, then," says Jane. "Give me your number, and I'll tell you what to do."

SEVENTY-ONE

I have money. Twenty thousand pounds. It was all I could extract in the craziness of what has just happened without drawing attention to myself. The feel of it in my bag, the heft, the weight, the freedom after these past few years of living in single sums of thousands. Twenty. There should have been more. Jessie has hundreds of thousands squirrelled away, but of course the blessed fucking children get that. I did not like having to be mean to Jessie. I did not like it at all. But I have told Martha I have money, and I have to prove to her that I have money.

So I was mean to Jessie.

And it broke my heart to do it.

She has always treated me like a king, made me feel like a god. And she's always been so, so kind to me. And generous too, but when I told her about my predicament, my poor mother, my perilous financial situation, when I cried again and allowed her to hold me while I told her I didn't know what I was going to do, that I was lost, that I was desperate, and she stroked my hair and said, "André, I am so, so sorry, but I just can't help you. I really can't," I saw red. Or some other color, in fact, a sort of bruise color, sick gray, violent purple, putrid, dirty yellow. And then I found that my hands were at her throat.

I know I said I wasn't a violent man. I'm not a violent man. Not until someone pushes me too far, to a place where I can no longer talk sense to myself. And in that moment—why couldn't she have just given me the fucking money? What was wrong with her?

I put my hands around her neck and I squeezed. I told her I would call her children right now and tell them all about their mother's secret life, the male prostitute she'd been paying to have sex with her for over fifteen years, the thousands of pounds she'd spent on him, the things she liked him to do to her, the objects belonging to their father that she'd given to him, the lovely Cartier watch, for example. Her eyes filled with the magical glistening tears that having a man's hands around your throat somehow conjures up, animal, beautiful, and I felt her nod, try to say something, so I loosened my grip, licked my lips, waited for her to find her voice.

"I have money, cash. But not much. The rest is in stocks and shares—I can't touch it. But you can have my cash. You can have all of it."

I tied her to a chair, and I took her cards to a local machine and checked her accounts. She was not lying. Twenty thousand one hundred and eighteen pounds in two separate bank accounts. The next day, I took her to her local branches, where I watched over her from a distance as she emptied them both, then we went back to her flat and I cooked her garlic chicken with mashed potatoes and we drank a bottle of wine, or at least I did, she just stared at her wine with big, glassy eyes. I told her that she was the greatest woman in the world and that her children did not deserve her, and then the next morning, I left.

The bag sits at my feet now as I stand on the platform at the train station heading home to Martha. I'll tell her that it's all I could free up in the short term, that I still have to sell my mother's house, that it's been valued at nearly £500,000. But at least we have something in the bank for now, and we can start working toward Martha's Garden on the Beach again. As I look up the platform to see if the train that is due in forty seconds is visible yet at the top of the track, I feel my phone vibrate and pull it out of my jacket pocket. It's Martha.

What's your ETA?

I reply:

I'll be home at midday. Just after.

OK, can't wait to see you! I'll be in our room.

I send her a throbbing-heart emoji and smile and tuck my phone back into my pocket.

Our room.

I can't wait to be back in our room, after all those days in Paddy Swann's bed with Paddy Swann's wife, Paddy Swann's pillows, Paddy Swann's beard stubble in the razor in Paddy Swann's en suite. I want to be back where I belong, where I am loved and appreciated, where I am wanted and needed.

SEVENTY-TWO

HASTINGS POLICE STATION

The woman sitting in front of DC Ian Langtry is around sixty-five to seventy years of age. She is well preserved, slim, and nicely dressed in fitted trousers, a striped sweater, and a woolen overcoat. Her hair is dyed a subtle blond and tied back at the nape of her neck. Her reading glasses sit on top of her head and her nails are painted a milky-coffee color. But despite her elegant appearance, it is clear she is in some distress. She seems flighty and panicked; her eyes will not rest on one spot.

"I've come to report an assault," she says, so quietly that DC Langtry asks her to repeat herself.

"Sorry. Yes. I've come to report an assault."

"And are you the victim of this assault?"

"Yes. Yes, I am."

"And what is your name, please?"

"It's Jessica Bland."

"Your address?"

She gives an address in an apartment block overlooking the sea.

"And can you tell me what happened exactly?"

The woman shuffles slightly in her seat. "I, er . . . it's very sensitive. It's . . . I mean, I need a lot of what I'm about to tell you to remain confidential. Otherwise, I'm not sure I can go through with this."

"Well," says DC Langtry gently, "why don't we start at the beginning and then see where we end up. But certainly, for now, everything you tell me remains between us. If you choose not to pursue your allegations, then that is your prerogative."

The woman sighs and grimaces slightly, then inhales hard and says, "I have been having a casual relationship for many, many years with a man called André. I do not know his surname—as I say, it has been incredibly casual. Last week, he came to my apartment and said that he was homeless, had nowhere to go, could he stay with me, just for a few days. In all honesty, I wanted to say no. But soft touch that I am . . ." She sighs again. "Anyway, it seemed fine at first. He was pleasant company. A good houseguest. We had dinner together every night. I felt very much that he was readying himself to leave. And then two nights ago, he . . ."

Jessica puts a hand to her throat and touches it softly.

"He got very angry, very suddenly. I'd never seen that side of him before. He had always been such a gentleman, so polite, so charming. But it was like these doors came down and a new version of him appeared. He was asking me for money, and I said no, I'm sorry, I can't give you money, and suddenly his hands were at my throat. I thought, I genuinely thought he intended to kill me. I thought it was the end."

DC Langtry sees the marks now: soft brownish pink spots in the flesh of her neck, the size and shape of fingertips. He makes notes.

"And then just as suddenly as he attacked me, he let go of me, and this is where, I'm afraid, this is where it gets murky, and frankly, I'd wondered if I could tell you about this without mentioning all the facts, but really, I don't think I can because it wouldn't make any sense, not without the full picture. Because the thing is, you see, André was slightly more than a friend. He was a friend with benefits. And the benefits were—well . . ." Jessica's face contorts with discomfort. "Paid for," she says finally. "André was a male escort and I had been paying him for many, many years for his occasional company, and, well, I have grown children, I'm a respectable woman, and André knew that and used it as a weapon to blackmail me. He blackmailed me into giving him all my cash, every penny of it. There'll be CCTV footage of me visiting two banks over the course of a day, emptying out my accounts for him, in cash.

"Twenty thousand pounds. I gave that man twenty thousand pounds and I tried to be pragmatic about it, I really did try so hard. But as time went by, well, I just got crosser and crosser and more and more disgusted with him. Yes, that's the word. Disgusted. And I thought, No. What's more important, your bloody reputation—or stopping this horrible man doing this to somebody else? And I really, really, really don't want him to do this to anyone else, because believe me, as he held his hands around my neck, I knew without any shadow of a doubt that this was not his first rodeo. Oh no. Definitely not. I knew then that he was evil and that he hurt women and that stopping him was more important than saving my reputation. And I'm sorry that I don't know more about him, I don't know his surname, I don't know where he lives, and I don't know who he is. But I have this . . ." She pulls out her phone and plays a small video of a man on a Ring app, the familiar *ding-ding-dong* ringtone playing in the background. The man is tall and has a thick head of silvery white hair and a neat silver beard.

"This is him. This is André at my door when he first arrived, just over a week ago. It's pretty clear, I think. And hopefully, maybe, you can use it to track him down. And at the very least, might the notes I gave him from my bank accounts be marked and traceable?"

DC Ian Langtry makes another note in his pad and sighs.

"I'm very sorry," he says, "that you have experienced this. If it's OK with you, I would like to take you now to have your injuries photographed. Would you agree to that?"

Jessica nods. "Yes," she says. "Please. Anything. Whatever it takes to get this creep off the streets."

SEVENTY-THREE

The cottage is quiet and sweet when I arrive. There are fresh flowers in a vase on the dining table, lots of shades of pink and cream. The Christmas tree is still up, looking sad now, too many days past Twelfth Night, branches drooping heavily toward the floorboards, a solitary bauble on the floor, sitting on a bed of dead needles. There is condensation on the kitchen window, the lasting impression of the family who were here this morning, eating breakfast, boiling the kettle, chatting, living and breathing, without me. But now I'm back, and we will be complete again.

I place my bag full of money under the settle in the hallway, I take off my coat and then my shoes, and I step quietly and slowly up the tiny central staircase to the landing, where I see that the door to our bedroom is closed. My heart sings with anticipation. My darling wife. I knock gently and then I hear her footsteps. She pulls open the door and she is wearing a simple lawn nightdress, her hair tied back loosely, no makeup, no jewelry, she is completely unadorned, and I scoop her up in my arms and I carry her to the bed and she wraps her arms and legs around me and she kisses me back and presses her fingers into my flesh and pulls at my hair and groans into my ear and I know, all the way through, I know she is acting. I can feel it. She is acting. And now, so am I . . .

Afterward, we lie together in each other's arms, me and my beautiful wife, and I put my nose into her hair and smell her, the scalpy essence of her, and there, deep down, I smell her fear. What is she scared of? What has happened in the days since she came to Nina's house and peered through the windows, looking to find me in the arms of my lover? She glances up at me and smiles, traces her fingertip across the hair on my chest. I can feel the emotional weight of the words she is about to say.

"You know," she says, her finger making tiny circles against my skin, "Grace said she'd collect Nala from the childminder's today. I've closed the shop. The boys are with their dad. You and I could take a drive down to Bangate. Have another look at our pavilion. Maybe have dinner somewhere. What do you think? I've had so many ideas about the new café. I've got mood boards. I've filled in all the forms to apply for a business loan, extend the mortgage. And I thought . . . since you're getting the money from your mum's house . . . I'm sorry if that sounds insensitive, I know she's only just moved out and I know you've been through such stress these last few weeks. But I just want to move on now, Al. I want us to get the dream rolling. Finally. You and me. And look." She turns slightly and points toward the window. "It's a sunny day. What do you think? It would be nice?"

I stare down at her and I see that she has softened. The fear has left her eyes. She was just nervous, I think, nervous to ask me about spending the money from my mother's house, scared I would be cross with her for her insensitivity. And the sex, I see now, was some kind of attempt to butter me up, to reassure me, and I suddenly feel myself relax.

"Yes," I say, kissing the knuckles of her hand. "Yes. It would be lovely."

She wears a soft pink sweater and loose-fitting jeans, with a padded coat over the top. I smile at her in the hallway, where she's lacing up her trainers.

"Are we bringing Baxter?"

"No," she says. "Let's leave him here. Just in case we want to go somewhere they don't allow dogs."

I smile and nod, and I take my coat off the peg and slip it on. As I do so, my eye is caught by the bag of money under the settle where I left it. I could show it to Martha now, a sign of my grand intentions. *Look,* I could say, *we're starting with this*. But then I think, No, that money is my safety net. My escape fund. Should I ever need it. Which I won't. Not now that Martha and I are back together.

But then a question mark of doubt pops into my consciousness. I am never complacent, I cannot afford to be, and while Martha goes to put the dog in the kitchen, I lean down quickly and slot as many stacks of notes into my jacket pockets as I can. I also fish out my escape pack, the one I carry with me everywhere. Then I push the bag back under the settle with my foot, hold the door open for Martha, and we leave.

SEVENTY-FOUR

Martha glances at her husband in the driver's seat of the car. He looks, she thinks, so carefree. He looks happy, unburdened. His blue eyes gleam in the January sun through the windscreen, and he turns when he notices her gaze upon him, and smiles.

"You look so beautiful," he says. "I love you so much."

"I love you too," she says.

They are halfway to Bangate and Martha's gut roils and churns as the coast gets closer and closer. Twenty minutes, she thinks, twenty minutes and then . . . but no, she can't bring herself to think of it, of what happens in twenty minutes. Right now, she is in the moment: the sunshine, the road ahead, the road behind, this moment of nowness and calm. She absorbs it, holds it inside, ignores the voice in her head that says, *You idiot, you idiot, you idiot*; the voice that says, *How could you be so stupid, so stupid, so stupid?*

Hers has not been a life of bad decisions and poor choices. Hers has been a healthy life, a functional life, a life of pleasure and joy. Her first husband was a good man, a good husband, and a good father. They split up because they'd outgrown each other and that was all there was to it. Her friendships were solid, her home was beautiful, her children were happy (well, on the whole), her business was successful. And yet, into this pretty picture, somehow, stage left, silently and without Martha asking one single question, a beautiful man had appeared. And Martha had made the first bad decision of her life.

How, she asks herself now, had she lived for four years with a man who claimed to have a job but never took a business call, never introduced her to a colleague, never took her to a work function, a man who went on business trips that required him to switch off his phone for days on end, a man who claimed to have severe ADHD yet managed to hold down an important job, garner respect, be given promotions. How did she not ask more questions? Push him? Corner him? Who was she? And more important, who the hell is he, this man smiling into the winter sun, with his loose body language, telling her he loves her? And why, she asks herself, does she still want his love? What does she want it for? What is wrong with her?

But now she knows she is not alone, that many more women have allowed themselves to be manipulated and used by this man, and in some ways she feels she may have had the best of him. He has not stolen from her, at least, not until recently and even then not very much, not compared to how much he has stolen from others. From Laura, from Amanda, from Tara. She thinks, secretly, privately, that Al loves her more than he loved any of the others, she really does. She thinks, even as it pains her to do so, that Al gave her the best of himself, the less sleazy side of himself, the side of himself that wanted a normal life and a normal marriage. She suspects that she is fooling herself to think these things, and she pictures Nina Swann sitting in her office at the flower shop, strong and formidable in black. Nina Swann would not have put up with a moment of this treatment, she thinks, and as she thinks this her phone buzzes and she pulls it out to see that there is a message from Nina, except it does not say Nina, it says "school," and the message, she sees from the preview in her notifications, says: `All ready. ETA?`

She types quickly. `Eight minutes.` Then puts her phone away before Al can see it.

A moment later, Al pulls the car over into a lay-by. Martha looks at him anxiously.

"Just need a pee. I'll be right back."

He gets out of the car and Martha watches him curiously. She has never, in all the four years she's been with him, known Al to pee outdoors. Literally never. Her heart rate quickens, and her breathing becomes tight and uncomfortable. What is he doing? she wonders. Is he running? Escaping? Does he know? But a moment later, he reappears from the undergrowth, smiling genially.

"You OK?" he asks, looking at her strangely as he gets back into the car.

She nods and smiles hard. "I'm just excited," she says breathlessly, to hide the adrenaline rush brought about by the subterfuge. "This is going to be incredible."

Al turns to her and smiles, and still, even now, she is blown away by the way he looks when he smiles, this handsome, charming man, the father of her child.

"It is," he says warmly. "It really, really is."

SEVENTY-FIVE

The car park at Bangate Cove is completely empty and the sun shines milky white through a thin veil of clouds, while the air is full of salt and promise. A new year, a new start. No more, I think to myself, no more running away. No more women. I've learned my lesson. I will dedicate the rest of my life to making Martha happy. And somehow, and I do not know how, we will find a way to make this dream come true, this dream of both of ours. And then it will be me who turns heads when I walk into the establishment, me who causes people to say, "It's Alistair himself." There will be photographs of me in lifestyle coffee-table books, pictures of me and my beautiful wife and our beautiful daughter in our iconic beachfront café and flower shop. And fuck everyone else. Fuck all of them, especially the Swann family. They can keep their money and their house and their restaurants and their perfect lives. I have one last parting gift to the Swann family and it's in a letter posted yesterday, addressed to Aisling. Fuck them. Fuck their dreams and fuck their self-delusion.

I wait for Martha to get out of the passenger seat, and then I close her door behind her and hold my hand out to her. She smiles and lets me take it. Together we walk through the path between the dunes and onto the beach.

SEVENTY-SIX

The old ice cream pavilion is cold and damp, the air still and pungent with disuse. They sit, all of them, on the cheap wooden chairs that had been stacked into piles around the edges of the room. Ash looks at each woman in turn.

First there is Emma Greenlaw, sitting next to Nina. Then there is Laura, who is with Lola, the elder of her two daughters. There are Sam and Joel, Amanda's grown-up sons, and there are the two girls from the neighborhood app who accused Nick Radcliffe of stalking them. And then there are the others, the ones who found out about the Facebook page that Nina, Emma, and Ash set up a few days ago called DON'T LET HIM IN.

It had been Ash's idea. She'd read a story in the news about some women in America who'd set up a Facebook page when they realized that they'd been the victims of a serial scammer and had eventually uncovered about fifty victims of the same man, each one knowing him by a different name, each one being caught in a web of lies and untruths so convoluted that they could barely think straight. And so, as well as the key players, there are other women here who claim to have been stalked by him: a girl called Kadija, who had to report him to her boss for making her feel uncomfortable in the coffee shop in Tooting where she worked four years ago, and another girl who'd been stalked on the street in Hastings by the same man just over a week ago. She claimed he'd followed her for five full minutes and then "sniffed the back of her neck." There are women here who claim he scammed them out of savings by offering them life-coaching training, women he dated for a few days, a few weeks, and left with their cash, their jewelry, their pride. And more incredibly than that, there is a woman called Jessica Bland, who was assaulted by a man she knew as "André" just a few days ago and blackmailed out of £20K of cash. The most remarkable thing about Jessica Bland is that she claims that "André" was a male escort who charged £500 a night for his services and traveled all around the country, with, she claimed, at least twenty or thirty other regular clients.

And then there is the issue of Joe Kritner's "Silver Man." Paddy's case is currently being investigated again by the police who'd done the original investigation, and they are looking afresh at the CCTV footage from that night and the eyewitness reports.

The Tara Truscott case has also been reopened, and the police are now looking into the disappearance of Amanda Law too.

This is their moment, these people here, now, who have been abused, manipulated, stolen from, lied to, and broken by this man. It ends now. And each one of them wants to bear witness to it.

There is a sound, just audible over the crackle of the surf against the beach, of tires over gravel.

Ash and her mother exchange looks. Her mother squeezes her hand hard and smiles. Ash smiles back and looks at the time on her phone.

He's here.

SEVENTY-SEVEN

I suppose you'd like to hear from me, directly, about how it feels to walk into that place, that space, with all those women looking at me, all those faces, those eyes, those expressions of distaste, dislike, fear, curiosity, rage. Well, the first thing I can tell you that I feel is like a fucking *idiot*.

I turn to Martha. I see what she has done. She has lured me into a trap with her lackluster sex and her talk of dreams and her stupid messages that, *God*, I cannot believe I fell for. I am better than this, is what I think when I walk into that space. I am better than this, and I am better than all of you. I cannot imagine for a moment what they want with me. What? I think. What do you want? What do you want me to say, want me to do?

You all wanted me, I want to say. *You all had gaping voids in your lives, and you all invited me to fill them. I did not force one of you to choose me. Not one of you.*

But I don't say anything, I merely stand with my arms folded and look from one to the next. I see my sons. Sam eyes me warily. Joel eyes me challengingly. They are both so handsome. I feel a kick of pride at the sight of them. And then I see Lola, my elder daughter with Laura, and my stomach lurches. I have not seen Lola since she was six. She is now a young woman, long and lean, dressed in black, unable to look at me at all. *Wow,* I want to say, *look at you! Just look at you!* But again, I say nothing. I see, much to my disgust, the girl called Kadija from the café in Tooting. What on earth, I think, is *she* doing here? And that's when I break my silence.

I turn to Martha and issue a small laugh. "What's going on, darling?" I ask her, in my softest, most vulnerable voice. "What on earth have you done?"

Martha looks at me and I see her sigh. "It's over, Al," she says. "This is the end."

I frown. "The end of what, exactly?"

I hear someone tut, someone else sigh.

I put my hand against my heart, and let my eyes fill with tears. "No, really," I say. "The end of what? The end of me just trying to survive in this world? Just trying to make people happy, give them what they want?"

The gathering is silent for a moment until a young woman—I think it might be the girl who reported me to the police in Reading—gets to her feet and says, "I'm sorry. You think I wanted you breathing down my neck in the dark? You think I wanted to feel like my heart was going to burst apart, explode out of my chest, like I might be about to be killed or raped, that my life might be about to end? You think I wanted that, *you sick fuck*?"

And then I see what is happening here. It is a reckoning. These women and children have come together to make me atone for my so-called sins. But these women and these children—they know nothing.

I sigh sadly and reply to the woman accusing me. "You know it wasn't me. The police know it wasn't me."

Then the woman called Kadija gets to her feet and takes three steps toward me, a finger pointed at me feverishly. "You made me not want to come into work in the morning. You made me feel like meat. You knew nothing about me, about my history, about the things I have had to deal with in my life, my trauma, yet you thought it was OK to come into my workspace and intimidate me and scare me and make me feel unsafe—"

And that is when I lose my cool. This stupid, stupid girl with her stupid, stupid sense of entitlement, to what? My respect? What on earth has she done to earn my respect? Nothing. Not one thing.

"Trauma!" I say. "You know nothing about trauma. None of you know. But you don't see me whingeing about it, complaining about people making me feel 'unsafe' because someone stood a little close. Jesus Christ."

Nina gets to her feet, and I see in her eyes that she is about to make some kind of a pronouncement.

"So, this trauma," she says. "The—what was it you told me—the waterboarding? The neglect? Your cruel father? The jibes about your appearance? Being cut out of the inheritance for no good reason?"

I clench my jaw and stare at her, waiting to see where she is going.

"Simon . . . ," she says, with almost tangible relish. "Simon Smith."

I feel the center fall out of my world. *She has my name.* But then immediately it jumps back into place. *Go on,* I tell Nina with my eyes. *Go on then.*

"Only child of Richard and Felicity Smith," she continues. "*Beloved* only child. Given everything. But nothing was ever good enough. Loans and more loans, until your poor parents were almost bled dry. Your mother changed her will because she was scared you were going to kill her in her sleep. Your parents were scared of you. You made their lives hell with your superiority complex, your insistence that they pave your way with gold. And then when you found out about the will change, you arrived at your mother's door blue with rage, you screamed into her face so loudly she swore she was being berated by the devil. She changed the locks the day after your father died. She was terrified that you would come back and finish her off. But she loved you so much, your mother. She adored you. Until the day she died."

I feel a wave of nausea wash through me at her words. Images flash through my mind. My childhood home so lovingly tended. The garden that was my father's pride and joy. The holidays that were so painstakingly planned for and looked forward to and which I always, always hated, and always, always spoiled. The attempts to find me friends, to buy me gifts that might make me happy. My mother's hand on the crown of my head. *"My beautiful boy,"* she would say. *"Look at you, you are the most beautiful boy in the world."* My mother had loved me. My father had loved me too. But neither of them had loved me enough to give me what I truly needed. They tried, but they couldn't. Small people they were, both of them, with small dreams and small ambitions. They thought that what they had should be enough for me, but it was not. Not nearly enough. And then they cut it all away from me and left me adrift.

"I assume," I say now to Nina, "that you have been talking to my aunt."

Now Emma gets to her feet. "Not just your aunt, Simon. Your cousins. Your neighbors. Everyone, in fact, that we could find in the village of Lower Dunton where you grew up. And all of them said the same thing. They all said you were a psycho. A monster. A user. And . . ." Emma purses her lips before letting rip with her finishing salvo. "A loser."

The word sits in my head like the imprint of a camera flash, and I stare at Tara's daughter, this woman who ruined my life, this ugly, ugly woman who set this whole sequence of events in motion four years ago when she told her mother to leave me. I feel a fire burning from the pit of my stomach and into the muscle and sinew and gristle of my arms, and I make a roar and I hurl myself at her. My fist connects with her face, and I feel some part of it crackle, satisfyingly. There is blood and some muted screams and then there are hands pulling me back, but everything has fallen apart, all the neatly stitched seams that hold me together are falling apart and bits of me are spilling out and I don't care anymore, I simply don't care, not one person in this room is worthy of me, not one person in this room means anything to me, not even Martha, not my children. None of them. And my body throws out blows and kicks as other people's bodies attempt to overpower me and then I am somehow on the floor and my sons, my strong, handsome sons, they have pinned me down and I stare up now into the dark eyes of Sam, his face a few inches from mine, and he hisses into my face, "Where's Mum? What the fuck have you done with Mum?"

"Nothing," I hiss back. "I've done nothing to your mum."

"Where's my mother, Jonathan?" Emma booms from somewhere out of my eyeline. "Where is she? Just tell us. We know you've killed them both. Just tell us where they are!"

I can see the pieces aligning. I can see the power that this group of disparate people hold. Through the sea of faces staring down at me, I see the face of Jessie Bland. What is she doing here? I wonder queasily. Has she told anyone about the money? About me throttling her? Has she given up her anonymity to get me into this room, to bring about this intervention? Has she told the police? I feel it all merging, all of it, all the connections hissing and popping, all the perfectly separated pieces of my life merging into a toxic black puddle, and someone has a match to it, the whole thing is about to explode, subsume, consume, and not only that but bring out all the other dormant pieces, the other people I have messed with and hurt. The face of Luke Berner flashes through my mind. Not my fault. Not my fault.

All of this swims through my consciousness and I know I cannot be here, not anymore. I use my heft, my substance, my terror, my rage, and I am not the small, spoiled, fey boy that the kids at school called Simone. I am Simon, Simon Smith, I am strong and I am tall and I can fight back, I can bend the world to my will, and I throw back the grips of the people who are holding me to the floor and I leap to my feet and I push Martha out of the way so hard that I see her stumble backward against the side of a table and wince, but I cannot care about her now, I just need to go. I stride, tough, solid, out of the pavilion and onto the beach and my feet hit the cold, hard sand. I start to run toward the sea, and I run and I run and I run until I feel the icy chill of seawater inside my shoes, leaching through the cotton of my socks, my jeans, my underwear, my jacket, my sleeves, my chest, my neck, the top of my head. It closes over me, the shock of it is awesome, my heart pounds, my thoughts still. I am gone.

SEVENTY-EIGHT

They stand on the beach in awe, all of them, watching the disappearing outline of the man they each know by a different name, and then the boys are in the water, Sam and Joel, fully clothed, going in after their father. They stride through the surf until the water is up to their thighs and then they dive, start to swim, thrash through the small waves, breaking the surface of the water into a foamy soup. They go down and come back up, go down and come back up, but there is a current and it tugs them away from the place where the man called Simon Smith was last seen, his silver hair swallowed up by the gray sea, like a light being extinguished.

Martha looks at Nina. "Where is he?" she asks in a loud whisper.

Nina simply shakes her head, her arms crossed tight around her chest, the wind blowing her dark hair across her cheeks.

They stand like that for fifteen minutes, watching the two young men in the water, until the women call them back. It's too cold. They will get hypothermia. Someone has called the emergency services and an ambulance arrives just as the boys finally pull themselves from the sea, and then the police arrive, followed by sea rescue and a police helicopter. Within half an hour, the tranquil cove is a mass of flashing lights and action and noise. The boys are wrapped in foil cloaks, someone has brought them hot drinks. But still, as Martha stands on the sea's edge, staring into the thin line of the horizon, there is no sign of him. Of the man she called her husband. Of the man she called Al.

SEVENTY-NINE

Jane clicks the link in the message that Ash has just sent her and scrolls frantically down the screen of her phone. The news is freshly broken, only three hours old:

> A man has been lost, feared drowned, in the English Channel in Bangate Cove, near Folkestone. Search-and-rescue teams have called off their search as night falls. It is believed that the man in question is Simon Smith, 55, who was wanted by Hastings police in connection with an assault on a seventy-year-old woman and financial extortion. He was also under investigation for the disappearance and possible murder of two other women, and conspiracy to commit murder in the case of a man who was pushed under a tube train in London fifteen months ago. Two men who attempted to rescue Smith were treated at the scene for mild hypothermia but did not require hospitalization. Witnesses to the tragedy have informed the police that Smith may also be responsible for other acts of financial extortion, coercive behavior, physical abuse, street stalking, and antisocial behaviors. One witness told a local reporter that Smith was the subject of a Facebook group that acted as a forum for women who felt they had been

victims of Smith's crimes and misdemeanors and that the other witnesses on the beach were all members of the same group.

The page is currently offline.

Jane lowers her phone and raises her eyes to the blue sky above. She's torn between triumph that Nick Radcliffe has paid for his crimes with his life and disappointment that there will be no public reckoning, no time in prison, and, more important, no closure for the children of Tara Truscott and Amanda Law, all of whom still have no idea where their mothers are. He has taken their fates with him into the cold, murky waters of the English Channel, taken those secrets, taken it all and disappeared. Death is an easy way out. But at least the world will now know, she thinks, they will know that he was a killer, a liar, a cheat, a loser, a reprehensible human being.

She lifts her phone again and goes back to Ash's text message.

`Wow,` she types. `You did it. You are an incredible human being, and your father would have been so proud of you. And so am I.`

EIGHTY

They got back from Bangate Cove an hour ago and Ash is still in a state of shock. She goes to the fridge for wine and notices that the bowl of vegan curry Nick Radcliffe had made for her is still in there, under cling film. She stares at it blindly for a moment. An image flashes into her mind of that tall, vital man leaning against the kitchen counter, blue eyes flashing, a tea towel over his shoulder, the lovingly tended curry on the hob behind him. Then she thinks of him just now, striding out into the icy water, plummeting into the depths, disappearing.

She pulls the bowl from the fridge and scrapes the contents with some relish into the bin before rinsing the bowl and putting it in the dishwasher. There, she thinks, the last traces, gone.

Her mother walks into the kitchen a moment later. She looks shell-shocked, gray, her hair tangled up by the wind and sea spray into a thick thatch.

"What a mess," she says. "What a horrible, horrible fucking mess." She sighs loudly. "And now we'll never know what happened to Tara. What happened to Amanda. Those poor boys. Poor Emma. The lack of closure is . . ." She sighs again. And then she looks straight at Ash and says, "But we're going to be great. Aren't we? You and I? You're going to be great. I'm going to be great. We're both going to be great? Aren't we?"

And they are going to be great. They really are. They've been talking a lot about the future these last few days. Nina is going to find a business partner to help her with Paddy's restaurants. She's going to sell this big old house that was bigger, she'd told Ash in the car just now, than she ever wanted or needed her house to be—Paddy's house, she told Ash, it was always Paddy's house. She will downsize to a modern apartment on the beach in Folkestone with a terrace directly over the sea, with bedrooms for Ash and for Arlo so that they will always have a home to come back to.

Ash knows now that her time has finally come. The weight she has been laboring under for all of these months since those letters started to arrive from Ritchie Lloyd, since the police turned up at her flat, since being diagnosed with a personality disorder, since her father died, and since Nick fucking Radcliffe walked into their lives—it's all gone. She is sane. She is clear. She is pure and unfiltered, and she is ready now, ready to leave the Riviera, her mother's protective bosom, her home comforts, and the shadow of her father's memory. Because that's another thing that's changed. A letter had arrived that morning in a handwritten envelope, addressed to Ash.

It was from Nick.

Dear Ash

We never did get around to those life-coaching sessions, did we? There was so much I would have liked to share with you if we had. But mainly this: your family was not perfect, it really wasn't. Your father was not perfect and your mother is not perfect, and really, if you want to heal yourself and find your jumping-off platform into the adult life you so want for yourself, I suggest you sit down with your mother and make her have a difficult conversation with you. She'll know what you're talking about and then it will be up to her whether or not she's capable of sharing the truth with you. And then and only then can you become the woman you are destined to become. Get out there. Own your truth. Seize the world by the balls. Be the best person you possibly can.

Yours, with good intentions,
Nick

Ash had read the letter twice in quick succession, her heart racing hard inside her chest. She'd looked at the back of her mother's head, staring at her laptop on the kitchen table.

"Mum," she'd said, sliding the letter on the table in front of her for her to read. "What does he mean?"

And her mother had told her everything. Every last thing. Ash had taken it in, held it inside her heart, her gut, her mind, felt it start to rip her into tiny pieces, but then she'd taken control of the feelings, turned them around and looked at them objectively and thought, Yes, of course. *Of course.* It had all made a weird, sickening kind of sense of everything, of the feeling she'd always had that her life was a story that someone was writing about her and not a real thing. But it was a real thing, it had been, all along. And she was not a doll or a puppet, not an actor playing the role of "soft-hearted daughter" in the movie of her life, she was a real person, with edges and spikes and layers and terrible truths to confront. And while she will always be her mother's child, she is also an adult, and it's time now for her to go. Nick Radcliffe might well have thought he was throwing a hand grenade into the glossy façade of Ash's fake golden world, but actually, he had done her a favor, her and her mother. Now they could walk side by side, holding each other up, as equals and as friends.

They'd embraced for a while then, and Ash had breathed in the scent of her mother, the scent that has always brought her to safety, to home. And then they'd set off together for Bangate Cove.

But something occurs to Ash now as she stares down at the letter still sitting unfolded on the kitchen table where they'd left it.

The font.

The layout.

The sheen of the paper.

She's seen a letter like this before, she knows she has.

She runs up the stairs to her bedroom and pulls open the bottom drawer of her desk, rifles through piles of stuff until she finds what she's looking for. The letters that Ritchie Lloyd had sent her during that insane, crazy summer when she lost her mind, her reputation, her self-worth—her way.

She holds the two letters up, side by side.

They are identical.

EPILOGUE

I see him, just there, on the hill that leads into the village. He pulls behind him a small case on wheels. His hair is brown. His face is clean-shaven. He is wearing a hoodie and shorts, has a bottle of water in his hand. He could be anyone, any tall, good-looking bloke arriving on his holidays at a quiet village ten miles inland from the coastal resorts of the Algarve. My heart races at the sight of him. With his hair that color, he looks like he did when we first met. I leave the door of my cottage open behind me and start down the quiet road toward him. I know I should wait, but I can't. I have missed him so much, this beautiful man—my husband. And I know that I am his only true wife. I am the only one with whom he shared his real name: Simon Smith. He shared it with me four years ago as a reward for my loyalty. "I have never given this name to anyone else," he had said, kissing the backs of my hands, his blue eyes limpid with gratitude, with love. I am the only one who has ever been truly loved by him and the only one who has ever loved him the way he deserves to be loved. I am the only one who knows him, who gets him, who would sacrifice everything for him. All the others, the ones I read about in the papers, Laura, Tara, Nina, Martha, they're nothing. They're nobodies.

The woman caught on camera leaving my flat the day that Tara disappeared was me. I was wearing Tara's clothes. We had the same build, the same overall look—I put the hood of her winter coat up and kept my face away from the CCTV cameras that followed me as I walked to the station, took the tube to Paddington and then the train to Reading. In the toilet on the train, I changed out of my disguise and back into my normal clothes, dumped Tara's clothes in a bin behind a shopping precinct, sat in a Caffè Nero for an hour, and then got a train back to London. Simon used Tara's phone to send messages to her daughter, and of course to his own phone. He'd made sure he was caught on CCTV in the local area in the hours after I left my flat dressed as Tara. Whatever anyone might have suspected, there was no way anyone could ever point the finger at us. We'd put ourselves beyond suspicion.

Simon stayed with me for a day or two and then he had to go. I thought he was coming here, to the Algarve. He told me he would call me when it was safe for me to join him. I had no idea, of course, that he was going to her place. That Martha woman. I only found that out later.

It was a weird time. I feel strange about it. I did some uncomfortable things at Simon's behest. All that business with the wine bar, leaving horrible reviews, pretending I'd been assaulted. And then I don't know what happened exactly, but the next thing I heard, it was all over the papers that Luke was dead. He'd taken his own life. I felt bad about that, even if his family did say he'd been suffering with his mental health for most of his adult life. I did wonder if it was something to do with the rat and the complaints. Something to do with me . . .

I drank a lot during those first few weeks to numb the trauma of what had happened with Tara at my flat. And yes, I have not seen my boys for four years, and who knows when I'll see them again. They thought their dad was dead for over twenty years and then they watched him die again in front of their very eyes. My poor babies. But they have their lives to live, and I have mine. It was all going to be worth it in the end. Simon would come and then we could be a family again.

Or at least that's what I thought.

My husband's beautiful face breaks open into a wide smile at the sight of me on the road. I feel a blast of happiness and then I remember that I helped this man dismember a woman's body, which I then, at his request, disposed of in three separate areas of woodland around the M25. I made excuses for this man, I loved him, stole for him, lied for him, and hated him. This man has made me miss four years of my children's lives, the first year of my only grandchild's. For four years he has been promising me that he was coming, that he was planning it, sorting it, making it happen. I'll be there next month, he kept telling me. Just a few things to tie up. I'm on my way. I'll be with you tomorrow. I've booked my flight. And then always the excuses about sickness and treatment and money and passports.

He called me a week ago with a story about a trap he'd escaped. He said he needed to lie low for a while, sort some things out. I thought it was another excuse, that he was lying yet again. But then he called last night. "I'll be with you tomorrow evening. Six o'clock. I can't wait to see you again. I've missed you so much. You have no idea."

My husband doesn't see the man emerge from my cottage, the plainclothes detective from London, he doesn't see the cars pulling up over the brow of the hill, shimmering in the near distance. He doesn't know that I'm prepared to go to prison to atone for my sins, and to ensure that he does too.

All he sees is me. His first wife. His only true wife. The wife who would do anything for him. Literally anything. Except this.

I take a step to the side and let them come for him.

ACKNOWLEDGMENTS

All through 2022 while I was working out of my comfort zone on my Marvel novel, *Breaking the Dark*, I was so desperate to start this book. I just wanted to write a simple psychological thriller set in a world that existed and that I understood. And from typing the first word of this book in October 2023 I felt a rush of relief and joy. It was good to be back!

So thank you, first of all, to all the readers who took a punt on my Marvel novel in 2024, I know it was a stretch, but God I worked so hard on it, and I'm so glad that you enjoyed it. Thank you for keeping the faith.

Thanks also to the usual suspects for getting this book into your hands:

First of all, to my editor in the UK, the incomparable Selina Walker, who is my first reader and my loudest cheerleader and who has built my career brick-by-brick through love and sheer bloody-mindedness. Thanks, must also go to my brand-new American editor, the amazing Kaitlin Olson—this has been our first collaboration, and I am already excited about the next one, and the one after that, and the one after that. You have such a clear vision and so much energy and I could not love what you've done with this book more. I am so incredibly lucky when it comes to editors, I really am.

And of course, thank you to the incredible teams behind the editors: to Claire Bush, Ania Gordon, Liv Thomas, Meredith Benson, Mary Karayel, and Charlotte Osment at Cornerstone in the UK, and to Dayna Johnson, Dana Trocker, Ali Hinchcliffe, Morgan Pager, and Camilla Araujo at Simon & Schuster in the US. You are all superstars, and I have loved working with you on this book, listening to all your incredible ideas and visions.

Thank you to Ceara Elliot for the jaw-dropping cover artwork in the UK and to James Iacobelli for the jaw-dropping cover artwork in the US. You are both geniuses.

Thank you to Joanna Taylor and Caroline Johnson for your combined copyediting magic.

Jonny Geller, my agent, thank you so much. When I was shopping around for a new agent fifteen years ago a friend suggested I see you, as you were "a safe pair of hands" and that has proved to be true over and over, but even more so in 2024. Thank you for keeping everything rolling along so that I can keep writing books. And thanks too to Jonny's brilliant team: Viola Hayden, Natalie Beckett, Sophie Storey, and Atlanta Hatch.

Thank you so much to Kate Cooper, Sam Loader, and Nadia Mokdad for getting this book into the hands of my wonderful foreign publishers; and to my wonderful foreign publishers, thank you so much for working so hard to build me in your territories and for publishing me so brilliantly and with so much care.

Thanks, as always, to you, my readers. I know for a FACT that you are the best in the world. Thank you for your loyalty, for spending your hard-earned money on my books, for showing up to see me at events, for sending me wonderful messages on social media, and for telling your friends and family that they should also be reading my books. Word of mouth is what keeps the publishing industry alive, so thank you, thank you, thank you.

Lastly, thank you to all the utterly TERRIBLE MEN in this world (no, not you, only good men read my books) for helping to bring Simon Smith to life in these pages. I have watched so many documentaries about men like you, listened to so many podcasts, read so many books, you are all appalling. How do you live with yourselves? What the hell do you think you're doing? Why do you behave like this? And believe me, Simon Smith is not an outlandish literary confection. He could easily exist in this world. He does exist in this world. Please see below for some recommended reading, listening, and watching if you want to dig deeper into the psychology of men like Simon Smith.

And in the meantime: be careful who you let in . . .

Documentaries

The Tinder Swindler

The Puppet Master: Hunting the Ultimate Conman

Stolen Youth: Inside the Cult at Sarah Lawrence
Who TF Did I Marry? (on TikTok)

Podcasts
Who The Hell is Hamish?
I am Not Nicholas
Dirty John
Chasing Charlie

Books
Sleeping With a Psychopath: Carolyn Woods
The Psychopath: Mary Turner Thomson
The Bigamist: The True Story of a Husband's Ultimate Betrayal: Mary Turner Thomson
No One Knew: My Emotional Journey of Being Married to a Sociopath and How I Learned to Heal: Renee Olivier

A note on the character name Justin Warshaw

Two years ago, the Spear Camden Charity offered me the chance to name a character in this book after the winner of a charity auction.

Spear Camden is one of the charities supported by the London Lighthouse Community Trust. It takes vulnerable local young people aged 16–24, who all have barriers to employment, and puts them through an intensive six-week coaching program, as well as offering a follow-up year of support. The result is that, despite coming from often difficult backgrounds—out of care, prison, escaping gang violence, struggling with mental health issues, or long-term unemployment—more than 75 percent of the young people who complete the six-week Spear program are in work, training, or employment a year later.

The money raised by this auction prize was enough to completely transform the lives of one and a half young people.

So a huge, huge thank you to the real life Justin Warshaw.

Who bears no resemblance whatsoever to my fictional one.

ABOUT THE AUTHOR

Lisa Jewell is the #1 *New York Times* bestselling author of twenty-three novels, including *None of This Is True*, *The Family Upstairs*, and *Then She Was Gone*, as well as *Invisible Girl* and *Watching You.* Her novels have sold more than fifteen million copies internationally, and her work has also been translated into over thirty languages. Connect with her on X @LisaJewellUK, on Instagram @LisaJewellUK, and on Facebook @LisaJewellOfficial.